Advocatus

Book one of the Culpa Magum series

A.R. Turner

This is a work of fiction. All persons, places, events are creations of the author's mind, or used in a fictitious manner. All resemblances to actual persons, living or dead is purely coincidental.

Published by:
Cloaked Press, LLC
P. O. Box 341
Suring, WI 54174
HTTPS://www.cloakedpress.com

Cover design by Fantasy & Coffee Design
https://fantasyandcoffee.com/SPDesign/

Dedicated to Anna,
Who showed me that lawyers could be magical.

Contents

Part One: Warlord

1 – The Courtroom

"Your Honour, does *that*," said Felix, pointing at his client, "look like the sort of man who would terrorise an entire *district?*"

He darted his eyes to the person in the defendant's chair, an enormous figure in black-iron armour, whose very posture dripped with malice. What wasn't covered with terrifying runes promising untold torment was dotted with spikes, curved and horrifying, or festooned with nightmarish trinkets, skulls and fetishes.

Felix gestured with his free hand, miming lifting something from his face. His client made to raise an arm, and the seven wizards that maintained the crackling cage of power that restrained him winced. As he moved, a squeal like the keening of the abyss emanated from him as metal ground against metal. An obsidian gauntlet reached slowly for the visor of his snarling-demon face plate, and began to lift.

~

This was his last case as a 'junior lawyer'. After this, he was no longer contractually bound to work for the firm randomly allocated to him upon graduation. From here, he could seek a firm of his choice, or, if he was feeling particularly entrepreneurial, start his own.

Kurrip & Kurripe was a decent enough firm, but he wasn't a fan of the South Country. He had thought to move out West.

Far from this stinking city.

Truth be told, he relished the challenge of starting fresh in an unknown part of the world. It's not like he had any friends to leave behind. Friends were something that happened to other people. It's not that he didn't want friends, it's just that he hadn't met any. Evenings were spent reading case law or studying precedent. There were people he knew, of course, but no one he *knew*. And, of course, by extension, no one who really knew *him*.

He had been told by Kurripe (or was it Kurrip?) that this last case was essentially a crapshoot, but as the client was quite happy to pay upfront and in cash, they were going to take it and 'might as well give it a go'. No other firm in the city was willing to touch it, which, on the one hand, made Felix want to run a mile, but on another, larger hand, sparked the bonfire of challenge in his head. Besides, he had a soft spot for the downtrodden. Though, judging by the details in this case, downtrodden was perhaps the wrong word.

This case was defending a young-ish lad called Bupp. 'Unlucky Bupp' was what Felix called him. 'Warlord Bupp The Devastator' was what others called him.

It had been quite a story.

~

Felix had been scribbling a few notes on his pad when Kurrip had gestured to him to follow, explaining that a gentleman had called upon the firm, and Felix was to be representing him.

"Don't be too frightened, lad," Kurrip had crooned as he swung the door to the defendant's interview chambers. "He's really not all that bad."

Felix had walked through the doorway and regarded a figure in menacing black armour, spiked and covered with ghoulish carvings. He looked like the sort of man-hunting monster that stomps from the deepest, darkest kingdoms of Beyond to collect souls for the Black Harvest. Felix was sure that if this *thing* lifted his horned helmet, a laughing skull, black with death, would greet him and chaperone him to a plane of torment.

The door closed behind Felix with the sound of promised horror.

Felix fidgeted with his notebook as he sat opposite the figure, who shifted his weight, causing the wooden chair beneath him to creak pitifully. His gauntleted hand rose to his face, and began to peel back his visor. Felix tensed, his soul bracing itself.

"Oh thank goodness you've taken my case, fella. I've had a right mare of a year, I have," said the figure in a voice broken with worry. The face beneath the helm was a scrawny, freckled one, lank haired and pale. Not with the pale clamour of death, just a bit ill-looking. He looked at Felix.

"Have we met?" he asked, peering at Felix's face.

"Uh—" Felix had begun.

"No, I suppose not. Name's Bupp. You can call me 'unlucky' Bupp, if you like."

Bupp… Bupp… Why did that name ring a bell?

Felix took a good look at the man opposite him.

Surely this wasn't THE Bupp?

~

Felix glanced at the carving above the front door of the courtroom. It was a small one, no larger than a cat, the features worn away from years of cold rain and harsh wind. A robed figure with long hair, blindfolded, yet averting its gaze downwards. It might have had wings, once, but they were long since eroded. Whatever it held it its hands had likewise been victim to the elements, abraded to stumps of nothing. Could it have been a sword? A set of scales? A glass of mead? A stick of rhubarb? It was impossible to tell.

It looked… sad. It did not swell Felix's breast with inspiration as it might have done to lawyers past.

"Wish me luck," Felix mumbled to it as he entered. The figure did not reply.

Passing through the doors, Felix looked up at the dock, where Bupp was chained. He was still in his armour; in fact, it was impossible to remove it from him. Bupp had explained that the armour was laced with sorcery, and cursed the wearer never to remove it until death. The best he could manage was lifting the visor, which he had now done at Felix's suggestion. He was fidgeting with his gauntlets, looking pathetic.

The prosecutor opposite Felix was a young woman about his age. She introduced herself as Ettyson, recently a partner of Jurviles.

He cursed inwardly. *They don't hire just any old person.*

He tried to suss out the competition in a subtle way, but failed. "This your first case with them?"

"Oh yes," she said. Every word she said sounded practiced, as if delivered to a script she had prepared the night before. "They gave me this case because it is so open-and-shut. Even a 'rookie' like me can oversee it without supervision."

"Uh, yes. Well, good luck," said Felix, returning to his desk.

The courtroom was, as courtrooms go, fairly meagre. There was the dock, where the accused normally waited alone (though in this case, very much supervised). The two desks, one for the prosecution, one for the defence. Behind them were the benches where members of the public could watch, if they so chose. It was full today, no doubt the thought of the notorious Bupp the Horrendous undergoing trial was hard to resist for the morbidly curious. Lastly, the raised dais at the front, where the Judge would oversee proceedings.

Some courtrooms had ostentation on every surface, from gilded candlesticks to great stained-glass portraits of Habeus, God of Judgement, bathing the unjust in bright beams of scrutiny. Placenamia courtroom had a small statue of a set of scales on the far-end of the judge's table, a sign that said "No Smoking" at the front, and a faint smell of old shoes.

Judge Gunter would be leading this case. She was a judge Felix had had plenty of dealings with before. She was one of the long-standing judges who were both seemingly minutes from death's door and apparently immortal at the same time. Felix had no idea how long she had been a judge. All he knew was that she had been presiding over courtrooms from at least the time his old university lecturer was still practicing, and he was ancient.

Gunter entered without ceremony, and Felix noticed the quiet sound of her shuffling footsteps a heartbeat after Ettyson did, and rushed to stand, as was customary. She regarded him and Ettyson without comment. She finally cast an eye over Bupp, looking like a nightmare king on a throne of obsidian. She narrowed her eyes a fraction, then turned to the court.

"Court is in session. Please read the charges, prosecutor Ettyson." Her voice was thin and reedy, but carried across the room.

4

The judge recognises her by sight? I thought she was new.

She stood, and lifted a roll of paper she had taken from the neat bundle of documents in front of her.

~

"Don't be fooled when they say 'alleged' counts," Felix told Bupp, who had calmed down a little since Felix entered the interview room. He was nursing a small cup of tea in his enormous, armoured fists. "That doesn't mean it's potential, or just hearsay. They'll only bring it up when they have evidence to prove it, so be prepared for the world to hear it."

"O-okay," stammered the Warlord. He sipped at his drink and winced at the heat. "Ooh, that's hot."

Felix almost went to ask Kurrip if this was some sort of practical joke, but then remembered Kurrip had absolutely no sense of humour. Instead, he flicked open his notepad, and readied his pencil.

"Now, what sort of offences list are we going to be looking at?"

"Uh…"

~

Ettyson unfurled the scroll. When it was fully unravelled, the bottom of it brushed against the cobbles.

"The royal district of Placenamia brings this case against the Warlord Bupp the Mangler, also known as Bupp the Family-Killer, Bupp the End Of Days, among many other names. The crimes we allege are, as follows. One count of Unsanctioned Warfare, seventeen counts of Attempted City-Sacking, two counts of Attempted Genocide, fifty-seven cases of General Nefariousness, one count of Evil Witchery…"

~

Felix rubbed his chin, pencil tapping on the paper.

"That's quite a list, Bupp."

"I know! Buh-but it's not worrit sounds like!" his client whimpered, eyes starting to moisten. Felix leaned over and patted him on the arm. The armour stung him where his hand came into contact with it, and began to numb slightly. He whipped his hand back, and tried shaking some feeling back into it. He licked his pencil and prepared to take notes.

"Okay. Start from the beginning. Leave *nothing* out," he said. His client looked nervous, but nodded.

~

"…and six counts of Theft."

Ettyson furled the paper into a tube and tied it with a green ribbon. She handed it to an aide, who tucked it into a bag.

Judge Gunter turned to Felix.

"How does the defence plead, Defence Counsel, hm..?"

"Sacramentum, Your Honour," he said, straightening himself and thrusting his chest out.

"How does the defence plead, Defence Counsel Saccharine?"

His stance faltered an inch, but he still proclaimed in a confident voice: "Not guilty, Your Honour, to all charges."

The assembled crowd of observing public began murmuring at this. Felix caught snippets of conversation before the judge shushed them all with a tap of her gavel.

"Not guilty? He's a flaming war criminal!"

"Bloody smarmy looking lawyer…"

"…my arse…"

"Order!" said Gunter. "The client is entitled to have his defence heard, despite the sizable list of charges. Now, if the prosecution would like to begin, please, with their opening statement."

~

Bupp looked close to tears. "It all happened like this, y'see. It were an accident."

Felix tilted his head and glanced at his notes.

"You accidentally committed 'Attempted Genocide'?"

"No, no—well, tha's not quite what I meant. I mean, like, this whole Warlord thingie. I'm not a Warlord, I'm a farmhand from yon village down Wart-Bottom."

"A… farmhand, hm?"

"Aye. I was just a normal lad, working the fields, courting my lass, normal stuff. Well, one day, I found this amulet down by yon river, I did."

"An amulet?"

"Yes, gurt big red stone on it. Beautiful, it was. I were going to give it to Zaya and ask her to be my missus."

"Okay, so what happened?"

"Well, it weren't no bloody ordinary amulet, were it?"

~

Ettyson swept from the prosecutor's bench to the open area in the front of the room, looking every bit the perfectly turned-out prosecutor. She took two deep breaths before starting.

"The man you see sitting in the dock is, perhaps, the most evil force to ever walk this earth. His wave of destruction began when, at the mere age of fifteen, he commanded the forces of darkness to lay waste to his village through dark sorcery. He was found standing, alone, in the middle of an untouched patch of grass, surrounded by death and destruction, flames and ashes. A trinket from which he drew his dark powers clutched in hand, an expression of delight on his face as he turned to the brave men and women of the Peacekeepers. Those brave, selfless souls laying their lives on the line to bring this creature to answer for his crimes. As you will hear later, the survivors still sometimes wake up screaming, so terrible was that sight."

Felix chanced a look at the judge, who was following Ettyson's every word with great interest. That was a bad sign. Gunter was normally half asleep, and that was on a good day. He glanced down at his notebook.

~

Felix scribbled a few things, then paused, tapping his pencil against his mouth.

"When you say it… went off?"

Bupp was well onto his second cup of tea by now. He had been offered something stronger, but had refused. ("It hurts me ol' tummy, I'm delicate, see").

Bupp clutched his black gauntlet to his chest, the metal grating on Felix's ears.

"Yes, it were awful. It was 'ot to touch, so I went to dip it in that bucket by the well, 'n'this awful swirlin' heat burst from it, burnin' and flamin' everything in sight, except for me. Oh, it was terrible, mister! I were so glad when th'Watch came for me. I just wanted to get away from them awful sights and smells, and from everything I held dear burnin' in front of me."

"So, you submitted to the Peacekeepers?"

"Yes I did, sir, yes I did. But, uh, tha's when it got worse…"

~

The crowd were spellbound by the prosecutor. She was like one of those famous actresses from the theatre.

I wonder if she's had stage training? I wonder if whoever gave those lessons is still taking on students? I wonder if I could afford them?

"However, this was merely a fraction of his malevolent scheming!"

A flourish of the hand.

"Allowing himself to be detained by the brave guardsmen, he waited until he was locked up, secure behind bars, before wreaking further havoc, freeing himself and all manner of terrible prisoners, binding them to his will. And thus, the seeds of his fledgling army were planted!"

~

Felix handed Bupp the Terrible a hanky, who accepted it clumsily. "What happened in prison?"

"Well, some of them other prisoners, horrible people they were, they saw I was young'n'skinny with long arms, and they said I should try'n fit through the bars. I wasn't *that* skinny, but I tried, because they said they'd hurt me if I didn't..." he sniffed, dabbing his eyes.

"...And?"

"Well, I reached me arm through, then some guard saw me'nd came over to tell me to stop, and he tripped, and I don't know how, but he landed badly, proper badly, and was stabbed by his own sword! His keys clattered over t'me, and I reached 'em. The other boys, superstitious like, had heard something about magic when I were led in, but not believed it. Now they started thinkin' I was some kinda awful wizard who bewitched the guard to kill his-self. Well, I held the keys in my hand, and one of them took the keys and unlocked the door, then the next door, until they was all unlocked, and there I stood, among a sea of villains. They all looked to me, askin' what I were gonna do next."

Felix took a thoughtful sip of tea.

"Right... so, what did you do next?"

~

Edison thrust her index finger on the table before Bupp.

"Leading this new prison revolt, he stormed Hillsgate Guardsquarter, slaughtering all who stood in his path. By the time he was finished, barely one man in ten lived. The survivors saw Evil Bupp being carried like a demon king through hell, high on the shoulders of the men he freed. He was carried towards the mountains, no doubt to carve out a *kingdom diabolus* fit for the monster he truly was."

~

Bupp blew his nose wetly. Felix mentally disowned the handkerchief.

"These criminals, *nasty* bunch they were, they thought I was lucky, or powerful, or both, and so they took me with'em. Turns out just the same day some bandit gang, the Black Eye, had been arrested, all of'em at once, and they all had a big hideout not too far from where we were. Their boss

9

had died in the arrests, so they needed someone else. They liked the idea of a wizard to lead them, so they chose me."

"Just like that? They chose you?" Felix said, frowning. Bupp looked at him earnestly, bottom lip starting to wobble.

"Yes sir, just like that. I couldn't say no, could I? They'd have killed me!"

"But didn't they find out that you weren't a criminal? Just a farm boy? No offence, but it can't have been that hard for them," Felix said, feeling a touch guilty.

Bupp fidgeted with the now-snotty rag and mumbled, "Well, not exactly…"

~

Ettyson strode to the centre of the room, her back to the defendant.

"Three long years of terror reigned on the district, with the newly formed Black Heart gang holding the area to ransom. Only when setting his sights on a greater prize was the county spared. Bupp the Conqueror led his evil forces southward to claim the jewel of the south: Placenamia."

~

Felix passed Bupp his fourth cup of tea. Bupp leaned forward to take it, his chair creaking in protest. He blew gently on his drink, which appeared to grow warmer judging by the steam, then sipped. Felix was trying to wrap his head around the physics of this—and was coming to the conclusion it was probably magic—when Bupp started speaking.

"There were this fella, see, called Chiv. He knew I were a fraud, and he held me by knifepoint once, and told me that the leader is the one who gets killed when things go sour, but if I did everythin' he said, I could stay leader and I'd be safe, while he made the choices and whatnot. So… I agreed. He told me what to say and when to say it, and, uh, the gang flourished…"

"So, you *did* lead a gang?" said Felix, raising an eyebrow, but not looking up from his pad.

"I never chose to! I feared for me life!" Bupp said, clutching his hands together and holding them to his chest.

The whole tale carried on much like this. Every few months some new bad bit of chance or coercion would see poor old Bupp take the next step on his terrible career. After four years, his meagre mountain home became a mighty citadel, and he spent his time on a great throne in armour black as midnight. His armour? A gift from a supplicated rival warlock gang, which he was honour bound to wear, lest blood spill between them. He only found out later that it was un-removable, and no amount of tugging or scraping would give him release. The screaming sword? Pressed into his hands by a necromancer who feared for his unlife, begging the mighty Bupp to leave him be. It had never been swung. By Bupp, that is.

As his notoriety grew, so did Chiv's coercions. Sieges, sackings, all manner of terrible crimes attempted, but, due to a lack of crucial tactical understanding or callousness, all failed at the last moment. Mostly these were split-second decisions that people expected Bupp to take in the heat of the moment, and, Bupp being Bupp, and with Chiv not always being present, he constantly made them wrong. However, no one was brave enough to call him out on it, content to hide their concerns in their cups. No one wanted to be the one to challenge their overlord.

Eventually, Chiv died under mysterious circumstances ("Nothin' to do with me, honest!", blubbered Bupp), so everyone assumed Bupp had killed him out of spite or boredom. From then on, his rule was absolute and his volunteer bodyguards, itching for favour, were plentiful. His fate was sealed.

Since then, his gang had committed no major crimes, the assumption being they were biding their time for the "big one." Why else would their evil wizard-king brood for days at a time on his dark throne, if not planning the raid of the century? The cult of the Black Heart swelled, and their reputation spread like an infestation on the country.

This was going to be an interesting case, thought Felix.

~

11

Back in the courtroom, Ettyson finished her lengthy and heartfelt tale of Bupp's exploits and returned to her seat. Felix stood, and at a gesture from the judge, took his place. He looked at the room, taking in the tense atmosphere. Fear, disbelief, anger. These emotions filled the room like mist, and he felt it fill his lungs as he breathed. He swept the court with his gaze, from the severe looking judge to the agitated crowd, disbelieving that anyone could defend such a monster. The only sound was the gentle fizz-crackle of the cage that held Bupp.

Well, here goes nothing.

He licked his teeth before starting.

Curtain up.

He flung an arm up, first finger extended in the sky. "Wrong place, wrong time. A phrase we have all used, and a phenomenon we have all experienced. I fear to say, Your Honour, it is a phrase I will be referring to quite frequently this afternoon.

"A series of dreadful, unlikely circumstances have led to this modest farmhand, this skinny, harmless nobody, being, quite accidentally, elevated to the level of terrible warlord."

~

Ettyson's first witness was one of the two survivors who apprehended Bupp at the village on Wart-Bottom Hill. Her name was Guardswoman Wellity, and she was a blocky, nervous looking person with a sandy dusting of short-cropped hair. Despite her clear discomfort at having to recreate that terrible day, she maintained the stiff expression of the veteran guardswoman. She didn't look up at Bupp as she marched in.

In the dock, she explained a distressing tale of dark magic and evil sorcery, much as Ettyson herself had described. The prosecutor would often ask for further details on certain aspects of the tale, getting the witness to repeat words like 'Malevolent', 'Dread', and 'Terrifying'.

When she was finished, Felix prepared to cross-examine her.

He gave her a good ten-second stare, trying to unnerve her. She did not falter.

"Guardswoman Wellity," he began. His voice echoed around the chamber, and the sound died off before she replied.

"Yes?" she answered tersely. She had large, scared eyes, like a deer, but the rest of her face was stony. Her guards' uniform was pristine, all reds and whites, not a speck of muck or a thread out of place.

"How did Bupp look when you saw him?" he began.

"He looked most sinister, sir."

"I mean, his expression. His face."

"Evil, sir."

Her responses to Felix, in contrast to those towards Ettyson, were guarded and brusque.

"But it was dark, there was fire and ash swirling around, you said. How could you tell?"

"I saw it, sir, no mistake."

"From a distance, at night, in the middle of a flaming village?"

"Yes, sir."

"I see." He paused, then started pacing slowly around the room. "Did the defendant attempt to fight you when you arrived to arrest him?"

She didn't answer, evidently trying to figure out how to obscure the truth without actually lying. Felix didn't give her the chance.

"Answer me, please, witness, yes or no will suffice," he snapped. "Did the defendant fight you, or put up any resistance at all when you went to arrest him?"

"…No, sir." She turned her eyes away, looking at the floor.

"In other words, he handed himself in?"

"Objection," interjected Ettyson, and Felix froze, waiting to hear her reasoning. "One does not mean the other. 'Handing in' implies he came to the guard to admit his crimes, which he didn't."

Gunter nodded. "Sustained. Felix, next question, please."

"Thank you, Your Honour," he nodded, discarding that line of questioning like an apple core. He turned back to the guard.

"Now, I wonder." Another theatrical pause. "Guardswoman Wellity. Are you a wizard?"

She blinked, and swallowed. "No sir."

"A witch?"

13

"No, sir."

He produced a strip of parchment of his own from inside his inner jacket pocket, and began theatrically crossing entries off of them as he made his way down.

"A relic-master? Archaeomancer? Necromancer, temporomancer, witch-doctor, curse-breaker, or any other kind of profession that casts or removes curses, spells or magic?"

His pencil scratched loudly with each line. He'd practised getting the sound *just* right. *Schwit.*

"Certainly not, sir." the witness answered, sounding more indignant with each reply. Felix took on the mannerism of an irritated schoolmaster, struggling to get a simple question from a misbehaving pupil.

"Perhaps you are an alumnus of a prestigious university, having obtained a degree studying the arcane or, perhaps, the mysterious ways of magic?"

"No, sir," she said through gritted teeth.

"Have you *any* part of your history, professional or personal, that might give you an insight into the specifics between different types of magic?"

"…No, sir.."

He scrunched up the paper and put it into a pocket. It had been completely blank, of course, but it wouldn't do for someone to notice.

"So, you wouldn't be able to tell at a glance, for example, the difference between a spell cast by a benevolent forest spirit and a, let's say, cursed amulet?"

"…Well, that depends!"

Felix considered this, and tilted his head in mock-overthinking.

"On what, witness?" he asked, genuinely.

"On, umm… Well…" she glanced at the Ettyson, who watched impassively.

"You couldn't, could you?" said Felix.

"…No, sir." She seemed less defiant and more deflated.

"So, this dreadful scene you took in… You say you saw a dark wizard flaunting his powers, whereas it could have been a cursed amulet, much like the one submitted as evidence, performing its own dark magics despite the handler trying to stop it?"

Her face hardened, her brow furrowing. She didn't look happy.

Good.

"I don't agree, sir," she said, firmly.

Got you.

He smiled. "In that case, would you be able to tell us how to differentiate between the dark magic of a mad sorcerer and the dark magic of a demonic amulet? To me, an inexperienced lawyer, they seem quite similar." He had reached his desk, and leaned back on it, arms crossed. "I'm dying to know the difference."

She fidgeted, before again looking to the prosecutor for help. Ettyson just stared at her.

"Uhm…" said Wellity.

"Please speak up, witness," said Felix.

"Uh, I… I couldn't sir."

"I see." he bowed his head, as if disappointed. "So, in answer to the previous question; Guardswoman, can you be sure you saw the defendant casting evil magic, or could it be something else, something perhaps being summoned from that terrible jewellery?"

"I don't know, sir."

"You don't know if you can be sure? Would it perhaps be more accurate to give a single word answer? Let me repeat the question. Can you, guardswoman, be *sure* you saw the defendant casting evil magic, or could it be something else, something perhaps"—he emphasised each word—"being summoned from some demonically possessed jewellery?"

Her face flushed, and her eyes flicked to Bupp, and back again. "No, sir."

Felix nodded. "That will suffice. No further questions."

~

The next witness for the prosecution was a shifty looking man, all sinew and suspicious glares. Darting eyes—short, greasy hair. He looked like a career criminal, if such things can be gleaned from a single glance. He wore an ill-fitting overcoat of an indeterminate brownish-grey, and it seemed to swallow him up, leaving only his head poking out.

"Name, witness, and profession," stated Ettyson in a flat monotone.

He slicked his hair back before answering in a husky voice. "Sticker, and I'm, ah, um… an insider, if you like.."

"Who for, and what does that entail?" She could well have been asking a stranger for the time of day, so direct was her tone.

"For the Black Eye, uh, I mean the Black Heart. I work with the townsguards though, help them and whatnot, information, and they protect me."

"Tell me what you know of the last ten years in the Black Eye Gang."

"Well, it's not called that no more, it's the Black Heart, on account of, er…" he nudged a head towards Bupp. "Oh. it's been the most terrible time. Since *he* took over, there's just this atmosphere, you know?"

"In that time, has the severity of the crimes you committed increased?"

"Oh, yes. Before, it was just some small robbings, a small amount of strong-arming, then it was all sorts. Capturing towns, burning bodies, oh it was awful. We might be crims, but we're not rotten, you know? There's a world of difference between nicking something and burning a city down."

He looked side to side, before leaning closer to Ettyson, though his voice was just as loud. "Also, between you'n'me, some very strange types turning up lately. Fellas in black cloaks, muttering about the end of the world, the final judgement, end of life as we know it, that sort of rubbish. Gives me the willies. S'gone to the dogs."

~

Felix strode to the witness, and tried not to imagine quite how one in such a dangerous profession managed to live to such a ripe old age. It can't have been luck.

"Witness Sticker." He enjoyed speaking out the witness's name before starting questioning. It always gave him a natural starting place, and he felt it focussed attention in the right way. "Did you ever, at any time, see the defendant personally command any member of the Black Heart gang to commit any of the alleged crimes?"

"Yes," said the crook.

"Ahem, okay." *Whoops.* Felix tapped his chin with a finger, eyes pointing upwards in a 'thinking' pose. "And… how did he *seem* when he did so? When he gave these commands?"

Sticker paused, and started moving his hands in front of him, trying to shape the correct word.

"Calculatin'." he settled on.

Interesting… Maybe…

"Calculating, you say? Calculating… or hesitant?"

"Eh?" Sticker wrinkled his nose.

Felix smiled as if he realised he hadn't quite explained the joke correctly. "Allow me to elaborate. What do you mean, when you say 'calculating'?"

Sticker shrugged. Something in his coat jingled when he did so.

"He spent a long time thinking of what to say, so he could make sure it was as evil as possible, I reckon." he nodded, jingling again, happy with his own interpretation. Felix shrugged.

"Or, perhaps he wasn't sure what to say, and was trying to remember what Chiv had prompted him with earlier that day?"

"Uh—", Sticker began.

"Objection," said Ettyson, rising. After a nod from the judge, she explained. "Who exactly is Chiv? I believe the defence has suddenly conjured this name out of nothing."

"Sustained. Defence counsel?" enquired the Judge, looking at Felix like he was genuinely an idiot.

Getting ahead of myself… maybe I can make it look intended?

He nodded to Ettyson. "A jolly good question indeed. Witness, do you know of a man called Chiv?"

"Aye, I do."

"Is he a member of the Black Heart gang?"

"Yes, he was." Sticker itched the end of his nose. "Was bein' the key word. Good riddance t'bad rubbish, I say," he muttered.

"What was Chiv like?" Felix asked. Sticker whistled, a long, low drawn-out whistle that carried on for a heartbeat too long.

"Oh, now he was a sneaky bastard. Always wanted to be top dog, but never wanted to be the one taking the heat. I always knew he'd end up with a knife in the back, I did." He spat, remembered where he was, and glanced up at the judge. She didn't notice. Felix continued.

"Could Chiv have ruled from 'behind the throne'?"

Sticker nodded, absentmindedly. "Oh, sure, he did it once a while back. The last leader was a right pushover, did whatever Chiv wanted, until Chiv got fed up with him and had him killed. Proper, hmm, wasstheword... *perfidious.*"

Felix was not expecting that sort of word from this sort of witness. He nodded, despite himself.

"No further questions, Your Honour."

~

Felix regarded his defence witness. There hadn't been many to choose from, and he had decided that putting Bupp on the stand wouldn't have done his case any favours. He'd have been painted as an actor, feigning weakness, and Ettyson would have ripped him apart.

He had scraped the barrel, perhaps, but something was better than nothing. And, who knows? Perhaps this would be enough.

"Just exactly what are the chances," Felix said, leaning back on his desk. "Of, for example, a butterfly entering through the top window during this case?"

The Aleaomancer twitched his hand in the air in front of him, mouthing silent calculations. Tiny sparks flickered on his fingertips. His white hair seemed to defy gravity, sticking almost straight up.

"Well, let's see. Any sort of butterfly, the case is likely to take X long, so multiply over and..." he paused. He spoke very quickly.

"...and?"

"Around two-hundred and sixty to one," said the small, frizzy haired man. He seemed to always be moving, unable to sit still for even a moment. Felix couldn't help contrast him to Ettyson, who sat as if carved from stone on the prosecutor's table.

"I see. And, based on the evidence you have heard, and the narrative given to you by the defence, what are the odds of our defendant, Bupp, experiencing the series of events as described?"

The chance-wizard whistled a long, low laugh.

"Well, those are long odds," he said.

"Please, just answer the question," Felix said. He never much cared for wizards.

The man was quiet for some time, suddenly still, larger sparks and crackles popping around him. He sat up as if shocked, then blurted out: "around four-hundred-and-seventy-five-thousand-billion, one-hundred-and-sixteen-million, nine-hundred-and-sixty-eight-thousand, six-hundred sixty-six to one."

"So, you're saying there's a chance?" Felix said, hoping he didn't appear as desperate as the argument sounded. "It's not impossible that things happened as described?"

"Oh yes, me boy, there's almost always a chance," smiled the wizard, playing with his collar. Felix thanked him, and stepped away.

Ettyson approached for cross-examination.

"Two questions for you, witness. Can you think of any event that you have encountered in your long career that has odds as unlikely as the one just described?"

The man considered. "No, sorry. It's very much on the high end of the sorts of odds we can, hmm, generate."

She nodded, then continued.

"What are the odds for the defendant being found innocent of all the crimes accused?"

"Probably around four-hundred-and-seventy-five-thousand-billion, one-hundred-and-sixteen-million, nine-hundred-sixty-eight-thousand, six-hundred sixty-eight... to one." He smiled again. He seemed to like long odds.

"No further questions," she said. Felix groaned internally.

~

Ettyson's closing speech was very much like her first, full of emotive descriptions of maimed villages and other poetic language. It was at odds with her style of questioning, but she delivered both speeches and examinations expertly.

Felix's close was succinct. After a quick round up of the evidence, he appealed to the judge directly.

"I implore you, Your Honour, please consider not what appears easy and straightforward, but what appears possible, and remember that, despite all this, my client, Bupp the Apparently Utterly Evil, *handed himself in*. He turned up, hands outstretched, to allow himself to be arrested, just so long as he got a fair trial. Would a true monster throw himself at the feet of justice? No, I move that he would not. Thank you for your time."

The judge waited for him to sit down, then stood up herself.

"I have heard all the evidence and arguments presented and shall now retire to my chambers to consider them. Expect a verdict within the hour."

And with that, Judge Gunter shuffled out of the room.

Felix stretched his neck out, sighing. It didn't look good for poor old Bupp. He'd done his best, but barring a miracle, he reckoned his last case for Kurrip & Kurripe's was going to be a blowout.

It's a shame, because I actually believe him.

He looked around the room again, trying not to make direct-eye contact with anyone in the audience. Heckling, he could deal with. He wasn't a fan of being pelted with rotten vegetables, however. The chance of that happening was low, at least in the courtroom itself, but Felix figured that if anyone was going to 'decorate' him just outside the building, they'd almost certainly be giving him an evil glare from within. He picked a few likely contenders out and made a mental note to avoid them if possible.

Bupp was still up in the dock, within the blue power-cage. He looked uncomfortable. The seven wizards keeping him in check had been swapped out a few hours ago for fresh ones. They'd been tense during the switchover, but it had apparently gone well, based on how Bupp was not rampaging through the city. Instead, he just sat, looking sad. He was perhaps naive in thinking the law could help him, but he had trusted anyway.

Felix wondered what would have happened if Bupp *had* decided to try and break free, and felt a slight chill.

~

Almost exactly one hour after leaving, Gunter returned. She didn't sit, and instead just looked out over the room.

"The prosecution makes a very strong case," she began, addressing the room in a solemn voice. "The mountain of evidence is almost as large as that in which the defendant has made his stronghold these past ten years." She took a deep breath. "There is some room for doubt, however."

Ettyson tensed, letting the mask of professionalism slip ever-so-slightly. For one as her, it was equivalent to another bawling and tearing her hair out. Felix felt the tiny flame of hope spark deep within his gut. *Surely not...*

"But, as our Aleaomancer friend has noted, the room for doubt is microscopically small. Sometimes, the law must understand that on the balance of probability, certain actions were likely to have occurred, and others are unlikely. In this case, disregarding as fantasy the infinitesimally unfortuitous series of events presented by the defence, this court finds the defendant Guilty of all crimes accused. Sentence shall be death, to be meted out in one week's time."

She struck her gavel on the plate, and nodded once each to Felix and Ettyson, before leaving again, much more quickly than the last time.

Cheers erupted from the audience, and Felix found it hard to look up at the dock. He heard the sound of something wet and hefty hit the cage, and it fizzled and puffed when it impacted, leaving behind the smell of cabbage.

Felix knew he should try to speak to his client, but before he could, Bupp was whisked away by the team of seven Cabal wizards, keeping him contained within a web of blue energy. Felix thought he could hear him trying to speak, but the sound was drowned out by the hubbub.

I'm sorry, Bupp.

~

Kurrip knocked lightly on the interview room door and poked his head around. He gave Bupp a nervous glance, then spoke to Felix.

"I'm about to head off, Felix. Have you got everything you need from our, eh, esteemed client?" He was trying a calm and easy smile, but it wasn't quite making it to his face.

Felix looked at this notebook. It was as full as it was likely to be, and, truth be told, his wrist hurt. He turned to Kurrip.

"Yes, I think so. I'll be out in a moment."

Kurrip nodded quickly and shut the door behind him. Felix waited until his footsteps receded out of earshot.

"Bupp," said Felix, putting down his pencil and flexing his wrist. "There is one question I haven't asked you yet."

The armoured figure of Bupp the Merciless gave Felix a tired look. "Oh?"

"Yes. Why exactly *did* you hand yourself in? You must know that it's not going to be easy to get the result you want." He tried to sound comforting, but that was never his strong point.

His client sighed and dipped his head.

"I s'pose I just thought, enough is enough, you know? And when I were a nipper, my folks, they taught me, they said: do the right thing, Bupp, even if it's hard. I been thinking about this for a long while. I decided it's about time I faced the music, so to speak. And it can't be too late for me, not if I believe in man's good nature."

He looked up at Felix, his eyes glistening.

"I got faith, sir."

~

Felix was gathering his papers from the desk, half-listening to the gentle bustle of the crowd as it shuffled from the courtroom. Some voices were excitable, some were fearful. What would happen to Bupp now? Ghoulish speculation floated from a few noisier punters. Execution, certainly. Maybe they'd draw it out, if they'd make him suffer.

You did your best, he thought.

Could he have done better? Did he miss anything? Did he say too much?

He knew it was pointless thinking this way, especially so soon after the sentence was passed. And, with time, this would just be another individual tried and found guilty, Felix's name a footnote at the end. Legally, this was the right course of action. On the balance of evidence, Bupp was guilty. Justice had been served.

Hadn't it?

A thought bobbed to the surface, and he paused, bag in one hand, document in another. Bupp, blowing on his tea, and it warming as a result. Why did that memory stick out?

He was aware of a presence behind him. He turned, and saw a middle-aged woman he didn't recognise, who appeared to be waiting for him. She was wearing her hair in a tight grey bun, and light gleamed from a single glass lens that covered an eye. She had a half-smile, as if privy to a secret joke. It irked him.

"I'm sorry, have we met?" he said, perhaps too curtly.

There's no need for rudeness.

"Sorry," he added, embarrassed. "I didn't mean to sound rude. You know how it is, you saw…" He waved a hand towards the dock.

"No offence caused, young man, and we haven't met. I must say, you fought a tough fight." Her voice was musical, and she didn't seem the slightest bit bothered by his attitude.

He shrugged. "I did my best, it's just a shame it didn't quite turn out how I had hoped. But there's always more clients in hopeless situations. Perhaps not quite as hopeless as that, but we have to try, eh?" He turned back to his papers, and began ordering them, ready to pack away. *Or I could just burn them.*

She nodded. "Quite. Might I enquire as to which company you represent?"

He stopped, and pursed his mouth. "Oh, well, no one, now. I'm currently looking for somewhere, as it happens."

She reached into a bag she was clutching and passed him a card. He took it, and it took a few moments to register what it was. She gave him a full smile.

"Well, if you haven't quite made up your mind, might I recommend Lunchers & Co. They're based out in the West Country, and I know for a fact they would gobble up a lawyer with your sort of spirit."

Felix looked at the card. It had old-fashioned lettering, and the corners were slightly dog-eared.

"Thanks," he said, "I'll think about it."

She smiled at him one last time, and she looked so genuine that he felt guilty for immediately dismissing her firm. When she was gone, he looked at the back of the card.

"Representing the downtrodden, the misused, the abused, the voiceless. Lunchers & Co: Lawyers for the Underdog."

He thought long and hard about that.

2 – Journal

I suspect you'll want to hear about my history, how I wound up like this—all the rest of it. Let me get it all out of the way to ease your curious mind. However, only on the proviso that you don't ask me again.

I studied Legal at the university, obviously. I'm sure, once upon a time, you have on occasion—perhaps under certain intoxicating influences—discussed the law and its many foibles. You might insist that certain results are clearly insane, and only conniving lawyers or senile judges could come to such conclusions. How could *that* result possibly be the correct, legal result, you cry, sobbing bitterly into your pint. It just doesn't make sense!

Unbeknownst to your good self, however… that is precisely how the law was designed to work. That's part of the allure. It's a secret language, hidden in plain sight, in which anything can be argued, nothing is irrelevant, and it's not what you do, it's how you phrase it. Lawyers hold a special power that others simply cannot fathom—the art of twisting words in just the right way that, suddenly, the innocent become criminals, or the guilty become irreproachable. That's why it takes a gruelling nine years to get qualified. They wouldn't just want anyone to have this sort of power.

The upside, once you're done, is the money, of course. Oh, and the ability to wield the weapon of the law to save the downtrodden, to slay the unjust mighty, to change the very course of life itself *etcetera*. But mostly, it's the security.

When you've grown up with nothing, that sort of thing is somewhat alluring.

Now, I wouldn't be a half decent lawyer if I let such an unsubstantiated character profile fly, especially if it is so clearly an exaggeration. *Objection, clearly the defendant had at least 'something', not 'nothing' as he so staunchly insists, else surely his esteemed person would have sadly died in childhood. Perhaps he is prone to embellishment?* Of course I didn't have *nothing*. I had *little*.

I was born to *et cetera* parents who didn't *et cetera ad nauseum...* you've heard it all a thousand times in a thousand ways. I had terrible parents who didn't care, and I was fending for myself from a young age. When you're in those sorts of circumstances at that sort of age in this sort of city you tend to go one of two ways: Dead, or crime.

I wish I could tell you I had a kindly uncle with large eyebrows who took me in and taught me the ways of the world, or a guild of mischievous yet charming rogues who assimilated me into their number, or perhaps that I drew a great blade from a stump and was gifted with destiny, but that's the sort of rubbish you only hear in fairy stories or awful novels.

No, nothing as thrilling. I wasn't much good at most crime, so I pretended to be someone else and finagled my way into a boarding school. There I learnt my books, focussed on the law, then managed to secure a placement (and a stipend) from an uninspiring small firm in the city (the aforementioned Kurrip & Kurripe's). After that, I'd passed the tests, got my qualifications, and found a place as a full-blown lawyer on the other end of the West Country. And voila, my new life.

That's pretty much it, if you want more details, get me drunk and sing me songs from my childhood, otherwise, that's all that needs to be said.

I've added a few entries from my journals to help give you a broader understanding of the sorts of cases I've worked on. Please find them attached. I've entered the correct dates and references, and as far as I know I've not included any inconsistencies or mistakes.

...

Now, as I write this, I'm a mere few hours from damnation. I'm preparing for a case. Probably my last. It's going to go terribly, awfully, cosmically wrong, so there's little to no chance of anyone actually reading this. I could be reading and re-reading the case, making sure every possible outcome is planned for, reinforcing every argument... Instead, I'm here, writing a journal that no one will ever see. Procrastinating? Escapism? Who knows. Human nature, I suppose.

~journal entry ends

26

Part Two: Sanctum

3 – Felix outside Lunchers & Co

The outside of Lunchers & Company was not inspiring. The lettering was precise and clean despite looking old-fashioned, but the edges of the window had started turning green. The wooden bracing was peeling. *Was wood supposed to peel?*

Felix was taking in the facade, and considering turning and leaving, when the door opened with a jerk, and a portly woman with a monocle peered out at him. She beamed a smile of recognition and beckoned him inside.

"Welcome, Felix. Lovely to see you again," she said warmly, in the same sing-song voice as before. "I was so very thrilled to receive your letter. Come on in. Can I get you a cup of tea?"

She was named Mrs Zwelee, he had learned, and was the 'talent scout' for Luncher. She travelled around, popping her head into any cases that looked interesting, trying to poach talent from other agencies. *All part of the business*, she had written to him. *We all do it, so don't fret.*

Felix removed his hat and strode in, attempting to make himself look purposeful and confident. No one noticed. A wave of warm smoky air buffeted him as he entered.

Inside, the building was bright and cramped. No less than four other clerks were stuffed inside a room built for three, reduced to sharing desk space and storing documents on the floor. The ceiling seemed low and divided curiously into many small sections. It was only when Felix saw one of the aides reach up and pull one of these sections down did he realise why.

Each section was the bottom of a recessed bookcase which could be extended fully from ceiling to floor. The one Felix could see in use was overflowing with bundles of papers, books, a few stamps and what looked like a skull.

A skull? What is this place?

Felix coughed, suddenly aware of the smoke. Every clerk, plus the woman who had shown him in, were smoking from short pipes. Some were resting on foldable wooden stands, which in turn stood dangerously on precarious piles of paper.

The smell, while not unpleasant, was immense. It was as if instead of plucking a flower to take in its subtle scent, someone had ambushed him and shoved them up his nose.

"Takes a little getting used to, but a bit of smoke is good for the soul," came a croaky voice.

A white-haired man had appeared at the foot of a staircase that Felix hadn't even noticed. He, like the lady, had a single lens on one eye, somehow secured by a small chain that swung freely in front of him. He was also smoking, but from a stout pipe with a bowl at least thrice the size anyone else's. He was dressed stylishly in a waistcoat of textured felt, thick corduroy trousers and a long, striped shirt. His hair managed to express itself in a way most unsuited to the gent's impeccable fashion sense, exploding from his scalp at a cacophony of angles. It was like he had gotten dressed from the bottom up, and by the time he reached his head, had run out of motivation.

"Well then call me cleansed and make me a monk," replied Felix, trying, with difficulty, not to blink or cough.

The man cracked a yellowed smile and shuffled through the buzzing hive of clerks to shake Felix's hand. His was a firm grip, not crushing like some people seemed to insist upon.

"You must be Mr Luncher," said Felix. "I have heard of your firm's success in winning some real against-the-odds cases, though I must admit it's not quite what I expected." He tried to look like he was unbothered by the insane surroundings, but wasn't sure if he'd succeeded.

Smile anyway..! First impressions and all that...

Mr Luncher chuckled as he shook his head, miraculously keeping hold of his monocle, and grinned broadly. Felix couldn't help but like this bizarre fellow, but no idea why.

"Life never is, unless you expect it to disappoint, but then we're dealing with paradoxes, and lawyers are allergic to those. Ever tried arguing one? Now that's an awkward subject. No, we're a little different, but just wait and see, we get the job done all right, and done well. Come on up and meet the boss."

At a surprised glance, Luncher's grin widened, and he explained before the question was asked. "No, I'm not in charge here. I have other, hm, skillsets… My wife's the one who runs the ship. We put my name on the front of the shop because there are still deluded people in this world who don't believe women are capable of Legal. I know, I know, but custom is custom, money is money, and we're in need of it." He clapped his hands together and shook his head.

"You've barely arrived and I'm already passing my worries onto you. Apologies young man, all things in time. I'll try not to scare you off before you've even picked a desk."

Picked a floor space more like.

He led Felix up the small staircase at the back to an even smaller room than the main office. It was behind a flimsy looking door, which Luncher knocked on gently before forcing it open with a jerk.

"Bloody hinges… aha my dear, here he is."

Felix saw a woman who must have been in her late sixties writing at a desk. She had a full set of glasses, her hair up in a tight bun, and was, of course, smoking. At her husband's entrance, she looked up and saw Felix for the first time.

Felix had the feeling of being appraised, as if he were a piece of furniture that had been brought home from the local Burning Yard just minutes before being engulfed. He kept up what he hoped was a 'good impressions' face, whatever that was. Sort of a neutral, vaguely positive expression.

She put down her pen and spoke.

"Who was at fault in the case of Henrig versus Gerring, and what was the penalty?"

It was a famous case, one that every child learns of when starting the path to Legal. Felix responded without hesitation.

"Henrig, but Gerring had died upon hearing the pronouncement, so no penalty was awarded."

Mrs Luncher didn't react.

"What are the levels of Legal, and how many of each level are there?"

"There are five levels of Legal: Student, of which there are countless; Journeyman-Legalite, of which there are an estimated fifteen hundred; Legalite, of which there are three hundred; Judge, of which there are fifteen, and the three Lord Judges. That is in this Country, as the laws and quantities differ between them."

This was important to know. The fewer permitted law-users, the fiercer the competition, and the higher standards one had to apply to oneself in order to practice and maintain the royal providence. Quite why these particular limits were in place was a matter lost to time, but rigidly adhered to all the same.

"Describe the outcome of Duggen versus Duggen and Duggen?"

Felix blinked.

That case was still being heard, wasn't it? I'm sure I read that in the paper... and judgement wasn't due for... three weeks?

That being said, he was good at his job, and felt confident of what was likely to happen.

"Well, Duggen Senior will almost certainly face prison time, and Mrs Duggen and Duggen Junior will, I suspect, be forced into exile. That was the result of Gershwo and, ah, Trellew—"

"Trewell," corrected the lady Luncher, sharply.

Felix carried on as if his ears weren't reddening.

"Gershwo and Trewell. The circumstances were almost exactly the same, and so the smart bet is a similar outcome."

She had stopped writing and was looking at Felix with impatience. *Had she blinked yet?* His gaze fell to the floor instinctively, and he tried to force it back. It was quite happy where it was.

"Finally, tell me about the case of The Crown versus Yerrin."

Yerrin... drunkenness? No, theft? Murder, no, divorce, no kidnapping, tax skipping, fraud, abscondment...

Argh!

I have no idea.

Felix frowned, then snapped his eyes back to hers.

"Lady Luncher, I am not familiar with that case."

A short pause, then she steepled her fingers in front of her.

"Not familiar? That's all? No apology, or excuse? Don't even want to hazard a guess?"

Felix stood resolute, and shook his head. "No, ma'am".

"I'm sitting here on your first night in this company, asking you a simple question, and you're telling me *awfully sorry, you don't know?*"

Felix was gritting his teeth, but kept his face neutral.

"I am, ma'am."

Mrs Luncher stood then, and walked to a cabinet built into the wall. She pulled open the top drawer and retrieved a pack of papers, bundled together. Ignoring Felix, she turned to her husband and asked:

"Dear, remind me. What sort of lawyers do I hate?"

"Stupid ones, my love."

"No, I pity stupid lawyers. Whom do I hate?"

"Misguided lawyers."

"No, I am irritated by misguided lawyers. Which kind of lawyer do I completely loathe? I will tell you."

She handed the pack to Felix, who took it with trepidation. Glancing down, he noticed it had a marking on it.

TCvY45

"I hate dishonest lawyers. I hate those who pretend, who obfuscate, who mislead, who blather. I'm not talking about within the courtroom, I am talking about inner dishonesty. If you do not know a thing, there is no shame in standing up and admitting the fact. Ignorance is not a weakness; it is a stage on the road to knowledge. First we are ignorant, then we are aware, then we are knowledgeable, then we are learned, and finally we are masters. And, of course, the more you know, the more you realise there is still to learn."

"Paradoxes," said Mr Luncher, giving Felix a wink. His wife continued as if he hadn't interrupted.

"It is only those that remain wilfully ignorant that should feel ashamed, and those who deceive themselves and others that should be reprimanded."

Felix let his breath out, which he realised only now he had been holding.

Mrs Luncher pointed at the bundle of papers in Felix's hands.

"We deal with facts. We deal with truth. That is what we need to succeed, both in the courtroom and out of it. Now, what I absolutely detest is *unprepared* lawyers." She took a seat and began writing again. "I expect you to master that case by the end of three days hence. Your client is waiting for you. I look forward to working together."

With that, she nodded towards the door, and Felix dipped his head in respect and hurried from the room. He walked to the bottom of the staircase, and only when he was back in the main office did he look at the bundle of papers in his hand.

"I suppose you'll be wanting a space to work?" asked Mrs Zwelee, who had miraculously cleared an area on a table in the corner. There were still precarious piles of books and papers on it, but at least there was a tiny surface for him to utilise.

Felix nodded, still feeling in somewhat of a daze. "Uh, yes." He walked over to it, and accepted the tea pressed into his hands.

"I'll leave you too it," she said. "First case is bound to be a biggie. Good luck."

He nodded, mumbled a thank you for the tea, shook his head like a cat drying itself, and began to read.

Journal Entry A: Frog

Reference case [GCvHh] (GreCro v. HH), year 1329, judge Jeckob presiding.

What is magic? I don't bloody know. Ask a wizard. I prefer to deal in that which I can see and hear myself, thank you very much.

Unfortunately for me, quite often I end up having to deal with both. Many of my cases involve some idiot who meddled with forces beyond their understanding, or the unintended consequence of some other idiot mucking about with forces they little understood.

I did once have an old witch try to explain how it works to me. She said it was more instinct than anything else. You just sort of tap into it, you exert your will, and if you're attuned to the mystical realm, you can make things happen. Things that shouldn't happen, things that break their own laws of physics. Like, for example, making an apple roll up a hill. Complete nonsense from a physics perspective, but here we are.

A common misconception is that magic is something that belongs only to those creatures with higher intelligence—your humans or goblins for example. I used to harbour this misconception myself for a while. That is, until the case of Great Croaker.

There was a town on the edge of the winding moors, up the western edge of the North Country. A hardy folk lived there, and they made their living as hunters and traders. They'd head into the swamplands, gather mushrooms and other unusual plants, catch themselves a few buckets of frogs and bog-fish and sell them as exotic luxuries and medicines to any passers-by, or by cartload to the larger towns and cities.

This town had existed here for generations, and the methods and lifestyles were handed down, parent to child.

One day, the hunters were going for their regular jaunt into the marshes, when they found themselves beset by a terrible power. Dark magics began swirling about their heads, filling their thoughts with monstrous visions. They ran, terrified, and told their town elders what had happened. This continued for weeks. Every time someone entered the marshes, horrible visions plagued them, and they fled.

One particularly tough hunter fought through the visions, but found his skin started to fester and break out in warts and boils as he pushed on, so he too withdrew.

Convinced the swamp had gained an evil sentience, the townspeople cobbled together enough money to hire a Purger from faraway Placenamia to remove the wicked spirit. However, when she came, she told them that no such phantom occupied the swamp, and therefore there was nothing she could do. She charged the full fee, regardless.

That's what started the whole legal case. The townsfolk demanded she exorcise the spirit or return their money, but the Purger refused both, citing that whatever lived there had the right to live there, but she hadn't travelled all the way across the country to this god-forsaken backwater for no recompense.

The case found its way to Luncher, eventually. We were working on the side of the townsfolk, them having little left to pay a more reputable firm, and, because the Purgers were based in Placenamia, here is where the case was being fought. We were happy to help, what with the Purgers acting in a manner most unbecoming of a respected professional guild.

We made the long journey to the swamp to conduct our own investigations. We had taken a friend of Mr Luncher's, an old cheerful wizard called Huppity, long past his prime, but always up for a bit of adventure. We arrived at the swamp, apprehensive of what we might find. We did not expect that to be a frog waiting for us.

Now, you might think 'Wow, a frog in a swamp, whatever next', but I assure you this was no ordinary frog. It exuded a… Presence. It was sat upon a rotted stump, on the edge of the village, as if it were waiting for us, and we were bang on time.

Huppity had stared, open mouthed, when we first saw it.

"This ain't no normal frog," he had whispered.

I had raised an eyebrow in what I hoped was an accurate level of sarcasm, and made a note on my pad. *Saw a weird frog.*

I not weird.

The voice had spoken in my own head and was really rather unsettling. I dropped my pad in alarm, and it landed with a splat on the muddy floor.

The frog was looking at me… and grinning.

"Wh-what!" I had stammered.

Maybe you weird?

The voice sounded deep and wet. Almost… warty. I looked to Huppity. "You're hearing this, right?"

He nodded. I turned back to the frog.

"Uhm, my pardons. I'm not used to speaking with amphibians."

Hmm. I not used speaking you. But think give you chance.

Huppity had taken off his jacket then and laid it down, settling on it in a cross-legged position. He beckoned me to do the same. We were eye-level to the frog.

"Tell us your story," the wizard had said.

The frog began. It was less spoken in Common, more a sequence of… feelings. It's hard to explain. I felt the emotions, I felt the urgings, I shared the memories, but the words weren't there.

When you look from the perspective of the swamp creatures, the local town comes across rather differently. Giant, horrible monsters that appear with alarming frequency, stealing your food, destroying your homes, stealing your friends, even your children… Using all manner of horrible traps and tricks to lure you into their hideous warm clutches. Those that manage to escape talk of nightmarish treatment and terrible fates.

This frog, who he told us goes by the name himself Great Croaker, had been born different. A monster had tried to take him, but he had been able to turn him away with a thought.

As he explored his powers, he found he could protect not just himself but his friends and families too.

He explained that the swamp dwellers understood the nature of things, that the strong eat the weak, but this was different.

This not natural.

He had been getting stronger the more he used his magic, for magic it was, and as long as he lived, he would let no human enter his swampland. He admitted that it was hard work, and he didn't think he could keep it up for much longer. He then asked us about us.

Who you? What do want?

We shared who we were and what we did. He asked if we could help him.

Now, it might sound ridiculous to you, but I felt a connection with that creature. I don't know if he used his weird swamp magic on me, or it was just my conscience, but I knew I wanted to help him. So, I offered. We exchanged details, or, rather, I explained what I could do for him, and he accepted my help.

A short while later, court day approached. We had two back-to-back cases.

In the first case, we helped the judge see that the townsfolk deserved their money back from the Purgers, who offered a service they could not provide. We didn't win that one, sadly, as it was all stipulated in the contract. The day was about to get a lot worse for the town.

The second case was on behalf of Great Croaker, who had travelled back with us in a nest of leaves, moss and swamp water. I stood up and argued that the land belonged to the creatures that lived there; as they held first claim to it, they were within their rights to defend themselves. Great Croaker even testified, which must be a first.

He sat on a stack of boxes, facing down this collection of humanity, and shared with them his thoughts and feelings. Waves of emotion washed over those in the room, judge and audience alike. The panic of the arrival of the monsters. The fear and powerlessness of what might be taken. The anger and frustration at not being able to defend yourself. The vindication of finally standing up to these *beasts*, these warm beasts with their spikes, and their cages, and their fires-on-sticks.

It was moving.

I don't know if it was some more slimy frog-wizardry that did it, but miraculously the Judge ruled in Croaker's favour. From this point on, for what is now called Great Croaker Swamp, no human is permitted to enter unless invited by the inhabitants, and any breaking that code will be subject to the will of the inhabitants.

The townsfolk were understandably furious with us, but… I think we made the right decision.

One of the stranger side-effects of the court case was the inexplicable return of the frog pie as the latest 'trendy' dish-of-choice for the fashionably up-to-date. I suspect it was to do with the newfound difficulty in obtaining frogs as ingredients in that region, leading to it being prohibitively expensive. As it was only to be found in high-end North Country restaurants, it was seen as something to be enjoyed by only those with more money than sense, ergo fashionable. Before you knew it, the revolting bloody things were everywhere, and still are.

Oh, and we were made honorary and lifetime members of Great Croakers Kingdom, official Swamp-Friends, forever welcome to enter and leave as we saw fit.

So made a few hundred enemies, but befriended a magic frog. Not the best deal, perhaps, but made for the right reasons. I hope.

~journal entry ends

4 – Furbo & Helda

Furbo stood staring up at the door. It was enormous, five men standing on each other's shoulders would barely reach the top. Every square inch was covered in shallow carvings, intricately detailed. Each of the two doors looked, to his eye, to be carved from a single slab for no visible seams could be seen. Furbo was fascinated by the sheer mechanics of the thing. Where would one source a slab this large? How did they bring it here? It must have been abominably heavy, so how on earth did the hinges work? How did they not snap when the weight was first transferred to them? Were there tests to see how heavy they could go, and they settled on this size? Did they carve it before they hung it, or did they hang it then carve?

He examined the carvings, walking slowly along the face of the door. He saw men pointing at men, he saw women planting shrubs, he saw cats, sheep, birds. As he moved, his perspective shifted, and suddenly the men were fighting, the women digging graves. There were no birds or fluffy sheep, but demons, and carrion beasts waiting for morsels.

How long did it take the artisan who carved this to discover that technique? How many years of practice, then how did he or she transfer that knowledge to a single piece of stone this huge? What if they made a mistake? Did they file it down, snap it off, or start from fresh? Did they work as an individual, or use a team? Did they carve in shifts? Did the carver work for a few hours, get bored, then give up for the day, going home to his or her family? Did their minds wander when they were carving, did they wonder what they would have for their supper that day?

Or were they forced to carve, every day and every night? Did they hide any secret rebellious clues in the fresco? Or were their spirits completely broken, simply responding to the wants of their master?

"What are you staring at?" asked Helda.

"The door," he replied.

Helda wrinkled her nose, scoffing. "It's just a door."

Furbo shook his head, but didn't elaborate.

There was a handle within reach situated in the centre of where the two doors met. A single vertical grip was visible, set into a recess formed from two semi-circular hollows, one in each door. It was wide enough for one arm, or two small arms. There were words scratched around the handle, written in an old dialect of the common language.

"They say: Turn, Hold, Wait," explained Furbo. "Do you mind..?"

Helda was undoubtedly the muscle of the pair. She was broad without being fat and seemed to have reserves of stamina that continually surprised Furbo. She carried the enormous pack containing their worldly possessions without complaint. Though, she did have a habit of hoarding—she tended to carry five where one would suffice—so if she did complain about it being too heavy, Furbo could tell her to leave some stuff behind. Perhaps that's why she didn't complain…

Helda dropped the pack, rolling her shoulders as she did so. She rolled up her sleeve, and swept her short brown hair back, out of her eyes. She flexed her wrist and fingers, clapped twice, then grasped the cold handle firmly. With a grunt she twisted it to the left.

"It's heavy!" She forced out between strained breaths and gritted teeth.

As she twisted the handle, the sound of grating stone and churning mechanisms filled the room. Helda's arm burned from the effort. Slowly, the handle turned, and turned, until it could turn no more. Helda could feel some yearning to force the handle back, fighting with her, trying to return to its starting position.

Furbo's eyes were wide open as he flicked his gaze all over the fresco, searching for something. Not finding it, he pressed his ear to the door, and his mouth hung open.

"Absolutely incredible," he whispered.

Helda's arm was fire. Her elbow would snap at any moment. She was uncomfortably aware of just how fragile the human form could be. She had proven that point many times to many people, and her mind was filled with images of her bones splintering and snapping like a bundle of dry twigs. The grating sound ceased suddenly, but Helda held on, bracing her legs, core, shoulder, her entire body.

"How long did it say to wait for!?" she gurgled.

Furbo stepped back, staring at the stone. He reluctantly scrambled over to Helda and re-read the writing. He read it again, muttering while he did so.

"Turn, wait, hold… hold? No, not hold, reverse? No, reverse isn't it… Undo? Scrap..? Oh! It doesn't say "Wait", Helda, it says "Release". I think you can—"

Helda roared and whipped her hand from the handle, flinging it behind her with such force she overbalanced and toppled over, landing heavily on her front, face-down in the dust. The door responded with a series of deep metallic clunks, before an immense squealing of hinges, and the gap between the doors widened. Dust and air whirled out of the room, settling on the swearing heap that was Helda.

She pushed herself to standing, shaking dust from her like a cat shakes water. She stomped over to Furbo, a face like thunder.

"'Wait'!? Idiot! My bloody arm feels like it's been bent backwards!"

Furbo waved her down in a poorly-chosen mollifying gesture that only infuriated her more. She grabbed the scruff of his collar with her good arm, dragging the gangly old man closer to her.

He was of average height, but trim—the sort of slimness that comes from a lifetime of wandering and never quite having enough to eat. While his late-middling age had compounded this, his salt-and-pepper hair making him often appear like a wiry old badger, his curiosity had never stopped burning, and he often lost himself in wonder at some contraption or other. Helda tightened her grip on his scruff, trying to snap him out of this latest trance so he could be properly terrified of her.

"What say I show you how it feels?" she snarled, grabbing his wrist.

"Helda, look." Furbo's eyes hadn't left the crack in the door.

Helda turned, her anger briefly forgotten, and beheld something no other eyes had seen for countless years. The sanctum was open.

She dropped him and brushed some more dust off of her heavy jerkin.

"Peh. Bloody arm…" she muttered, trying to remain miserable despite the anticipation bubbling within her guts. Furbo wasn't interested, so she gave up, and followed him through the doorway.

Inside, the room was ascetic; no carvings were on the walls (which disappointed Furbo no end), no statues adorned the dais, no carpet or tiles covered the floor. The only object in the dark room was an old stone plinth, worn and rubbed smooth. On the plinth was a skeletal corpse, draped in mouldy cloth, slumped awkwardly forward.

They approached it slowly, Helda scanning the room for anything that could spell danger. She was rubbing her elbow with her good hand, angling herself towards Furbo. Helda was clearly trying to elicit even a shred of empathy, but her efforts were wasted. A mixture of reverence, curiosity and fear battled on Furbo's face, giving him a look of terrified wonder as he inched closer to the dead relic.

"That would be him, the Fetter," he spoke quietly. "A quiet life of solitude, meditating on the mysteries of the universe, both human and otherwise. Only once every two years could this seal be broken, and two questions asked of him, which legends tell would be spoken in truth. They may not answer the question directly, but whatever wisdom they imparted would be reverently received by whichever person, usually the monarch, had asked."

"Well, it looks like we're a few hundred years too late," Helda muttered. "I suppose we'll not get the answer we wanted."

Furbo shook his head and sighed. "I fear not."

"What did he eat?" asked Helda, looking around the room for any evidence of habitation. "No kitchen, no toilets… How did they survive? Well, I guess they didn't," she added, staring with disgust at the skeleton.

"They were in tune with the great unknown, they were beyond such earthly needs as food and sleep. They were sustained by wisdom, nourished by starlight," he whispered.

Helda looked up at what could have once been a window to the stars, but was now a crusty lump in the ceiling. Besides, they had been descending gradually for hours. How could a window reach this far down?

"Starlight, hm?" she said. Her face showed exactly what she thought of that, but Furbo was off.

"Quite so! And when, at the start of…"

Furbo went on, but she had stopped listening. She tried desperately to quash the wave of disappointment that washed through her.

I should be used to it by now.

Trying to distract herself, she began examining the skeleton more closely, looking for any signs of damage or combat. Mysticism was one thing, but not her thing. She knew battle, and pain, and injury, and evidence. She peered at the form of the skeleton.

He was stooped unusually, his upper body and head face down, but his lower body in a sitting position. He was sitting when he died. Was he stabbed, or poisoned? No, the angle was too sharp, the neck and upper back shattered. Perhaps bludgeoned from behind by someone or other who didn't like his answer?

"Bingo."

Furbo stopped, and asked, "Sorry, Helda?"

"I didn't say anything," she replied.

"You said bingo."

"I don't say 'bingo'."

"I said 'bingo'," came a soft voice.

Both of them stared at the body. It shifted, and they both leapt back, Furbo with his arms flailing around him madly, Helda drawing her hammer by instinct.

The skeleton's right arm braced itself against the plinth, followed by the left, and with a dry crunch, the creature pushed its upper body to an upright position. The head flopped sickening around on a clearly-broken neck, but the eye sockets fixed the pair with a stare only a skull can manage, a faint green glow coming from them. Once it was settled, it grabbed its head and lifted and twisted it, so it rested more-or-less correctly on its shoulders.

"Hundreds of years of saying nothing, then I say 'bingo'." The voice was dry and breathy, the stuff of nightmares. The mouth didn't move when the words came out, but the sounds came from the skull. The creature considered the two figures in front of it.

41

"Is this what man resembles these days?"

"Uh, wha, wha, when, wha, uh," blurted Furbo.

"I knew this would happen." The voice slowed, speaking with great deliberation. *Did it just roll its eyes?* "I - am - not - familiar - with - that - dialect," it spoke.

"I mean, that is to say, sir, I wonder if, who are you, what are you?" Furbo's words tumbled out of a trembling mouth, tripping over each other in their reluctance to be said.

"Oh, you do speak Common. And, 'madam'."

Helda started. "Me?"

The skeleton shook its head, the motion of which made Helda's stomach turn.

"No. You called me 'sir'. I am not a 'sir', I am a 'madam'," the figure plucked mildly at one clump of rotten fabric, lifting it, and watching it fall to pieces. "I suppose there's no need to tell you I was beautiful. You wouldn't know either way. Fat lot of good it did me, anyway."

Furbo was blinking and stuttering still. Helda put her mace away.

"You're a woman?" she asked.

"Yes. Is that so surprising? You are too, I gather? What a pair we make. I think your friend needs a lie down."

Helda tore her eyes from the spectre and saw Furbo wavering, his balance teetering forward and backwards as if drunk. She caught him as his legs gave way and lowered him gently to the ground. Her elbow hurt as she did so, but she didn't notice.

She eyed the creature with confusion. "I think we need to talk."

The creature shrugged. "I would, but I'm afraid I have such a busy schedule."

Helda didn't understand. "Uh…"

"Not much of a sense of humour, hmm? Never mind. Let's talk."

It flourished an arm and bowed as best it could.

"My name is Racelsus."

Journal Entry B: Goblin

Reference case [BvD] (Bur v. Drak), year 1331, judge Verxi presiding.

I might have said once already, but I hate bullies. I took this little guy's case because he had nowhere else to turn, and I'm a sap. His auntie had knocked the door of Lunchers & Co one chilly evening and asked to see the owner.

"The real owner, the one with brains," she had added.

Descending the staircase, Mrs Luncher had clapped in delight upon spotting the stunty, reddish-green creature in the doorway.

"Oh Depinity, it's been years," she had exclaimed in a girlish way quite unlike her normal demeanour. Realising this, she had cleared her throat and straitened to her full, formal height.

"Do please follow me, madam," she had intoned with a slight bow, leading the goblin away to her office. I swore I saw her trying desperately not to giggle as she walked past.

It turns out they knew each other when they were young, and became fast, lifelong friends. Depinity the Goblin had a caustic sense of humour but a kind, motherly attitude, and they'd got on like a barn on fire.

"Believe it or not, the esteemed Mrs Luncher was quite the troublemaker in her younger days," Mr Luncher had explained to me during that day's walk, with a conspiratorial glance around. "You wouldn't believe the sorts of mischief they got up to. I'll tell you more about it another day, when I'm absolutely, positively sure that she won't overhear me."

It transpired that Depinity's nephew was in a spot of bother.

Burrimo is, obviously, a goblin. A shifty looking bugger that, despite assumptions and appearances, did quite nothing wrong and has been the target of a cruel prank, which may cost him his life.

He was a new, proud member of the Drakarian Household Guard. Admittedly a minor member, but a member, nonetheless. It was largely down to the Princess's direct interventions. She had, by chance, been passing through when he had presented himself to the Guard Captain and offered his service. Instead of being laughed out of the building, the

Princess had accepted his offer of service with a dignity not often shown to goblinkind.

He served dutifully, guarded fervently, and obeyed diligently. Every penny of his meagre wage had gone onto his uniform, which had been given to him, on loan, until he paid it off.

"It's not cheap making goblin-sized breastplates, you know," opined the quartermaster, with a sad shake of the head. "You understand, of course."

Burrimo had not, but had gone along with it. He was desperate to find a place for himself in this civilised society, so had upped-sticks and left his homeland, deep in the mountains, to settle in the East Country, in the city of Great Pave. There is a certain view of goblins by outsiders (which is perhaps not entirely unfounded), and Burrimo had encountered endless bullying, suspicion, rejection and outright xenophobia. But, brave little soul he was, he had dug in his heels and persevered.

One night, his bunkmates had woken him to tell him he needed to get dressed, and quick! The princess was in mortal danger!

A child assassin had snuck through the sewer pipes and was threatening her life, and had barred and locked the door to her bedroom. He needed to sneak in the same way the child had, fight him off, save the princess, and earn the favour of the whole country. Quick—there's no time to lose! But go quietly—in case he cottons on!

Burrimo had grabbed his gear and snuck like a shadow through and out the castle until he had come to the river where the sewage pipes began. Clamping his shortsword in his teeth, his mind raced with fantasies of him, a lowly goblin, saving the princess! He could repay her faith in him by doing the unthinkable—rescuing her!

Maybe he would be promoted, and human-goblin relations could be cast anew from the iron of his deed. Tears welled, but he forced them back, for now was a time for bravery and action.

He had crawled through fetid water until he arrived at the princess's tower and crept through out of her privy. Breathing heavily, eyes darting madly, he had slowly, slowly pushed the door open, and gently, gently grasped his shortsword, ready to leap in and save the one person who had ever shown him kindness. The room was dark, black as pitch, and his heart was hammering in his ears as he searched frantically for any sign of the assassin.

A sharp thump at the door, and the sleeping princess awoke, lighting a lamp, to find a small, stinking goblin brandishing a sword, eyes darting around in determined fury. She had screamed then, and the door was kicked in. Three members of the guard had accosted him, stripped him of his arms and armour and thrown him out the window.

He had survived, no doubt through luck more than judgement. He'd landed on a wheeled cart full of sponges, which had wrecked said cart. The understandably upset merchant waggled a finger at the goblin, demanding recompense, causing an already overwhelmed Burrimo to go into full emotional meltdown. He'd been seized, beaten, then thrown in prison, ready to be executed in the next available slot.

Word had travelled of the would-be Goblin Assassin, and it had reached his aunt. Being an enterprising goblin, she had left immediately to find her nephew to convince him that staying in the city would be untenable for a goblin with this news.

You can imagine her surprise when she could not find him at his home, his friends' houses, his favourite pub. When she visited his place of work, she was met with pompous condescension, she had treated the guards to a little goblin hospitality, and they had graciously informed her of her nephew's predicament.

She found him, got his story. Then, sparing no time or effort, came straight to us. I was selected to represent him, and I was told his execution was scheduled for two days hence, so I had better get down there and sort it out fast. I was going to have to prepare my case on the road.

~

It was not going to be a simple case. I fully believed Burrimo, but there was so little evidence. Our case would hinge on whether we could prove the guards in question were demonstrably speciesist—try spelling that correctly first try—and it would therefore be reasonable to think they could have and would have engineered a circumstance in which they could, without interjection from onlookers, injure or kill this goblin. I

45

suspect they thought that if they had just murdered him in his sleep, the chances of being caught would have been high—for, if they cannot guard themselves, how could they guard the (minor) royal family of Drakaria? So, kill him in plain sight, but do it in a way no one would question.

Sneaky buggers they were.

I arrived at Great Pave with a day to spare, so, with Depinity's help, I conducted my research and prepared my arguments as quickly as I could. There is a feeling of excitement when time is against you, even when the stakes are high. I probably hated it at the time, but looking back I can't help but feel that same excitement again.

There were three guards in question who had talked to Burrimo that night. Getlock Hominy, Jayce Yellowman and Sweetness Fenneldaughter. We had a suspicion Sweetness was the brains behind the operation, and I use that word loosely. Her colleagues went along because of a mixture of wanting to impress her, wanting to kill something, and bare-faced pig-headed speciesism.

It didn't turn out to be difficult to prove Sweetness's bone-deep hatred for anything non-human. A cursory investigation into her private life (via a few swapped silvers to a few 'sympathetic' associates of Depinity) found she regularly attended 'self-defence' groups. The topics of discussion at these classes were specifics like the weak spots of anything not-human (apparently for goblins it's the ears), and political meetings of parties singularly obsessed with the purity of humanity (a point easily disproved if you actually met any members of humanity.) A check through the barracks records showed us a whopping seventeen similar cases of non-humans being expelled/executed for seemingly sudden crimes with few, if any, witnesses in Sweetness's time as Guard Captain at the Drakarian Estate. Each time the case was labelled as 'Unsolved Due to Non-Human Conspiracy.'

The two dregs she hung out with were clearly infatuated with her, and she strung them both along in whatever schemes she concocted, often pitting them against each other in their quest for her affection. Again, this turned out quite easy to prove. The first out-and-out told us she was his one and truly, and the other would spend his evenings painting dreadful romantic portraits of, guess who, our Guard Captain.

All we had to do was string it together, combined with a heartfelt account of Burrimo's quest to find a life in the big city, to find a respectable job to make his poor old mum proud. It was hard not to feel sorry for him, all small and weedy looking. He looked like some poor, sick child.

Now, as mentioned, this case was to be heard in the East Country. The laws are more or less the same, but they have this bizarre practice of not letting the Judge decide if someone is guilty on the balance of evidence, but instead choose thirteen random citizens who watch the whole trial, have no input, and must deliberate among themselves, in secret, and declare whether the client is guilty or not. I know, it's insane. How are thirteen random strangers, with no legal training whatsoever, going to come up with a verdict that's better than a judge would deliver? But there we go.

The jury was selected, as is normal, and, by some cosmic stroke of luck, of the thirteen jurors, seven of them were goblins.

I explained how it had gone to Mr Luncher in the pub after our victory, and of the good fortune for our now-exonerated goblin client. He laughed and took me aside, an arm on my shoulder, and leaned close to speak quietly.

"Hah, yes, well. It was clear as day that our little friend was innocent, any halfwit can see that. Prejudices, though, nasty things. You remember the aunt? The one who went to university with Mrs Luncher? I caught up with the missus after she returned home in the early hours this morning, I mean the really early hours. She and the aunt had had a busy night it seems. Do you know, she gave me a wonderful gift. Goblin powder tastes simply marvellous, and look—"

He lit his pipe, dragged deep and let out a fantastic cloud of red smoke. It smelled of earthy pebbles.

I gave a meagre wave in an attempt to try to move the smoke away from my face. "Expensive stuff, isn't it? Goblin powder? How could the aunt afford it?" I asked.

He looked at me then, a dastardly twinkle in that old eye.

"I hear that after university Depinity quite defied expectations and became something of a skilled bureaucrat. In the civil service, apparently.

She oversees some aspect of the postal system and has a small hand in a number of other departments. Now, I'm *not* saying she selects jurors, we all know that's a random process, as sacred as the law itself. All I'm saying is she oversees the people who send the letters."

He sighed.

"Troublesome things, letters. So easy to get them muddled up."

He saw the look in my eye and patted me on the back. "As I said, as far as we know, nothing dodgy happened. But, even if it did, I would sleep soundly, my lad, knowing that the right people got what they deserved."

With that he called for more drinks, leaving me to mull that thought over for a good many minutes. Was my skill, or lack thereof, completely irrelevant? Did I make any difference at all, or was it… the luck of the jury?

If I had had two years to forge the perfect case, could I have won? Or was I doomed from the outset? Was I as good as I hoped I was, or was I completely wrong?

I gladly accepted the drink from Mr Luncher and didn't let my smile drop as he raised his glass to me.

~journal entry ends

5 – Racelsus's Story

I am Racelsus.

This cave we are in has been my home for… I honestly do not know how long.

Allow me to quickly clarify something for you both. I'm not a wise man of the mountain, or a wise woman of the woods. I've been called a witch, a hag, a harridan, and, most recently, 'necromancer'. Or, I suppose, if we're being pedantic about it, they should have called me a 'lich'. What's the difference? Well, a necromancer communicates and reanimates the dead to serve all sorts of nefarious purposes, and a lich uses those similar magicks to perpetuate one's own longevity: that is, they grant themselves immortality.

Now, let me get this out there right away. It was an accident.

My twin brother and I were swamp dwellers. We lived in a damp shack out west, a place no-doubt long lost to time and progress. We each had some small ability in mysticism. Nothing to bring nations low or invite the wrath of the temples, mind you, simple provincial tricks to earn a living and a modicum of wary respect from the locals. I could read thoughts and move objects a little, he could steal the heat from one thing and move it through the air to something else.

I don't know if anyone's ever explained this to you before, but using these magicks isn't some skill you can study, or some logical puzzle you can unlock. It's pure instinct. Look, let me give you an example. Pick up that stone over there, that's right. Now, I want you to throw it up in the air at an angle and pin your arms to your sides. When the stone is falling and is level with your head, catch it with one hand.

I mean it, go and try it. I know your elbow hurts, just humour me.

…

49

Well done, and first attempt, too! Answer this: How did you know at which time to dart your arm out? How did you know exactly where to put your hand so it would intercept the stone in its flight?

A fiendishly complex series of events happened without your knowing about it. The stone was in flight. Light entered your eyes and was transmitted to your brain. Your brain took this stimulus, interpreted it as motion, and sent signals to your muscles in your body to contract or extend in just the right way so your physical arm would move at exactly the right speed and in precisely the right way. Your open hand reaches the stone, and a further signal causes your fingers to clench. Cosmically, your hand and that stone occupying the same space is such a small event, infinitely unlikely, and yet it happened.

Not to mention hairs in your ears vibrated in the right way and you understood exactly what I asked of you in the first place.

Now, can you explain why all of that happened, *exactly*?

I can't.

I'm sure some doctor or scientist would give theories. They would explain the *how*, but could they explain the *why*? They can't.

In a similar way, I can't explain how I can make that pebble rattle and bounce without anyone touching it, or how I knew you were thinking about my broken back. I think about it, I urge it to happen, and it does. Sometimes it's easier, sometimes harder.

Perhaps you have some power you just haven't discovered yet?

I am getting side-tracked. It feels nice to talk to someone again. Rocks and walls are good listeners, but not great conversationalists.

I was talking of my brother and I, and our talents.

Some days the strength of these 'powers' ebbs or flows, like the tide. Sometimes they work differently to normal. I suppose this is like a chef having a good day or a bad day. Sometimes they cook the dish perfectly, sometimes it burns for reasons they can't understand.

We were having a rare day of tranquillity. We had decided to take a long walk around the distant fen. We were in good spirits; the weather was perfect for long walks: bright and chilly. The sounds of life were filling in the air around us, buzzing and clicking and wheep-wheeping.

He had made some joke about frogs, I can't remember what it was, but it made me laugh. He could spin a joke from anything. The clouds parted briefly, and I had raised my face to feel the heat of the sun on my closed eyes... when I stumbled. I caught myself before I fell, and my brother rushed to aid me. I was unhurt, perhaps my pride had taken a small hit, but nothing new there.

When he had helped me to my feet, we stopped and listened. There was no sound. It was cold and dark. We looked around us. There was a ring of mushrooms, great bloated black and yellow things, crooked and warty and leaking. They formed a perfect circle around me. In my carelessness I must have wandered in, and my brother's selfless nature led him to follow.

We had heard of mushroom rings, but hearing is one thing and experiencing is another. We could not leave. We were trapped.

There was a heavy sense of something in the air, both my brother and I could feel it. Something was looking at us, trying to get our attention. Something beyond our comprehension, but we could feel it. It felt old and bitter.

The darkness crept from the horizon to the edge of the ring, until it seemed as if we were trapped in a well. A deep well, a well without bottom. Ironic, considering what happened to him. Or maybe it was portentous? Ah, but that's a story for another time.

A great sound, like the air itself tearing. I could feel my thoughts dribbling from my head, my very spirit spreading like spores from my body to the ground. My brother looked as if he were similarly afflicted. His face was locked in a primal contortion, the image of which will never leave me.

His hand grasped mine, and he pulled me close. He held me and I clutched him, all the while our souls were pulled from us by some greater power.

Our essences coalesced, mixing in the air around us, protecting us both. It burned.

Abruptly, it stopped. We stayed holding each other for some time yet, reluctantly taking in the world around us.

All seemed the same, but we were changed.

A tightness under the skin, as if in our blood. A feeling that we were never quite… here. Our skills in the arcane arts bloomed, and we could achieve things we previously could not.

And, of course, everlasting life. We noticed that we did not age as others did. It took us decades to realise this. The townschildren we had helped birth had grown up and we were unchanged. Generations had grown and died, yet we were the same.

Once, my brother had been involved in a fight, and had been stabbed through the chest. Yet, he lived. He lost heartsblood, but still, he lived.

This shook us, and we became recluses. But… words spread, and we were hunted.

They found us eventually. They called us demons, witches, and more besides. I suspect them jealously at the supposed gift of immortality irked them, and that manifested itself into hatred. We must be dealt with. Yet, how could they kill us? They dared not slice us to pieces, for our ghosts would haunt them, or crush us to powder, lest our angry spirits drag them to hell.

Better to keep us alive but separate, under control but helpless. I was banished here, to this cave, and my back was broken, so I might never leave. Yet… I lived.

My brother? I cannot say for sure, but I can feel him in some way. He was falling for the longest time, but no longer. Now he is climbing, and I can feel that he has nearly reached the top.

What he will do once free, I have no idea. I hope he'll find me, and we will again be reunited. I… haven't heard from him in so long.

As for me, I have no purpose. I seek not revenge. I just… am. I don't want to die, but I don't know if I want to live.

So, I wait. I wait for something to happen, or someone to come along, or I suppose for the universe to end.

And thus, here I am, waiting.

Until you walked in.

6 – Felix at Lunchers

"**S**he's incredible, isn't she?" asked Mirandhe, exhaling a devilish cloud of smoke while she spoke. Her eyes sparkled with jealous mischief. "I hope one day to command such, such... Ah! I don't even know what to call it. But whatever she has, I want it. I want people to fear me."

Felix coughed delicately, trying to hide the fact his eyes were streaming from the acrid smoke. Mirandhe's herb of choice was particularly grating to one not used to it. It was called 'Yellow Wheat' by those that enjoyed it, or to others that didn't, 'arseroot'. "She certainly scared the socks off of me. I never want to get on her bad side, let me tell you."

A few of the clerks took daily walks in the nearby woods. They had invited Felix to join them, and he had accepted, partially to enjoy some fresh air.

"Wait until you see her in full swing," chuckled Dago, chewing the end of an empty pipe as he chatted. "Hoo, boy."

Dago and Merindha had been legal clerks at Luncher for quite some time, around six and seven years, respectively. Dago was lanky, preferring tight, form fitting clothes that make him look almost skeletal. He had a slow way of speaking, as if considering each word separately before he said them.

Merindha was almost his complete opposite. Small, wide, with a quick tongue and a love for the dramatic. She preferred bright, billowing outfits, and she seemed to speak without thinking.

She spun to Dago. "Do you remember the last new guy, what was his name, Ferrin or something? Anyway, she did the whole, tell me this case, tell me that case, and he had tried to fudge his way into convincing her he knew about the unrevealed one she always keeps secret until the end. The more she probed, the bigger the hole he dug for himself, until she eventually shouted him out of the office and all the way down the street! Poor kid," sighed Mirandhe, who didn't seem to display any outwards signs of sympathy, and in fact seemed to relish the memory.

They had filled him in on her history as they walked through the pleasant forest path. Jucinda Luncher, formerly Jucinda Diero, had been a formidable lawyer in the East country for ten years, first as a take-any-comers lawyer, then specialising in fraud cases. Somewhere in those years she had developed a real bee in her bonnet for dishonesty, injustice and 'punching down'. Nothing ignited her blood like seeing a large, powerful individual bending the law to get one over on the little guy, particularly doing so dishonestly.

Unfortunately, it's not easy to make a living as a lawyer who hunts the big fish and preaches honesty. Why? Most clients have either got something to hide that they would very much like to remain unsaid, or they thought spreading a few lies and mistruths about a legal opponent was all part and parcel of the system, and having a lawyer who insists on full disclosure and one hundred percent honesty can cause a few tense conversations. Also, the little guys didn't have much money to begin with.

Additionally, Jucinda was a woman. There are a lot of people that don't like being told what to do, and even less so by a woman, especially a young woman.

"A lot of *idiots*," Mirandhe had added, flourishing her hand above her in a gesture of genuine vehemence.

This meant that eventually, Jucinda ran out of clients, and out of money, and was forced to widen the net, so to speak. She joined a firm, and met a young, optimistic Mr Luncher, and that was that.

Since then, they had formed their own company, and had built a successful career and solid reputation defending the underdog, the little guy, relying on costs recouped from the other side to pay their dues.

Mr Luncher is the face, Mrs Luncher is the brain, and the Layers and Juniors are the hands, teeth and claws.

Mirandhe tipped her spent pipe on the ground, scuffing it about with the toe of her boot.

"Of course, there are rumours about her time in the South Country…"

"Oh, here we go again," said Dago. "Always with the rumours."

"Shut it, you," she snapped. "I happen to think they're true. I just daren't go digging for evidence…"

"What are the rumours?" Felix said, genuinely curious, despite the nagging voice in his head telling him to ignore them.

Glancing about her, Merindha came closer. The smell of her brand of smoke was almost overpowering, and Felix resisted the urge to gag. Satisfied no one else was listening, she began.

"I heard she used to be a prosecutor, and she used to be good. Really bloody good. But she prosecuted some case, and won, and as a result, people died. Good people just trying their best. After that, she hung up her prosecutor's apron and completely changed her ways, dedicating herself to the 'little guy'. No more representing the powers-that-be, as it were."

"Look," said Dago. "If that were the case, we'd know about it, and even if it were true, it doesn't matter. Lawyers aren't responsible for the fallout of their cases. They fight for their client, for justice and that. Even if it's not pretty, or not what the guy in the pub might agree with, they do what's right by their client. Even if the guy who looks guilty as sin, who almost certainly *probably* done it, even if he is practically *asking for it*, it's up to us to make sure his side of the story gets heard. We do *our* bit, and the other side does *their* bit, and the judge puts it all together and comes up with a result, and we call that justice. So, Mrs Luncher was just fulfilling her role as a lawyer, she wasn't responsible for what happened after. End of, in my opinion."

Dago shook his stocky wooden pipe with rather more irritation than normal, before stuffing it roughly with tobacco and lighting it, all without looking at the others.

"Blimey Dago, I've never heard you speak like that before," said Merindha, nudging Felix. "It must be love. Infatuation. Fancy that, fancying your boss."

She narrowly avoided the pipe being thrown at her, before Dago stomped off back the way they had come, muttering something.

She was still laughing when she stood up, brushing leaves from her coat. She was holding Dago's pipe, which was still smoking.

"For what it's worth, I agree with him," Felix said.

Her smile dropped an inch, but returned swiftly. "Me too. Just like winding him up."

Felix raised an eyebrow. "Tugging his pigtails?"

She shoved him over, and he fell heavily on his arse.

"Nice try," she said, before strolling back to Lunchers & Co.

What an odd bunch, thought Felix, standing and gingerly feeling for bruises.

"Hang on," he called after her. "You haven't told me what happened to the last lawyer that joined Luncher!"

Journal Entry C: Temporomancer

Reference case [CEvCE] (CulMen [pre] v. CulMen [fut]), year 1328/58, judge Merita presiding.

There was one case that I think about from time to time. It was about a temporomancer—that's 'time-wizard', to you and me—who successfully travelled into the past. Now, time travel is, from what I understand, somewhat complicated. Most of the time we don't really know it's happened. Either the traveller has got lost somewhere in the past, or he has affected the future in some way, and we, living in our current time-splinter, don't know either way. Events simply happen to us; we are not privy to alternative dimensions where events happen to us in slightly different ways. I also know it takes a good half-century to learn even the most rudimentary of time-magicks. Any less and, well, goodbye, thanks for all the non-existent memories.

Anyway, this particular enterprising late middle-aged gent had lived his whole life as a penniless academic, barely a coin to his name. He was sick of it. He had managed to calculate that if he left a certain amount of money in a certain number of bank accounts, he could travel to the past, deposit the cash, return to his present (our future,) collect the interest and live the life of luxury. Time travel requires some specific, incredibly rare and hard-to-produce reagents. This meant that our wizard, having sold all of his possessions, had just enough frog's ears or snake's knees or whatever to jump to the past once and then jump back again—but that was it.

So, this is what he did. He jumped backwards forty years, but found he couldn't earn a single coin, as no one was hiring a seemingly mad old academic. Even trying to pass himself off as an old beggar had failed. Time for 'Plan B'.

He found where his younger self lived and robbed him blind. He knew exactly where he kept all the good stuff and the spare key, so entered one afternoon and took everything that wasn't nailed down.

Well, Past Mr Time Wizard wasn't best pleased, as he himself was saving his money to invest in his study into Temporomancy, which would now have been all for naught. Arriving home and seeing this intruder rummaging through his things, he grabbed the old man before he could disappear, and dragged him before the courts.

I was acting as prosecution for the younger man. We had to first determine that these were exactly the same people, just displaced in time. The method we came up with was fairly barbaric, in my opinion, but it got the job done. The judge declared the young man would have to have a small, permanent tattoo, secretly administered. Then someone else, someone from the public, would examine the old man's body to see if he had the same marking. Sure enough, with a screen between them, a tiny blue cross was marked on the young man's ear, and it was determined that the older man had the same tattoo in the same place. So that was settled.

It was hard to define whether it was possible to steal from oneself, as the law assumes another person taking your belongings, and if they're yours, well, they're yours. We argued that this older man had used time travel, and had thus split reality, meaning he couldn't be from the same reality as us, and thus, metaphysically, he was not the same man. That didn't work (judges aren't too hot on metaphysics), so we tried arguing that they weren't the same actual physical body, but that didn't work either.

Eventually, I tried my last-ditch attempt at making them settle. A tie is better than a loss, right? I explained to them that if the older gent took this money back from his younger self, he would never learn Temporomancy, and so would not have the ability as the older man to travel back and steal his own money in the first place. Therefore, they *must* have already settled this amicably, else this very sequence of events could never have happened.

They concurred, then agreed to split the money between them, leaving the old man just enough to get rich. The elder gave a long stare to his younger, and I remember him muttering: "Maybe this time it'll work out. No funny business."

Once it was all settled and our old traveller returned to his time, his younger self took me aside and told me he had taken my fee from the old man's account, leaving him with nothing, the thieving grey-haired git.

Upon seeing my face, he explained.

"If it's already predetermined that I end up poor, there's no point in trying to save for a rainy day as I know I'm going to lose it all."

I tried to explain that perhaps this course of events would lead to him travelling back in time to rob himself, but he seemed nonplussed.

"I'm learning a lot about Temporomancy. I'm certain I'll be able to adjust the course of time, just a smidge, to avoid all this nasty business," he said to me. I don't know whether he noticed his own logical fallacy, but then again, I don't think that's something time-wizards focus on too much.

I wished him good luck and he went on his way with a curt nod. As I was leaving, an ancient man tapped me on the shoulder with his cane and folded down his hood. His eyes were almost blind, his skin creased and crinkled, and he had a mischievous smile as he whispered to me in a voice croaked with age.

"He doesn't manage it. Just thought I'd let you know." And with that he chuckled, and as he shuffled off I couldn't help but notice the smallest, barely perceptible blue cross on his ear.

~journal entry ends

Interlude – Corney Buys Some Seeds
~ *Very Long Ago*

"Hanging baskets, hanging baskets! Freshly made." The seller tipped a wink at the man approaching, adding: "Very impressive, our hanging baskets, sure to turn an eye or cause jealousy among your friends."

Her customer scoffed.

"Seems bloody pointless if you're asking me, why take the time to heave a good clump of earth and suspend it so, broken from the sod it recognises? Our unlucky plant will be happy for a short time, but it'll not be able to drink up its goodness from mother ground, once the basket itself is wrung dry. So? So, you have to keep filling it with new earth, good earth, yet more taken from the ground where it belongs, and swapped with the dead soil in this infernal hanging nonsense. A complete, total waste of good wicker."

The shopkeeper, unsure of how to respond to such an outpouring of opinion on such an unassuming topic, didn't respond, though her face took on a hurt expression. The other man sighed and continued.

"Here now, I didn't mean it all like that. For those as have the time and inclination I'm sure they're not all bad, and I understand you have your own path to tread and your own money to make to look after you and your own. I'll not begrudge you a moment for it, especially as your own vocation impacts me naught. Each to their own, I say, and why concern yourself with a furrow in a field unless you're the one sowing the seeds, if you understand me."

The shopkeeper still looked upset. Corney, for that was his name, felt a little guilty for his rudeness. He was a good man, an honest and decent man, and not one who intentionally spread unkindness. He believed one good turn deserves another, and a bad act, swiftly mended, was all even in the eyes of God.

He did not deserve his fate.

"Look, how about those seeds you've there, how much're they?" Corney gestured to a small, sad pot, not larger than a pepperpot, seemingly full of large, dull, grey seeds. He reached for this moneybag, which, though light, was enough for a stroll through town. Provided he wasn't about to be ripped off, he could still afford the new thresher he'd come here for.

"Thirty-five."

Corney coughed.

"Thirty-five. It's a good price for a pot of Sunless seeds."

Corney could tell these were slow movers based on the dust he had only just noticed on the pot. Still, he'd committed to this act of reconciliation, so how could he refuse now? But what were Sunless seeds?

"Sunless seeds? Never heard of 'em," he said, perhaps a little too quickly.

The merchant smiled again, full of warmth that she doubtless didn't feel.

"Ah, wonderful things. Special plants with medicinal qualities come from Sunless seeds. They need no sunlight; in fact, they suffer in it. What they need is earth, some small water, and time. Grind up the berries, and ha!"

Corney was no fool, but felt he was about to be taken for one. "Ha?"

"Ha. A juice to cure any illness. It's bitter, but so are all good things, no? And worth thirty-five silvers, at least."

Corney considered a moment. If he removed some of the chains from the enclosure door, he could probably strap them to the head of this old scythe and thresh that way. It'd be hard work, but...

"All I've got is three."

"Well, that's perfect, all you really need is one seed, plus one spare. I'll do you two seeds for three."

Corney remembered words he'd heard when he was young. 'Stick with your gut. There's wisdom in you that you don't know, and your gut is your way of telling you what you need to do.'

He emptied his money bag, the three coins landing with a heavy clink on the table in front of the merchant. The woman nodded her head, as if a solemn oath had been sworn to her, and gestured at the pot.

"Please, help yourself."

"Aye, to my two magic beans…" muttered Corney. He dug a finger into the pot and scooped out two at random. He nodded to the shopkeeper, and left.

Only when he was halfway home did he stop and look more closely at the seeds. One was as he remembered, large and grey. The other… was not.

It seemed grey, but was laced with red. When held up to the light, it almost shimmered like ore mined veins of copper. It was quite unlike anything Corney had seen before.

"Well, here's something pretty. Is this the same seed, or a stowaway? And does it feel warm, or have I finally gone mad?"

Once he returned home, he grabbed a pot, filled it with earth, pressed each seed deep into the soil, put them in his run-down old barn—the one that had been half-burned out nigh on a year ago, leaving nothing but the ancient millstone—and promptly forgot about them.

They didn't forget about him, though. How easily they slipped his mind one day, and that was that.

It was some weeks later that the accident occurred. Corney wasn't much of a baker, content to sell his flour to the baker. He enjoyed the process of baking nonetheless, those rare weeks he found the time. Most of his direct produce in that regard ended up lumpy, blackened messes, but *the journey is as important as the destination.*

A bag of wheat, ready for milling, split and tumbled its contents around the base of the millstone, knocking over a small, forgotten pot in the process. The pot broke, and a seed escaped. Not one to waste good seed, Corney scooped the grain back into the sack (once repaired) and proceeded to grind the seeds to make the flour loaf.

It was a curious thing. The seeds ground as normal, the low rumbling of the stone filling the air with a familiar and satisfying crumbling. At once a crack sounded, like the stone splitting, but when inspected—all was well. *And that's a relief! Mills sure ain't cheap.*

When the flour was ready, the bread produced was a marvellous loaf. Corney had surprised himself with it.

"I'm not a baker, by troth, but if I can make these willy-nilly then perhaps I'm in the wrong vocation, and that's not a thought I think often!

Maybe I'll share it with the baker. Naw, he'll take it wrong. I wouldn't want to offend. More for me, then!"

It hadn't tasted as good as it looked, but not one to waste food, Corney had polished the lot off in a single day.

The day after that, the compulsions started.

7 – Journal Interlude

Regarding the last lawyer at Luncher… It wasn't as exciting a story as I imagined it to be. Loya Numblety. She was a good fit, got on famously with the staff, but after ten years, wanted something different, so moved out East. That was a few months ago, and so they were casting the net out.

For the next few years, I got used to Luncher, and I like to think I settled in fairly quickly. They're bizarre, with odd notions of how to behave. Sometimes, their smoke smells as bad as the devil's own farts, but they're good people.

I've included some writings from my journal for you to read through. I've tried to cut out a lot of the boring stuff you won't care about. A lot of law is reading statute and precedent, and only a small part is arguing and one-upping.

After my suggestion to Mr Luncher that a second lawyer might help the firm in the long run, and convincing them that student lawyers get paid peanuts, they agreed to take on a Junior.

She started a year or so after me, coming from the West University for her placement with Luncher: a young woman named Yetty. Before you ask, no, we were never involved; our relationship was entirely professional. I mention her because she and I became a strong partnership. Not friends. Not quite friends. But we were on a similar wavelength, and I found her invaluable for bouncing ideas off. Although…

Although I could see it was almost always coming from a place of logic, she had a certain callousness I found worrying at times. I once joked with her by posing a 'philosophical question': would she kill a child to save two? Her answer frightened me. Without pausing, she had said: "Would I be able to use a weapon, or can I do it with my hands?"

"…don't you mean, 'would' I do it with my hands?" Dago had asked.
"Yes, what did I say?" she had said, all brown eyes and innocence.

8 – Furbo, Helda & Racelsus

Racelsus finished her story without flourish.

"So, you aren't the all-knowing Fetter?" asked Helda.

"No."

"Hmm," Helda hummed.

No one spoke for a minute after that.

The skeleton clacked its teeth and wobbled its head in an irritated way. The crunching sounds were disgusting. Dust and other aged detritus fluttered from her as she moved.

"Well?" it asked.

Furbo was sitting up, pale but recovered. His voice was thin and tremulous. "Er, well what?"

Racelsus grated her teeth. "Well, are you going to kill me?"

"What! No!" Furbo said.

"I'm not even sure we could," Helda mused.

"Then what are you going to do with me?" Racelsus asked with a forced air of calm. "You can't just leave me here…"

Helda and Furbo looked at one another. Silence hung in the air.

Helda shrugged. "We could."

Racelsus clacked again. "If you will not end me, then take me with you. I yearn to see the world again." Her voice lowered to a whisper. "Please. I beg you."

Furbo furrowed his brow. Helda looked at him, and shrugged, then said. "Sure, why not? It's no skin off my nose."

Furbo turned to the skeleton. "Perhaps it was destined that we come down to rescue you, Racelsus. Who am I to ignore the will of the universe? It hasn't steered me wrong so far… mostly… Though, how are we going to manage it? Your body's destroyed. We didn't bring a coffin with us, and Helda is strong, but not that strong. Besides, if she tries to carry anything else I fear her back will break. Uh, no offence."

Racelsus swung her head down to look at her mangled remains. Her neck crunched as she did so. She sighed.

"You're right, of course. Fear not, I've had a good while to think about this. Do you have any sort of lantern with you?"

Helda dragged the huge pack into the room. It left a dusty trail as she brought it to the plinth. She unlatched the metal candle lantern strapped to the back. It was similar in design to a birdcage, but it was stuffed with candles. Some rolled away as she fidgeted with it, and she sheepishly tried to catch them as they scattered.

Furbo shook his head. "Do we really need all of those candles?"

Helda scowled and muttered. "One day, we're going to need something that you made me throw away, then you'll be sorry."

"Empty the lantern and get your hammer out," spoke Racelsus.

Helda looked at the skeleton and raised an eyebrow.

~

Furbo and Helda left by the same ornate door they had arrived by, leaving it open behind them.

"I'm not moving that bloody thing," Helda had said, before she was even asked. Not wanting to argue, Furbo shrugged.

As they made their way through the dank corridors, up the way they had come, the darkness crept in. Helda lifted her lantern, and a pale green witchlight illuminated the path in front of them. Odd rocks gleamed as the light struck it at the right angle.

The light emanated from the two eye sockets of the skull as it rested in its new casing. Rags had been stuffed behind it to keep it from rattling against the metal of the lantern. Helda had to turn it to keep the beam of light steady.

"This is exhilarating!" Racelsus's skull breathed. "Ah! I have missed this! The wind on my face, the feeling of motion!"

Helda's face screwed up. "But it's so dark and mouldy down here…"

Nothing could deflate Racelsus's mood. "Not to me! I am skipping along the fields of paradise! I might just float away if I'm not careful!"

Furbo couldn't help but laugh. The witch's mood was infectious.

As they ascended through the cave complex, Racelsus and Furbo talked of the pre-times, the time where Racelsus walked among her fellows. They talked of the times between, and Furbo explained about the falling of the empire, the rekindling of the new empire, the splitting of the clans, all of it. They reckoned Racelsus had been trapped for perhaps four hundred years.

"I'm amazed the language hasn't changed," she said. "I was worried whoever discovered me wouldn't be able to understand what I was saying."

Helda shrugged. "I sometimes can't understand what that one says anyway." She gestured her head towards Furbo, who gave a sheepish smile. "Tell me, skull. What was the world like four hundred years back?

"More than that, my dear," said Furbo. "Remember, she was imprisoned four hundred years ago, but lived for many more years before that." At a glare from Helda, he quickly added. "Oh, but she doesn't look a day over two hundred, of course."

Racelsus laughed, a high, dry chuckle. "Quite the charmer, you are. To answer your question, Helda, my world was a small one. I rarely ventured from the swamplands I grew up in for fear of being persecuted. I was content to wander my home, exploring the secrets of the fens, filling my days with wandering and nights with hobbies. Weaving, baking, mushroom-gardening."

"What sort of things did you bake?" asked Helda.

"Pastries, cakes, oh all sorts! My speciality was a frog pie. You had to find just the right sorts of frog. Not too big, not too warty."

Helda paused. "I wonder... No, it doesn't matter."

"Your mother used to make you a frog pie, and you want me to teach you how to make it?" asked Racelsus.

"What! How did—" spluttered Helda, before remembering. "Oh, eh, yes, the mind reading. Well..." she coughed. "It's one of the only things I remember about her or my childhood, so..."

"I'd love to!" squeaked the witch. "Oh, this will be fun!"

The hours drifted away as they chatted, and before long the distant beam of light that signified the entrance to the cave was visible. Racelsus began chattering, unable to hide her excitement.

"Oh, sunlight! Real sunlight! Rain! Wind!"

Helda couldn't help but feel a smile tug at her. Her mood really was contagious. She tried to imagine being trapped underground for four hundred years. It wasn't easy, or pleasant.

As they stepped into the sunlight, Racelsus gasped.

"It's just how I remember it," she whispered.

The cave mouth was near the sea, and emerged on a wide-open grassy field that ended with a cliff, a stone's throw from where they stood. A cold breeze swept through them, rustling the trees in the copse behind the cave, carrying the scents of the ocean with it. It was around mid-afternoon, and the warm autumn sun was a welcome change from the dankness of the cavern.

Helda and Furbo glanced at one another and both cracked smiles. *A good deed done is food for the spirit*, Furbo often said, and *the best feelings come from the knowledge of helping another.* Normally Helda ignored these philosophical nothings, but today, she believed it.

Her gaze focussed on something over Furbo's shoulder, and her smile fell immediately. Behind Furbo was a man on horseback, dressed completely in white, armour gleaming, a cape of bright blue streaming down the back of his horse. Flanking him were seven similarly dressed men, some aiming crossbows at them, some idly hefting shortswords. Furbo swivelled where he stood, following her gaze.

The leader held a mace of office. Its heavy bejewelled head glittered in the sunlight as he swung it about him with no apparent effort. As he did so, the light bounced from the three purple diamonds arranged in a row on the handle.

That's a symbol of the church, thought Furbo, and knew Helda would have spotted it too.

"Surrender the witch or die immediately, so demands the Great Apostolry," he spoke in a deep voice, used to command.

Helda hated authority wherever she found it, and she hated religious authority even more. Furbo knew this, but he also knew that, despite her great skill at arms, seven-to-one (as he didn't count himself) was poor odds.

He held his arms outstretched, palms up.

"Please, noble hierarch, there must be a misunderstanding here. We are neither of us witches." His voice was subservient, mollifying, calm and reasonable. His whole pose changed. No longer hunched and twitchy, he now stood with confidence, like a butler.

"No? What's that then?" the horseman gestured at the skull in the cages, with its eyes glowing greenly.

"What we bear here is a simple relic, a good luck charm." Furbo smiled, rapidly assessing what sort of a churchman this man on horseback was. *Would he respond better to challenge? Prostration on his mercy? Outright lies?*

The man didn't look convinced. "Then why does it gasp and speak?" his mace stopped swinging, his fingers opening and closing on the handle.

Furbo side-glanced at Helda, who had pursed her mouth petulantly. She knew these sorts of things were best left to him. *Until it comes to face-smashing.*

Furbo flourished an arm. "We are travelling performers, ventriloquists, what you heard was our craft," he said, with an utterly undeserved air of pomposity. He thrust out his chest and bowed. "Lady Vanilla's Finest Circus, at your service." He raised his voice a touch. "Observe how we throw our voices to this inanimate skull!"

Please, please, please…

"What ho, kind strangers," said Racelsus, in a mock-mummery voice that was easily five hundred years out of date.

Their accoster didn't look entertained or impressed.

"And just why were circus performers in that cave?"

Without missing a beat, Furbo gave a haughty sniff.

"'Tis well known that the most potent Grungeroot grows in this cave, and it's *common* knowledge that the only way to keep a feral Frog-Beast subdued is copious amounts of the stuff. We are here to collect it for our animal trainer."

The templar shifted uneasily. He was clearly having issues believing this tale, yet didn't seem to have the confidence to call it an outright lie.

Thank God for the devout! Furbo thought.

"So where is the Grungeroot?" he said.

Furbo took on a maudlin face of theatrical horror.

"Alas! We found none! Despite hours of searching… what a waste. Our masters will surely be most unhappy with us."

"And, so, you were just practicing your… craft… as you wandered out of the cave?"

"Yes, my good sir."

Furbo hoped he didn't look as concerned as he felt. He was aware of an itch on the back of his neck and didn't know if it was sweat or the possibility of a crossbow bolt.

The mounted man tapped his saddle irritably. A fellow horseman sidled up to him and began speaking in a slightly-too-loud whisper.

"We were told there would be a powerful witch escaping, and all I see are, well, two clearly insane wanderers. Mayhaps we leave them, they're clearly not our quarry."

"Sergeant…" said the leader, eyes narrowing.

"Sir, after the incident with the cultists, we really have to be careful…"

The leader seemed to be thinking hard about what to do. He looked at the pair of them, and the skull again. He sighed heavily, and latched his mace to his belt.

"Did you see anyone else in the cave?"

"No sir. We didn't travel that far into it, though."

Did it work?

With an irritated wave, the soldier dismissed them.

"Okay, you can be on your way."

Furbo let out a sigh of relief. Helda shifted her pack and turned.

"…Once we give you a ward of safe passage. Let it not be said that the Orthodoxy does not bless the *clearly* needy."

Racelsus rattled nervously in her cage.

Furbo brightened. "Ah! Thank you most kindly." He turned to Helda and Racelsus, the smile never leaving his face. "Run."

With a sprightliness unbecoming of a man of his age and bearing, Furbo began sprinting away from the horsemen towards the woods behind the cave. Helda was behind him in a flash.

"Why — running?" Helda snatched out between breaths.

"Never — bless — a — witch!" Furbo spluttered. The shouts behind them began mingling with hoof beats. A crossbow bolt thrummed into the ground between his feet. He hopped, never daring to look back.

How Helda kept up with him with that enormous bag of hers, he did not know. However, he knew that with steadying the bag in one hand and Racelsus in the other, she would not be able to reach her weapon easily if required. Furbo fumbled in his inner pocket and found what he was looking for: a little bottle full of red, gritty liquid. He unstoppered it and threw it behind him blindly. It exploded into thick orange smoke, and shouts and cries were replaced with sounds of coughing and choking.

I've always wanted to use that. I hope it works!

He stole a glance behind him to see the results of his experiment, but all he could see was an enormous orange cloud that appeared to be growing exponentially. The cloying, sickly smog was spreading like ink poured into water. His mood dampened.

At least it's non-toxic… Or was that the blue bottle?

A strong hand grabbed him by the arm and yanked him sideways into a wooded crevice. He saw Helda's furious eyes in the shadows as she pressed a wet rag over his mouth. She had an identical one over hers. He stood there, suppressing his body's urgent need to take deep breaths after his exertion. He could see Racelsus, eyes glowing faintly. He glanced around. They were in some sort of hollow tree stump. The smog crept around them, engulfing them from top to toe. Breathing through the rag was nasty work, but better than the alternative.

They remained there for some while, waiting. They heard commotion outside, but no one found them. The commotion and the smoke faded. When they felt it safe to leave, they did so slowly, peering around for stragglers. Furbo was astonished that once he had taken three paces from their hiding place, he couldn't see it among the brush.

"How did you spot this?" he asked Helda, coughing.

Helda pointed to a branch above them. Barely visible was a tiny glyph, shaped like an antler.

"Secret hiding place. Old Forest-Ganger rune, that," she said.

Furbo shook his head and clapped her on the arm. "You are full of surprises, Helda."

She winced, gripping her elbow with her other arm. "Careful!"

He looked at Racelsus then.

"Now, who were they exactly?"

Racelsus looked as sheepish as it was possible for a skull to look.

"When I was placed *there*, I suspect wards were woven on me. The moment I left the plinth, or the door was opened, *people* were warned. Not nice people. People that want me contained until I am nothing but dust."

"The Orthodoxy?"

"In my day they were the Covenant, but I suspect they're the same sort of person."

"And now we're mixed up in it."

"Yes. Sorry about that. You might not have freed me if I had said at the time, and—."

Helda's face reddened, and she lifted the skull in its casing so it was eye level, rattling and bouncing in its cage.

"How about we just leave you on the forest floor here for squirrels to hide their nuts in your eye sockets, you selfish, arrogant scoundrel? Perhaps the church will pay handsomely for your delivery?"

Furbo kept quiet, but couldn't help entertaining the thought.

Racelsus's voice was broken. It sounded like she was on the verge of tears.

"I'm sorry! It was completely garish of me. I'm so sorry. Once you opened that door, they would have come anyway, but I didn't want to worry you. You're such wonderful people. Let me make it up to you. Please."

Helda's fury ebbed, and subsided.

"How?"

"I can help you find what you seek. You have lost a friend of yours, some time ago, correct? You journey to find him?"

The two looked at each other. Their expressions hardened.

"…Aye," Helda said. "How did you..?"

"I can help you," Racelsus repeated. "I can find… Gerridge."

Helda said nothing, then Furbo sighed heavily. His eyes closed. His head dropped.

"We have been looking for so long. Don't give us false hope," he whispered, staring at the ground. There was still a sticky orange residue in parts on the ground. It was dissolving into harmless sludge that would wash away when the next rain fell. *If one were to mix three parts Alterhime root, it would—*

"I can help you. I promise," Racelsus said.

Helda's eyes widened.

"He lives?"

"Yes."

Helda's face contorted with a combination of fury and joy.

"*He lives...*" Furbo muttered, squeezing his eyes shut again. He wouldn't cry. He had promised himself he wouldn't ever again.

"For my help, all I ask is one thing," Racelsus said.

"Huh! First we save you, then you ask for more? What should we do for you, besides not leaving you to the squirrels?" Helda spat. "What do you want, witch?"

Racelsus's eyes dimmed. "If we discover some way of finding where my brother is, we pursue it. I owe it to him."

Helda paused, and turned to Furbo. Helda's anger flickered with a split-second of despair. The anger had melted away instantly, before she turned to look at Furbo with a forced face of neutral consideration. Furbo nodded. She shrugged and turned back to the skull.

"...Okay, skull," Helda said. Racelsus sighed with relief. A rustle in the undergrowth caused Helda to snap to attention, the embers of her anger smouldering. "But know this: if you're lying to me, I won't kill you, but I'll make your life an even bigger misery than it is now."

She looked around at a sound in the brush.

"But first, how do we get these God-Botherers to leave us alone?" she muttered.

Racelsus paused, then spoke carefully. "Well... now the ward is broken, I suspect they'll be able to track you down, wherever you go— not instantly, but eventually. You'll have to get them to remove it, somehow. I... don't know the way."

Helda spat. "So, we're doomed! Furbo, what are you thinking?"

Furbo thought. He watched a squirrel skitter on the branch above them. It didn't know whether to run or freeze, so flitted between the two.

We can't do it by force, I suspect. Or by subterfuge...

The squirrel scuttled along the branch, disappearing from view. Furbo snapped his fingers.

That means asking them politely.

"I have an idea. Let's head to town. I know a place we might be able to get the help we need."

Helda had noticed the forced positivity in his voice but knew better than to question him on it now. He would talk about it when he was ready. "Mercenaries? Assassins?" she suggested.

Furbo cleared his throat delicately. "Not quite..."

Journal Entry D: Kidnapped

Reference case [TTvHH] (TyrThr v. HelRie), year 1331, judge Jeckob presiding.

Dragon exists, dragon steals princess, hero slays dragon, princess is saved. It's a cliche every child is already bored with.

Mr Luncher waved me over, explaining I was to be looking at a new case for him.

A nobleman's daughter, Bella, was seen walking the meadows, dallying amongst the flowers, or whatever else young noble-daughters do. As she bent to no-doubt fondle a lily, she was bathed in darkness. The great silhouette of Tyranathrix the Burning Cloud blotted out the sun, and swooped down, roaring, and back up... with the 'princess' nowhere to be seen.

Enter our handsome hero, a knight's son called Herid. Strong of arm, noble of purpose, wide of brow, thick of head... (you get the picture). He went off to find this kidnapper, rescue the fair maiden, and perhaps earn himself some sort of reward in the process.

It wasn't hard to track the dragon down. I understand they tend to leave no secrets as to their lairs. You just follow the path of dead farm animals and shed scales or skin until you can see the smoky plume on the horizon. Then you're almost guaranteed to find a dragon beneath it, if you get close enough. Of course, most people are more sensible than that.

Herid approached the cove near the beach, bow in hand, arrow at the ready. He cautiously crept towards the mouth, eyes never leaving the open cave. Deep rumblings could be heard from within… and girlish giggling?

He tripped on a crab, and let loose the arrow he had nocked and drawn in preparation. Thrummmm! Swiiiish! Splat! Eurgh!!

This barbed and notched arrow flew deep into the darkness, impacting meatily with something soft. Out stampedes our dragon, smoke and fire pouring from its face. In its mighty clawed paw is clasped our fair maiden, an arrow in her head, quite dead.

Herid screamed then, and tried to run, but Tyranathrix had other plans. Grabbing the lad by the ankle, it started to angrily berate him for murdering its best friend, roaring and spitting flames. Herid collapsed in terror, weeping and pleading.

Rolling its eyes, the dragon flew back to town with the body of Bella in one claw and our gibbering hero in the other. Upon landing, a quick flash of light consumed the great beast—and where there once was dragon, there now was girl. A young girl, teenage, upset, confused, and wanting someone to blame. Marching up to the nobleman's house, she kicked the door open and started yelling for justice.

Our nobleman, leaping downstairs, saw many things at once. He saw a large crowd outside, gathering to see where the dragon had landed. He saw Herid, the strong son of Detson the Bold, in a crying, shaking heap. He saw a young, angry, fiery stranger yelling for the guards. Lastly, he saw his daughter, dead, an arrow protruding wickedly from her delicate head.

In the furore, the guards decided it would best serve the town if *everyone* in the house was detained while they sort out the mess.

Tyranathrix, or 'Tilly' as she preferred to be called, was our client. Despite being a dragon, she had no money. She was young, even by human standards, and practically a baby by dragon. She wasn't a murderer; she only killed for food. She wasn't a thief; she had no hoard. The only draconic stereotype she filled was that she was terribly lonely.

Dragons are born, taught how to fly and to spit flame, then kicked out by their parents, all within the space of a few meagre years. From then on, it's down to the fledgling lizard to survive by itself.

It's not easy making friends as a teenager anyway, let alone when you're a great, scaled beast—cursed with intelligence, power, and a hell of a temper.

One night, whilst in her cave and feeling sorry for herself, the dragon had heard Bella singing while walking along the beach. She cautiously approached her and the two had struck an unlikely friendship. Perhaps it was their shared feelings of being trapped, or lost, or whatever else teenage girls have in common. Either way, they became fast friends, despite the difference in species.

They met up frequently, and Tilly would show Bella what it was like to be a dragon, and Bella would show Tilly what it was like to be a human. Tilly learned to change her form, as most dragons do eventually, and they would spend many hours whiling away the evenings talking about everything and nothing.

Of course, you know what happened next.

We argued that just because a dragon was a dragon, that didn't mean it deserved to be slayed. 'Intent' is a funny old word in legalese. We used it in this case to say that, while the young Herid went off, thinking he was saving this young woman from certain peril, it did not justify the presumption of deadly force. Tilly had just as much a right to live as he did.

The other side tried to argue that the reasonable person would assume that the young lady was in mortal danger, and so deadly force was justified, even without all the facts.

Despite the best efforts of our esteemed opponents, it really was very difficult to conclude anything other than the obvious chain of events. Besides, with the greatest will in the world, would you want to be the judge that declares a dragon guilty of murder, and then asking— 'would you please kindly submit yourself for execution?'

Judge Jeckob declared that, good intentions regardless, when it comes to meting out death for any purpose, it should only be as an absolute last resort. In this case, due diligence had not been performed by the young hero-wannabe, and his carelessness had tragically resulted in this most grievous of accidents.

Tilly asked the judge to not be too harsh on Herid. He was only a boy himself, trying his best to find a place in the world. The punishment settled upon was thirty years serving in the national army, starting immediately, which seemed to suit everyone fine.

So, a happy ending, all things considered. Except for Bella, obviously, and her father. But you know what I mean.

~journal entry ends

9 – Felix, Furbo & Helda

Felix sat at the table, pencil poised over his journal, waiting for the other party to begin speaking. They had been here for several long, silent minutes. Unsure of whether he should prompt them, he waited.

There were two of them, a man and a woman. The man was dark-skinned, and on the old end of middle aged, but possessing a curious energy that animated his face. He had a look of someone who either missed nothing, taking it in with eagle-eyed scrutiny, or missed everything, lost as he was in the chasm of his own mind. Felix found it impossible to tell which, and so waited for him to make the first move.

The other was a woman, and quite a woman at that. Her face was a mess of scars, her bright hair cut short, and her build looked like she spent her days either wrestling bears or splitting rocks by hand. Despite saying nothing, Felix suspected she was the sort of person that was quick to anger, and so he said nothing, waiting for them to speak.

Quite why they were travelling together eluded him. Quite everything about them eluded him, including the reason they were here in the first place. They had shown up at the door, allegedly asked to speak to a lawyer on a matter of some importance, and Felix had been volunteered by Mr Luncher. They had been led to the only private-client-discussion room in the always-too-small building, and so here he was.

Time had passed, but no one in the room had spoken yet.

A small knock at the door, and Mr Luncher poked his head around. A waft of smoke followed him into the interview room.

"Everything alright in here?" he asked, bushy eyebrows raised.

The couple turned to look at Felix, who suddenly felt very awkward.

"Uh, yes thank you, Mr Luncher. We're, hm, just getting into the real detail of the matter."

The woman snorted, then began laughing loudly.

Smiling, Mr Luncher nodded and left. As he shut the door, the smoke swirled behind him in heavy patterns.

"So, Mr Lawyer, are you going to take our case?" the woman asked in a rough voice, index finger pressed into the table. She laughed again.

In spite of his professional bearing, Felix started laughing too.

"Sure, why not. Shall we set the fee at fifty thousand golds?"

She howled, slamming the table. The older man jumped, and looked around, startled.

"What? He's taking it?" he mumbled.

"I haven't even told him what it is yet," the woman added, wiping tears from her eyes.

The old man added his chuckling too, and all three of them began laughing at nothing together.

After they had calmed down, the couple introduced themselves.

"I'm Furbo, this is my traveling companion, Helda," spoke the man.

Felix offered his hand. "Felix, I'm a Lawyer here at Luncher."

Helda's grip was iron. "Let me answer a few questions that I'm sure you're thinking." She counted them off on meaty fingers. "One, we are not an item. Two, we are not family. Three, neither of us is hired by the other. Four, we are not criminals. Five, we are not crazy people. Actually, ignore number five."

Felix lowered his eyebrows, which had raised without him realising. He blinked twice. "Okay."

Helda shrugged. "It's just simpler to get that all out in the open."

Felix looked down at his empty journal. "Great. So, remind me why you're here."

Furbo leaned forward. "How can I remind you if you have never been told?" He had a mischievous twinkle in his eye as he said this.

Felix sighed and put down the pencil, but grinned as he spoke.

"Much as I am enjoying this frankly maddening conversation, you did come here for a reason, I trust?"

Furbo's expression lost its good-natured tinge. He reclined back again and grunted.

"Yes. Forgive us. We've seen a lot, and we've found that nothing quite helps a dire situation as much as a sense of humour. Isn't that right, my one-and-only?"

He turned to look, starry-eyed at Helda, who returned a stare so full of malice Felix was worried she might rip his head off. When Furbo turned back to Felix, however, he spotted her fail to suppress a smile.

"We are wanted by the Orthodoxy for fifth-level sacrilegious graverobbing and witchery," Furbo said.

Felix eyed them both. They didn't look the type to commit blasphemy. Fraud, maybe…

He scribbled a few words. "I see. And did you? Graverob, that is?"

Helda stood up. "It's a little more complicated than that."

Before Felix could ask, Helda reached behind her enormous travelsack and planted a birdcage onto the table. The cage contained a human skull.

Felix blinked, then asked: "What's the complication..?"

The skull answered then. "I wanted to be stolen."

~

Felix hadn't remembered jumping from his chair and knocking his papers over, yet here he was, and there they were. His heart raced.

"Sorry, didn't mean to scare you," the skull said, plaintively.

"That's quite alright, I didn't mean to be scared," Felix offered, pathetically.

Calm down, man. This is hardly the eeriest thing you've dealt with. Remember the ghost?

He sat down again and picked up his pencil.

"Start from the beginning," he said.

~

They laid out their adventure from the moment they entered the cave system to their encounter with Racelsus, and how they escaped from the Covenant's men. Felix listened attentively, making notes on a piece of parchment as he went. He was well onto his third sheaf when Helda asked him:

"How do you find so much to write about? We've only given you a basic account of what is really only a small part of one day…"

Felix flexed his wrist. "Oh, I disagree. There's a lot I can work with here. I can stretch this out into a three-hour speech if required. Though… I have to ask. You seem to have missed out a rather important detail."

"Oh..?" asked Furbo, with a look at Helda. "What would that be?"

"Why exactly were you in that cave in the first place, and what were you looking for?"

Helda slammed the table, making Felix leap out of his skin, knocking over his pot of ink. With a curse he righted the pot and tried to stop the flow of black with a few extra sheafs of paper.

"I wish you wouldn't do that," the skull muttered.

"Damn it! Does it matter?" Helda said, ignoring her. "It's our own private business."

Felix gave her an exasperated look as his sleeves began to take on more of the ink in his futile attempt to restore some dignity.

"Well, yes, it does matter. If I'm going to go up there and tell the church where to stick it, I need to know all the facts, or we end up looking like enormous pillocks—and losing, by the way."

Helda tightened her glare at him but said nothing. Furbo offered Felix a ragged old handkerchief and began.

"We were looking for a friend," he said.

Helda hissed through her teeth.

Felix reached for a new, clean page.

Furbo raised a hand in a stopping gesture. "Please, let us explain first. It's not easy to do so."

Felix paused, but did as he was bade. He mopped with the kerchief as best he could, then sat down again, pen and paper out of reach and out of mind.

Helda had turned her back to them.

"We have to trust him, Helda," Furbo said to his friend.

She looked at the floor, shrugged, then stormed out the room.

"Will she—"

Furbo turned to Felix.

"We were looking for a very dear friend of ours, a young lad called Gerridge. We lost him."

10 – Furbo's Story

Gerridge was only a whelp when we met him. Oh, but I should explain first. We used to live in a town on the other side of the North Country. We were… We lived and worked with a small group of like-minded individuals. We did a special kind of work.

We used to redistribute the wealth of those that had too much to those that didn't. Don't look so surprised, young man. Heh.

I'm loath to use the word bandits, but… We've heard it often enough, so perhaps there's some truth there. Indeed, to some, that is precisely what we were. Thieves and robbers, scoundrels deserving of the most severe of punishments.

But we did it for the right reasons, and to the right people. We never robbed the poor or the destitute, or even those one or two rungs up. We didn't leave anyone in need. We took only that which was in excess from those who wouldn't miss it… no matter what they might claim.

You can see Helda's talents from here, I suspect. She's a brawler through and through. I've only seen her bested a handful of times, and I've been traveling with her for fifteen years now. She's a crack lockpicker, she can swim, climb rocks, fashion a shelter out of twigs… a real talented lady, in that fashion. She's also got the eyes of an owl. She could spot a tick on a mouse's back.

Me? I'm a thinker. An architect. I'm a tax-man. An accountant. A circus performer. I can plan, I can plot, I can scheme, I can act, I can blend in. I flatter myself by calling myself learned, but… I am. I seem to be in a minority of educated people that think helping others is as important as helping oneself. Bleeding heart, I know.

Together, we started out small. We actually met in a pub, typical as it is to say. We both got completely smashed, started putting the world to rights, and realised we both hated those with too much to go around. The next morning, a little tender-headed, we talked again—more earnestly. After a few weeks, we had become fast friends and confidants.

That's when we decided to try something. To put our money where our mouth was, so to speak. Our first target was the local smithery.

It was a well-known secret that the smith was stealing the metal from people's carts and gardens, tools, anything he could reach, and melting it down to sell on. He did this all over the region and had become rich. He started moving away from smithing and began lending money. Soon, he had cronies, and if you couldn't pay... you get the idea.

So, we hatched a plan. I posed as a tax collector, Helda was my bodyguard. We walked right up to him and knocked on the door, bold as the brass he stole.

Obviously he wasn't keen to meet me, so we made it clear we could be bought. He was all too happy to pay us off, and he did so. Meanwhile, Helda was taking a good look around for any loose floorboards, any... 'unusually hanging ornaments'. She gave me the signal, we went on our merry way, and five hours later we were back.

'It's the bookshelf,' she had said as we left. 'Scuff marks on the floor, carpet a little dog-eared at the edge. Plus, I'd bet my left arm that those books are fake. They're too uniform.'

After sneaking back in, Helda had slid away the false bookshelf in his front room. We found the box of silvers and golds, and we were out within minutes. We'd left him a little note telling him he'd been visited by the Cheerful Woodsmen, and that he should change his ways unless he wanted another visit. Forgive me a touch of theatre, but there is something so exciting about letting them know we had been there.

We never went back, we're not idiots. We had donated the money to a few local worthy causes, and paid a couple of mercenaries we knew to hang around and 'keep the peace' as it were for a few months, just so the smith didn't try to get any revenge.

Anyway. We had discovered our true calling, and began performing these sorts of deeds wherever we wandered to. It was only ever just the two of us. We saw the full length and breadth of the country, becoming true nomads. We lived off the land, bought what we needed, foraged the rest.

Then we found him. We were giving the latest sack of goodies to a convent-orphanage. It was a measly place, but the people who worked there did their best. We saw this young lad, probably eight or nine, smaller than the rest but with a certain fire about him.

We'd caught him that night trying to follow us stealthily, and returned him. We couldn't bring him with us, could we?

He told us then of the dark secrets the convent held. Terrible secrets.

It turns out, when you're at the very bottom rung, you have no one to defend you. No one.

I say, are you okay, my boy? Yes? I'll continue.

Knowing this, some people take sick delight in making your life a misery. Others see you as nothing but vessels for their disgusting perversions. It's especially abhorrent when those who are in positions of trust... I apologise, it makes my blood boil.

We returned, and demanded to speak to some of the other children. It was easy to see they were beyond miserable. They were practically haunted.

So, we adopted them all. The wardens tried to prevent us, but we reminded them of the generous down payment we had just made, and they couldn't say no.

That night, as we made camp under the stars, we had close to twenty children in tow! Quite a sight I'm sure. They enjoyed their freedom instantly. We let them choose their own names, their own clothes, gave them each the attention or space they had needed but been denied. Some left to pursue their own destinies, and we didn't stop them. I hope they found what they were looking for.

Our focus changed then. We could still perform the, hm, redistributions. But we wanted to give these kids a life. Our idea was thus: We could help those under the heel of the greedy upper classes, and in return ask the people we helped to consider adopting one of the wretches we travelled with in return for some of the money.

We would sometimes find more children in need of homes, so we took them. They joined our merry band.

It worked well. We rehoused the children, which soothed our souls. We helped the poor and needy, which calmed our consciences. We were smart and careful, and we didn't get caught.

Well, almost.

The lad from before, the stealthy one, chose the name Gerridge. Gerridge brightened up our life. We had long since decided that we wanted him to stay with us forever, if he also wanted. He was funny, kind, smart and an all-round great kid. We asked him on his eleventh birthday, and he had hugged us both, saying it was all he ever wanted. We were content.

By that time there were around thirty children in our entourage. We'd had to hire a nanny to travel with us! We'd found a great lady who had spent her life looking after spoilt brats and had been desperate for a little adventure.

As the number of children increased, the nanny needed a little help. And so, we looked for another. The second woman we had hired had seemed perfect... Carefree, dedicated to making the world a better place.

Gerridge hadn't got on with her, saying she acted funny, but we hadn't noticed. Like I said, smart boy. I think we had become complacent.

We had planned a 'redistribution' against a landowner who had been squeezing and squeezing his peasant workers. Someone had actually heard of our little troupe and had starting sticking posters in the neighbouring villages asking for help.

We were unsure, but our new nanny convinced us to respond. She was persuasive, and seemed so earnest. How could we refuse a direct and plaintive request?

Helda and I were scouting one evening. We'd left our campsite in the woods in the capable hands of our nannies. We weren't overly concerned with bandits. We had nothing worth stealing, and who would hurt children and their old nurses?

We'd returned when the moon was full, and our heads were full also. Full of ideas and plots to get one over on the cruel landlord... What we needed was a few hours of lively discussion around a roaring campfire. We rounded the final corner, eager to tell the group of our plans.

We returned to a massacre.

The children...

I... I'm sorry, I'll be okay in a moment.

...

Thank you, yes I'm fine, now. Bless you for asking. Tea? Oh, yes, that would be wonderful. But, let me just... I'm almost finished, my boy.

...

They had all been killed, mercilessly. You... don't need the details.

The old nanny as well.

We didn't find the newer nanny, but we did find her note.

"You get what you deserve, bandit scum. Enjoy your nightmares."

Helda wailed, I wept. We searched for any survivors, but their work had been brutal and thorough.

It was dark. The moon had slid behind the clouds, as if unable to bear witness to this night any longer.

We lit a torch and checked each child, counting them.

They were all accounted for, except Gerridge.

Helda had roared then, bellowing a challenge for anyone to fight her. To return her boy. To come and kill her, if they were brave enough.

None answered, and we had sat, our backs to each other, until sunrise.

With the new day's light, we once again checked the bodies. Gerridge wasn't there.

We headed right to the landlord's house, and Helda kicked the door down. She was like a whirlwind. I tried to help, but I am no fighter.

We scoured that house, room to room, but found no sign of our little lad. Helda unleashed such devastation on the people she found. She broke arms, snapped wrists, all the while demanding to know where the boy was.

Even the baron himself was not safe. She had incapacitated his guards easily, and threated to rip him to pieces with her bare hands. She would have, too. The baron gurgled something about him being taken, but we heard the sound of the guard arriving outside. I managed to get through to Helda, and she dropped the fat baron, though not before breaking his nose with a headbutt.

We escaped through the back window, me clinging to her back like a lizard, and disappeared into the forests.

That was five years ago. The search for Gerridge hasn't stopped. We've been keeping low, discrete. It's been difficult. Helda and I have become more lost, more desperate. Less *hopeful* with each passing year.

There were old rumours of an old wise man living in the caves beneath Grey Hill. We'd tried everything else, so we decided to explore. We didn't find him, but we did find Racelsus.

And that, dear fellow, brings us up to today.

Journal Entry E: Defamation

Reference case [QTvDW] (QueTer v. DaiWhe), year 1333, judge Ki presiding.

Fame is a funny old thing. Some people would kill to be famous, some people would die to be famous. For many, though, it's not just being well-known, it's what you're known *for*.

Humanity loves a scandal. We can't help it. It's planted deep in our brains at birth. Newspapers also love scandals. They see them as a great opportunity to reap reams of cash, and won't let something as inconvenient as the truth get in the way.

Quetrietta is a charming young-ish woman of varying reputation. The papers seemed to get it in their head she was some delicate flower that liked to get herself kidnapped for attention. In reality, she had never been kidnapped at all. The papers didn't care. It's what sold copies, and what attracted their dedicated readership to collectively tut and shake their head whenever her name came up.

One paper was particularly diligent: The Weekly Wheatsheaf. Quite why it had decided this was the hill it wanted to die on remains a mystery. But, regular as the seasons, every third or fourth issue would contain a page or two of hand-to-forehead prose, bemoaning the state of the youth of today, always going and getting themselves kidnapped for attention.

She got so fed up with this incessant character-assassination that she decided to take them to court to get a judge to make them shut up. Despite being such a 'prissy attention-seeker' (the paper's words, not mine), she wasn't wealthy, and just wanted a quiet life where she could live in peace. She came to us, and we agreed to help.

Three days before the case was supposed to start, however, Quetrietta went missing… presumed kidnapped.

Two days before the court date, a letter surfaced in her bedroom, allegedly in her handwriting, explaining to her mother that she would be back in a few days, but if anyone asked to 'tell them I was kidnapped by a group of men in masks'.

One day before the court case, and she was still nowhere to be seen.

The trial went ahead anyway without her present. Her lawyer, who was me, found it a mite tricky to argue that his client is so clearly not the type to get herself kidnapped for attention, despite the fact she appears to have been kidnapped through her own machinations.

Like some tawdry play, just as the judge was preparing to wrap it all up, she bursts in through the doors. She was dirty, dishevelled, and, alarmingly, blood-soaked.

She was carrying a sack that was oozing something dark and slimy. I've seen enough in my time to recognise a sack of flesh when I see one.

She upends the bag, and sure enough, body parts come squelching out. A few hands, some feet, a collection of fleshy lumps that didn't merit closer inspection unless absolutely necessary. A flabbergasted courtroom stands frozen during this macabre display.

She rooted around in the, eh, mound, until she found a small, wrapped piece of cloth. Unfolding it, and flicking the viscera from it, she handed it to the opposition attorney, who read it wide eyed, then to the judge, who read it even wider eyed, then to me.

It was a press-pass for a number of employees of the Weekly Wheatsheaf, complete with a sketch of their face and a stamp of authenticity, wrapped in a letter from the chief-editor explaining exactly where Quen would be and where to take her.

Without prompting, she takes the stand and explains how she was minding her own business at home, when her door is kicked down and she is bundled into a sack and kidnapped. She is taken on horseback to an unknown location.

Unbeknownst to her would-be kidnapper, Quetrietta is a master of Gueppo, a bare-knuckle fighting method taught by a select few to an even selecter few. It is a frightening practice focussed on maiming one's opponent in all manner of creative ways. For self-defence, of course.

She had stated on the dock that if the papers had *actually* done their research, they'd have known she was a Gueppo master, and not just that, but taught other masters at her secluded forest dojo. Consequently, the kidnappers deserved everything they got.

After being taken, it took Quen only a short while to free herself and overpower her would-be abductors, despite her small size and reputation. I hear the scene of the crime was officially reported as 'grisly'.

A few hours later, she had extracted the whole story from her unlucky companions. Not wanting to return without proof, she took a few souvenirs, then came straight to court.

The nervous-looking judge ruled in her favour, saying her response was appropriate. She also fined the paper a year's income and instructed the chief-editor to attend court for a hearing of his own. Mysteriously, he appears to have gone missing, and as of the date of writing, has not surfaced.

As for our 'kidnap magnet' Quen?

It is safe to say that Quetrietta no longer has that reputation and is no longer mentioned in the papers at all.

~journal entry ends

11 – Felix & Racelsus

Felix had suggested they take a break, and Furbo had accepted. A mug of tea and a short stroll, and within the hour, they were all back in the interview room. Someone, probably Mrs Zwelee, had found them a plate of biscuits, which improved the atmosphere in the room quite miraculously. By the time the minty crunchers were eaten, Helda was less quiet, and Furbo was back to his amiable self.

Racelsus was in her cage, resting on the table. The cage was not dissimilar to a bird cage. It was round with thin metal bars. Some padding had been placed to help the skull stay upright.

Felix stared at the skull. It was old, that much was obvious. If he were a medical man, he supposed there would be no end of interesting facts he could glean from a mere glance at it. However, he wasn't, so that was more or less all he got.

He was preparing to address the witch directly for the first time. At Felix's request, Yetty had accompanied him into the room after the break. *Moral support?* Felix delayed the inevitable by making introductions. To her credit, she barely reacted when Felix introduced Racelsus. He could put it off no longer, so Felix prepared to question the witch.

Should I make eye contact? Why am I so nervous…

"Could you describe the prison you were held in to me," he said in her direction, pen in hand. He was focussing on the paper, mostly so he didn't have to look her in the…

In the socket.

Her voice was dry, somehow breathy, despite her clear lack of lungs. Like a loud whisper. It made the hairs on Felix's neck stand on end.

"It was an austere stone room with only one door."

"A bloody marvellous door," interjected Furbo, nodding. "I have many notes and theories on it, for example—"

93

"Not now, Furbo," Helda said, patting his hand. Furbo stopped and gave an embarrassed cough. Racelsus continued.

"A tiny square of light would sometimes reach from a window in the ceiling. The window was very small, so small a cat would have trouble fitting through it."

Felix was nodding as he notated. Her voice had the mildly terrifying quality of appearing to overlap over itself, almost like an echo, but in reverse. You'd hear the back end of the word she hadn't said yet before she'd finished the last word. Felix did his best to ignore it while he took notes more fastidiously than normal. Any excuse not to have to make...

Eye contact.

"And tell me of the cell. How deep was it embedded into the mountain?"

"It wasn't in a mountain, it was in a cave."

She explained it took several hours of walking through passageways to reach the room, and that on a constant decline.

"I would guess it was several hundred feet below the solid rock. Long ago, I heard discussions that there were several emergency measures to flood the passages with rocks or water in the event of an escape—my escape—but I never saw them used. I was most well behaved."

Felix looked up at her without realising, and found himself staring into those green lights. It struck him suddenly how unsettling this was, and he suppressed an involuntary shiver.

"Oh, come now, I'm not that bad am I?" asked Racelsus.

Felix blinked, and colour rose to his cheeks. "I'm so sorry, I didn't say that out loud, did I?"

"Oh, I forgot to mention, she does that. Reads minds. You get used to it," said Helda. "She doesn't delve deep, just surface thoughts. At least, that's what she claims." She narrowed her eyes at the skull.

"Maiden's honour," Racelsus purred.

Quite unbidden, Felix's head immediately filled with all manner of incredibly embarrassing thoughts that spread to fill his whole consciousness. Hidden secrets floated by like jetsam from a sinking ship, and he realised that, if he didn't control himself soon, he was going to have to find Racelsus's old cave and live there forever, or die of shame.

Felix shook his head as a dog might when drying itself.

Pure thoughts, pure thoughts. Dogs, cats, trees, sunshine, rainbows…

"Okay… I'd request that you don't do that to me, as it will throw me right off my flow. Or the opposition; remember, this is the clergy we're dealing with. It won't help our case at all if we're found out to be using actual mind-reading witchery. Erm, no offence intended."

The skull clattered its teeth together. Unsure of whether this was a 'Yes, no problem' clack or a 'No, stuff you' clack. Felix proceeded.

"…right, so. The rest of you, your body, is that still in the cell?"

"Yes. I was bludgeoned from behind, breaking my spine at the neck, and my body rotted from under me while I watched. The…" Her voice broke suddenly. She paused, working her jaw open and shut a couple of times. "I succumbed to despair. You cannot know the complete misery of watching yourself… unable to intervene. Watching yourself… just…"

"It's okay, Racelsus," said Furbo, soothingly quiet. "We'll not ask you to recount that."

She clacked her teeth sharply and continued "I was able to move in small ways, but not enough to escape. When they found me, they carried only my head as it was the only part of me left worth taking."

"Wait, wait a minute!" Helda said. Her eyes were moving left to right, up and down, as if thinking about something, something complicated. "When we found you, you were moving your arms about… how could you do that if your back was broken, and you couldn't move? Are you being honest with us, skull?"

That's a good point. Something the prosecution might ask… A prosecutor in the making?

"Helda," said Racelsus. "Turn me round so we are looking at each other's eyes."

Helda paused, brushing crumbs from her lap. She pursed her mouth petulantly.

"Helda," she said again.

The large woman slowly, gingerly, reached a hand over and swivelled the cage. It scraped as it rotated, and Felix was torn with wanting to prevent scratches on the table and with getting in the middle of this confrontation.

The skull was staring hot iron at Helda.

"Helda. You saved me. I owe you. I will be nothing, *nothing*, but honest with you. I promise. You know that, don't you? Both of you, Furbo as well."

Helda looked a little bashful. She dropped her gaze.

"I'm sorry, I didn't mean…"

"I will never, never give you reason to doubt me. You understand?"

"Okay, okay…"

"Good, I'm glad we got that out of the way," finished Racelsus.

Felix tapped his finger on the table.

"I'm sorry, but I'm going to play demon's advocate here… Imagine if I'm the prosecution, that's a question they might well ask. Racelsus," he said, putting on a serious voice, "what would you answer?"

She clacked. "I'd say: it was magic. I can move objects a little. I was able to animate my own body to give the illusion of normal movement. I didn't want to completely scare them off, did I? Furbo was enough of a wreck as it was."

"It's true," Furbo said. "I was *most* perturbed."

They chuckled in a good-natured way.

These guys have a nice bond. A weird one, I'll admit, but nice.

Felix scribbled something out on his pad.

"Silly question, but just to reiterate—you did actually want to be removed, yes?" Felix said, rubbing his eyes with his finger and thumb.

"Absolutely," declared Racelsus. "One hundred percent."

"Why?" Felix asked.

"*You* spend four hundred years in a cave, then ask me again."

Felix nodded a few times, bobbing his head absent-mindedly. He made a few notes, then stood up, placing one hand on his waist and one on his chin. In this thoughtful pose, he addressed the room.

"Good. Right. Okay. I think our defence is going to have to be a twofold matter. One: you're not a danger, so your imprisonment was, in fact, carried out under false pretences. Second, it's a matter of consent. You were not robbed because you are not property, and you are able to give consent, so you cannot be 'stolen'. That's going to be the crux of our argument.

"They're probably going to argue point one like a terrier with a rat. Unfortunately, the church tends to overreact to anyone with any sort of magical ability, especially if they're not registered with the university. More so if they're from a swamp. We don't have anyone who can vouch for your, hm, purity, so that's going to probably go nowhere. But we have to present it. The strongest argument will be the consent matter. If you cannot be robbed, the whole case falls apart. The rest of the charges, Heresy and whatnot, that's just filler to make their case look more important. We can't argue it either way, and they have no proof, so provided you don't perform any actual heresy during the trial... That means no magic... and if we can remove the graverobbing charge, we should be laughing."

Helda peered at him, eyes narrowed in anticipation. "So... you're taking our case?"

Felix stared at her, before chuckling. "Oh, yes. Absolutely. This is right up my street," he said smiling with a twinkle in his eye.

"Uh, we don't really have much money..." Helda mumbled.

"Don't worry about that. We'll counterclaim for the costs, and if that doesn't work, we'll do it for free."

Furbo stammered. "Are you sure, my lad?"

Felix smiled and nodded. "I am. Sometimes, you—"

He slammed his open palm on the table, making everyone jump. He waved a hand at Yetty.

"That's it! Queily v Builder's & Co." He turned to her. "You remember that one?"

Her eyes scanned from left to right, seeing nothing, searching the library of her mind for answers. "Uhh... The fountain case?" she said.

"Yes!" said Felix. He turned to the trio.

"Queily was a mad old wizard who turned himself into a statue so he could live forever. He couldn't move, but could still speak, sort of, in a manner of speaking. Assuming he had died, his house was sold for developments by his next of kin. The people who bought his house after he, hm, 'disappeared' tried to demolish it with him in it. But they found they couldn't, due to some form of ward he had placed on his surroundings before his statuification. He also refused to allow himself to be moved, as he wanted to watch his garden grow until the end of time, or some such. The builders argued he was just an object, and was not allowed to object, having no rights.

"Eventually, it found its way to court, and it was decried that sentience begets consent. IE, an object, regardless of what it was, was deemed able to agree and consent to things provided it could prove it had sentience. Old Queily was permitted to stay, and the builders had to sell the land… of course, no one would buy it, except Queily himself, for a much-reduced price. Sneaky bugger, Queily."

Yetty spoke. "So, either we argue that Racelsus is an object, in which case she can give consent to her own theft, or she's not an object, and so is a person, and so can give consent, and so can't be stolen. That means we have precedent… So, it should be simple?"

"Yes, I think so!" Felix smiled. "So long as the judge isn't some insane god-botherer that ignores precedents, we should be in for an easy ride."

His smile dropped and morphed into a frown.

"Before we pat ourselves on the head too soon, do we know who will be presiding over the court? Tell me it's not an insane god-botherer," asked Felix.

"Let me check the proclamation that we got yesterday… I think we might have skipped the presider when we first read it," said Yetty. She retrieved it from a precarious pile of papers, brushed the ash from it, and began reading.

"Judge presiding… the judge will be… HJ.H? Who's that?"

Felix scrunched his eyes up and sighed.

"Holy Judge Helmellia, Bishop and Deacon of the Order of Apostolry, Habeus's Chosen. My own fault, I shouldn't have jinxed it," he muttered.

"That's bad?" asked Helda.

"That's bad," grumbled Felix. He flipped the paper over and read the back. "And, to make it worse, it's being heard in the bloody Temple of Habeus. Still let's not give up until we've actually tried, right?"

However tempting that might be. We're in trouble.

He noticed the skull looking at him.

Sorry. Natural pessimist.

He could have sworn the skull smiled.

Interlude – Corney Carves
~ *Very Long Ago*

A figure was crouched at the stem of a tree. One tree among thousands nearby, though this tree was marked by its size and eminent majesty. The figure was hacking a small shape from the bark with a sharpened rock. The sound was muffled by the heavy moss that carpeted both the floor and every trunk in the surrounding glen.

It stopped, considering the next mark. It looked up, taking in the full grandeur of the Great Tree. It certainly was great, there was no denying it.

"Great means big," it muttered to itself. "Big doesn't mean good, and no mistake."

It spat, then cocked an ear. Having made up its mind, it began chipping the next shape in the sequence. This one was carved with dirty, rough strikes of the stone.

A shift of the stance, and the third symbol began. This time, instead of the haphazard, manic strokes of the last, these etchings were slow and gentle, the stone being used more like a piece of chalk than a brutal tool of destruction.

"Do you have something against trees?" came a voice, sounding resonant but tired. Stopping to place the rock thoughtfully on the floor, the figure replied.

"Eh, not trees in general, or wood, leaves or any other vegetation. I daresay I'd be somewhat of a hypocrite if I started spouting nonsense about detesting plants, what with seeing how without 'em all life on this here great marble would cease, and do so most abruptly."

It picked up its rock again. "Man cannot live on meat alone, for then what does the meat live on?"

It started on the fourth symbol, stabbing the stone deep into the bark with a thrust, then dragging it with both hands. It was clearly difficult, for the figure was muttering and sweating before long. The sonorous voice replied.

"Not trees in general, then. So, it must be these trees in particular?"

"Aye." A pause then, as the fifth rune was started. "'Spose you'll be asking me why?"

The figure turned for the first time to find an elderly man, clad all in green, standing a few paces off. His beard was wrapped in a knot that hung freely, swinging pendulously from his stooped posture.

"I would settle for you simply stopping, and you can keep your reasons to yourself."

Considering for the briefest of moments, the figure set his tools down, and brushed his hands clean of detritus. Clearing his throat, he stood up, and approached the old man with his hand outstretched.

"Habe," he offered.

Common decency transcended all manner of traditions, cultures and creeds, and the old man completed the greeting with a small shake of the hand.

"I am Habeus."

"Ha! What are the odds? We're name-brothers. Tell you what, you call me Corney, and I'll call you Habeus, and we'll not get confused with whom's carving what into whom, lest you find yourself on my homestead digging some swearwords into my outhouse!" He laughed then, a filthy, raucous laugh that belonged in an inn.

Habeus smiled in spite of the situation, for humour also transcended cultures. "So, why are you doing this?"

Corney's wonky smile dropped an inch but didn't disappear. "Well, that's the strangest part. I can't really say, if I'm being clear, which I know for a fact I ain't."

Habeus stared at the full length of Corney, taking him in. He had a sun-burnished look, like one who has spent years under the sky, and hardened into leather. His cracks and creaks showed a fellow who laughed often, but his eyes were shrewd, and didn't waiver. He had the clothes of a simple man, and indeed the tools of the simplest of men. He did not seem the type to carve wanton rituals into ancient forests.

"To tell the truth, I find frequent, eh, compulsions seem to grasp me these days. I'll be at home, just having lit a pipe, or taking the fresher air outside, or perhaps setting to carving something fancy, when I'll be gripped by the urge to go and cause mischief of some kind. Usually it's vague, so I'm settled by some minor crime, like stealing an apple or trampling a flower bed, but of late they're much harder to quash. It's like some voice is in my head, and what once was a whisper is now a shout. I can't get it to quieten down, except by doing exactly what it wants. What the voice wants now, more than anything, is for me to finish this here last carving in this very particular tree. I tell you, the urge is strong. It's like falling off a cliff. I can't stop, the ground is coming, no matter how I wriggle and writhe, I still plummet, and there's only one way it ends." He paused. "That is, until you came over. Since then, it's like the voice has, well, come and gone, wandered off, and I'm back to myself again."

Habeus nodded. "Yes, I suspected as much. I can influence you somewhat, but I fear the demon inside you has grown considerably. It's quite a marvel that you still retain what portion of your soul you have left."

Instead of stammering or quavering at the revelation that he was possessed, Corney just sighed. "Figured it was some nonsense of that like. Gah, fancy getting your soul infested with sommat like that." He squatted on his haunches, passing the rock from hand to hand. "Live honestly, want only what you deserve, hope for the best. Words to live by, and I daresay die by, said by them that's wiser'n me."

He looked up at the old man, staring at that ancient face.

"I can't end it, though. I'm still falling, don't matter that I know what I'm falling on."

"Yes."

"I suppose you can't stand there forever, soothing my unquiet spirit, hm?"

"No."

"Pity." Corney stood, holding the sharpened stone so tightly it caused his hand to bleed. "Might as well you get on with you then. Busy man I expect, if a man you are, though even forest sprites must have agendas and chores, errands and whatnot. I will be honest as well—this hand hurts

101

something fearsome, and if I must complete this, I'd rather do it quickly."
Veins bulged in his arm, encouraging the bleeding to worsen.

"I'm sorry," intoned Habeus, shaking his head.

"I'm sure you are, though I, hrmm, expect you'll be sorrier soon, for
which I in turn.. Will say I'm sorry..." Blood smeared into the final stroke
of the final rune, and the moment it was done, each rune disappeared into
the bark, like footprints in the mud.

"Will it, ah, hurt much longer... Habeus?" asked Corney, with great
effort, as he looked at his mangled, twisted hand, black sticky blood
swelling at the palm.

"No. You are very brave."

"For what good it done me."

Corney swayed then, and toppled over, but by the time he hit the
floor, he was dead.

12 – Practice

Felix talked to them for some hours more, going over the same details time and time again, adding notes, removing notes, filling reams and reams of paperwork with large, scratchy lettering. Evening was rolling in, and his clients were getting irritable. He was getting irritable. Yetty, somehow, wasn't. She could have just strolled in after a nap.

Perfect time for it.

He lowered his pen, slapped his thighs, and stood. "Okay, it's getting late. I suspect we're all tired."

Helda leaned her head back. "And bored, oh so bored."

"You'll be wanting to head off to bed soon, maybe a nightcap first?" he mused.

"Yes! God! Please!" she laughed. "And not a moment too soon!" she stood, and smiled at Furbo, relief dripping from her. Furbo hadn't moved, but regarded Felix with tired eyes. "You not coming, Furbo?"

Furbo looked from Felix to Helda. Her eyes looked a little more strained and desperate the longer he paused. "Come on, what's the hold up?" she said.

He stretched and sank further into his chair. "I think our lawyer has a last trick for us."

Felix held a hand up. "Guilty, Your Honour."

She rounded on him. "Are you serious? I'm hungry, tired, and bored *out of my mind!* Can't this wait until tomorrow?"

Felix shook his head. "Sorry, but no. We need to talk about cross examination." He gestured for her to sit. She didn't.

"Why?"

He yawned. "Cross examination is where the case will be made, or it will be broken. It's when the lawyer, either me or the other guy, will listen

103

to what you say, nod politely, then try to break your story to pieces, whilst simultaneously making you appear to be the worst sort of person ever to grace a court, using every lawyer trick in the book."

He started pacing the room. Helda watched him.

"You will be tired, hungry, bored out of your mind. You will want nothing more than to leave, to go home, to lie down and think about something else, a nice drink in hand, the day's unpleasantness just a bad memory. That's just where we want you. Lawyers will make you recount your experiences, beginning to end, and we will dedicate ourselves to pulling-it-to-pieces. We'll infuriate you, deliberately pushing your buttons, trying to get a reaction, trying to prove you a liar, a scoundrel, a person so unbelievable that it should be a *crime* that we even let you walk into a courtroom. And, if you rise to it, you'll help us."

He scraped a chair to the corner of the room, making sure it grated as loudly as possible, causing Helda to flinch, and gestured to her to sit.

"We are going to cross examine you now."

"Now?" Helda said. She looked scared.

"Now. We need to decide which of you is going to take the stand, and we need to do it now."

Helda looked to Furbo, who nodded, and to Racelsus, who didn't react at all. She grunted, and stomped over to the chair.

"Try to be as calm and reasonable as you can, and remember—don't rise to it. Saying that, you have to answer every question truthfully. Don't lie, and try not to take what she says personally."

"She?" said Helda.

Felix turned with a flourish to Yetty, who had stood up. She had swept her hair to the side, wearing it in a short ponytail that jutted from her head, unlike her normal style, which let her hair flow down her back. Her face was that of complete distaste, sprinkled with pomposity. She managed to look down her nose at everyone in the room, which was impressive, considering she was the shortest.

"Prosecutor," said Felix, bowing deeply, before taking a seat.

Yetty strode over to Helda, sniffing haughtily. Felix sat on the table facing them, putting his best judge face on. "Cross examination of the witness will commence. The floor is yours, Prosecutor Yetty." He stamped his foot on the floor in a mock-gavel.

"Thank you, Your Honour," she droned.

She turned to face Helda, who squirmed in the dock.

"Name and occupation?" she spoke in a nasal voice she reserved just for this occasion.

"Uh, Helda," said Helda.

"Occupation, witness, or are you *simple?*" said Yetty, with a withering stare.

"I'm not simple…" growled Helda. "I'm Helda. I'm a wanderer."

"Where do you wander, witness?"

"All over, wherever we want."

"Going wherever you want, doing whatever you want, I suppose?" sneered Yetty, turning from her to pace up and down the makeshift courtroom.

"I guess, I—"

"So, you don't much care for the law, then?"

"I didn't say that!" rebuked Helda.

"You said, 'We do whatever we want, wherever we want, did you not?"

"Now hold on, I—"

"Yes or No, witness, please, or do you need it explained more simply?"

Helda's face was starting to redden.

"Prosecutor, next question please," Felix said. Yetty nodded.

"Do you ever get into brawls, witness?"

Helda coughed. "Uh, sometimes."

"How often, let's say, in the last year?"

"Uhm… uhh…"

"It's a *simple* question."

Her face darkened. "About seven times…"

"Seven different brawls at seven different times, with seven different victims?"

"I didn't start—"

"Were you or were you not involved in around seven unique brawls in the last year, yes or no?"

"Yes…" she was getting really quite angry.

"So, a strong fighter like yourself, why is it you didn't fight these churchmen who stopped you when you left the cave? Was that not your instinct?"

"I didn't want to fight."

"Oh, you didn't want to fight? So, the other seven times, those were fine, but this was too much?"

"Yes." She was trying to calm herself down.

"Were you scared?"

She leapt from her chair. "Look, what's the bloody point in these bloody questions!?" she yelled.

Yetty whirled to Felix. "Your honour, the witness is clearly hysterical and prone to violence, I move she be reprimanded in custody immediately, for our own safety, and her testimony stripped from the record."

Felix nodded sagely. "I agree. Guards." He gestured to imaginary bailiffs. Helda flicked her eyes towards her would-be reprimanders, then from Felix to Yetty, back to Felix, then screwed her eyes shut. The sound of her teeth grinding made Furbo wince.

He shook his head. "Helda, my dear, are you okay?"

She flumped into her seat, deflated. "I don't know."

Yetty undid her ponytail. "Sorry, Helda, I didn't mean it. I was just trying to be horrible to you to show you what it could be like."

"Well, you did a great job!" she said, laughing nervously.

Felix stood. "You only get one chance in the dock. You have to be ready to be attacked like that, and keep your cool, sticking to the facts. I think, Helda, we might be best served if we keep you on the bench."

She nodded, and looked exhausted. She waved her hand at Yetty. "You're good. Is she going to be doing that in court?"

Felix gathered his papers that were strewn on his desk into a bundle and walked to the door. "No, I'll be doing it. I think we should actually call it a night. You're tomorrow, Furbo. Goodnight, all. See you in the morning." He strode from the room, whistling as he went. The room started standing, stretching, getting ready to head off to a well-deserved rest.

Helda turned to Yetty. "Why is *he* doing it? You're so good at being utterly horrendous. You made me want to rip your head off. Why him?"

Yetty paused in the doorway and flashed her a mischievous grin. "Because he's much, much worse than I am."

~

After more grilling the following evening, they decided that Furbo was made of the right stuff for cross-examination. He was cool and calm under pressure, and answered the questions precisely and without fuss, rarely getting muddled and not rising to the bait.

That's good. I needed one of them to testify, at least.

He looked at Racelsus.

Maybe...

He imagined the Holy Judge's face as he announced his intention, declaring them heretics and sentencing him to immediate execution via mob disembowelment.

Maybe not.

~

He didn't sleep the next few nights. Long evenings spent revising and gathering his documents, obsessing over the smallest of details. The worst part though was the fluttering nerves, the anticipation.

The excitement.

Journal Entry F: Barbarian

Reference case [BBvJB] (BerBru v. JefBel), year 1325, judge Merita presiding.

"My client was merely expressing his sentiment in the custom most suited to his tradition, your ho-urk"!

That last noise was due to said client deciding he hadn't quite fully expressed his sentiment in the custom most suited to his tradition and needed to further explain the matter. More specifically, he was doing this by grabbing me by the arm and hefting me bodily across the dock and into the prosecution.

After the intervention of four of the guards (who really were earning their pay this afternoon), my client, the terrifyingly styled Bertruk the Pummeller, once more sat calmly in his designated chair, albeit slightly more covered-in-chains than he was previously. In fact, it was hard to see his body at all, just a head and two hands poking out of a large mound of iron.

Bertruk was barbaric, and I mean that in the nicest possible way. He was enormous, terrifically hairy, and had not an ounce of fat on his body. Both of his ears were mangled, his face was covered with scars and his hair was matted and patchy. I'd managed to count five real teeth, the rest seemingly mis-shapen lumps of bone or metal that someone, somewhere had hammered into his gums. He was utterly menacing, indescribably brutish, and completely innocent.

It began around four weeks prior. The town of Gurlton, just on the outskirts of Pleg Ford, West Country, had a monster problem. Every three weeks, some unlucky townsfolk would wake up to find their neighbour's door had been torn from its hinges, and the neighbour themselves reduced to a bloody stain. Local government was useless because of the war, consequently no money was diverted to improve security. It has nothing at all to do with the fact the town mayor lived five or six towns over and was thus unworried for his own skin, so don't even think that, you cynic.

So, the townsfolk had banded together, and tried to track the beast down themselves. It had ended poorly.

After that, they had the much more sensible idea of hiring some professional talent to rid them of their beastly problem.

Enter Bertruk.

He's one of these nomadic types, wandering the country, earning their way through skill at arms. Much less romantic than it sounds, but if you're half-way decent at the job, you can make a comfortable living. Also, generally speaking, the ones who aren't good at the job end up dead, so there's plenty of work to go around. Times had been hard for Bertruk though, and he was hungry.

People down the pub often give these wandering mercenaries a bad rap. They assume they're nonchalant when it comes to killing, theft, extortion, etc. They assume that just because one has set oneself aside from 'civilised' society, then one must have no qualms with breaking whatever inconvenient laws prevent you from simply taking what you want. This might be true for some, perhaps, but never any that I've met. However hungry he got, Bertruk had a code of honour. He was not a thief.

They had found him, half starved, a few towns over. After listening to their story, he had been moved by their plea for help, and their offer of payment: one animal of his choosing from the town and a basket of fruit tilled from the town's good earth, was more than enough for him. In truth, it was way beneath the going rate for this sort of work, but the desperate hero agreed, and the deal was struck.

Bertruk had no difficulty tracking the monster to its lair (like I said, a professional). Planting his feet and unlatching his club, Bertruk spat on his hands and rubbed them together. After instructing the villagers to wait outside, he muttered a few words to his patron spirit, performed the short Western Dance of Protection, and stomped into the cave.

His adversary had met him at full charge, and the two titans clashed! One, a chiselled hero straight from the books (an old dog-eared and stained copy, perhaps, but no less majestic in its content), the other, a snarling, biting, grasping mound of flesh and fur, pulled from a nightmare. Fifteen full minutes they fought, until Bertruk stood victorious, standing limp, snapped club hanging by a splinter. He must have struck an inspirational sight, all bloody and triumphant, looking down at the body of his vanquished foe.

The villagers had taken his words to their logical conclusion, and were nowhere to be seen. He willed himself back to town, dragging the body of the creature with him, limping and wincing the whole way. The townsfolk, seeing him in such a piteous state, thanked him quickly and directly, then ushered him to his reward. All the animals in the village were gathered up in Farmer McWurt's pen, all ready for Bertruk's inspection and collection.

Imagine his surprise when all he saw was a table with a bucket, and in that bucket, three rats. This town, he was informed, was not a farming town that raised animals, but a quarry town, and so the only animals in their village were unwanted ones.

To add insult to injury, they gifted him a basket of rocks, hewn from the town quarry, free and given gratefully to their saviour, now could you please move on, you're scaring the children?

In my opinion, I think his response was actually rather restrained, considering. All he did really was dish out a few bruises and help himself to a bit of food from the locals, which is, in all honesty, what should have been given freely to him from the outset. The peacekeepers, suspiciously present upon Bertruk's arrival into Pleg Ford, hadn't quite agreed, and had forced him under threat of crossbow into chains. And, here he was.

~

What had caused the outburst just now? Well, the prosecutor had suggested that the defendant was perhaps not intellectually cognisant enough to understand the obvious inference that there was no actual mention of 'food', so he, morally, deserved what he got. I had explained this in simpler language to Bertruk, and I had begun my response to my counterpart, then…

I think the prosecutor deserved what he got as well.

~

Obviously they were pushing for the death sentence, but I'd managed to get him off scot-free in the end. It came down to what the sympathetic judge described as Clear Intent in the offering. To hint at the provision of needed foodstuffs to a starving yet helpful contractor was simply not the done thing, not in the West Country, he opined. What's more, it was important that people understood that you shouldn't bite the hand that feeds, and so this case could work as an example to any other townsfolk looking to get one over on the honourable Monster Hunting profession.

So, after many weeks of frustrations, Bertruk finally got his basket of apples and his goat. Of course, by this point he had been held in chains for almost a month, and had been fed by the jailors in the meantime, so he'd refused all but one apple.

"I only take what I need," he had said, in a heavily accented grumble.

He caught up with me afterwards, while I was packing up my things. His heavy brow was low and dark as he talked to me.

"I never asked. Why did you help? I don't know you," he said, regarding me with unveiled suspicion.

I didn't look up as I replied.

"Well, it's my job. I earn my money this way."

He shook his huge, shaggy head. All manner of trinkets woven into his hair or pierced into his face tinkled and jangled as he did so.

"No. I mean, why this? You could have been anything. Why a lawman?"

I stopped and thought about it. Actually thought about it. The money, to start with. At least, that's what drew me to this job. I suppose I could have moved into something less adversarial, more clinical… But, cheesy as it is to say it…

I looked up at that craggy, weather-beaten face.

"I suppose… I like helping people. Standing up for the little guy." I eyed him up. "Or, the not-so-little-guy, sometimes. I hate seeing the guy who can't defend himself getting taken advantage of. I hate seeing those with the money and the power using that to get what they want all the time, not caring about those whose lives they ruin on the way. Yes, I know, it's cheesy, clichéd rubbish…"

Bertruk's face cracked into a smile. A terrifying, nightmarish smile, but a smile nonetheless.

"Hah! You big softy." He playfully poked a massive finger into my chest, which actually hurt quite a lot. "You're like me. We fight the big monsters that hurt the townsfolk, hmm?"

"I suppose… but in this case it was the townsfolk who were the monsters, eh?"

111

Bertruk shook his head again. "I don't think so. I think they were just desperate. Like you said in your talk, I think their Lord worked them too hard, and they had to become cunning. It was that, or die. I don't blame them."

To demonstrate this, he waved cheerfully at a few stragglers at the back, visitors from the village come to see what was going to happen. They gasped and shuffled away quickly. Bertruk shrugged.

"Well, Bertruk, you can't be everyone's friend, unfortunately. Sometimes you have to make a stand, and people dislike you for it. I reckon that Lord of yours is not going to forget me in a hurry."

Said lord had attended once he had heard Lunchers & Company was defending Bertruk. He had lurked in the back, and I had clearly heard him loudly mutter 'outrageous' at least five times. He had long since stomped out of the room, not before staring bloody murder at me.

"What matters is standing up for the right reasons, and doing the right thing. That's all I did," I said, turning back to my bag. I stopped, then regarded Bertruk.

He looked down at me, a thoughtful look on his battered face. He put down his axe then and reached into a leather pouch strung to a belt. From it, he withdrew a tiny bottle of brown powder.

"What's this?" I said.

"Shh."

He unscrewed the tiny topper and carefully laid it down, before pouring the smallest sample of the stuff onto his grizzled palm. He considered it briefly, then poured out around a tenth the contents.

"I have a feeling you will need this," he rumbled.

"Need what?" I didn't know what he was doing, and I don't like not knowing things.

"Take a deep breath," he commanded.

Wanting to get whatever this was over as soon as possible, I cautiously opened my mouth to comply. His hand whipped up, palm down, spraying me with the fine powder. It was heavier than it looked, and warm. A lot of it went straight into my windpipe, and I started coughing. A heavy hand went over my mouth, and another patted my back.

"Breathe it in, law-man."

It stung, it burned, it tasted awful. Every instinct of mine wanted to vomit. I scrabbled at his hand, but he was too strong. My eyes watered and I felt close to passing out.

He released me then, leaving me to cough, gag and scrape deep breaths at the same time. Not the most dignified pose.

"Whu… hua… mm?" I asked him, eyes streaming.

He looked solemn. "You saved me today. I will save you one day. That was a gift from an old friend of mine. It used to let us know if either of us was in danger. It let us help one another."

He looked skyward. "He died eventually."

He faced me once more. "I have passed this onto you. I will aid you one day. With this, I will know if you need me."

I had managed to wipe my eyes and mouth almost dry.

"Thanks, Bertruk," I croaked, and I hoped I sounded sincere. I mean, I wasn't, but I didn't want him thinking that. Mumbo jumbo. If his old friend had died, it clearly didn't work.

He nodded and smiled again.

"I will be going now. Thank you, Felix."

And he left.

I turned to my new legal aide, Yetty. "Five silvers I never see him again." She shrugged, and accepted.

A judge's aide scuttled over to me then.

"His Honour suggested you might want a napkin."

I gave him my most withering look, but took the napkin anyway

~journal entry ends

13 – Outside The Courtroom

Felix looked up at the columns either side of the door to the temple. He had his clutch of papers under one arm. It was a chilly morning, and his breath misted in the air.

"Marvellous things, doors," Furbo said, stepping up beside him.

Felix didn't hear him.

"I said, marvellous things, doors," Furbo repeated, a little louder. This time Felix turned to Furbo, almost surprised to see him there.

"Oh, morning Furbo," he said, distantly.

"I suppose we'd better head in?" the older man prompted.

Felix nodded, and straightened himself up. "I suppose we had."

He climbed the three steps to the door and pushed. Despite the size and apparent weight of it, the door moved easily and without complaint.

"Fascinating," Felix heard Furbo mutter as they passed in.

~

The courtroom was set up inside the main chamber of the Church of Holy Habeus, God of Judgement. It had clearly not seen much use these past decades, judging by the thick layer of dust that coated everything. Behind the raised dais, where the judge would sit, was an enormous stain-glass portrait of Habeus himself, staring down upon the assembled—watching, judging. It was bearded, balding, and gazed sternly upon all that was before him.

The effect was only slightly minimised by the thick layer of dust covering him. He looked less magnificent and intimidating, more old and sad, perhaps wondering why all these people have suddenly turned up to make noise and cause a fuss in his lovely quiet temple.

It wasn't unheard of for churches to be used as courtrooms, especially the Church of Habeus. Before the judiciary and apostolry were formally divided by Queen Kinnian the Unbeliever, there were no separate courthouses. Of course, Kinnian hadn't quite thought that through at the time, and what followed was a period those interested in legal history call 'The Pub Judgements'. It was said cases were tried and fought in inns and pubs, those being the only non-residential non-religious buildings large enough and common enough to be of use.

It mutated the system somewhat, with some particularly bilious landlords acting as stand-in judges for local cases, since the townsfolk equated pubs with justice, and the one on the right side of the bar as being the one with the power. It only lasted a few months before the first proper courthouses were built, and the days of sinking a pint while watching the local criminal squeal for his life came to an end.

Despite all that history, some vestiges of the unity of justice and belief remain, namely in the (hitherto assumed) ceremonial position of Holy Judge, that hallowed individual said to be the arbiter of the soul, the earthly representative of Habeus, God of Judgement. Often they will move from the judiciary to the position, having curried enough favour with the church, usually from outspoken opinions on certain issues the church finds particularly interesting. Cue many years of easy living, making a few appearances a year, and eventually dying old, fat and stress-free.

Helmellia had been a judge for twenty years when she was called, and has been acting as Holy Judge for nearly double that. She had not presided over a single case in that time.

Until this one, obviously.

~

Felix walked quietly through the gangway between the pews, which were filled with figures in the light blue raiment of the church. They rustled slightly as he passed them, their heavy robes hiding their faces which, like a wave, turned to follow him.

Normally, members of the public were permitted to view proceedings in court (excepting private cases, of course, but those were *awfully* expensive). Today, only members of the church were in the audience. While the public were, of course, *welcome*, if they couldn't find a seat, they were kindly asked to wait outside. Not a square inch of bench was free of blue-robed bottom.

Prosecutor Ettyson nodded to Felix as he arrived. She was, as ever, immaculately turned out, her light blonde hair wrapped and arranged in a modest plait. She dressed in a timeless style, simple colours with simple cuts, but modelled them perfectly. Her sheer preparedness and quiet confidence made Felix feel like he'd arrived fifteen minutes late already, despite being ten minutes early.

"Only ten minutes?" her demeanour seemed to say *"I've been here since last night. Do keep up."*

"Felix," she said.

"Ettyson," he replied. "Quite eerie here, isn't it?"

She considered, then shrugged. "Beats the normal rabble."

Felix turned to take in the scene. It was like being at a funeral, and he had the corpse-eye view. He placed his folder down on the table, from which a small puff of dust was the response.

"Mm," he hummed.

He was then aware of heavy footsteps behind him. For a heartbeat he imagined himself being seized from behind and thrown into a penitent cell, to spend eternity in ceaseless toil to obtain his absolution.

Guilty conscience?

When he looked, it was just Helda and Furbo, carrying Racelsus in her cage outstretched, like a lantern. The light from the sconces along the wall reflected in the bars of her birdcage, and Felix wondered if they would leave her behind these bars if they convicted her. Bars within bars.

A flash of reflected light caught his eye.

"Did you polish the cage?" he asked Helda.

She fidgeted. "Well, first impressions count."

Felix couldn't help but smile.

The large door to the hall slammed shut without warning causing Felix to almost leap out of his skin. A figure starting shouting from the end of the hall.

"Are all who are to be judged gathered hither?" he yelled.

There was a short pause while Felix tried to decide if he needed to respond. Things were done differently in church-led cases. Far more ceremony and pomposity, and that was saying something.

I think that's my cue.

"Ye-s." His voice cracked as he said it, making him sound like a teenager. He cleared his throat and said again, more loudly. "Yes."

Ettyson echoed the affirmative.

"All here to be judged," intoned the speaker at the back.

The congregation all chanted as one. "All will be judged."

The door behind the dais opened.

Holy Judge Helmellia herself entered the room without fanfare. Whereas a normal judge would wear the severe black robe of the judiciary, she instead wore the black robe striped with the dark purple of the church, coupled with a frankly enormous hat of office. The effect was equally intimidating and ponderously ludicrous. She was old and shrivelled but moved without tremble or hesitation.

Plus, she must have a neck like a rhino to hold that damn thing up.

When she spoke, her voice was low and had that quality that, despite being quiet, carried it to every corner of the hall.

"We are gathered here today upon the sacred ground of Habeus the Just to hear the case of The Apostolry and Racelsus, the witch, Furbo, the wanderer, and Helda, the wanderer."

Felix swallowed. He always spontaneously developed a dry throat when a case started. He also always forgot to pour out a glass of water before the judge arrived, and so had to stand in parched discomfort while the judge continued.

"They have been confirmed as in attendance, and thus will leave this room as the condemned Guilty or the forgiven Innocents. This case, being wholly within the jurisdiction of the church, may be tried and convicted based on the interpretations of the evidence and assertions by the Holy Judge, which is myself. The charges are:"

She unfurled a piece of paper that she appeared to produce from nowhere.

"One count of heresy, one count of graverobbing, one count of theft, one count of witchery."

Helda shifted nervously beside them. Furbo gave her shoulder a reassuring squeeze. *"Give her a rhino, and she'll charge at it, brave as anything"*, he had told Felix after her cross-examination practice. *"But tell her to speak to a crowd with confidence and she turns to jelly."* Helmellia rolled the paper up again and it disappeared into a pocket or a sleeve.

She'd make a good magician. Felix mused.

"The maximum penalty for these collected crimes is Death, or Life Imprisonment. Leniency will be shown to those who admit their crimes in front of God."

Even Furbo's cheerful expression looked strained, despite having been warned of this the day before.

"Do the defendants wish to confess their sins?" she added, in a warm, forgiving sort of tone.

"…No, Your Honour," said Felix.

"I see. Pity," the judge said, before continuing.

"Prosecuting the case for the Church of Apostolry will be Prosecutor Ettyson, who shall undoubtedly deliver the holy truth backed up with irrefutable evidence to assist in His Divine Will. Defending the accused will be Defence Counsel Felix, who will look to assert the rights of the defendants, despite the seriousness of the charges and the weight of evidence against them."

I'd offer an objection, but it's the bloody judge making the assertions, Felix thought. Instead, he bit his tongue, and put on his best attentive choirboy face.

"We will begin with opening statements from both sides, then we shall hear witness testimony and evidence. Finally, both sides will deliver a closing statement and henceforth I shall deliver my judgement. So sayeth I, Holy Judge Helmellia."

"All will be judged," chanted the congregation.

That's going to take some getting used to.

She turned to Ettyson, who nodded her head in respect.

"You may begin."

14 – The First Day

Ettyson stood up, all grace and favour. A slight incline of the head to show reverence, and a respectable pause before she began.

"It is the church's position that the crimes of Heresy, Graverobbing, Theft and Witchery have been committed against the Apostolry, the Crown, and thus the Kingdom, and so we seek the highest punishment in the name of Habeus."

"Noted. Your opening statement, please," replied the Judge, gesturing at a scribe who made notes on a slab of vellum.

Ettyson had her papers in front of her on the desk, perfectly arranged, but she didn't look at them.

"The charges are, in order of severity, Theft, Graverobbing, Witchery and Heresy. We allege that, on the 27th of Coldmonth, the defendants Furbo and Helda did knowingly enter the Sanctum of The Fetter, and did remove the corpse of the witch known as Racelsus, for their own nefarious purposes."

"I object to the word nefarious," Felix said, standing.

Before the Judge could reply, Ettyson conceded, and responded with a cool, uncaring tone. "Very well. They removed the corpse for their own mysterious purposes."

"I object to the word mysterious," Felix said, standing once more.

"Defence Counsel Felix," growled Judge Helmellia "Do please be quiet."

Felix stared at her. She stared back. He decided to sit back down, clenching his teeth. Ettyson watched Felix with raised eyebrows, then, satisfied he was not going to interrupt, continued.

"As I was saying. They removed the body of the witch Racelsus for their own inscrutable purposes, and then fought off a squad of Holy Warriors who attempted to challenge them, by use of unlicensed witchery.

This theft was against the Church and is thus Heresy. This we shall prove beyond doubt through the evidence we have prepared."

She paused again, another incline of the head, then sat down.

"And you?" the judge said, turning to Felix.

Felix stood, allowing a short pause and his own gentle nod.

"Get on with it," the judge snapped.

Feeling his ears turn red, he cleared his throat and began.

"I move that all the charges be dropped. Theft and Graverobbing are one and the same in this context, so charging for both is duplication of offence. Without the initial charge of Graverobbing, the charge of Heresy is subsequently moot, especially as we intend to argue that the imprisonment of Racelsus was, in fact, unlawful in the first instance, and thus we seek to correct a grave miscarriage of justice. As for the witchery, none such event occurred. It was instead human ingenuity, and a reasonable response to the circumstances."

The judge held a finger up. "I note that you wish to drop the sin of Graverobbing, yet you give no reason as to why?"

Felix blinked. "Your Honour, I—"

"Holy Honour."

"Apologies, your, Holy Honour. I move that a sentient form cannot be stolen if they provide consent to be removed. I will explain this position during the defence's witness stages."

"But you do accept that the contents of a grave were removed?" she leaned forward, talking at him, not to him, as an impatient teacher might correct a child.

"Your Holy Honour, I humbly request that I answer that question, in full, during our witness stages, if it pleases the court," he replied, more meekly than he would have liked.

Must watch my tongue…

The judge sniffed, and waved a hand. "Acquiesced. But I shall be waiting for your explanation. Are you finished, Defence Counsel?"

Felix nodded, bowing slightly as he did so. "The defence's opening statement is concluded, your Holy Honour."

"A simple 'yes' would do, man," she chided.

Felix said nothing, simply straightened himself and then sat down.

She pointed at the prosecutor. "Please call your first witness."

She stood, then bowed. "It pleases me to call Captain Hyacinth, Order of the Apostolic Guards."

"Oh bugger," said Furbo, sliding down in his seat to hide behind Felix.

The doors were opened and in walked the captain. He was bedecked in armour of the purest blue, with a long white cape trailing behind him. His haughty expression completely ignored Felix, instead turning to Ettyson, nodding. Felix wondered how he was supposed to be taken seriously with such a ludicrous moustache, but no one else seemed to care.

He took his place on the stand, his heavy boots thunking into the wooden steps. Each step echoed around the room. When he was settled, the prosecutor strode over to him.

Journal Entry G: Cat

Reference case [GGvCR] (GreGre v. ColRob), year 1334, judge Neffin presiding.

I wish I could say it was the most bizarre case I'd ever been involved with, but I once helped a family sue their pet cat.

Life as a cat is one of endless pampering and luxury, provided you find the right family to look after you. 'Gurning' Greta was a cantankerous, lecherous, debaucherous old woman who fancied the life of a cat would suit her down to the ground. She strong-armed the local witch into transforming her into a great ginger cat, thinking it was to be a permanent change in circumstance. However, the clever and annoyed witch had short-changed our feline-wannabe.

Humans act in a way around cats that they wouldn't with other humans. I feel it's worth emphasizing this. They answer calls of nature, they get intimate with loved ones, they feel no need to hide their shame when a cat is in the room. Animals don't care, so people act naturally around them. Humans also give them belly rubs, kisses, and will perform such disgusting acts as cleaning up after them or general veterinary procedures, some including the words 'glands' and 'squeeze' that I don't particularly feel obliged to explain in more detail.

Not long after the initial transformation, Gretty, as her collar now proudly said, was adopted by a loving family of herbalists. Gretty was not the world's greatest cat. She could barely catch pests, she took a liberal approach to toileting and she had a habit of stealing the best cuts and warmest spaces to sit. When you would perhaps act in an uncivilised way while she was in the room, she would *watch* in a way that other cats simply didn't. She yowled, she scratched, she stank.

Despite this, the poor family, for poor they were, showered her with love, warmth and affection. She formed a particular bond with the youngest son, Wisty, a small, blind child with a big heart. He didn't care that she smelled or moulted, he loved her just the same. She slept on the bottom of his old, uncomfortable bed, and gave him solace through the long, chilly nights.

A little over six months later, Wisty, after waking from a nightmare, reached out to take comfort in Gretty's calming presence. What should have been warm and furry had been cold and hairless... What should have been soft and fluffy had been clammy and wrinkled.

"Gretty!" he had gasped, and cried, and his parents had burst into the room to find a naked old woman sprawled, snoring and dribbling, on the end of their son's bed. Around her neck was a collar reading: *Gretty*.

Our investigations had managed to track down the original witch who cast the spell, and she was all too happy to be a witness for us. Greta had abused and threatened her mercilessly until the witch had caved and acquiesced just to shut her up.

Instead of the spell lasting thirty years, she had woven it to last thirty weeks. Long enough for Greta to be far, far away by the time it wore off.

"My mother always told me never to annoy a witch," I lied to the witch. I didn't have... it doesn't matter.

"Your mother was very wise," she had returned with a sage nod. "Bet she was pretty too, you being such a lovely young man and all."

I had blushed just enough to be polite and gently made my excuses.

"Come and see me any time, dear," she had purred after me.

The case was fairly open and shut. Greta got six years manual labour, and Wisty got sixty years of trust issues.

~journal entry ends

15 – The Captain

The church shouter sidled up to the captain, and placed his hand on the guard's helmet, before beginning in a loud, booming monotone:

"Do you swear this oath to speak only the truth before the hereto assembled, as well as noble Habeus, lest your soul be found wanting and sacrificed to the Dwellers for eternity?"

"I do swear," he spoke.

The speaker nodded and backed away. He gestured to Prosecutor Ettyson.

"Captain Hyacinth, please state your full name and occupation for the courtroom," she began.

"Gregor Hyacinth, Captain of the Noble Ecclesiarch of the Apostolic Guards, commonly called the Apostolic Guards."

His voice was gravelly but sing-song, the sort of voice that belongs to elderly bards. When he spoke, his face didn't move, save for his mouth.

"Captain, please explain to me, in your own words, the events of that afternoon."

"Certainly. I was stationed in Guard Chapel Seven, located on the intersection of the Royal Road and the town of Herridgeton. We were performing our normal duties, when one of the Ward Alarms was triggered, instructing us to respond with immediacy."

"By Ward Alarms, witness, you mean one of these?"

Ettyson produced a small jar, filled with some gloopy liquid, and held it for the room to see. It looked like grey, gone-off jam.

"For those of us unfamiliar with Ward Alarms, could you explain them?" she said.

"Certainly. They are jars of essence that look similar to small clouds when active. Normally, they are clear, slightly white. When triggered, they turn red. They are triggered by some twin of the bottle being disturbed somewhere else. They have been sanctified by the holy orders, praise be to them, and we use them to keep an eye on Holy Sites that should not be disturbed."

"In simpler language – once could say, almost like a bell, signifying trouble?"

"Yes, prosecutor."

He hadn't moved a muscle since taking his seat.

"And this specific ward, can you tell me what it signified?"

"Certainly. It was on a shelf with a sealed note, and we are under instruction, if the ward were ever to be activated, to break the seal and perform the instruction with urgency. This one contained detail of a site close to the chapel, held deep within the caves near the coast. It told of an ancient and powerful witch that had been imprisoned there centuries ago. We were under instruction to apprehend, and, if necessary, destroy the witch."

"Like they would have been able to…" said Racelsus, quietly. The captain continued.

"Consequently, we hurried with all haste to the site, and thereupon we did spy the trio emerging from the cave."

"Did you suspect they were the cause of the alarm?" she asked, waving an arm at the defendant's bench.

"Yes, and we moved to apprehend them with speed." His voice started rising, becoming almost feverish. "Yet, they bewitched us with devilry, smoke and obfuscation, and did escape, disappearing before our very eyes… using sorcery!"

Rustles of fabric indicated that the congregation were shifting. They muttered to each other, and Felix heard someone whisper 'Witchery!' to a neighbour.

"That's not what happened at all…" said Helda to Felix.

"I know, but wait. We'll get our chance to make him regret those words," Felix whispered to her.

The prosecutor waited for the excitement to subside, then resumed her questioning.

"Please explain the nature of the sorcery you saw, captain."

"Certainly. It was threefold. First, our brains were clouded, and the nature of these individuals was hidden to us. We were unable to form clear thoughts, and their poor deceptions withstood our challenges.

"Secondly, sinister witch-smoke, bright and orange, filled the air, choking our men and scorching our pure lungs with foulness. In the chaos, they did weave some spell and vanish into nothing before us, that vanishment being the third instance."

She leaned back on her desk, in a casual way. *Trying to give the impression that this is so straight forward, no real effort need be exerted?*

She tipped her head to one side, as if thinking.

"Did you examine the cell, captain?"

"Certainly. We found the skeletal remains of the witch and some tatty rags, minus the head."

"Tatty indeed…" Racelsus quietly mumbled.

"Did you find anything else?" asked Ettyson.

"We found the matching ward, the signal jar. It was knocked over, and the cloud was red. We also found some candles that were strewn on the floor."

"Thank you witness. Did you have anything else you wanted to add?"

The captain sat taller in his chair. "We did offer a blessing to the trio, but it was refused!"

More murmurs from the crowd.

"What traveller of noble purpose would refuse such benediction?" spluttered the captain, not trying to hide the disgust. He looked at Helda for the first time, who stared back.

"Thank you, captain. I will not keep you any longer. I am sure you have many important duties to attend to. You may leave."

"Thank you captain," said Holy Judge Helmellia, dismissing him with a hand. The captain nodded and made to stand. Felix practically leapt from his seat.

"Judge, uh, Holy Judge, may we be permitted to cross-examine the witness?" he said, only slightly flummoxed.

Helmellia rolled her eyes at the suggestion and sighed, heavily.

"If you so desire, but make it quick," she intoned.

16 – The Captain II

Felix paused briefly before nodding his thanks. He glanced at the prosecutor, who was examining her papers for the first time. Finally, he looked at the captain, whose gaze was fixed ahead. Felix flicked through a few pages in his dossier, before finding the statement he took from Helda and Furbo upon first agreeing to take their case.

"Captain," he began, giving the man a smile that was not returned. Upon receiving nothing from him, Felix began.

"You are, as you would describe, a holy man? Devout?"

"Yes." He still was not looking at him.

"Living a life of duty and honest toil?"

"Yes."

"For to do otherwise in such a position as yours would be… what do you think?"

He didn't respond.

"Witness, please remember you are obliged to answer my questions unless excused by the judge."

He frowned.

Felix continued, "And not answering such simple questions in the court of Habeus himself? Could that not be seen as..?"

He didn't have to say the word. *Heretical.* He let it hang in the air.

"I will answer all your questions," the captain grunted.

"Excellent. Let's get on with it then, shall we?"

Felix flicked through a paper.

"Have you ever had much dealing with cultists?"

"Objection," said Ettyson. "No one in this case is, was, or has been accused of being, either now or in the past, a member of any cult, and thus this line of questioning is irrelevant."

The judge tapped her finger on her desk. "I'm inclined to agree…"

Felix had dug up some old reports that said this captain was a little prone to heavy-handedness when it came to dealing with those he called 'heretics'. Only recently, he had overreacted to an alleged cult gathering, and been reprimanded. Felix wanted to paint this man as an overreaction-prone fanatic... but perhaps, in these surroundings, he'd best steer clear.

"I apologise, your holy honour. I shall skip that line of questioning," he said.

"Good," she replied.

Does she always need to have the last word? She's like a child.

Felix tapped his chin in mock thought.

"Captain. I wonder if you might describe the smoke you saw. You described it as... 'sinister witch-smoke, bright orange'. You also asserted that it burned your lungs?"

"Yes, it did."

"Would you say the smoke was more liquidy, or foamy?"

His brow creased. "Uh... foamy, I suppose."

"I see. Did it have a particular smell?"

"Yes, it smelled of the devil's own produce!"

Helda guffawed, and Furbo tapped her on the arm urgently, in a *shut the hell up you madwoman* sort of way. Felix carried on as if he hadn't heard her.

Felix produced a small bottle from his pocket. It was in a brown paper bag. He moved to unstopper the cork.

"Captain, I'm going to open this bottle. I wonder if you might smell it for me, and let the court know if..?"

He popped the bottletop as he spoke, filling the room with a foul stench within seconds. As Felix approached the captain, he wafted a white-gauntleted hand in front of his face.

"Ugh! I can smell it from here," the captain coughed. "I know *not* what nefarious unguent you have in that bag, but it's the same pungence as that dastardly witch-magic. I'd recognise it anywhere," he finished, his face crinkling with disgust.

"Quite a distinctive aroma, you would say?"

"Yes, man! How clearly do I have to spell it out?"

"Would you say the smoke smelled of Mrs Haggerty's Wound Cleansing Poultice?" Felix said, producing the small bottle from the bag, holding it up for all to see.

"Mrs... what?"

"This is Mrs Haggerty's Wound Cleansing Poultice. No doubt familiar to an *experienced* soldier such as yourself, used as it is to soothe cuts and prevent infection. I wonder if you might verify that it is indeed Mrs Haggerty's?" said Felix. He unstoppered it, and a foul stench filled the room within seconds.

It does wonderful things for wounds, apparently, but stinks like the devil. *That's how you know it's still fresh!* Claimed the bottle.

"Captain, what you have just smelled – and declared to be a product of witchery – is none other than a commonplace medicinal ointment, found in every guard-cabin and barracks in the land."

The captain didn't speak. He glowered at Felix.

"Oh!" Felix said, in mock forgetfulness. "I realise, of course, that I haven't asked a question. So, allow me. Would you say the smell of Mrs Haggerty's was similar, if not identical, to the smell of the cloud of 'witch-smoke'?"

The captain paused.

"I remind you, you have oathed to speak the truth, captain."

"How dare you! Such insolence. Of course I will speak the truth! Yes, the smell is the same," he muttered.

Felix nodded, and stoppered the bottle.

"I wonder if you would tell the court if you are familiar with Alchemy."

The man didn't react. "I know alchemy. 'Tis the mixing of potions and whatnot."

Felix nodded. "I also wonder... do you know what is created when one mixes Aquagen Twice-oxide with Oxygen?"

The guard shrugged. "I do not."

Felix considered this answer. "Allow me to demonstrate."

He gestured to Yetty, who produced a small box, lifting the lid to reveal some bottles. One was large and empty, and a smaller one contained a bright orange powder.

"A key ingredient of Mrs Haggerty's Cleanser is Aquagen Twice-oxide. Over 90% of it, in fact. This bottle here, this is pure Oxygen. I have had it independently verified by registered alchemists, which I have detailed in the evidence log, should you need proof of the authenticity."

He picked up the third bottle. It tinkled in his hand.

"And this little bottle contains copper groundings mixed with drakelung filings."

He gestured to Dago, who was standing by the back door. At receiving the signal, Dago pushed the door open, gestured to someone, and began wheeling a large, glass box to the front of the courtroom. It was large enough to fit a grown man lying down, arms outstretched.

When it reached Felix, he thanked Dago, and unscrewed a small hatch on the top of the box.

"When one mixes these particular ingredients, not much happens," he said, pouring each bottle save the orange one into the bottom of the box. It settled in a little, sad puddle.

"That is, until one adds the copper and drakelung. If one does, then…"

He upended the last bottle, and the court watched it land with a splat in the stinking puddle. Instantly, orange foam exploded from it, quickly expanding to fill the box. Felix stood back, allowing the captain a view of the reaction.

"Captain, is this what you saw?"

The man's eyes were wide, disbelief wrestling with his impassive features. Felix screwed the lid on before it overflowed.

"If we cut off the oxygen, the foam dissolves."

Sure enough, the moment the lid was screwed shut, the foam immediately stopped growing and instead bubbled to an orange slime.

"Captain? Was that what you saw that day?"

The captain looked at the box. Without taking his eyes from it, he nodded.

Murmurs from the crowd. The judge banged her gavel, much harder than was necessary.

"The court will be silent. Is that all, Mr Sacramentum? After all, this is a courtroom, not a classroom," she said, venomously.

Felix opened and closed his fists.

"Honoured Holy Judge, I have but a few more questions for the witness, if it please the court," he said, with forced calmness.

She didn't speak, but waved at him to continue.

Dago wheeled the box out of the room. Felix started pacing.

"Simple science, not witchery, Your Honour. In addition, it was a purely defensive manoeuvre that my clients used as they feared for their lives. Did you, or did you not, Captain, threaten them with your bejewelled mace of office, using the words 'surrender or die immediately'?"

He began to fidget. "Yes, but—"

"Do you accept that these people, innocent of any crime, would have been startled to be met with a squad of armed and armoured soldiers, threatening them with instant death by bludgeon and crossbow?"

"I don't—"

"And is it therefore not reasonable for people in such circumstances to flee to safety?"

The captain stood up.

"I wasn't going to kill them!" he shouted.

Felix whirled to face him. "Then why the crossbows, the threats, the mace?"

The prosecutor stood up.

"Your Holy Honour, he is haranguing the witness."

The judge nodded.

"I agree. Stop at once, Felix. This cross-examination is over."

"But—"

"It. Is. Over," she said, lowering her glasses. "Do not make me say it again."

Felix furiously clamped his jaw tight, before nodding, and sitting down.

Furbo leant over to him. "Is that normal? For the examination to just be… ended?"

Felix whispered back. "No. Still, chin up."

This is going to be harder than I thought.

"Captain," said the Judge. "You may leave now."

He did, marching smartly from the room, sparing Felix a stare like a rusty dagger. Felix didn't bother returning it.

"We didn't even get to explain what happened!" Helda spluttered. Felix held a hand up.

"We will, we will. Just wait."

~

The church called several more witnesses, mostly members of the clergy, who explained in no uncertain terms the official stance on graverobbing, which can be summarised as: It's Definitely Not Allowed, except for a Few Good Reasons, such as re-burying a saint in holier ground, that sort of thing.

As the day drew to a close, Holy Judge Helmellia called the proceedings to an end.

"And so, taking into account the evidence, this court is under no illusion as to the severity of the crime, and so judges—" she ministered.

Felix sprung to his feet. "Honoured Holy Judge, if I may—"

"Oh, what is it now?" she whined.

Felix coughed. "Pardon my interruption, Holy Judge, but we have not yet had the opportunity to call our own witnesses."

She regarded him with undisguised irritation. She glanced at the large clock on the wall, displaying that evening was fast approaching.

"I suppose you should get that much. We will all meet again, same time tomorrow, for the defence's witness."

"Uhm pardon oh Holy Judge, but it's witness*es*. We have several—"

"Enough! I'm sick of the sound of your voice, Mr Felix. I have already granted you the chance to call witnesses, or do you wish me to revoke that privilege?"

Felix froze, not daring to speak. His heart hammered in his ears.

"Better. We will meet here tomorrow morning. Court is adjourned." She slammed her gavel on the plate.

"All will be judged," moaned the congregation.

~

Felix reclined on the sofa bed at Lunchers. He was quite alone, which suited him fine. He stared at the ceiling, running the events from the day over and over, trying to find angles that weren't there, or hidden meanings he hadn't caught first (or fifth) time around.

He worried about the next day. The judge clearly wasn't on his side. The judge wasn't meant to be on anyone's side. But this one...

Felix absentmindedly flicked through some of the books about clergy-law he had borrowed from Mr Luncher's collection. The book was yellowed with age and smelled exactly like the temple.

He found nothing that could help him garner some respect from Helmellia, so he would just have to hope his witnesses were enough. He looked at the wall where a small, smoke-stained portrait of Habeus hung above the window.

"What are my odds, big man?" Felix asked.

He got no response.

17 – The Second Day

The courtroom was very much the same as the day before, all dust, pews and robed figures. Felix wondered what time they all arrived.

Ettyson was there again, of course, despite Felix's efforts to arrive twenty minutes early this morning. *Why do I bother!*

Once everyone was assembled, the judge entered, and called the proceedings to order.

Okay, it's a fresh, new day. I will remain calm and professional, and view the judge with the respect she deserves.

"Defence, call your witness."

Felix stood.

"Good morning judge. We—"

"Get on with it!"

Rrnnngh!

"For our *first* witness, I call Furbo the Wanderer to the stand."

Journal Entry H: Spirits

Reference case [HFvJC] (HerFed v. JetCom), year 1336, judge Ki presiding.

Ghosts are funny old things. From what I gather, they hang around in some other-realm, skirting the line between this life and the next, doomed to endlessly bemoan some unfulfilled desire. That is until either A) that desire is fulfilled, B) the universe ends or, C) An irritated haunt-ee hires a professional to give the spirit a little 'push' in the right direction.

Take this case I had once worked on. Man lives life. Man dies. Man has regrets. Man becomes ghost. Ghost haunts people. People have enough.

The people he was haunting were his old workmates. He had been some bureaucrat or other overseeing some specific trade-based tariff collection for overseas shipments… or something. I know law isn't always the glamorous page-turner you hear about in awful legal fiction, but even I have to admit that even the phrase 'supply chain management' is dry and boring.

Anyway. His colleagues had put up with his ethereal sobs and plaintive rattles for a few weeks, hoping that he would resolve whatever inner turmoil kept him here. When that was clearly not going to happen, they tried speaking with him.

Spirits are not easy to engage with. They have the benefit of being able to literally disappear at any given moment, so they're really the ones in control. They often have to be deferred to. One has to give them centre stage. We're there, hanging on their every word, and the dramatic so-and-sos don't half milk it.

After trying, and failing, to talk to him, they hired a spirit medium to give him a gentle shove 'over the edge'. The medium arrived, only to find a spectral letter floating in mid-air. It unfolded itself and explained that Hermin Fedder (deceased) was taking the entire company of Jetterson & Co to court for attempted phantomicide and confirmed murder.

I was defending Hermin. He had been able to pay in full up front for our services, utilising his skills in money management to filter some of his pre-death wealth into our accounts. When we were chatting, he seemed a perfectly conversational client, explaining in great detail the plans he had overheard from his colleagues.

"Jjust bbecause I'm ddead, tthat ddoesn't mmean I'm nnot a pperson wwith rrights." When he spoke, his voice had a bizarre reverse-echo. I could hear the beginning of his words before he actually spoke them, and the ends of his words simply cut out, despite the surroundings. It was, well, spooky.

He went on to say that in his life, he had been treated badly. His workmates had used his gentle demeanour and poor-social skills to bully him, piling on massive workloads and making him the victim to a lifetime of nasty jokes and cruel pranks. To them, he was a nobody.

"I didn't top myself, if that's what you're thinking. It was some sort of poisoning," he said. He'd retreated back into himself before continuing. "Perhaps by accident, maybe as part of a prank, but I'm pretty sure one of them did it. They want to push me on, so I don't get them in trouble. I gave them ample time to come clean, but none of them did."

I offered him a biscuit without thinking, before realising my mistake. He didn't seem to mind. I asked him what he wanted. "So, Hermin… Why are you still, erm, here? Why not move on and simply forget these nasty people?"

He looked at me then with an intensity achievable only by the dead.

"I'm not ready to move on. They didn't see me as a person, didn't treat me as a person, and they killed me for no reason. I want the world to know that you can't just *do* that to people."

I had felt a chill in my spine at that, and had resolved to be a lot nicer to the interns at Lunchers & Co.

~

The case focussed on two facets. One, whether we could prove they had killed my client in the first place, and two, whether they had effectively tried to 'kill' him again when procuring the services of the medium.

The first case was quite straightforward to prove. Hermin had full memory of the last day of his life, and had watched while his co-workers discovered him and panicked. He had stood, incorporeal, while two of them bickered about how much Frogroot would give for incontinence and how much would kill you, before they agreed to say he just collapsed of a heart attack.

The defending lawyer argued that it was impossible to tell at this stage what had killed him, and that's when we brought in our trump card.

"Could we not refer to the autopsy?" I asked.

"As the case was so open-and-shut, there was no autopsy," the prosecutor informed me snootily.

"That's interesting," I replied. "My client informed me that it was in his death-wishes, which were updated yearly, that a full autopsy would be conducted in the event of his untimely death. It had all been paid for. Yet, when I asked the town morticians, they told me that the contract was amended by his next of kin, who, despite my searching, I have not been able to locate."

The opposition didn't respond to me, as I suspected they wouldn't. It was all too late to prove this he-said-she-said stuff.

"With that in mind," I said, turning to the judge. "We would like to present evidence of poison."

I just want to state now, that this was all c idea.

The doors opened and a casket was carried in by a few dockhands who had known Hermin, and who had received an envelope with a good handful of silvers from an unknown benefactor. The casket was set down at the front of the courtroom and the lid lifted. The stench of three-week-old body was… indescribable. Bad as that was, what happened next will stay with me forever.

Summoning whatever horrific netherworldly energy was available to him, Hermin moved his spirit back into his own body, and began moving his dead limbs in a gross mockery of life. His corpse was still very much a corpse, lolloping and sagging in all the expected places, but, like a drunk puppeteer with the world's sickest puppet, he stood himself up and hobbled over to a wide, clean silver table we had set up.

He plunged his hands into his own rotting abdomen and began pulling apart his body, spilling entrails on the table. There were shouts and gasps and vomiting from the stands. In the chaos, he found what he was looking for. A kidney. He held it up in a wobbling hand. The kidney was dark red and covered with yellow spots.

Once all eyes had settled on the gruesome sight, the body abruptly collapsed in a steaming heap, then Hermin's spirit floated nonchalantly over to me, and nodded.

I stood up, discreetly pocketing a scented handkerchief I was using to settle my own gorge. I produced a sheaf of paper.

"'The specific and distinctive side effects to Frogroot poisoning is an inflammation of the kidney, characterised by a series of bright yellow spots,'" I quoted. "So says page two hundred and six of Terrant's Complete Guide to Poisons, a well-respected book by a world-famous doctor."

I left the part out about him being a complete psychotic poison-obsessed maniac serial killer.

It took some while for normality to return to the court. When it did, the court indeed found the defendants guilty of unintentional murder. The prosecution had tried the suicide angle, but with the actual ghost of the defendant able to attest that 'No, I very much liked being alive, thank you', that argument didn't hold much water.

The judge bashed his gavel on the plate and made to speak. "As to the second charge…"

My client had stood then, raising a ghostly hand.

"I withdraw my accusation of phantomicide. I have my justice, and am satisfied."

The judge had raised an eyebrow, but nodded.

"Very well, spirit. Do you wish to add anything?"

He had shaken his head then, turned to wave to me, then fizzed away into nothing without so much as a 'goodbye'.

I had caught up with the medium after the case. He was looking a little shaken up.

"Thank God you didn't push for phantomicide. That would have been my whole profession up the swanny," he said, wiping his head with a sodden rag.

I asked him, with perhaps a little distaste, whether he ever gave any thought to ghosts he 'pushed on'.

"No, I try not to. I provide a service for people who need it. Once they're gone, they're gone, departed forever into the next life, never to be seen or heard from again."

He had paused for a moment then, before giving me a mournful look, adding:

"Except for in my dreams."

~journal entry ends

18 – The Wanderer

Furbo sat at ease, as if this weren't a court case for his life, but instead a cup of tea and a catch up with an old chum. He smiled at Felix, he smiled at the judge, he smiled at the prosecutor. Something about this strange man made Felix feel comforted.

"Witness, please state your name and occupation for the court," Felix began.

Furbo started, as if suddenly remembering where he was.

"Oh yes, of course, sorry. I'm Furbo, and my occupation is, well… wandering."

Felix nodded, Ettyson stood up. "I object. Perhaps the witness could elaborate on his profession?"

The judge agreed. "What sort of wandering, witness?"

Furbo moved his eyes around, as if searching for an answer.

"Well, to be honest, the indescribable kind. I, and my partner Helda, explore the land, live off nature's bounty, and go where the universe takes us. We take jobs, here and there, we right wrongs that are within our power, and we try to leave the world a better place than how we found it." He considered his own words and nodded, happy with his own interpretation.

He looked at the prosecutor in a grandfatherly way. "I hope that answers your question, my girl?"

She didn't react, other than to raise a single eyebrow., and so Felix continued.

"How long have you been wandering?"

"Oh, my. Perhaps thirty years?"

Felix turned sideways on to Furbo, addressing the room.

"Please tell the court what happened on the day in question, the day you met Racelsus, in your own words."

It was important to use words that humanise Racelsus as much as possible. The more human she seemed, the less likely she'd be treated as an object. Words like 'met' were good. You didn't 'meet' an object. Only people.

Or, I suppose, animals.

Whenever he thought something like this, his eyes flicked over to the skull, worried she was reading his mind and would hear him and his stupid thoughts.

Furbo closed his eyes and took a deep breath.

"We were exploring down Westernby Caves. I had received a sign that we should head down there and see what we could find."

"What sort of a sign?"

"Oh, you know. An eagle calling from the west, a patch of grass in the shape of an island, that sort of thing."

"Objection," said Ettyson, rising swiftly. "The witness is being deliberately vague."

"Granted. Please *clarify* yourself, witness. Details, man, details," said Helmellia.

Felix looked at Furbo with an expression he hoped was encouraging, but instead just looked pained. He had hoped to be able to breeze past these wishy-washy details. He stretched his neck out as he questioned Furbo, tipping his head from side to side..

"Witness, I wonder… could you explain the nature of the sign you received, and specifically how it pointed you towards Westernby Caves?"

Furbo brightened at the prospect. "Oh certainly, my boy. It was a dream. Helda, in fact, was the dreamer." He waved at her. She looked embarrassed. Furbo didn't seem to hear the mutters from the audience, and so carried on quite happily. He gestured with his hands as he spoke, as if telling a ghost story at a children's party.

"She dreamed of a dark, cold night, and great barriers of stone. She dreamed of a light in the darkness, of a great treasure hidden from view. She dreamed of tunnels of history, and when she awoke, she said the word: Westernby. So, I knew the universe was guiding us in that direction. Will that do, my lad?"

On the one hand, Felix didn't want to be called 'my lad' in this setting. It undermined his authority. On the other, he had never really had a father figure, so a small part of him glowed whenever he was referred to like that.

"Yes, witness, that will suffice. Unless my colleague wishes further clarification?" said Felix, turning to Ettyson in an over-dramatic turn, eyes wide open, eyebrows raised. She did not respond, so he turned back to Furbo.

"And what did you know of the caves before you arrived?"

"I knew that it was said to contain 'The Fetter'; an ancient wise man who could answer any question. I didn't know anything else. Oh! That's a lie."

The room tensed. Helmellia peered at him intensely. It was as if the room held its breath. No one would dare admit to lying, in the witness stand, in the Temple of Habeus… Would they?

"Witness?" Felix hesitated.

"I knew there was meant to be a lovely beach out front of it, too. So, I did know something else. Awfully sorry," he said, sheepishly. The room let out its breath.

Felix thought to carry on before anyone thought to question that.

"And did you have a reason to seek out this Fetter?"

Furbo hesitated, his smile dropping a fraction.

"Well, in a manner of speaking. But it's a private matter, the full extent of which I believe is not relevant."

The judge leaned forward.

"I will decide what is relevant. What did you want to obtain an answer to?" questioned Judge Helmellia.

Furbo paused again, frowning.

"I wanted to know where my son was. I haven't seen him in years. He was lost to me. Taken from me, too soon. I have searched for him, but not yet found him. That is my great purpose."

There was a silence, not a tense silence, but one of reverence. After leaving just enough time for the silence to feel significant (according to Felix's sense of drama), he began to question Furbo.

"Furbo, please explain what happened when you arrived at the caves."

"We entered the cave through the opening by the woods, up from the beach," Furbo said.

"Were there any doors, or signs? Perhaps warnings, or visible wards? 'Keep Out', that sort of thing?"

"None whatsoever. It was bare as the top of my head."

"And then what happened?"

"We passed through the cave. We walked for a few hours. There were a number of forking paths, tunnels that split into two, or three, or more. Lots of snaking ways in the caves. We just picked whichever one felt right, and eventually came to The Door."

"The Door?"

"The Door." Furbo's face took on a wondrous expression. "Oh, my boy, now *that* is a Door. Would you like me to tell you about it?"

"Uh, briefly, please, Furbo, sticking to the size and overall nature of the carvings."

Felix had heard about this door a lot in the past few weeks. When Furbo was in the mood, he could talk about it for literally hours. He had, once. Felix wanted to hear it all, just in case some part of it was relevant.

None of it was.

"Well, it was large, around as big as the door to this hall. Pure black stone, hinged, and covered top to bottom in all manner of carvings, from animals, women, monsters, demons—"

"Thank you, witness. Was the door locked?"

Furbo was only slightly deflated upon being stopped, but Felix had warned him that would happen.

"Not really, Felix."

"Not really? Can you elaborate?"

"Well, there was no key, no lock as such. There was a handle within easy reach, and Helda turned it, and the door opened."

"Was there any indication on the door that you *should* not open it?"

"No, nothing."

"Objection," said Ettyson. "Was there any sign insinuating you could or should open it?"

Felix was surprised at this. He had expected better from his counterpart. Furbo gave the response that had been drilled into him by the defence team, on the 'just in case' practice sessions.

"No, prosecutor, but surely a door without a warning or 'no entry' sign is an invitation in itself? One does not build a door where one intended a wall."

Ettyson worked her jaw, then sat down.

Felix clasped his hands together, steepling his fingers in a thoughtful expression.

"Witness, what did you find behind the door?" he said.

"Racelsus."

A few murmurs from the crowd.

"And what happened then?"

"We chatted."

More murmurs.

"What about?"

"Oh, you know. Life, the universe… just about everything. The nature of her imprisonment, all that sort of stuff." Furbo's casual demeanour was completely at odds with the surroundings. Felix took confidence in that.

He considered the next question, wanting to give it the gravity it required. "Would you say that she was… alive?"

Furbo considered this in return. Felix had advised him to do so. *Don't be afraid to take your time. Better to think and answer correctly, especially when it's my questions.* "Yes, I would. She certainly wasn't dead."

"And did she coerce you into releasing her from her cell?"

"No, I would say not. She asked politely if we might bring her with us, we said yes. But we couldn't carry all of her, so Helda emptied her candle-holder and we put her skull in there, and off we went."

"I suppose that's why there were a few candles lying about?"

"Yes. Poor old Helda was miffed she had to leave them behind, but there was no space for them."

Felix nodded. "And then what happened?"

"Well, we left the same way we had come. We were met by some churchmen, who asked who we were and what we were doing."

"What were the first words they said to you, do you remember? As precise as you can be, please."

Furbo furrowed his brow, closing his eyes.

"'Surrender the witch or die immediately', I believe," he said calmly.

Murmurs.

"And then what happened?"

"I told him we were travellers, we had seen no witch, and that we would like to be on our way."

"But you knew the nature of the skull's history, so why did you say that?"

Felix had warned Furbo of these awkward questions. But better they come from him than from Ettyson.

Furbo shifted uncomfortably.

"Well… I'm a little loathe to say it here…".

The judge leaned over again. "You will speak, witness. The truth."

"All will be judged," intoned the crowd.

Furbo wiped his head with a sleeve.

"Well, church people, particularly the ones with armour and weapons – in my experience – tend to be a 'smite-first-ask-questions-later' type. If I told them we had brought the 'witch' with us, they might have smitten her, and us, before we could explain that she was not dangerous. So… I hid that fact to protect us."

Felix had drilled that into Furbo. *Self-defence, self-defence. You were only doing what you had to do to defend your innocent lives.*

"Did they let you go freely?"

"Well… no. Not until they had blessed us, and I knew that if they tried to bless us… with the witch, it could cause a serious problem. 'Never bless a witch', my mother used to say. So, Helda and I fled."

"Were you pursued?"

"Yes. Crossbow bolts flew at us, horses charged… I had to use one of my alchemical formulas to help us escape – I believe you demonstrated it earlier, and did a splendid job, too," he smiled. Felix couldn't help feeling a slight warmth.

"The guard captain maintains you 'vanished'?"

"We didn't, we just hid in a stump. When you travel for a living, you get used to making yourself unseen. We did that, and waited for them to leave. They left, and so did we. Then we saw the wanted posters, and we came to your firm. That's all, really."

"Thank you Furbo. That's all from me, Holy Judge," said Felix.

That wasn't so bad, he thought, wrongly.

19 – The Wanderer II

Prosecutor Ettyson strode to the concourse in front of Furbo. She took a long look at him.

"Witness. Please explain how long you have been a registered alchemist."

Furbo shrugged. "My dear, I am sad to say I never registered."

She nodded, folding her arms. "And would you say drakelung filings is the sort of thing amateur alchemists should be handling?"

Furbo chuckled at this. "I agree, but I assure you, I am not an amateur. I have been handling drakelung powder, and much more dangerous components besides, for almost three decades."

"In laboratory conditions? With the correct safety measures?" she said, one eyebrow raised.

"Where possible, yes… it is not always so easy, out in the field. You build up certain tolerances, though, so don't worry about me," he added, again smiling.

She nodded once more and flipped open her pad of notes for the first time. Felix got a bad feeling that Furbo had just walked into a trap, but he didn't see how. *What obscure piece of alchemical law is she going to use to discredit Furbo now? I knew I should have done more research…*

"Please describe the nature of the relationship between yourself and Helda."

Or… not?

Furbo blinked, then shrugged. "She is my compatriot. My travelling companion."

"Has anything romantic ever passed between you two?"

Felix raised a hand. "Objection, how is this relevant?"

The judge, reluctantly, turned to the prosecutor. "Miss?"

"Holy Judge, I was curious as to where the witness's child came from."

The judge raised an eyebrow, then nodded. "Proceed."

She turned back to Furbo. "Witness. Were you ever romantically involved with Helda?"

"On my honour, I tell you 'no'."

"In that case. Can you explain where your child came from?"

Furbo chuckled. "I'm sorry my dear, but that's a conversation your parents should have had with you a long time ago."

The prosecutor did not rise to the bait. Only Helda giggled, and Felix would have, if he didn't feel so nervous. *Where was she going with this?*

"How old was your son?"

Furbo's mood darkened for the first time.

"He *is* around fourteen. We lost him when he was around eight."

She picked up a sheet of paper. "I have a sworn expert testimony from a respected alchemy firm in the city here that states prolonged inhalation of drakelung filings causes infertility in men."

Helda guffawed. "Someone better tell the guard captain. I hope he didn't want kiddies," she said, to hurried shushing from Felix.

"So, witness, I ask you again. Where did your son come from?"

Furbo pursed his mouth, unsure of what to say. Considering.

"Do you often have difficulty answering basic questions, witness?"

"No!" he said.

"I move that it's a simple question, so why the hesitation? Coming up with more lies?"

"Objection! This is clearly badgering the witness!" Felix said, perhaps too loudly.

The judge waved him down. "Carry on, Ettyson, but perhaps skip that question. However, witness, please answer where your child came from."

Furbo rubbed his head again. He was starting to sweat.

"We adopted him."

Uh oh.

"Did you adopt many children?"

"We, well, we did, then when they were old enough, we let them forge their own path. They travelled with us," he said. He was starting to unravel, and Felix could see it. Furbo was like a tapestry, and Ettyson was a cat; slowly pulling and picking at the threads.

"How many at a time, would you say, did you have with you?"

"Uh, well, sometimes a few…"

"A simple number will do."

"Fifteen..?"

Hushed mutters from the pews.

"A large number of children. You must have a kind heart," she said. "How did you say you funded your lifestyle? Living off nature's bounty? Interesting choice of words. 'Bounty', you said… A word often used by pirates and criminals."

Furbo was starting to look pale. The prosecutor walked over to her bundle of papers and pulled a sheet out.

"I wonder if the witness recognises this?" she said, passing the paper to Furbo, who began to read silently. She turned her back to him.

"For the court: it is a wanted poster detailing a gang of youths, led by an elderly gentleman and a large woman, who travel the country thieving, robbing and blackmailing their way to wealth. Does the witness agree this could describe himself?"

Furbo wiped his brow.

"No! That's not true."

"So how did you survive, I wonder? Travelling around, a swarm of hungry children underfoot, no stable house or income? How, if not crime? Please, tell us."

"Uh…"

The prosecutor turned to the judge. "I suggest that this man is a criminal and a gang-leader, not an innocent traveller as he asserts. His purposes for visiting the prison of the witch were almost certainly nefarious in nature. The exact details of which, I suspect, he will never reveal. He expects us to believe he was led straight to her because of a dream? Yet, he has lied about his profession, he has lied about his son and he himself has *admitted* to *lying in the stand*. I move that *he* is the figure from the poster, and is a rogue, a scoundrel, and a criminal, through-and-through. As such, anything he says must be viewed through the lens of dishonesty."

155

The judge considered this. "Agreed. Anything this witness says will be struck from the record, and the court shall, at a later date, remand him for crimes against the country. Provided, of course, he has not already been put to death for this case. For now, however—witness, you may leave."

Helda stood, furious. "This is a complete farce! How dare you—you skinny, sour, manipulative—"

Furbo held up his hand to her, in what he hoped was a mollifying gesture. "Helda, my dear, please be quiet."

"Much as I am loath to agree with criminals, you have the right idea, witness," said the judge. "Another outburst like that, miss, and you will be imprisoned for contempt. Do I make myself clear?"

Helda's face was bright red, and Felix could hear her teeth grinding. She collapsed into her seat with a *flump*. Felix tried to catch Furbo's eye, but the older man didn't look up.

Furbo slowly stood and shuffled back to the defence's bench. He lifted his head and smiled weakly at Felix.

"I suppose that could have gone worse… Right, my lad?"

Not really.

"Of course, old man. Chin up," Felix said. He tried to sound genuine. After a few moments of gentle hubbub, the judge addressed the defence.

"Does the defence have any other witnesses?" she asked, peering at Felix like an owl peers at a mouse.

I think I'm going to have to…

"Yes, Your Honour."

"Perhaps one of a less controversial history, this time?" she added, to polite titters from her sycophantic staff.

About that… Nibble on this, you sour old fruit-bat.

Felix offered an obsequious smile.

"We would like to call the witch Racelsus to the stand."

20 – The Witch

The judge's eyes boggled. "What!?"

"We would like to call—"

"I bloody heard you, you imbecile! You can't call that... *thing* to give testimony!" she shrieked.

"Honoured judge, there is precedent. A frog-magi was called to give testimony in the case of—"

"Yes, I know, I know." She looked ready to bite someone's head off. She was breathing hard, a strange mixture of panic and rage. After a pause, Felix prompted.

"...judge, may we?"

"We will have Sanctifiers standing either side, ready to obliterate her at a moment's notice. The *slightest* reason, and they shall do so. It is only through my respect to the sacrosanctity of law that I do not order such a procedure immediately," she rasped, out of breath with fury. An eye twitched as she looked at Felix.

"You are on *very* thin ice."

Felix made his face a mask of calm acceptance, as if this was a perfectly reasonable thing to have shouted in his face.

She waved a frantic hand at him. "Hurry up then!"

Felix nodded his thanks, and whispered to Helda, who brought Racelsus up to the stand. The figures in the pews made all manner of gestures and mutterings when she was turned to face them. Her eyes glowed a faint green. She looked... nightmarish.

Thank goodness her cage is shiny, or what might they think?

~

"Witness, please state your full name and occupation for the court."

Racelsus rattled in her cage. When she spoke, her mouth didn't move with the words, but opened slightly.

"Racelsus, and I have no occupation."

Her voice was like purple velvet.

"How old are you?"

"A gentleman never asks, and a lady never tells," she said, coyly. Helda chuckled, Felix smiled. No one else reacted.

"Witness, please answer the question."

"I am at least four hundred and thirty years old, but actually much older, I think. It's hard to be exact."

"How did you come to be that old?" he asked.

For a moment she appeared as if she were about to admonish him for asking such a rude question, but she resisted the urge. "It was an accident. A spell was cast, not by me, and when I awoke I was changed."

"Changed how?"

"I found I could not die."

The room was silent. Each member of the congregation was listening intently, drawn between terror and the excitement of listening to heresy in a controlled environment. Felix nodded, as if this was the sort of thing that could just happened to anyone, and continued.

"What happened then?"

A slight pause. "The church found me, and I was imprisoned. My back was broken, and I was locked in a prison for all time."

"What happened after that?"

"Then, these two found me. Furbo and Helda. We talked, and they agreed to take me with them if I helped them find the missing child. I agreed."

"Why did you agree to that, witness?"

She hesitated, but spoke without prompting. "I'm not a monster. A lost child is a heart-breaking story. Plus, they could offer me a way out, and so I owed them everything. If it was in my power to help them, I was going to do it."

Felix let this sink in. *Show them your humanity.*

"Are you a witch, Racelsus?"

She rattled again, clacking her teeth together. The sound echoed throughout the chamber and caused a few of the audience to wince.

"I am *attuned* to certain magical ways. But I lived and practiced out in the swamps, far from the reach of the church. I have used my abilities to help those in need, and never in spite or anger. Additionally, I have not practiced magic since I was released from my prison, and, despite what the church would like to allege, being a witch is not illegal."

Judge Helmellia bristled but didn't say anything.

Careful, Racelsus… No use being technically right if you can still be executed by an angry judge.

"Let us move onto the 'why'. People, even witches, are not just thrown into cells for no reason. At least, that is what we like to believe. So, why were you arrested?"

The skull didn't say anything for a few moments. The glow in her eyes darkened.

"People were scared of us. We didn't ask to be this way, we didn't want to be this way, so we kept to ourselves. We helped when we were asked, but we mostly stayed alone. We bothered no one and no one bothered us. But, some local dignitary, some jumped-up clergyman decided to make a name for himself, so looked out for weak people he could victimise 'for the good of the realm'. He found out about us, and punished us for existing. I was imprisoned, my back broken, he was promoted, and thus my life, as I had known it, was ended."

Felix walked slowly around the concourse in front of the dock. He didn't speak for a few moments. It was important that all of Racelsus's words were heard and understood, not rushed, not spoken over. He stopped and turned to her.

"'We'?"

"My brother and I. He was also imprisoned, but on the opposite side of the world. I… don't know what happened to him."

Felix nodded. He could tell Racelsus was starting to get tired. He didn't fully understand her, but he knew that she needed downtime. A prolonged interrogation like this wore her thin. To be honest, no one likes being in the dock at the best of times. Add to that the fact that she's talking for her life, in a manner of speaking, and that she's a great bloody witch in a bloody great church, and you can understand why she might want this to be over with. He sometimes wished he could reach over to his clients, give them a supportive pat on the arm and let them know it's all going to be okay. Sadly, that sort of thing wasn't permitted. He could question, he could dig, but couldn't empathise in that way.

Not much longer now. Hang in there!

"Did you, or your brother, do anything to draw the ire of the church?"

"No."

"No dark spells, curses, evil magicks? Hexes on livestock, that sort of thing?"

"No, not once."

"Were you given a trial after you were accused?"

"No."

"Any chance to defend yourselves?"

"No."

Felix paced again. An unconscious habit, or a theatrical trick? Maybe it was one earlier, and is now the other.

"I would like to ask you a hypothetical question. If, in theory, you *were* a dark witch of some renown, some great power... do you think you would have used your dark magic to overcome these clergymen and escape, before your first imprisonment?"

"Yes, but I'm not, so I didn't."

Felix had hoped Ettyson would try to object on the grounds that the Apostolic Guard were too powerful to overcome, and he was quite looking forward to reminding her their own captain was outsmarted by a bottle of ointment. She didn't rise to it, however, so Felix continued.

"And the same question, but for your escape?"

"I answer in the same way."

Felix stopped, and leaned on his desk.

"To summarise: Based on your attitude, history, and circumstances, and the nature of the way you were treated... Would you say you were *unlawfully imprisoned?*"

"I would."

Murmurs rose like a mist from the ground. Ettyson's face was dark, her eyes narrowed. She made some notes on her pad. *I've never seen her do that before...*

"How long were you kept in that prison cell, against your will, having received no trial?"

"Around four hundred years."

A few outbursts from the audience. *Preposterous! Ludicrous!* To her credit, Holy Judge Helmellia tapped her oversized gavel twice to shut them up. Felix resumed pacing around the room. He shifted his weight in such a way that his footsteps made almost no sound. A slow transfer of weight from heel to toe, almost like a glide. He had heard somewhere that getting eyes to follow you around the room makes people pay attention more. Whether it was true... well, who knows.

"What happened when you reached the surface with Helda and Furbo, after you finally tasted freedom and fresh air for the first time in almost half a century of false imprisonment?"

Ettyson stood, tapping her pen on the table. "Objection, Your Honour. The imprisonment has not been proven to be false, and for my colleague to refer to it as that adds credence that does not exist."

Felix grimaced. He had hoped she would miss that one.

"Agreed," said the judge. "Do not do it again, Felix. Perhaps try to stick to the facts, such as they are? I do not want to remind you how to do your job. Again."

He nodded, feeling the heat rising in his neck. It was an effort to be deferential in the face of such clear bias, but he would not let an ill-timed retort cost him his good standing. He visualised the heat rising up his body, only to sink and dissipate through the cold, grey stone under his feet. His inner calm returned.

He would *not* snap at this judge, however much she might deserve it.

He addressed Racelsus again. "Let me rephrase, witness. What happened once you were carried out of the cave?"

"We were accosted and threatened by members of the Apostolic guards."

"Do you think that if you had submitted to them, you would have been arrested again?"

"Yes."

"Of course, being arrested is one thing. Naturally, given the option to defend yourself in a trial…" Felix opened his arms wide and gestured at the room. "Do you think you would have been found innocent?"

"I do."

Felix nodded and dropped his arms.

"Do you think you would have received a trial this time around?"

"I highly doubt it."

"Or any chance to defend yourself, offer your side of the story?"

She clacked again to show what she thought of that. "No."

Felix darted his eyes to Ettyson, but she wasn't falling for the traps he was setting her. Instead, he gave a wide, slow shrug. "So, what did you do?"

"We made our escape… to defend our lives and lawful liberty."

That was one of Yetty's suggested lines. Too many L's, thought Felix, but it was best to let it be said out loud for her to realise. He flicked his eyes to her, and she was pinching her nose.

"To avoid," he added the next part anticipating an objection. "In your opinion – unlawful punishment?"

"Yes."

Felix scratched his chin. He was happy with how it was going, but Ettyson's behaviour worried him. She was usually quite eager to knock him off his stride. What was she planning?

Still, perhaps she was just having a bad day. He tried to keep his thoughts to himself, not wanting to appear smug. He needed every point he could score with this judge. If things carried on this way, his team might just get away with it after all. Felix switched track.

"Racelsus, are you alive?"

Racelsus did something unexpected then, which caught Felix by surprise. She laughed.

"Yes, very much so."

"Did you consent to being removed from that unlawful – in your opinion – imprisonment?"

"Yes."

He returned to his desk and faced her.

"Would you identify yourself as a corpse?"

"Not at all."

"So, would you argue that the phrase: 'you were grave-robbed' is inaccurate?"

"Yes. I am not a corpse, and I was not robbed."

Perfect.

"Thank you witness. I have no further questions."

The two armoured Sanctifiers relaxed slightly and rubbed their shoulders. They had been poised, holy potions at the ready; their arms must have ached.

This next part was the one he was worried about. Racelsus was tired, and her cross-examination could make – or more likely, break – the case. It was a worthwhile risk, though. She had been a good witness, and after Furbo, they needed one.

As prosecutor Ettyson approached, Felix stared hard into Racelsus's eye sockets.

Remember: NO mind-reading.

Felix thought he saw her roll her eyes. Though quite how he understood that gesture, he didn't know.

21 – The Witch II

Ettyson looked at Racelsus. For the first time, the prosecutor seemed a little uncertain. Interviewing criminals is one thing, but interviewing a skull in a cage… that's quite something else. She cleared her throat, then plunged in, her voice loud and confident.

"Witness. What are the extents of your powers?"

Racelsus rattled. "I don't know."

"How can you not know?"

"I've never attempted to find out."

"Why is that?"

Racelsus clacked her teeth together.

"I have never felt the need to. How many peanuts can you fit up your nose?"

"I – excuse me?" said Ettyson, knocked off-course somewhat.

"It's not a question you have ever felt you needed to answer. You *could* find out, so why haven't you?"

"I don't think that's the same, witness," she retorted, regaining her composure with lightning speed.

"Then we will have to agree to disagree. I have never found the limits of my powers because I did not ever want to. I had no need to."

Ettyson paced the room, much more slowly and deliberately than Felix had. He wondered if she was trying to formulate precisely *how* to ask the next questions she was thinking of.

"What magicks do you know?"

"I don't understand the question."

"Spells, witness. What spells can you perform?" she said, irritated.

"I don't know, prosecutor," Racelsus replied, sweetly.

"You must have some idea!" she snapped.

"I'm sorry, I don't. It's all instinctual."

Ettyson frowned, and shrugged before continuing, once again the image of professional calm.

"Could you perform some magic for us now?"

"I could, yes."

The Sanctifiers looked nervous, and tensed. The judge leaned over and stared at her.

"But I won't. I don't want to be reprimanded for illegal witchery, especially in these circumstances. And, as I said… I'm out of practice."

She's good.

The prosecutor's hand brushed some hair from her eyes as she wandered over to her desk and flicked open her stack of papers. Felix watched her, confused. Her hair was as immaculate as ever, wound in a tight braid, secured with a simple ribbon. Something didn't sit right. In all the cases they had been fighting against one another, he had never seen a single hair out of place on Ettyson. It's just something that didn't happen to her.

Why does that unsettle me?

She continued, unaware of his scrutiny. "You said you were arrested by a – using your words – 'local dignitary'. Would this be… High Priest Restintute?"

"Perhaps. It was a long time ago, I couldn't say for certain."

"In his diaries, he writes…" she flipped to another page in her bundle. "'I did then apprehend two most foul witches that did plague the township, casting all manner of sinister magicks for their sick pleasure'. Does this ring any bells?"

Felix felt, rather than saw, Racelsus shrug. "Not to me. Perhaps you could call the High Priest as a witness?"

"He's been dead for hundreds of years!"

"I suppose it's my word against his, then."

The prosecutor tapped her fingers on her arm in annoyance. Felix noticed something catch the light in Ettyson's ear. It was a small, light metal disc, carved in some manner, small enough that it could cover one's eardrum entirely while resting inside the ear.

Bizarre type of earring? What on earth..?

Something set a tiny alarm bell ringing far in the recesses of his memory. He began thinking furiously to find why.

"Witness, you mentioned you have a brother who was similarly… detained."

"…Yes."

"Would it be of interest to you to know he resurfaced recently?"

"What?" the skull's eyes lightened.

"Yes, and he was apprehended and destroyed by the church."

That disc… Realisation dawned on Felix.

She's wearing a mind alarm!

They were invented after a case, some years ago now, involving telepaths. They're essentially anti-magic, and are attuned precisely to react to any attempt to pry into the wearer's brain. If they do, a thin ribbon on the inside vibrates, and the wearer hears a tiny ringing sound. Felix had heard of them, once, but didn't think they worked. He wasn't an expert though. Ettyson was the sort of person who didn't try something like this unless she *knew* it worked.

He slammed the table. "Objection! She is trying to bait the witness! The line of questioning is irrelevant!" said Felix, darting to his feet. *I can't have her give in to temptation! If she tries to read her mind…*

The judge shook her head. "Well, which is it? Baiting, or irrelevant? Calm down, Defence Counsel. It will stand. Carry on, Ettyson."

He did not sit. "Your Holy Honour, I suspect that—"

"Overruled, Felix! Now be quiet."

"Judge, may I *urgently* speak to my client?" Felix said, desperately.

"No, counsel. For the last time, *sit down* and *shut up*," snapped the judge, as if to a naughty grandchild.

Felix collapsed into his chair and stared at Racelsus.

I know I told you not to read minds, but if you're going to, read mine now, and I'm telling you, don't read hers! It's a trap!

Racelsus was silent. Ettyson smiled. She didn't smile often.

"Well, witness? Do you have any opinion on that?"

He knew he should object again. The question was vague, irrelevant… But he also knew it was pointless.

Was the disc quivering, or is it just catching the light?

"You're not speaking true," said the skull. Her breathy voice was cold and distant.

"You seem very certain."

"I just *know*… You wouldn't understand…" Racelsus whispered.

Ettyson pointed her finger at the skull.

"How could you be so sure… unless you are reading my mind? Practicing the very witchery you maintained you did not practice?"

"I don't know how, I just know!" spluttered Racelsus, losing her cool.

"So, you admit it, you're casting witchcraft right now!" snarled Ettyson.

The court became animated with worry. Signs and prayers of protection filled the air. No-one made to leave, though.

"Witness! Cease this witchery now or be purged!" yelled the Judge. The two Sanctifiers kept flitting their eyes between the skull and the judge.

Felix jumped to his feet.

"Judge! She is not—"

The Judge slammed her gavel on the plate in front of her, causing dust to rise in small clouds.

"All will be silent!! The witness will be dismissed, her testimony struck from the record! Add another count of witchery to the charge count, bailiff!" she screeched, waving her gavel at the astonished bailiff beneath her. He began scribbling on his slab of velum.

Voices were still chanting prayers of protection, and some people shuffled to their neighbours to clasp each other's arms.

Felix was angry. His anger slithered around his chest and up his neck, writhing inside his head, before his reason forced it down with cold willpower, and it coiled up inside his stomach, waiting, but not gone. His breathing returned to normal.

Helda quickly jogged up to Racelsus and carried her back to the defendant's bench, both arms clamped around her cage. Her eyes had turned from dark green to a blood red.

Felix whispered to her. "You didn't—"

"Of course I bloody didn't, I'm not an idiot," she snarled.

"All will be silent!" barked the usher. "Silence!"

Felix glanced over at Ettyson. He saw her scratch her ear, then nonchalantly reach into her bag for something. Her ear looked normal again. She looked up and caught his eye. She didn't react.

Order was restored to the hall. Felix stood, and made an effort to unclench his fists. He opened his mouth to speak but was cut off by the judge.

"There will now be a *short* recess while I consider the evidence submitted to me. I shall then deliver my judgement. You will retire to your chambers and be summoned when required. Dismissed."

Felix sat down again. He had nothing to say.

Journal Entry I: Thief

Reference case [UpvCR] (UntPen v. CroReg), year 1274, judge Fyringe presiding.

Law in Placenamia was steeped in tradition and precedent. Impartial, decisive justice passed through the years from judge to judge; irrefutable, precise, clean and fair. Punishment, however, was archaic and brutal, with the development of technologies and magicks only serving to multiply the cruelty of the legal system. Some of the more eccentric professors described the relationship as like having a conversation with an ogre that had a voice like velvet. Utterly mesmerising and engrossing, but don't open your eyes, and don't sit too close.

I'll give you an example. Take the case of Unter.

Unter was a self-proclaimed life-long criminal. However, he always maintained he only stole from the rich, swindling those who had plenty to swindle, and never 'punched down' – at least, he was never caught punching down. What he was caught doing in the case in question was seventy-seven counts of Majestic Theft, which is not as complimentary as it sounds. It is, in fact, stealing something of great value from the Monarch's estate. A single sentence would typically be losing a part of a finger, or a whole finger if this was the second instance.

The presiding judge, a Judge Fyringe, instead offered an alternative arrangement. A sentence of three years per stolen item, to be served sequentially. Unter accepted with some great relief, not least because he was an old man now, and trying to rob the King had been a 'go-out-with-a-bang' affair that was supposed to cement his place as a figure of folkloric legend. He knew the prisons were rotten, but he had many friends and acquaintances there, and even was on good terms with most of the guard. He imagined passing the last decade of his life without fear of finding food, paying bills, or the worry that the law was going to boot his door down and kick his remaining teeth in.

Imagine his surprise when, no sooner had he happily accepted the chains that would accompany him for the rest of his days, the judge beckoned to a lady in the stands. The lady was dressed in dark green laced with purple, and had a large, worn bag with her, full of what sounded like bottles. Unter recognised her as some sort of witch, and started to feel a little less rosy.

Judge Fyringe explained that, upon request by the plaintiff and with agreement of the monarch (which, let us remember, was the same person), the Law had obtained the services of a Temporomancer, who would extend Unter's life by exactly two hundred and thirty-one years, give or take a little, so he could serve his sentence completely.

Unter was held down and force-fed seven potions of longevity, (which taste foul, apparently), and began the horrifically cruel process of progressing from late-late-middle age to old age over the process of some two hundred years. His body had already begun to suffer before sentencing from seized frozen joints, poor eyesight, a weak bladder and crunchy back pains. There are, of course, some potions that'll cure you of those problems, but, as of today, some one hundred and thirty years after the sentence was passed, none of those have been given to poor old Unter. All his 'friends on the inside' had died of old age, and Unter was now completely, devastatingly alone.

Like I said, archaic and brutal.

~journal entry ends

22 – The Chambers

Felix slid down onto the bench in the defendant's chambers.

"What happened?" he said out loud.

Furbo was next to him. "You did your best, my lad, what more could we have asked for?"

A slight knock at the door went unheeded. Helda looked pale. She was still holding Racelsus's cage close to her, arms wrapped around it. Racelsus herself was silent. Helda sniffed. "What now?"

"Now, you wait," came a voice from the door. Felix sat up straight and saw Mrs Luncher peering through the now-open door.

He cleared his throat and stood. "Mrs Luncher, I didn't realise—"

"There isn't time for that," she said. "I was watching the whole thing. You've done remarkably well, considering the circumstances."

Felix didn't agree. She looked at him curiously.

"You're familiar with Barlotti's Gambit, I presume?" Mrs Luncher asked, one eyebrow raised.

Felix nodded, but didn't elaborate.

She turned to Helda and Furbo.

"Barlotti was a maverick amongst lawyers. Or at least he tried to be. Was renowned among certain circles for coming up with some rather ingenious defences. One of his most famous was when he was defending some peasants who were the figureheads for a case of attempted regicide. You see, two rival kingdoms had been eyeing each other up for some time, and war, it seemed, was inevitable. Several enterprising so-and-sos decided that they didn't much fancy getting drafted and likely killed in some pointless war, so they came up with the plan to assassinate the king. Their own king, that is. A sort of... pre-emptive strike. Plans were hatched, knives were purchased, and the day rolled steadily closer.

"Inevitably, someone in the conspiracy blabbed, and the king, or rather, the king's unctuous cronies, caught wind. The plotters were hauled in front of a magistrate, who was quite happy to condemn them to death for treason, when up jumps this little fellow who explains, calmly and slowly, that to do so would contravene laws set in place by this very same king treason was being declared against, and so to circumvent proper judicial process would, in fact, constitute treason."

Furbo scratched his pate. "So, hang on. The defence against treason was… more treason?"

Mrs Luncher shook her head twice. "No, dear fellow. That was just the beginning. What our enterprising lawyer was doing was ensuring the case got a proper chance for a defence in the first place. You see, the king's men were trying to rush this through, make an example of these schemers, try to quash this sort of thing, fuel for the propaganda machine. That way, when the war did come, people would be less reluctant to 'volunteer' for the army. More willing to defend their strong, no-nonsense ruler.

"So, the magistrate couldn't very well turn around and argue against this point, and thus a court date was announced… for later that day. This is not normal! Ordinarily, court cases are given dates that are weeks, commonly months, even *years* in advance. This gives both sides plenty of time to get their facts straight and build their cases. For it to be scheduled on the same day… Well, thankfully, our man was the prepared type, and had already built his case around a singular, iron-clad defensive position.

"Not two hours later, he was in court, his two baffled clients behind him, his opposing prosecutor opposite, and it all came down to this one argument he was going to make. One for all the marbles, as they say."

Helda was leaning forward, hanging on every word.

"Well? What did he say?" she asked, spellbound.

"He said that it was a well-known fact that war was inevitable, and it was also a known fact that the army recruited via forced conscription during wartime. Furthermore, or an average peasant conscript, chances of survival in any given battle was around 3-to-1. He also suggested that a war of the expected magnitude would consist of at least fifteen sizable battles, of which any one conscript could expect to be present in around half of them. Thus, he said, any given unwilling conscript, forced to participate in around eight battles, each of which gives him a 1-in-3 chance of dying, could expect a six percent chance of survival over the course of the war, on average. Thus, by removing the cause of the war – in this case, the king and his alleged *casus belli* – they would therefore be protecting themselves from harm and death. So, to conclude…" Mrs Luncher held her arms open wide, waiting for an answer.

Furbo laughed. "You don't mean…"

"Self-defence," Felix finished.

Helda whistled. "That's pretty, uhm, ballsy, pardon my language," she added with a glance at Mrs Luncher.

"Did it work?" said Furbo.

Felix sighed, then answered. "No. The prosecution maintained that it was *not* a well-known fact that war was inevitable, as it had not yet broken out, and destiny is fickle, meaning we cannot make predictions of that type and treat them as fact. Without that certainty of the danger of death, it could not be called self-defence. So, all the defendants were sentenced to be hanged, and Barlotti was banished from the realm."

"Of course, war did break out two days later," Mrs Luncher added pensively. "Of the near hundred-and-thirty-five thousand conscripted recruits, only eight thousand came back when the war finally ended."

Furbo's fingers jerked back and forward in some complex calculation. He mouthed silent numbers with his eyes closed. With a gasp, he opened them.

"Six percent," he said, quietly.

Mrs Luncher nodded. "We call that Barlotti's Gambit. A claim so bold, so risky, that it's a pivotal winner-takes-all last-chance attempt to swing the case."

Felix's eyes swivelled to hers. "Any reason why you feel like bringing up that particular case, ma'am?"

Mrs Luncher shrugged, then stood up. "No… why, do you see some connection?"

When Felix didn't answer, she left. As she was shutting the door, she paused.

"Of course, the reason we remember Barlotti is not just for his failure. The fact is, the defence was quite amazing. His ability to turn it around, to offer a whole new *perspective*. Absolutely no-one saw it coming, and it very nearly worked, if not for some, if I might add immodestly, stellar counter arguments from his opponent."

She shut the door before anyone could respond, and Felix realised his mouth had been hanging open.

She was the..?

Furbo cleared his throat.

"Felix, judging by your face, we're in deep trouble here. If you have some, eh, 'gambit', I think I speak for us all when I say: it's worth a shot."

Felix didn't speak, but if his brain had been working any harder steam would be blowing out his ears.

"Please," said Helda. He had placed Racelsus on the table, and watched him, but didn't say anything.

Felix began pacing the room. Several times, he appeared about to speak, raising a finger, but then silenced himself again.

A knock at the door, and a clerk poked her head around.

"Court will resume in five minutes," she said, glancing twice at the skull. The clerk gulped, shook her head and left.

Felix couldn't look his clients in the eye. He sighed. He had nothing.

"Come on, we'd better go back."

No one spoke on the way back to the courtroom.

23 – The Verdict

Judge Helmellia sat up on the dais, staring down at Felix. Everyone had gathered and was waiting for what seemed the inevitable verdict. She began to speak, and all other sounds died out instantly.

"I am ready to deliver my judgement. Prosecution: Your case has been made, and you have submitted compelling evidence to the court. I thank and congratulate you for the professionalism you have exhibited. Defence: You have made your arguments, and they have been found wanting. Do you have anything to say before judgement is delivered?"

Felix stood at this podium and stretched his neck from side to side. He thought of Mrs Luncher.

Barlotti's Gambit. Felix's Gambit? But what could he argue that he hadn't already tried?

Perhaps I've overthinking it. I need to simplify.

"Mr Felix? What is the meaning of this delay?"

His mind raced over the facts of the case, searching for something. He didn't know what it was, but when he found it, he would know. *What is the meaning of…*

Meaning of…

He took a deep breath.

"Just this, oh Holy Judge. The definition of Graverobbing by the great and noble Apostolry states: 'The removal of a body from a sanctified place of rest, unless for purposes defined by the holy sacraments.' Those purposes are explicitly stated within the holy texts, and include things such as beatification, returning of remains to a loved one, among several other, specific circumstances."

The judge explained in a bored voice. "We have already covered this, Felix. The church's position on this is very clear. Now-"

Felix carried on as if the judge hadn't spoken.

175

"The definition of 'body' by the Order of the Turellitus Medicalus is: 'The physical structure or remains of an organic entity.'"

The judge didn't respond, but peered at him. He could feel the weight of eyes on his back.

"The definition of 'body' from the University of Medicine in Restastine, North Country is: 'The main mass of the physical constituent parts of a living or dead organism, structure or collection.'"

The room was watching him. Felix knew he had to get this exactly right.

"The two organizations clashed on that point, as academics are wont to do. Eventually, however, it was the University that won that debate, and their definition of 'body' stuck, and is still in use today, adopted by all major organizations that need such things specified.

"The definition of 'main', according to the Standard Language Society of Placenamia is simple: The largest or more prevalent section of a larger whole.'"

"Felix, get to the point, before I lose my temper," warned the judge.

"Please, Your Honour, I am entitled to continue, and I shan't be long," Felix said, to sharp intakes of breath from the other attendees.

A vein started to bulge in the judge's head. "You have fifteen seconds," she growled.

Felix cleared his throat and stood up straight, arms clasped behind him.

"I therefore move that what happened was not 'graverobbing', as the church understands it, as the 'main' part of the 'body' of Racelsus remains in custody, deep within the caves, as can be confirmed by the first witness for the prosecution, Gregor Hyacinth, Captain of the Noble Ecclesiarch of the Apostolic Guards. Therefore, I move to strike that offence from the charging record as it is, in essence, incorrect, and therefore unjustly accused of my client."

Felix stood, defiant in his conviction.

There was no sound in the courtroom while the suggestion percolated into the consciousness of the assembled.

"Completely – preposterous!" spluttered Holy Judge Helmellia. "Utter and total drivel!"

Felix stood his ground. His fists were clenched. Blood rushed to his head. He had to stop his hands from shaking.

"Your Holy Honour, *may it please* you that I—"

She stood quickly, her glasses sliding down her long nose. Her eyes bulged, and her teeth were fixed in a rictus snarl.

"Graverobbing! Heresy! Witchcraft! Don't you lecture me on what the bloody law is!" she spat. "Last time I checked, I was the judge here!"

Felix had gone too far.

She reached into her robe and pulled out her necklace, an enormous symbol of the Church. It shook and bounced with her rage.

"Not only that, but I am also Habeus's representative! Don't presume to know his will, what is unjust or not! He speaks through me, and me alone. He is speaking to me now, and he instructs me to find you and your 'compatriots'- Heretics Extremis, an offence punishable by death!"

Felix felt his guts turn cold. He was holding his breath, his nails dug into his hands. The judge held her gavel out in front of her, pointing it at Felix.

"So judgeth I, Judge Merrity Helmellia—"

With a face red as a beetroot, she flung her hand backwards, white-knuckle fingers gripping the handle of her ceremonial gavel, preparing to strike the plate with the same force a blacksmith might use to flatten a lump of iron, or an angry god smiting the smuggest of unbelievers. Once it did, his fate, and the fate of his clients, was sealed.

On the backswing, the head of the gavel, loosened through some cosmic twist of fate, flew in an arc behind the judge, and sailed directly towards the stained-glass portrait of Habeus the Judge. It impacted with the sound of a thunderclap, and a great plume of dust exploded from the window, obscuring the view of the window.

The dust cloud blocked all vision of the window, and for a few moments, of the judge herself. As it cleared, she was staring out among the pews. As the dust cleared, the congregation began to gasp and speak prayers, making signs of benediction with both hands. Some lay on the floor in supplication, chanting 'all shall be judged' over and over. Felix felt his eyes widen as he looked behind the judge.

She followed their gazes. "What are—" she said, swivelling on the spot to look at the window behind her.

The window was, by some miracle, largely unbroken, save for the head of the figure. The head of Habeus the Judge was completely missing, sprinkled into glass fragments on the floor. The sun behind the window emblazoned the portrait in a penumbra glorious colour, whilst a single beam of light shone through the head-hole landing on the gavel plate. The body of Habeus glared down at them, no less stern for a lack of head.

I'm not normally one for religious signs, or signs from the universe, what have you.

He allowed himself the smallest of smiles. *But, that…*

The judge had her back to the assemblage. She was staring right at the window, unmoving. The gavel handle dropped from a limp hand. Excruciating seconds passed.

She slowly turned back to Felix, a look of pure hatred in her eyes combating the instinct of terror she was feeling having drawn the wrath of Habeus. She reached under the dais in front of her and lifted another gavel.

"How many of those tiny hammers do they keep in there?" whispered Helda, receiving an elbow in the ribs from Furbo.

Helmellia lifted the gavel slowly, very slowly, and hovered it mere inches from the plate. When she spoke, her voice was strained and hoarse.

"The court finds the claim of graverobbing to be inappropriate. All charges are dropped. Dismissed," she whispered from trembling lips.

The gavel made the tiniest of *taps* as it touched the plate. The judge swivelled and *ran* out of the room.

Felix looked at Racelsus. She looked back at him.

"Awful lucky for that gavel to fly like that," he said.

"Yes," she said back. Felix thought he saw her smirk, but her bones didn't move.

"Did we win?" asked Furbo.

"We won," said Felix.

24 – The Pub

The Duck In Flagon swilled with mirth.

"Cups up for the legal eagle, the lawyer of legend, Felix!" yelled Helda, waving her tankard with much beer-spilling gusto, while Felix waved her down, an embarrassed smile on his face.

Everyone around the table launched their drinking vessels skywards, ignoring Felix's protestations. This added a wordless roar of triumph to the cacophony of scrapes and clanks as people stood, kicking chairs behind them.

Yetty jumped up on her chair, brandishing her smoking short-pipe. *Oh, I hate it when they do this.*

"Pipes in, peeps!" she yelled, before jamming her pipe in her mouth and inhaling.

All the locals did the same, pipes in hand, sucking, inhaling, filling their lungs to bursting with their own particular choice of smoke. Felix, with practiced swiftness, grabbed a handkerchief from a pocket, dunked it twice in an uncovered ale-pot and slapped it over his mouth. A relative newcomer to the area, he was still not taken with the locals' obsession with smoking, and this specific ritual tended to overwhelm his – as Mr Luncher had put it – *'delicate foreign senses'*. Helda and Furbo, despite not being local, seemed to know this tradition well, and joined in with their own smaller pipes.

After a good ten seconds of inhalation (which is a long time, even if it doesn't sound like it,) all those with pipes-in-mouths removed them and held them in two hands behind their backs. At some unspoken signal, they all expelled great clouds of smoke at the same time, some shaking their heads side to side, some aiming them at Felix, others straight up into the air. The effect was that within seconds, the room was a smoking, stinking, coughing mess. This was supposed to be some great honour, and Felix

179

had heard some people trying to explain that it is a serious ritual steeped in folk tradition, but mostly he just thought it was an excuse to show off.

It's often seriously joked that whoever is the last to finish exhaling is the winner. A silly game that most pretend to ignore, but after a few drinks, there's always some fool who wants to prove he's the one, and makes it plain that they intend to try. Tonight, it was Dago facing off against, of all people, Mrs Luncher. The matron of the firm wasn't much for drinking (besides a few short glasses of something dignified) but made sure to show up for the celebrations after a tough case had been won.

Dago was staring her right in the face, mouth pursed, a steady stream of dark grey blowing from him. Mrs Luncher had her mouth closed, and two thin spouts of white jetted from her nose. There were many unwritten rules to this game. Felix had, despite showing no interest at all, somehow picked them up from somewhere, the same way one sometimes just *knows* the latest pointless gossip, despite making zero effort to do so.

The first – and most important – rule being that you couldn't just let the smoke wheedle out of you in a meagre, pathetic dribble. No, you had to push it, you had to show you had the capacity to not only store it in great volumes, but force it out.

Dago's eyes were red. His hands, still behind him, were gripping his ludicrously big pipe with unrelenting purpose, fingertips whitening. Mrs Luncher's face was passive, almost condescending, giving precisely no indication that she was having to exert any particular effort at all. She didn't even blink.

After a half-dozen more heartbeats, Dago finally coughed and spluttered, and dropped his head to bang loudly on the table in front of him. Mrs Luncher opened her mouth to let out a tiny ring of smoke, before reaching over and patting him on the head.

"Maybe next time, eh?" she croaked in a scratchy, quiet voice. Everyone cheered and raised their glasses again, and Felix couldn't help but feel the smile tug at the corners of his mouth.

~

The Duck in Flagon was famous for three things. First, a speciality 'cocktail', named the Rusty Smuggler. Bert, the landlord, would never tell you what was in it, but insisted it was made of the finest ingredients you can find.

"Note how he said 'find', not 'buy'," Dago muttered, tapping his nose.

"I reckon it's mushrooms," said Yetty, nodding. "Big, plump, red ones."

Whatever it was, it was thick, pink, gritty, and tasted like milk on the turn. But, saying that, if getting absolutely blasted was your goal, it was a fantastic means to an end.

The second thing was its 'special' dish – the bizarrely named 'Froggoboggo Pie'. They had made Felix order one on his first week here, telling him it was a local delicacy. It was a wide, flat pie made from frogs, toadstools, pastry you could stab a man with, and all manner of other greenish wet clumps that Felix did not find palatable.

He was at the bar with Helda, when he pointed at the specials board. Perhaps 'specials' board was casting too grandiose an air, as there was only one special on it: the aforementioned Froggoboggo pie.

"Now, that," said Felix, several Smugglers deep, "Keep away from that, it's the most revolting, disgusting, hideous dish I've ever had the misfortune of being in the same country as."

Helda had looked at him, fury flashing across her face, and stomped back to her table.

What was that all about? Thought Felix, as the barkeep thunked down his round.

The third thing the pub was famous for was the sign above the door.

~

"The Duck In Flagon, eh? Curious name," said Furbo, looking at the sign that hung by a single nail above the bar. It portrayed a smiling yellow duckling, all fuzz and beaming innocence, poking its tiny head out of a tankard. It looked almost like the sort of thing a child might paint.

Mr Luncher waved a slightly wobbly hand at it. "It was a mistake, you *know*. This place used to be *called something* else."

"Oh?" said Furbo, with the earnest interest of the curious drunk.

Mr Luncher had a tendency to put emphasis on the wrong words when he was a little up-the-pole, so to speak. He pulled his monocle off, gave it a wipe on his top, leaving it more smeared than before.

"Yes, a while back, long ago now, gosh, long back, they hired some sign painter to do them a new sign as someone had nicked the last one. Or was it that it blew away in a storm? Oh, I don't remember. The important part was they needed a new sign, right? They were a bit short of cash though, what with all their accoutrements blowing away in the wind. So, instead of getting some decent artist to paint them this fantastic new sign, a real nasty, scary one to lure in the adventuring type, instead of that, they went to this old fella, half-deaf, the same old boy who used to paint the fences, and asked if he'd do it for a few pints and a free dinner. 'Sure', says he, 'happy to.'"

Mr Lunch took a thoughtful sip of his whiskey. "He beavers away for a few weeks, and the publican is getting right excited, can't wait to lure in the fierce warrior nomads, the wandering heroes, that sort of punter. His was a pub with a reputation, see, a nasty place where you can get a good, stiff drink, and maybe an honest fight. Or was it you could get a good, stiff fight, and maybe an honest drink?" he contemplated this for a minute, before shaking his head. "Doesn't matter. So, two weeks pass, and up walks the painter, hands it to the young chap out front, who scrambles up his ladder to hang the new sign, then calls out for the landlord. He almost drops his rag and cup in his excitement, he rushes outside, looking to see what promises have bought him, practically counting the returns already. Imagine his face when he saw this cute little duck poking his happy beak out of this cup. Ha! Anyway, the new name stuck."

It was a story the staff at Luncher had heard plenty of times, but they still laughed politely.

"...well, what was it meant to be called?" said Furbo, swilling his pot, spilling his grog, lost in thought.

"Think about it. The deaf old sign painter misheard him. Got the letters at the start swapped around, didn't he!" Mr Luncher raised his eyebrows, mouth hanging in a smile, waiting for Furbo to laugh.

Furbo still didn't get it. Yetty leaned over to whisper.

He spluttered into his beer. "The 'What'-ing Dragon?!"

~

Felix was outside the front of the pub, taking in a few gulps of fresh air. He peered through the front window at the motley crowd from Lunchers. They were chatting and drinking, smoking and laughing. As if Helda could sense his gaze, she looked out the window and met Felix's eyes. She stared daggers at him, then shifted her seat so her back was to him.

He signed and leaned back against the wall of the pub. Why had he never got the hang of making friends? He had thought it was going well with Helda, but all of a sudden she hated him. Why?

He could try asking Furbo, or even Racelsus. The witch could read right into her skull, and tell him exactly…

No, not this time.

He was a trained and qualified lawyer. If he could successfully argue the wings off a butterfly, he could figure out how and why Helda was angry with him.

The facts of their relationship arranged themselves in his head like evidence in a case. Pieces of paper sprawled on a table, with snippets of conversation or facial expressions and reactions portrayed as pictures on parchments. With a thought, the documents arranged themselves into date order.

The top one had a picture of Helda on it. Underneath, in Felix's own handwriting, it said: *"Short Hair. Strong Frame."* Annotated in large, bold letters, it said: **FACT**.

The next had a picture of Helda wrestling a bear. Underneath, it said: *"Could wrestle a bear."* **OPINION**.

There were thousands of documents on the table. Felix frowned.

It must have been today. We were fine earlier.

In his mind, he swept away everything older than a day. The documents whisked up and away into nothingness. A few hundred documents remained.

No, more than that. It was in the last hour.

More papers vanished. A dozen or so were left.

We were fine… until…

He picked up a picture from the table. They were leaning on the bar, chatting. The caption said: "Discussing the specials." Helda's face was furious. It said **FACT** on it in bold, black letters.

Was it the pie…? Why would someone get upset about a pie?

He screwed his eyes and held out a hand. When he opened them, he was holding a new bundle of papers. The top had a picture of a wet, dark, leaking pie. It had a toad's leg poking out of it. Underneath, it said: *"Froggoboggo Pie."* **FACT**.

He placed the document on the table. The second paper had another picture of the pie, dripping with slime, and the words said: *"The most revolting, disgusting, hideous dish I've ever had the misfortune of being in the same country as."*

FACT.

Felix held the paper up in one hand, and the picture of Helda and him discussing the food in the other. His eyes moved drunkenly from one to the other. He rolled his eyes. The words under the picture of the pie morphed, reluctantly, into **OPINION**.

He looked at the pictures again. He placed them on the table and moved them so there was a space between them. Felix blinked, and a third picture was between the two already set on the tabletop. It had a picture of Helda holding a pie, and underneath it said: *"Helda loves Froggoboggo pies."*

Felix slapped a hand to his head.

Oh, bugger.

~

Felix slumped opposite Helda, who sneered at him, and made to stand.

"Wait!" Felix said, and put a hand on her arm. She looked like she was about to thump him.

"I'm sorry," he said, looking deep into her eyes.

She slapped his hand off him. "Pah," she spat.

Felix gulped. *Here goes.*

"I was wondering if you were hungry, and if you might want to help me finish this—"

He was interrupted by the landlord thwacking the largest Froggoboggo pie Felix had ever seen on the table in front of him, between Felix and Helda. Felix suspected the landlord thought he was doing a nice thing for him by giving him the biggest, plumpest, slimiest, ripest pie he had in the larder. The landlord winked at him as he sauntered back to the bar. Felix felt his gorge rising. He cleared his throat, and cut two thick slices. Lifting one, he began.

"As I was saying, would you fancy sharing a delicious pie with me, Helda? This particular variety is among my favourites."

She eyed him up and down, squinting. Slowly, she lifted a slab of dripping, quivering pastry. Her face cracked into a grin. "Aye, Felix, I think I would."

Felix lifted his own slice, and they clinked them together in the same way one would with glasses. Instead of a clear, crisp note upon contact, the pies slapped wetly against each other.

Felix grinned through gritted teeth and took a huge bite of pie.

In his mind, the word morphed back to **FACT.**

~

"I still can't believe that bloody window," coughed Helda, waving a puff of smoke that had floated over from somewhere. The night was on the slowdown now, with everyone well and truly cross-eyed and cheerful, but not in a tear-the-walls-down way. Rather, a make-the-world-right sort of way. Racelsus had been with them all night, unable to drink, but certainly able to laugh and chat with the rest of them. Helda looked over at her. "I just can't believe it."

Furbo laughed warmly. "I tell you, those with an ear to hear the universe often find the universe speaks to them. Sometimes, though, people don't listen, and the universe has to shout a little louder. Sometimes it even has to yell and ring bells, so to speak. In this case, it really had to hammer the point home!"

Merindha cocked her hand to her ear. "Hellooo? Hellooo, it's the universe speaking, are you listening? Oi! I'm the bloody universe, stop ignoring me!" She started tapping Dago on the head, who was flumped on the table, snoring.

Felix finished another measure of spirits. "I thought that judge was going to have me killed! Right there and then! Summryexcecu… summaryexicyut… summarily executing!" He struggled with those words, but everyone seemed to know what he meant. "And you know what the worst part is?" he added, a twinkle in the eye.

"What?" asked Helda, eyes blinking independently of one another.

"I bet she would have done it by beheading!"

Their laughter carried far into the streets, filling the night with warmth.

~

Felix stumbled down the street supported by Furbo, who was being supported by Helda, who was merrily swinging Racelsus in time with a raunchy song called "Dig My Spud". Mrs Luncher pretended not to know the words, but Felix spotted her mouth moving along to it.

All of them (save the witch) were pissed as farts, and didn't quite care who knew it. Today was a good day, and life is short (unless you're immortal), so drink, sing, and celebrate.

They weren't aware of it, but above them, they were being watched by inhuman eyes.

~

Back at Lunchers, Felix, Furbo, Yetty, Helda and Racelsus were arranged on the chairs in the main office. They were past 'roaringly pissed', and were surfing their way to 'sleepily sozzled'. Felix knew that he was sitting down now, but if he had to stand up again, that would be it: the very last time he was standing up before finding somewhere to collapse and sleep. Tired as he was, and mushed as his brain was, he felt happier than he had for a long time. Not just because they had won the case, but because he had felt like he belonged. Genuinely belonged for the first time in... in...

"Bloody ages," he spluttered.

"Eh?" slurred Helda.

"Look, I want to tell you all something." Felix stood. "And I'm not just saying this because I'm drunk, but I am drunk, so, well, use that information in whatever way you want."

"Objection!" said Furbo, and chuckled.

"Yes, well, overruled. Now, listen, you lot." Through the fog of drink, a single beam of light illuminated the ocean of his thoughts. A guideline to steer this particular conversation in precisely the way he wanted it, avoiding all the rocks and traps that could damage or sink it. He looked at each of them in turn, making sure they were paying attention. Satisfied, he began.

"My childhood was... was... awful. I spent time in one of those convent orphanages you were on about, Furbo. When you said you used to save us from them, er, them from them, the kids I mean. That's when I knew. This is a good man, and I will fight for him."

He sat down again. "Grew up there. Got picked on. By kids, by the matrons. Didn't matter. I wasn't big enough or fast enough to avoid it. No friends to defend me. No parents to protect me. All I had was this."

He jabbed a finger at his head.

"It wasn't fair. It burned and churned inside of me, day and night. I knew it wasn't, but I couldn't do anything about it. It wasn't fair that they didn't feed us enough, but what could I do? We didn't have enough clothes, but what could I do? I got beaten up every day by the bigger boys, and the matron ignored it. But what could I do? We relied on the kindness of strangers donating money and other things, but it all seemed to vanish before it ever reached us, the kids. What could I do?"

He stood again. "One day, this skinny guy comes in. Dressed as smart as anything. He walks around the place, confident. Not in a fighty-way, but in a self-assured way. He knew what he was looking for. He walks room to room, tailed by the head matron and three of her cronies. They're all looking like they're chewing wasps, but they're saying nothing. He looks each room up and down, and makes a few notes. I was hiding from the other boys in the bedroom, and when he comes in I hear him ask a question, he says:

"'And this has been the standard for how long?'

Felix sat down once more. "I didn't hear the mumbled reply, but it was spat at him. He didn't react, he just takes a note, and makes to leave. As he's heading for the door, he spots me.

"'Hello, lad,' he says. 'What's your name?'

"'Felix,' I tell him. 'Who're you?'

"'I'm a lawyer,' he says. 'Representing – oh, you won't know them. Yet – someone who wants to make sure you're well enough fed and clothed.'

"I was gonna ask him how, but I was shy. Why would this adult listen to me when no one else had? So I just shrugged and stared at my shoes. He knew what was going through my head.

"'Hey,' he says, and I look up. He had a twinkle in his eye. 'Do you know what the law is, Felix?' he asks. I shake my head.

"'It's a set of rules made by the king, or the gods, or whoever's in charge. Right at the top. They make these rules, and everyone in the world agrees to them. It's things like: Don't kill people. Don't steal things. You understand?' I nod.

"Then," he says, turning to the matron. "If people don't follow those rules, those in charge march up to them and tell them to sort it out, or else."

"Or else what?" I say, spellbound. "Or you go to prison, or worse."

"I was amazed. This small, unassuming person had all that power! All that ability to make a difference. To help me."

"What if the people try to stop you?" I squeak at him, eyeing the matrons.

"Well, I have a whole lot of friends who happen to look very angrily on people who try to do that. They're called the peacekeepers. You might have seen them walking around, big fellows with the blue capes, yes?"

"I nodded. How could I learn to do what this stranger could do? The feeling of being in control, of knowing every possible outcome and confidently knowing he was going to walk out of there intact. He patted me on the arm, then nodded back to me. That was the last I ever saw him. He kindled that spark in my chest without even knowing it."

Felix was playing with a pipe on the desk, eyes down.

"Once he'd gone, they beat me black and blue. That spark didn't die, though. A few weeks after that, things changed a little. We ate a bit better. Our clothes had less holes in. They even started bringing in books for us to read. All because of some stranger making sure that the people followed the rules and did what was right. That was it. I dedicated myself to the law from then on. If he could do it, I could do it. Whatever it took."

He placed the pipe on the table. "I found a few huge, old legal books on the pile and studied them. It was my reason for living."

He pushed his chair back and stood tall. "If I can give one person that same spark of hope that that stranger gave to me, then I will call myself a successful lawyer. I don't care about the rest of it, the money, whatever. I just want to be a good person."

He turned to regard his friends, who were concentrating on him as well as they could.

"I've never told anyone that," he said. He wiped his eye, collapsed into his chair, and rested his head on the desk. Felix was asleep within moments.

His friends exchanged glances, smiled, and joined him.

~

After waking much more quietly and slowly than they had gone to sleep, they all decided to head out for breakfast together. Racelsus stayed back in the lodge but wished them all a lovely morning in a voice perhaps a little higher and more grating than normal.

"God I feel horrendous," muttered Furbo as they hobbled to town. The morning was bright and pleasant, exactly the sort of morning that they didn't want. They wanted dimly lit. They wanted grim.

"Hrngh," grumbled Helda, scowling.

Felix tried to respond, but a croaky groan was all he could contribute.

They wound up in Gutcher's Ale And Breakfaster, a dirty but homely old boozer/breakfaster on the edge of town. It tended to open late and stay open right until midday, so you would sometimes get the same people staying all through the night and ending their revels with a hearty slap-up breakfast.

Breakfast was a solemn affair, with many nursed heads and sensitive stomachs trying to survive this self-imposed misery, with many a mumbled mantra to never touch a drink again.

By mid-afternoon, spirits were restored, and Felix found himself strolling through the nearby flower park with Helda, Furbo and Racelsus, the latter having joined them after passing by the offices post-breakfast.

"So, what now for you two? Now you've cleared your names and are free people?" he asked, genuinely unsure as to what they might say. He had earnestly begun enjoying the company of these two, but if he knew people, they weren't the sort to hang around for long.

"Back to wandering, I suppose," Furbo said as he flicked a stone into the lake they were circling. "I find that life tends to give us direction as and when it fancies, and we've never been ones for waiting around. I'm sure something will come up soon."

Helda nodded. She was still a little sore from the night before, and wasn't saying much.

"And what about you, Racelsus? The nomad's life for you?" Felix asked.

The skull clacked its teeth. "I promised I would help these two find what was lost to them, so I will travel with them until such time that I can uphold that promise. And, I will state here again, that time *will* come."

Helda nodded again and Furbo smiled.

Felix sighed. "I will admit, I'll miss you three. You have a certain outlook on life that I think the staff of Lunchers & Co will miss, much to the detriment of any future clients, and of the staff themselves. Are you sure I can't convince you to stay?" he asked, knowing their answer already.

"No, my lad, we've gone over this. Our place is the great unknown, so head into the abyss we must, so to speak," Furbo said, not with sternness, but with a resolution that would not be shaken.

Their walking had taken them back to the outside of the offices. Felix tried to ignore the feelings he had about his new – *and only* – friends walking out of his life forever. He hadn't quite felt at home with the other lawyers at Luncher. They were lovely people, but it's as if they just weren't quite linked up with him. There was a certain missing something that stopped them being actual friends. When this unlikely trio had turned up, that had all been forgotten, and he had, for the first time in quite a while, felt as if he *fitted*. He had half-entertained the idea of asking if he could go with them, but he knew he wasn't cut out for that sort of life. No, this was for the best.

Helda grabbed his arm in a grip like iron. "So long, Felix. I'm sure we'll meet again, and soon. Thank you again for everything you've done for us." Her eyes looked moist and red, but that could have been the hangover.

Furbo embraced him, and added: "if we can ever do anything for you, and it is in our power to give, we will do it. We owe you, Felix."

Racelsus concurred.

Felix gave them all a smile, and said: "Thanks guys. I'll be fine, so long as I don't have any more cases quite like yours for a while. Maybe some nice, simple murders."

As soon as he said it, he realised it was a mistake. Furbo gave a small, pained smile, and Helda looked at the floor. Of all the crimes he could have plucked from the air...

I'm such an insensitive, unthinking—

Don't worry so much, came a soft voice in his head. *They know you don't mean it.*

Felix looked at Racelsus, who was regarding him calmly. He stared at the floor, sheepish. A pat on the shoulder and he looked up, and saw Furbo's creased, smiling face. Now Felix was this close to him, he could see that Furbo's dark skin was looking considerably older and more wrinkled than when they had first met.

"Aye, lad. Fingers crossed. Take care, Felix."

He gave his shoulder a squeeze and turned to leave. Helda followed, with Racelsus swinging from her pack. Felix watched them go with a heavy heart. He hoped he would see them again.

~

That evening, when Felix was feeling rather melancholy, he had decided on a moonlight stroll around the forest paths behind the office. It was a beautiful clear night, and he could see every star in the sky. He wondered what his friends would have said if he had expressed a desire to follow them.

One star was brighter than the others. Felix fixated on it.

I wonder if they're looking at that star, using it for navigation.

Despite his beliefs, or lack thereof, he said a tiny prayer on that star, asking that his friends find their son. He also added a slightly guilty wish that their wandering brought them around to see him again, when the time was right.

The star grew brighter.

It also grew larger.

Felix blinked a few times, but he was definitely seeing a bright light, getting brighter and bigger.

He heard clumsy footsteps behind him, and turned to see Furbo, Helda and Racelsus approaching him, looking worn out, as if they had been running.

"What—" Felix began to say.

"All in good time, my lad, all in good time – but look," said Furbo, out of breath, pointing at the star.

It started to form a shape, a human shape, as it got closer – not larger, Felix realised.

What on earth is that!

A figure descended to land gently in front of Felix. It exuded pale white light of brilliant purity, so bright he had to shield his eyes. It was the figure of a woman, dressed wholly in white, an aura of serene perfection coating her. The forest filled with pale purity, illuminating everything in a ghostly half-luminescence. It looked as if Felix had entered a dream.

She reached out and took Felix by the hand, pulling his hand away from his eyes. He looked at her face, and he felt his soul being comforted and softened by being near her. Looking deep into his eyes, she spoke in a voice like the birth of clouds.

"Felix, we need your help. Every life in the universe is depending on it," she said.

"…Sorry?" Felix replied.

Journal Entry J: Chosen One

Reference case [MNvMD] (MegNeg v. MadDus), year 1327, judge Detson presiding.

We've all heard it, the tale of the farm boy who is destined to save the world from evil. All very compelling stuff for cheap stories, but only the very gullible actually believe it.

I've never had much stick with Fortune Tellers. Most of it is vague mumbo-jumbo designed to make you feel heroic or worthy, all to scam you of a few scraps of coin. Or, so the self-styled mystic can parade themselves around feeling all other-worldly and mysterious.

This case was concerning the family of a young woman named Lagerty. She worked on her parents' farm far out in the North Country, and dreamed of bigger, better things. She heard the stories from the wandering tale-spinners about destiny and knew that, one day, she would be the one they sang songs about.

She practised her sword fighting, her wilderness survival techniques, all so she would be ready when the time came. All she needed was a quest, some noble purpose to spur her into adventure.

Along came the circus. A travelling group, you know the type. Acrobats, freaks, and, crucially, a fortune teller by the name of Ancient Madame Dustillia, Mystic of the Farthest East. Apparently, she was well-respected in the profession. A complete quack, but a well-respected quack. Lagerty caught wind of this, and set off on the long journey to find her destiny.

One stormy, atmospheric night, the air thick with promise, Lagerty the Wanderer drew aside the curtain to the cloying, incense-laden tent of the greatest prophet in the East.

"You will go on to great things, young hero," she crooned, eyes closed, hands waving left to right, crossing each other like the destinies of so many souls.

"You will travel far, and do much good," she continued, accompanied by the tinkle of jewels and bottles of unknown purpose.

"Remember this, when faced with the Peril of the Flame-Wielder of The Night-Fields, when all seems lost: Look up and to the west, for there you will find your salvation!"

For Lagerty, this was the sign she had been waiting for. She wrote a letter to her family, explaining it all, gathered her sword and possessions, and set off for a life of noble heroism.

Not three nights later, she was sleeping under a tree, when what did she see, but! Oh, great destiny, trouble afoot! A miscreant, holding a flaming torch, setting light to the stables of the local innhouse. The name of the innhouse: The Farmer's Dream.

The Night Fields!

Her prophecy singing in her ears, she drew her blade and marched to the villain.

"Stop, evildoer!" she yelled, standing triumphantly. The figure turned to her, arm outstretched, a black silhouette surrounded by flames.

"This doesn't concern you, outsider!" came the hoarse reply. "Bugger off!"

"No, I shall not! Cease this criminality, miscreant!" She wasn't a wordsmith, our girl.

"Nay! Get y'allself lost! Please, this ain't your business!"

When all seems lost...!

Fate spun in her mind, and she turned her head to the left. Squinting at the sky, she tried to make out the sure-sign of her destiny's approach.

She was so engrossed in this, she didn't hear the arsonist pad over to her from her east. He clubbed her on the back of the head, leaving her to bleed to death with the torch placed in her lifeless fingers. It was all an insurance scam, apparently. Crafty.

Her family, upon learning the news, were horrified. They demanded to speak to the Fortune Teller who had so clearly predicted this, but had left the part out about getting murdered. Lagerty had revealed all in her letter, from the dreams of adventure, to the prophecy itself – word for word.

In court, under threats of 'Death By Deliberately Misleading Prophecy', Madame What's-Her-Face broke down, admitting it was all a con, an act she put on, and her actual prophecy skills were non-existent.

She confessed that she had one or two go-to prophecies she reeled out for punters, and the 'Flame Wielder' one had been one of her favourites.

"It doesn't actually *mean* anything, it's just a b-bit of nonsense!" she bawled in the witness stand, managing to elicit equal parts disgust and begrudging sympathy from me.

"But you sent this poor girl to her death! What do you say to that?" I demanded of her, not giving into the small human part of me that wants to comfort the crying.

"It was just an awful, terrible coincidence! I didn't know there was a place called the Farmer's, uh, something, or that an arsonist would… oh, please, you have to believe me!" Her mystic makeup ran down her face, making her look like a maudlin clown. Even I had found it hard to continue with the finger-pointing at that point.

In the end, the ex-oracle was released without charge, but banned from ever performing soothsaying in any form ever again. Upon appeal, she was permitted to practice fortune-telling, but with the proper caveat beforehand. I can't remember the exact wording, but it was something like:

"Please note that fortune telling is not a guarantee of actual events. The customer waives any right to legally challenge any fortune hitherto dispensed, and any events that do transpire in a way that is in any way similar to events transcribed by the act is purely coincidental."

~journal entry ends

25 – Explanations

Felix took a sip of tea. It burned his mouth, but he didn't notice.

"Explain the part where you said all of the things you just said again," he said.

Helda raised an eyebrow. "Such unequalled wordplay must be why you were chosen."

The woman shook her head. "No, it wasn't that."

Helda sighed, then reclined. The chair creaked worryingly under her considerable weight.

The figure continued in a voice like a summer's evening.

"We have been observing you for quite some time. Not just you, but all the lawyers... well, everywhere. Whenever we saw one fall below our high standards, we took them off the list. We repeated this thousands of times until we had only a few left, then compared them, and you came out on top," she had a half-smile that didn't reach her wide, bright blue eyes.

Felix watched the steam curl from his mug in lazy spirals, and replied. "Yes, okay, that part I can comprehend. Just about." He twitched a finger in the air, pointing at nothing in particular. "It does raise questions, but it's the next part I meant. The part about the reason *why* you've been spying on me."

Her smile didn't move, but her eyes slowly looked upwards, as if looking for the right words.

"Of course... Put simply, we need your help to save the human race, and subsequently all existent life, from being destroyed by evil forces bent on mankind's obliteration. And only you, Felix, can save them."

Felix picked up a pipe, unlit, and chomped on the end. He didn't know why. It wasn't even his pipe. He cleared his throat.

"Nope, didn't work. Try it again."

It was as if someone was trying to fit a round peg into a square hole in his brain, but hadn't realised that someone had swapped the peg with a lemon. They just prodded against each other, and the more he tried to make sense of it, the less it made sense.

The figure descended to sit cross legged on the floor. She sighed deeply. She raised her right hand in front of her, and a small ball of light materialised, hovering above her palm, no larger than a grape. The room watched her closely.

"Let's try a wider perspective. First, there is creation." She lifted her hand slightly. "Energy coalescing together to form matter, which forms larger matter, which forms physical objects, from planets to pebbles." More lights, swirling around each other, to form a larger, brighter ball. Eventually, it darkened, becoming something else entirely – a solid shape. When she was finished, she held it up. It was a seed.

"There is also the balance." She lifted her other palm, where no light shone. She dropped the seed onto it. "You cannot see or feel it. There are those who can, but we cannot. The balance is its own force, it moves where it wills and acts according to its own design." The seed remained still. She gazed at it, and continued in a quiet voice.

"There is good in the world. There is also evil. I suppose you could call them life and death... that's too simple, but it will suffice in this example. These forces pull the balance in different directions. Are you following so far?" her eyes moved to Felix.

He nodded, though his eyes looked glazed. She smiled.

"I know this is a strange conversation, and it doesn't help that the words in your language don't perfectly represent the topics. No language does. Regardless. These opposite forces exist as a... scale, in perfect, well, balance. There is always greater evil, but there is also greater good. I exist on this scale, fairly close to the top, but I am not *the* top. I exist, born from life, and it is my purpose to ward off those who would spread death and evil wherever I can, but not so much so as to upset the great balance of life. For if we were to simply remove death, if such a thing were even possible, life would spiral out of control, and would end itself."

The seed started spinning, energetically bouncing in her palm, and steam started leaking from it. Small green shoots spurted from it, and the seed ripped apart its own casing, forming a small green tangle of roots.

She considered the plant, pausing. She continued.

"Once the balance is tipped, there is no going back. This plant will die. It grew too quickly, and now cannot support itself."

She stood, tipped her hand and let the plant land on the table.

"What should have happened is it should have sprouted carefully, taking what it needed, not spreading too quickly or too slowly, acting in balance with the soil, the other plants, the creatures that eat it to survive. It has a place in the balance, and too much or too little will kill it. Too much life or too much death, and nothing is left."

She frowned at the plant. Felix had no idea what she was talking about. He was still trying to figure out the lemon.

"This is all very interesting, I'm sure, but the last time I checked, we were in Lunchers & Co, the law firm, not a first-year philosophy class," added Yetty, eyeing the glowing figure suspiciously.

She returned the look with a smile. Yetty softened slightly, her shoulders lowering. The figure began again.

"Don't worry, I'm nearly finished, and I'll answer any questions you have later." She turned back to Felix. "Sentient life, in its many forms, holds a special place in the balance of life, with humanity at the epicentre of it. You, alone, are able to grasp the higher consequences and meanings of life. You walk up and down the scale of morality, and position yourself all along its length. You are the worst of all beings, and you are the best of all beings. You are uniquely aware of the structure of morality, and yet you use this to better yourselves and gain advantage over others, human or not. Some of you, anyway. Some of you are not aware of the grand scheme, and yet devote yourselves to goodness anyway. *That*... that is humanity."

"Erm, thanks?" added Felix.

The figure shook her head.

"It is not a complement. It is the truth, laid bare."

Felix handed his pipe to Furbo, who began filling it. He looked at the figure and began tapping his hand on his chin.

"You haven't explained why you're here," he said.

The figure looked up at him. Her aura was turning from white to blue, the cold blue of winter. She closed her eyes and nodded her head.

"I understand your place in life. I understand my place. I also understand the place of those opposite me on the scale. Recently… something has changed. A great demon, one by the name of Jurrekker, has appealed to Habeus, the Judge."

"Appealed to… Habeus is real?!" Felix exclaimed.

She nodded, smiling.

"Oh yes, he's real. He's as real as you or me."

Helda looked at the figure, and prodded her with a thick finger. "I'm still not convinced about you, truth be told…" The figure didn't seem to notice the poking.

"Who actually is Habeus?" asked Racelsus.

The figure looked towards the skull, and raised her eyebrows, as realising someone was there for the first time.

"He was there when the world was created. He set in motion the original universal laws that govern existence," she said.

"He's also mentioned in practically every law textbook that cares for history," Felix added. "I assumed he was made up."

The figure laughed and continued.

"He will find that funny." Her smile dropped. "Actually, no he won't. Once, he would have…" she took a deep breath, before continuing.

"It doesn't matter. What does matter is Jurrekker has approached him and declared that humanity is beginning to slide down the scale towards evil. He is arguing that they – that you – threaten to tip the scale, and will therefore upset the great balance, and thus all life will end. You stand all along the scale, but if you shift your weight the wrong way… it will be the end of it all."

Felix shook his head. "But where do *I* come into this?"

She stood then, and filled the room with her presence. Her aura reddened, the red of blood and determination.

"Habeus has agreed to hear the arguments Jurrekker was making, and to sit in judgement of them. Mercifully, we found out this was happening before…" she paused. "We successfully argued that we should present our case that humanity be left to exist in peace, and, thankfully, Habeus agreed." Her face darkened, and her aura began to darked with it.

"This is not some cosmic duel between champions of good and evil, flaming swords at the ready. No, this is a different kind of battle, where words are the weapons. This is a battle, a legal battle, for your very *species*, for the fate of *humanity*. If it goes wrong, if you lose, humanity will be wiped out, and that may well tip the scales, leading to the destruction of *all life as we know it*. That is why we need you, Felix."

He looked at her, watching him. She had such purpose, such passion.

"No pressure, then," Felix said, deflated. He looked up, and she looked deep into his eyes again, and his soul felt caressed, but the fear remained like a splinter in his heart.

How could he do it? What sort of man could shoulder that burden? Representing a single person was hard enough. The implications of what happens to them, win or lose, are enormous. Would they survive? Would their whole world be ruined? It was something lawyers had to live with, the idea that *your* arguments could make or break someone's entire life. But that was for just *one* client. How could someone do that for an entire species? His hands started shaking slightly.

Furbo coughed, and Cherinda, for that was her name, looked at him. "Pardon me, miss, I have a question. If humanity is, as you say, on the scale, spread thinly, then wouldn't it be better if we were all to disappear? Not that I want to, you understand," he added quickly.

She looked pained at that.

"To tell the truth... I don't know. Humanity was a sort of... experiment. Granting advanced sentience to a creature, permitting it to forge its own destiny. While you spread around the balance, who can say what will happen if you are removed, instantly? It could cause a more extreme unbalancing."

"Then... why does Jurrekker risk it all to see us removed?" he said, a deep furrow on his wrinkled face.

"I wish I knew, but I do not. All I know is he has made his move, and we must respond, or we are doomed. To take no action is a risk we dare not take."

Felix lowered his head in his hands.

"I don't know if I can do this," he muttered, and he meant it.

"Oh, for pity's sake!" came a voice like a whip-crack. Mrs Luncher stormed in, past the figure and grabbed Felix by the arm, turning him to face her.

"You have ahead of you the greatest possible opportunity ever given to any lawyer in the history of mankind! You have been *personally selected* by *cosmic powers* as the best we can offer. You should be proud! I'm proud, I can tell you. I'm prouder of you than I've ever been. I have no doubt you can do it. You have a fantastic mind, a razor-sharp wit, and a team of the best legal minds in the business. Plus, these three to keep you in line." She gestured at Furbo, Helda and Racelsus. She looked at him and smiled. "Felix, you can do this. Now, stop moping and bloody well get to business."

Felix looked at her, scanning her face for dishonesty. He breathed deeply and turned to take in the room. A sea of faces from all parts of the world looked at him. He saw friends, colleagues, mystical travelling partners, beings from beyond the mortal realm. All waiting for him. For his answer.

Mrs Luncher was right. What greater stage than this? And what more deserving client?

He grinned, his apprehension melting away.

"Sure, why not. Where do we start?"

~

Felix sat with a fresh cup of tea. He looked at Helda and Furbo, and frowned.

"You know, you two look just like my last clients."

"Har, har," said Helda.

Felix's face lost some of its forced mirth, and his voice filled with concern.

"What happened to you three? Last I knew you were heading off to find your boy."

"We were not one league away when Racelsus shouted that we needed to head back," said Helda. "It gave me a fright, I don't mind telling you. I'd never heard her scream before. I didn't know she could."

Racelsus would have blushed, if she could.

"I merely channelled what the message being sent through the heavens, through me. I didn't know the full meaning of it, I just knew that it was the most important thing I had ever heard."

"She told us to head back, and she sounded genuine, so we did, as fast as we could. When we arrived, we saw you, and that brings us pretty much up to speed. Looks like you're stuck with us, Felix!" laughed Helda, punching him on the arm.

Felix yelped as the pain darted through him. "Ah, yes, but… in the nicest possible way, and don't think this is me not wanting you here, because I do, but… why? What are you here for? You aren't lawyers."

Furbo answered. "Didn't I tell you we go where the universe decrees? Normally it's in quiet signs, or signals in dreams, but this time it literally shouted at us to do something, so who are we to argue?"

Felix looked at their earnest faces. They looked back.

"Thank you," Felix said, and they embraced.

"No, thank you, Felix," said Furbo. "You saved us once. Let us help you. And, if we get to save humanity while we do it, so much the better, eh?"

"Any objections?" Helda asked, grinning.

He had none.

Interlude – The Pit
~ *Long Ago*

His first vision had been of a butterfly. He was a child, barely walking. He had tottered over to a bright yellow flower, a pretty flower, and had gone to stroke it. Before he reached it, he stopped and closed his eyes. He didn't know why, he just wanted to. It didn't hurt. He just wanted to. When he did, he saw the yellow flower in his head. A beautiful fluttering butterfly, bright berry red, landed on the flower. It stretched its wings – then flew off. The insect swiftly stopped mid-flight, turning to him, and sighed, a sigh full of sadness, before dropping dead. The sky blackened and boiled, a faint screaming from the horizon. Emotion filled him, and he started to cry. He opened his eyes, but there was no butterfly. His mother had come at his crying, stroking his hair, then whispered to him, look! And he had looked, and there was a beautiful, berry red butterfly. It fluttered over to the flower, stretched its wings, then it had flown off.

"It's dead," he had said, "it's dead."

"Hush, look my love, it flies away." Silence then, as the butterfly was snatched from the air by a darting blue bird. The stroking of the hair had stopped. The tears did not.

~

He had been climbing for years. Muscles that had once ached had long since calcified and crumbled to nothing. Nerve endings that should be screaming bloody murder had curled and dropped off, one by one. Hoary tendons swung limply from blackened bones, worn thin, impossibly thin. Yet, still, he climbed. Fingertips worn short from constant gauging of holes in the rocky surface darted from one familiar handhold to the next.

His empty mind shifted back to the last time he had reached this high. He stopped, hanging, body frozen in place. He turned his head slowly upwards, rotten neck bones scraping with the unfamiliar movement. He silently scanned the cliff, scrutinising every black inch.

Eventually, he found it. A craggy hole, almost impossible to spot. Unless, of course, you knew where to look. And he knew where to look. The last time he had reached this high, he had gripped that familiar hand hold and it had shifted, taking him with it, casting him furiously down in a shower of pebbles and failure. The hole looked far too precarious to risk that again. The creature attempted to grunt, but managed an airy wheeze.

Forehead pressed into the wall, he released his left hand from its hold and slowly wiped it across the area above him. Finding no suitable gripping point, he tried again. He returned his hand to the wall.

He shifted his balance as slowly as he could, gradually putting more weight on every anchor point, feeling which was strongest. After concluding that his right hand was best suited, he lifted it. He formed a point with his remaining fingers, stumpy that they were. He began to tap the stone above him. Softly at first, but gradually harder. A sandy residue was flitting from the wall as he worked. His sense of time had completely vanished. What good was timekeeping in here? Saying that, he knew that it took a long time to create handholds in stone. It took a very long time to create thousands.

It was deep enough to place his palm flat into it. He tested it by slowly lifting a foot and leaning into it. It seemed solid enough. With a shake of the head, the creature pulled itself up. He reached out his left hand again, feeling for a ridge, but finding none. His teeth clacked in frustration. He braced, and formed a point with the bony fingers on his left hand.

~

The pit wasn't supposed to have a bottom. It was supposed to be an endless drop, leaving the victim spiralling for eternity. This had turned out to be false. It had taken weeks, just falling, bouncing off of walls, crashing into jutting bricks. He should have died long before he hit the bottom. He thought this often in the falling days. Whenever he was snapped to waking by hitting the sides, or just from getting a solid hour of sleep, he would wonder why he was still alive. He was starving. He had had nothing to drink. He had answered his calls of nature, cried, screamed until he bled, all while plummeting down.

Hitting the bottom had been a shock. The mind plays tricks in total blackness. It thinks it sees things, it tries to make sense of it. He thought he was going to land countless times. So, when he finally did, it shook him. The impact exploded with pain, and his searing limbs were matched by his sense of all-consuming nausea. His eyes ran in involuntary circles, his sense of balance completely reprogrammed to fall, not to stay. He rolled feebly, his emaciated frame battling with these damning circumstances, and wept until he lost consciousness.

~

When he awoke, the hunger and thirst had faded. Not entirely, but they held no urgency over him. He had concluded that he must have finally died. Grasping about him, he felt bones. Small joints, large limb bones, teeth. It took him many minutes, but he brought himself to a sitting position, back against the cold stone wall.

There was absolutely no light. The silence consumed, this time without the flapping of his clothes and the rushing of wind that had been his only conversation. He tried to speak, but a pained croak is all he managed. He felt the wall behind him without standing. It was brick, but mostly smooth. Some bricks jutted perhaps far enough to grip. He shook his head, sending pain through him. He had been falling for god knows how long. How on earth could he climb out?

It had taken four days for him to try to climb the first time. He had found a likely set of bricks, and had pulled his reduced form up to reach the next set. This was not something he was used to, and so lost his grip on the greasy stone almost immediately. He collected some smaller bones to use as grips, digging them as best he could in the tiny gaps between the bricks, and tried again. He fell from a little higher, crashing on the bone pile. One sharpened femur pierced his lower back. The pain was distant. He grunted and pulled the fragments loose. His body did not seem to bleed. At least, not much. And it was cold. He stood to try again.

He had realised that he no longer seemed to feel the urge to sleep or eat. He just felt boredom. His life, if you could call it that, consisted entirely of climbing, falling, climbing, falling. He tried to sing to himself to help the days go by. His voice was a gurgling croak, but he could still just about form a tune. He knew what the words were meant to be. Who would notice if the sounds were a little off?

This became harder when his lips were sliced off after a fall. He had landed face first on a ribcage, and they had been clean severed. Wordless growls were all he could muster.

His days turned into weeks, and presumably into months, and years. He wasn't counting any more. Just climbing.

As he did so, memories of his life returned. The reasons why he was cast into this pit eluded him. The pain of it. The injustice. He had stopped climbing when he remembered. Swinging madly, he beat his hand against the cliff side, not caring that it caused him to fall. He screamed as he fell, punching and kicking whatever he could, grabbing handfuls of hair and ripping them from his receding skin. When he had hit the bottom again he had wailed, and cried, and sobbed, and eventually lain in silence. When he then opened his eyes, he could perceive a faint green glow. The glow was coming from his eyes. It gave him the subtlest of lights to guide him, stopping when he blinked. He didn't need eyelids. He ripped them off without thinking. There was no pain. Green light now flowed unrestricted from his sunken eyes.

He examined his surroundings. *They* had done this to him. *They* had thrown him here. *They* had judged him. They *scapegoated* him. They would pay.

But she was going to save him.

No.

The word struck him. He recoiled, falling backwards.

"No?" he said, but it came out as a breathy crunch.

She isn't coming.

He had frozen in place. He said nothing. The words were not being spoken. They were just inside his head. They were not his thoughts.

You are abandoned.

He pressed his head against the stone wall in front of him. If he had had eyelids, he would have closed them. He didn't move for a long time.

He laughed, and let go. He was still laughing when he hit the bottom.

~

When he reached the top, the surprise of having no further ledge to grip almost caused him to fall. His hand dug furiously into the floor over the lip. Then the right foot went higher, followed by the left hand gripping the floor, then a heave, and… he was out.

He rolled onto his back, one arm dangling into the opening. The weight of his body, desiccated and papery as it was, was crushing. He was free.

His mind emptied. He was peaceful. A figure was waiting for him.

Part Three: Judgement

1 – Grudge

~ *Very Long Ago*

The hunched figure was cold and hungry. He had found nothing in his searching, not for several moons, and it pained him. He examined the flesh on his hands. It had grown taut and lean. Too lean.

The night was dark and bitter cold. Since his tribe had been killed by some unseen predator, he had been alone.

Aimless wandering, then. Would he fall tonight?

He saw something. Glowing, like the great sun, but not up above… somehow, below. Yet how could that be?

He approached, and saw the glow. It darted, licked the sky. The heat from it startled him, even from this great distance, but drew him nearer. It felt like day, safety.

He then saw he was not alone. Others were nearby, strangers, holding sticks and stones. He walked up to the bright heat, his head down, and sat quietly by the glow. He closed his eyes and lifted his face to the warmth. It flowed through him, washing his spirit in waves of security.

Emboldened by his inattention, they beat him with their sticks and pelted him with rocks until he left. Three more times he tried to approach, and each time was bloodied.

His spirit broke, and he left. He walked away, far away, and curled up to die on the floor.

But he didn't. He lived. And he never forgot.

2 – Muster

Felix was outside the front of the building, talking to Mr and Mrs Luncher. He leaned against the doorway, upwind of the proprietors to avoid their acrid pipe fumes. Autumn was on the way out, and a cold winter breeze carried the offending smoke far up and away. He held a steaming mug of tea in both hands, partially for warmth, but partially so it hurt slightly; a constant reminder that he wasn't dreaming. His attention almost drifted away with the steam, but his companion spoke again, snapping him back to focus.

"Look, my lad, this one's on you," Mr Luncher said, not for the first time. "It's logical. This, hm, *exotic* client said they've been keeping an eye out for the right lawyer, that they've been watching *all* lawyers, so that includes me and the better half." Mrs Luncher nodded in agreement. "If we assist, we're likely to end up taking control of the case. That's just in our nature. You'll naturally want to listen to our experience and whatnot, so you'll think it's best to do what we suggest." He stabbed a finger into the air. "But! That's not what *needs* to happen. That lady chose *you*, *not* us, because you have *something*, something we don't. If we run the show, it won't be your case, it'll be ours, and that's not right. It might even cost us all rather dearly. So, we're going to sit this one out, and let you take the reins. The whole sled, even."

"Besides," added Mrs Luncher. "You're more than capable, Felix. We really can't keep doing all the hard work for you all the time, can we?"

"But—" Felix said.

"No more buts!" she said, forcefully flicking out the contents of her pipe to scatter on the paved floor. It sizzled slightly as it landed on the cold stone. "You're just going to have to figure this one out alone. Well, not alone. You will have your counsel aide, your friends, etc."

"Plus, a Celestial," added Mr Luncher.

211

"Yes, that too. Now, go on, get. No more bellyaching," finished Mrs Luncher, in a tone that brooked no argument. She holstered her pipe expertly to a pouch on her belt.

Felix sighed, then nodded. "Okay, okay." He sipped his tea, taking a long, deliberate gulp, then narrowed his eyes. "But if humanity gets destroyed, then I'm apportioning some of the blame to you two."

"That's fair. Hurry up, now," she said, smiling. Mr Luncher opened the door and beckoned his wife through, bowing low. She rolled her eyes, but Felix noticed her tiny smile as she did so. Felix followed her, then turned to the right to head to the back of the building, squeezing through the tightly packed desks and paper stacks.

Felix opened the heavy door to the deliberation room, the same one he had been in for Racelsus's case not a few weeks prior. Only this time, it felt much more... *what was the word...*

Significant.

Cherinda's resplendent form bathed the room in warming light as she stood in the corner, chatting to Yetty. Yetty herself perched on a stool on the far end of the table, a stack of papers in front of her, leaning her elbow on them, head propped on an arm. She had a pencil ready, and an even larger stack of blank paper beside her. She looked focussed, undaunted despite all they were to discuss. It looked as if she wanted to take some notes, but wasn't sure how to tell this Celestial figure to bugger off.

Furbo and Helda sat in the same chairs as before, with Racelsus in her customary birdcage on the table in front of them. The cage was starting to get grubby again as some of the polish was wearing off. Furbo had asked if she would prefer some other method of transportation, perhaps a wooden box, but she had refused, saying she was quite enjoying her new home.

"It's nice and airy, with a pleasant breeze. Plus, three-sixty-degree views," she had mused, and that was the end of that.

They all turned as Felix entered. He regarded each of them. They were an odd bunch, that much was obvious. But, as he thought about it, he reckoned he could do worse for finding a team to help him save the world.

'Save the World'. What a ridiculous thought. When did I become a walking I?

He had a sudden mental image of himself wearing nothing but a chainmail thong, standing astride a mountain of corpses, gore-slicken blade in hand, screaming into the blood-red sky. His nose wrinkled involuntarily.

He closed the door behind him and set his tea on the table. Everyone went silent, looking at him. He licked his teeth before speaking.

"Okay, gang. No pressure, but if we don't get this right, we're all dead."

They chuckled politely, and Felix took a seat.

I was being serious.

~

Once he was settled, with paper and pencil at the ready, he turned to Cherinda. She was already watching him. He tried to ignore the strange 'scrutinised' feeling it gave him. He cleared his throat.

"What is their exact argument?" Felix asked. "About why... you know," he gestured with his pencil in a 'humanity needs to be destroyed' kind of a way.

Cherinda reached into the air in front of her, and a tiny pinprick of light appeared. From it she pulled a small roll of paper, and unfurling it, read it out.

"The continued existence of Humanity must end because it violates the first universal truth – namely that: 'Each entity is entitled to exist upon its own terms and meet its needs for survival.' We assert that humanity impinges with abandon upon that right for practically every species they interact with, that they do so willingly and wantonly, and that they show no sign of stopping. Indeed, with each passing year, their impact increases exponentially. Thus, we move that humanity must, in its entirety, be extirpated."

"It means 'completely eradicated', my dear," Furbo whispered to Helda, who let out a low whistle.

Cherinda laid the paper down on the table in front of Felix. "This is in Common, so you can understand it."

As he read, something made him blink. He read it again before handing it to Furbo. "Can you read that line for me, Furbo?"

The older man peered at the document. "Court shall be heard by Habeus. The place of hearing shall be Placenamia Royal Court-house."

"I thought it said that. They're hearing it there? Of all the courts in the world, and probably beyond, they chose *there*?" Felix said, to no one in particular. It was a run-down building more suited to petty boundary disputes. If it was any more decrepit it would be a literal ruin.

The Celestial shrugged. "They had to do it somewhere, so they chose there. I think it was because if you tried to travel to the Highest Court, your human frame might have been ripped apart by cosmic winds, your soul plunged into eternal swirling nothingness, and that would have probably impacted the case," she said matter-of-factly.

She was looking from astonished face to horrified face. "What?" she asked, oblivious. "Either way, better safe than sorry," she finished, with a nervous smile.

"…Okay," said Felix. *Best not think about that too hard.*

Yetty clicked her fingers and jumped to her feet. Her face was intense, and she grinned maniacally. "I've just thought. We don't actually need to prepare a defence at all."

"Oh? Why's that?" said Furbo.

"You remember case…" she referred to her stack of papers, pulling one from the top somewhere. "HC583, RX v. RX?"

"Ah yes! Temporomancy," said Felix, nodding. "Awkward bloody thing."

Yetty was almost tripping over her words in her excitement. "Yes, that's right! That case involved someone travelling from the future to steal from his younger self, so if he did that, there must have been a future for him to travel from, so therefore humanity must survive! That means we could prepare the worst defence ever made, or just nothing at all, because whatever we do will win regardless!" She sat down, looking smug.

There was a short pause while the room tried to come to terms with this.

"Hang on," said Furbo, crossing his arms. "I don't know if we can be so certain. Temporomancy is a tricky business. There are some that argue that each time one travels through time, as it were, one creates an alternative reality that can happen differently to the reality one travelled from, meaning the direct effects aren't felt by the home timestream at all."

Yetty didn't miss a beat. "Ah! But in this case, the temporomancer, and remember he was a *qualified* temporomancer, tried that himself. Even with his extensive knowledge, he couldn't affect his own past or future. That's with the benefit of a whole lifetime's study on the subject. Therefore, we must win!"

Furbo raised his palms. "Let's not be too hasty. What if that only happens in one time stream, and in every other one he has been able to affect his past successfully? Perhaps we just happen to be living in the one where it didn't work?"

Yetty shook her head. "Listen…"

"I'll stick the kettle on," said Helda.

~

Two hours later, they were still debating. Yetty's hair was dishevelled, and Furbo was red faced. They were both standing, almost yelling at each other. They had gone over every argument possible, it seemed to Felix, and yet had discovered nothing and progressed nowhere. Even Cherinda was looking a touch fed up.

Felix stood, and clapped his hands together once. "I can't take this anymore. Both of you, sit down and shut up!"

They stared daggers at each other, but did as they were told. Yetty turned her face to the wall, eyes closed and mouth drawn tight. Furbo flumped into his chair bodily, like a sack of wet rags thrown into a wagon.

As Felix looked between them, he noticed Furbo's flustered jowls and Yetty's frustrated gestures. Rubbing his eyes with a finger and thumb, he continued.

"Look. We both know time-wizardry is—for want of a better word—dodgy. Agreed?"

They both paused, then reluctantly nodded. Felix relaxed a little.

"Great. You are both making good points. The problem is, we just don't know for sure. I—hold on, Yetty—I know there are theories, many theories, and there is a certain logic to the argument of our fate being pre-ordained. But… Is it worth the risk? Even if there's a zero point zero zero zero one percent chance that your theory is wrong, I say it's worth us giving it everything we have, because we're going to look like a right bunch of numpties if we turn up, smile, wave, coast on through, and accidentally doom humanity." He walked over to his apprentice. "What do you think, Yetty?" he said to her, trying and failing to disguise the pleading tone from his voice.

She pursed her mouth even more tightly, clearly trying to find some argument. Helda's chair creaked as she reached for a biscuit. Eventually, Yetty sighed and shrugged. "I suppose…"

Felix softened. "Good. So, let's assume that we're not going to be able to rest on our haunches and let fate sort this out. We're going to have to do this one the hard way. Agreed?"

"…agreed."

Furbo at least had the good grace to not look pleased.

Felix smiled a tired smile, and sank into his chair. "Great. So, let's get started."

"I still think—" began Yetty.

Helda slammed her fist on the table, her biscuit clenched in her fist exploding in a shower of crumbs.

"Enough! Argh!" she shouted, shaking her hand, sprinkling Racelsus in chocolate sprinkles.

"Watch where you're banging, you great oaf!" said Racelsus.

"Oh, for goodness sake!" said Felix, jumping to his feet again.

The Celestial opened her arms, and the room brightened. Each of them was filled with a quiet serenity that flooded into their chests. Each limb felt lighter, each harsh thought and hot emotion was regarded as if through a sheet of soothing ice. Distant. Someone else's problem. Everyone stopped shouting, and just stood in a peaceful quiet.

"That's better," Cherinda said, smiling. "Now, I know you're all a little tense. But remember we're all on the same side. I suggest we take a quick break, maybe grab a drink, perhaps a biscuit, take a short walk, then we'll come back and start again. Yes?"

Everyone nodded slowly.

"Good. Let's meet here in twenty minutes," she said, exiting the room.

Furbo and Yetty both looked around each other, neither quite making eye contact. They both tried to apologise at the same time, which made Felix smile. Helda was suggesting adding a layer of padded leather underneath the cage to muffle any potential buffeting.

Maybe there's hope for us yet.

He went for a walk in the forest to clear his head. The sun was setting, and he found a beam of sunlight stabbing its way through the treetops. He let it land on his face, eyes closed. Despite the winter chill, it felt warm. He enjoyed the warmth for a moment, forgetting where he was or what he was in the middle of.

Without knowing why, for her feet made no sound, he knew Cherinda was behind him. He exhaled, a long slow breath, watching the steam curl up into the sky.

"Do we have a chance?" he asked her.

She hesitated, and he turned to face her. Her aura was a deep green, almost blending in with the foliage. "Yes, you do. Humanity is remarkable in its ability to preserve itself."

Felix tried to figure out if this was an insult.

He tilted his head to the side. "I remember hearing a story about Celestials once. In the story, the Celestial couldn't lie, and it meant the Celestial ends up sacrificing itself to save another. Can Celestials lie?"

She laughed. Felix loved the sound of her laughter. It was like the sound a river makes, or raindrops on a rooftop when you're warm and dry. "You know, what, I don't know. I've never tried."

"Not even once?" he said, eyebrows raised.

"Well…" she looked down, looking bashful. She started fiddling with her fingernails. "There was one time where a friend of mine was trying a new hairstyle. It looked… inelegant, but she was so happy with it, so I said it looked lovely."

"What!? And they didn't kick you out?!"

She waved a playful hand at him, but smiled. He leant back against a tree, eyes closed. The tree was hard, cold and damp, but it didn't seem to matter.

"It's an awfully heavy weight," he admitted. "I'm not used to these sorts of stakes." It was true. It kept him awake at night.

He opened his eyes as he felt a hand rest on his shoulder. She was close to him, her face filling his vision. She was beautiful, with such vibrant features. It was like looking at a painting, a piece of art that had been lovingly shaped over months and months. It brought comfort to him, and he felt his anxiety melt away.

"I believe in you," she said, smiling, and then lightly walked away. Once she left, the anxiety returned. He let it wash through him and considered his place in the grand scheme of things.

He focussed on a leaf on the tree above him, moving gently in the breeze. If a man chops down that tree, that leaf will die. Does the man care? Does the leaf? Is humanity the tree, the leaf, or the man?

I need a drink, he decided.

~

When he got back, forgoing the sought-after detour via the Duck, the sun was fully set. The cold was seeping into him. Inside, everyone was tired, and, despite Cherinda's involvement, some rattiness hung in the air. Racelsus suggested they all head to bed, and regroup in the morning, which was the first thing everyone had agreed on that day.

Helda and Furbo stayed in the spare room of the local inn, and received favourable rates because Luncher had helped him through a number of relatively minor legal troubles he had found himself in over the years.

Wasn't everything relatively minor, now? How can you compare something as inconsequential as a publican's troubles to what we're about to be going through?

Cherinda and Racelsus stayed at Luncher. When asked, they both had explained that they didn't need sleep, and so would spend the night talking.

Felix rarely lost sleep over a case. He was normally able to detach himself enough to make sure he was well rested. One thing Cherinda had said played around his head over and over, stopping him from drifting off.

"We repeated this thousands of times until we had only a few left, then compared them, and you came out on top."

Confidence was an important part of a lawyer's arsenal. You had to convince everyone, even yourself, that you knew everything, and were absolutely correct in the arguments you were making. Even if it was all horseshit, you had to pretend.

He knew he was good at his job, but this?

How could he accept he was the only option? He constantly second-guessed himself. He often convinced himself that his arguments were weak flimsy things that, only through a series of unlikely miracles, seemed to stick. Just that morning, he had stubbed his toe on the door frame and managed to spill his breakfast on himself at the same time. How was *he* the best choice?

"…You came out on top."

He watched the sunrise crawl up his window.

I'm allowing myself one morning of self-pity, then it's super-confident, champion-of-humanity Felix from here on out.

He clutched the blankets over himself, swaddling himself up like a new-born.

Maybe two mornings.

Journal Entry K: Pre-emptive

Reference case [JLvSR] (JusLes[f] v. SerRie), year 1331—[?], judge Lestere[pre] presiding.

Time travel? Again? Well, I do have another case dealing with it… I suppose they are considered some of the 'sexier' cases out there… Very well.

This one is all the more interesting because it actually involves a judge.

Judge Lestere was in his office one day, when a sharp rap at the door announced he had a letter. To his surprise, it was a letter from himself. It read:

Lestere,

This letter comes to you from the future. You will preside over a case involving a criminal named Serenity. During the case, her alibi will appear unbreakable. However, the prosecution will, at great expense, hire a temporomancer to travel back to the time of the alleged offence and will confirm the defendant's involvement. Therefore, in the interests of time and of justice, I am informing you of this result via the same method.

P.S. I know you are sceptical of this message's authenticity. I can prove it in fact to you by telling you something only you know. Thus: you dress your cat up in robes and pretend he's the king, you call him Majesty Fluffikins and you feed him from your own mouth.

Yours,

-Lestere

Okay, I admit the last paragraph is an invention of mine. All we know is he wrote something that instantly and completely convinced himself of the authenticity of the note. He scribbled it out before submitting it as evidence. Who knows, it could have been that?

Anyway, being a sensible judge of sound character, Lestere immediately called for the arrest of the accused, a woman called Serenity. This poor lady was dragged from her bed and thrown in jail for a crime she had not yet committed.

Precisely what had transpired here, o student? A judge had arrested someone on concrete evidence that didn't yet exist, on a crime that had yet to be committed. But, we argued, as her representatives, this false imprisonment would therefore mean she was unable to commit the offence, thus she was (or, would be) innocent of this alleged crime.

This didn't float with the judge, one, erm, Judge Lestere, who inferred we were disrespecting his judicial authority.

The case became very messy. We had to call that judge as a witness, which meant we had to find *another* judge to stand in while that was happening. Then, someone had the bright idea to pay for a temporomancer to head into the future, bring the future Lestere back, interview him, then send him home and use his testimony as evidence.

I tried to argue that this case had gone too far, and if we tried to muddy up the timelines even further we were in grave danger of serious consequences. That argument failed, so I tried to spin it on the argument that it would cost a bomb, and that one worked.

In order to convict a judge, you need three other judges to agree, unanimously, that the judge is guilty. Rounding up that many wigs in one place at the same time is no easy task, especially when they have the awkward business of judging one of their peers. I don't know how Mr and Mrs Luncher managed it, but a few quiet conversations with the right people and before we knew it, we had a practical panel of justices.

They closed ranks, of course, and declared that Lestere had acted in good faith, and should not be punished.

Our client? Well, she was released, citing lack of evidence. Then, I like to think out of pure frustration, she went and committed the alleged offence in the exact time and place that she was destined to.

Still, it wasn't all for naught. We managed to set a precedent for future cases, namely that:

Submitted evidence for cases must be obtained from the same time-stream as the alleged offence. No exceptions.

~journal entry ends

3 – The Rules

It was no simple task, proving humanity deserves to exist.

In theory, as the defence, they had the easier job; the other side had to make their case, providing enough irrefutable proof that their argument was the only conclusion. The defence only had to poke a few holes in it, enough to leave that doubt, and they were done. It was like sailing over a wide lake. If the prosecution can get the boat over without sinking, they win. Poke a couple of holes in the right place and let the water do the work; that's the defence counsel's philosophy.

Of course, it's often not as simple as that. Sometimes, it's not a sailboat, it's a dirty great ironclad rammership, and all you've got is a courgette. Sometimes it's less of a lake and more of a puddle.

This was a puddle case.

It was the second day. Yetty was off looking for precedents in the Luncher's Library. It was somewhat of a forlorn search; how often had these sorts of cases happened? But you never know, she had said, so off she went. Furbo and Helda, along with Racelsus, were off getting supplies—which had turned out to mean biscuits, beer and tobacco.

Felix was alone with the Celestial. Her aura was a clear, subtle white. He still didn't know what to make of her, but had told himself that once the case was over he'd have all the time in the world to find out. For now: he needed evidence. And for that, he needed to know the rules of the game. He picked up his pencil and flipped a clean sheet of paper in front of him, and offered her a cup of tea, which she politely refused. He cleared his throat, flexed his wrist, and began.

"For now, please just answer yes or no, if you can. If I want more details, I'll ask. Is that okay?"

"Yes," she answered, perfectly at ease. She folded her hands over her lap, and sat up straight, awaiting the questions.

Wonder if I can cross examine her..?

"Can we call witnesses?"

"Yes."

"Can I call anyone?"

"No."

"What are the limitations?"

She counted them off on her fingers. "They have to be alive, or at least able to speak. Not 'moved on'. They cannot be a higher power—that's me, Jurrekker, Habeus, and a number of others who you probably haven't heard of anyway. They have to have some level of sentience. Lastly…. lastly…" She held her three fingers out, face furrowed in thought. "There's one more… Aha!" She smiled suddenly. "Lastly, they cannot be Kel, the Spirit of the Infinite Word."

"Spirit of the..?"

"Yes, you can't call her for obvious reasons," she said, as if he had just asked if he could call the moon to give evidence.

He made some notes. He wanted to know about Kel, just from a curiosity point-of-view, but didn't want to waste precious time. They had been given a month to prepare their case; not as long as he would have liked, but it should be long enough. Especially if Felix didn't spend it all bellyaching or getting lost in rabbit holes.

"Okay. And if I call them, they will attend?"

"Yes."

"Can I supply physical evidence?"

"Yes."

"What if it's something I don't have, or can't find?"

"Yes."

He nodded, scratching away.

"Can we use existing, hmm, 'human' precedent?"

"Yes."

Felix hadn't expected that. He was going to assume that all bets were off, so to speak. He put his pencil down and stared at her.

"Can you elaborate on that, please?"

She nodded and flicked a non-existent strand of hair away from her face with a hand. *Was that a humanising gesture for my benefit?*

"Habeus is a creature of precedent. If it exists, he will almost certainly follow it. He knows every case that has ever been judged, between man, beast, or other. He takes their previous rulings seriously. As he believes that every judge is a descendant of his own divine will, so are their judgements part of him, and thus his own judgements. He's, uhm... somewhat of an optimist in that regard."

"If he knows them all, why preside on this case at all, why not just make a decision?"

"He is not omnipotent, and he earnestly believes in the power of argument. Law is a weapon, and the one with the biggest sword doesn't automatically win the fight."

Felix considered this in return. He scribbled a few notes.

"How will we know if we win or lose?"

"There will be a series of votes. Myself, Jurrekker and Habeus will vote to approve, deny, or abstain. Once there is a majority, the case is settled."

"Okay. So, if you vote for, Jurrekker against, we only really have to convince it to Habeus?"

She considered this, hesitating. She finally nodded.

"Yes, I suppose that's true."

Had she paused a little too long, then?

This questioning went on for several hours. Felix filled piles of papers, writing down the specific rules; the things you can do, the things you can't do, the things that count, those that don't. It was a convoluted, outdated, complex mess of rules and procedures.

He was used to it.

Both sides were able to call witnesses, but it wasn't like a normal case. One could call witnesses out of the arranged order in response to something, similar to an objection. You hear an argument and think "Gosh, if only I could call Mr McGuppery in to ask him a few questions..."—well, now you could. As it was possible to call any witness from anywhere, with the full power of the cosmic jurisprudence at your beck and call, one could see a piece of evidence, and call a surprise witness as a reaction, and turn the whole case on its head completely out of the blue.

That's the benefit of having these sorts of resources, I suppose!

Of course, it could be used against him, too. This is why the strength of the argument and the wit of the lawyers was so important; these trials could go anywhere, instantly. You had to be on your toes. It was exciting, in its way. A case where you could call any witness at any time.

I wonder if I'll eat those words.

~

The data gathering dragged on, and days bled into weeks. Without being able to magically summon their potential witnesses, Felix was going to have to rely on questioning them for the first time on the day itself. Hugely risky, but what choice was there?

It was the last day of week four. The day before the case to save humanity would be heard. Winter had arrived in earnest, and the uncaring frosts had greeted them every morning for the last week. Breath steaming in the air, Felix shouldered the front door open, made himself a warming spiced tea, and headed to the 'war room' at Luncher.

The interview space had been completely converted into a storage room/planning space/buffet cart. The whole crew were there, and each looked tired and nervous. As he entered, they stopped talking and watched him settle down.

He looked at Cherinda, pale glow and easy-going expression looking slightly ragged at the edges. You wouldn't know it unless you'd spent the last month with her. She had never complained about cramped conditions, the late nights, the stink of smoke, the diet of biscuits and sandwiches.

Yetty was opposite him, her accustomed scribing-pose at the ready. Her fortitude had surprised him. Despite being a relatively junior lawyer, she had shown an astuteness and an eye for detail that put some contemporaries he knew to shame.

He sighted Helda and Furbo. They had found it much harder than the rest. They were the wandering type, utterly unused to staying in one small room in a small building for any longer than was needed. And maybe that was it. They *were* needed. Felix had found their companionship, their optimism, their camaraderie in this difficult time priceless. On the nights where he had not only burned the candle at both ends, but stuck another wick in the middle too, it had been them who had gently prised him from the pencil and guided him to the pub, or bed. They understood him.

Lastly, he beheld Racelsus. She had been a font of suggestions of those he could call as witnesses. Her experience as an outcast gave her a certain perspective on humanity, and she was uniquely placed to understand the position of the prosecutors. Yet, despite this, her loyalty to Furbo and Helda had proven her a sturdy, reliable asset to the team.

All in all, they'd worked their socks off. If it hadn't been for their efforts, he wouldn't have lasted the week. They had worked, laughed, yelled, fought, and built the sorts of bonds that can only be created through shared hardships as the days ticked by and the deadline approached. Felix surprised himself by thinking that he and his friends might actually have a chance.

Friends.

He sipped his drink, slowly, savouring the warming spice. He found the ritual of making and drinking tea to be a welcoming grip on normality that he could latch onto when feeling particularly out of his depth.

He stood, placing his drink on the table.

"Ladies, gentlemen, heavenly beings, creepy animated skulls in cages." He nodded to each in turn. They watched him, desperate for confident reassurance. "The last four weeks have been a relentless, punishing slog. We've had to view humanity, our very species, through the worst possible lens, to try and understand what our opponents might throw at us. We have seen terrible things.

"Yet... what did you do with this perspective, when the worst of the worst was laid out before you? You said, 'I see, and now the other side of the story'. And you flipped the page, and started writing notes. You wrote the story of the best of humanity. The honourable, the kind, the selfless. You wrote about it, yet you also acted like it. You became the thing you were researching. Your selflessness in the face of this challenge has been inspirational. You have worked on a defence that I would be proud to use if I were in the dock. Which, of course, in a manner of speaking, I am.

"I will be up there, arguing with the very best that the Below can throw at us. Judging by a few of the lawyers I know, that could be quite an opponent. If you'd asked me to do this two months ago, I would have broken down. I'd be a gibbering wreck in the corner of the room, clutching my knees and trying to escape the world.

"But now, with you lot behind me, with my hand holding the file that you have helped create, not only am I able, not only am I willing, but I'm bloody *excited* to stand on the greatest of stages in front of the greatest of judges, *excited* to represent each and every one of you, and, most importantly of all, I'm *excited* to point a sturdy finger at this Jurrekker and tell him where to shove it, and say: Sorry mate, Humanity isn't up for debate."

He didn't want a round of applause, or a salute, or some other 'meaningful' over-used symbolic gesture. He didn't really know what he wanted, other than to tell his friends how he felt. His spirit lifted when he saw the light in their eyes return, and the spark in his belly ignited.

He grinned widely and clapped his hands once. He pointed at the board behind him.

"Let's go through it all, just one more time. This is the dress rehearsal. Tomorrow, the tickets are bought, the audience is here, and we're on stage. I say—Let's put on a show."

4 – The First Morning

Waking up on the morning of the case, Felix dressed in his best. He pulled on his comfiest socks, focussing on the ritual of dressing. The winter sun was slow in rising behind a wall of cloud, and he had breakfasted alone in the semi-gloom of a single candle.

A single grapefruit. This wasn't his normal breakfast, but today, for whatever reason, it's what he chose. He regretted it after the first bite, but told himself that if he can't handle a grapefruit, how could he handle the burden he carried?

By the time his companions had arrived, his nerves had twisted and curled into mush. He tried not to show it, but made a poor attempt.

"It's okay," said Helda, arm on his shoulder. She was carrying her customary travelsack, stuffed full to bursting. She hefted it onto the floor. "This time in a week or so, we'll be laughing."

"Or," said Yetty, "We'll all be dead, so we don't care."

Felix laughed despite himself. He looked around. "Anyone seen Cherinda?"

They all shook their heads and waited for her to arrive. They chatted about small things until Furbo spotted her walking down the street towards them. Her expression was plain, unreadable, but her aura was pulsing slowly between dark blue and dark red.

"Morning," Furbo said to her. She smiled, nodded, and raised an arm.

"So, how do we—" Felix said, before his ears were ripped out, and his brain impaled on a beam of light. His mind filled with sparks and lights, and he glimpsed colours and shapes normally beyond the human spectrum. His life, his whole experience, birth to death, spun in upon itself and twisted, the juices of his being coagulating into lumps of forever. Endless swarms of eyes watched as he—

He was yanked from this experience by a sense of tremendous falling, and, blinking, found himself standing on a stone floor. Washing feelings of nausea buffeted him.

He, along with Furbo, Helda, and Yetty, collapsed onto all fours. His brain felt like it had been frozen, and was melting, piece by piece.

"Oh, sorry," came a mellifluous voice. To Felix's ears it was warbled, garbled, like the voice of a nightmare. A clap, and his focus immediately returned to him, the aftershock of his nausea dwindling to nothing. Shaking his head, he stood, staring at his surroundings. It was the courtyard outside the courtroom at Placenamia.

He stared wide-eyed at Cherinda, standing a few feet away. She smiled innocently.

"I've been told that Transporting can be quite a bizarre sensation for humans. I'll give you a bit more warning next time."

"I-I… I saw such things…" gasped Furbo, still on the floor. "Wh-what… did we…"

Helda stood, and dragged the old man to his feet. "Oh, we've had worse," she said, despite looking a little boggle-eyed and pale.

Felix swallowed, thankful for his light breakfast. "Well. Here we are then." He looked around him, taking in the sights. The courtroom looked the same dishevelled, decrepit building it was the last time he saw it. There was no one hanging around outside, which was not normal. It's as if the world was not awake, yet the South country was bright. There should be activity, but Felix had other things on his mind.

He rubbed his hands together against the chill. "Shall we head in?"

~

Upon pushing open the familiar door to the Defence Counsel's chambers, Felix's heart skipped a beat. What he saw was completely different to what he had expected. It was definitely the right door into the right room, but it was like the door led them somewhere else, not the slightly-damp chambers he had spent dozens of nervous hours in. Inside, they found all their prepared documentation was already waiting for them, stacked neatly against a far wall.

The defendant's chambers were always austere, but never in quite so intimidating a way. What used to be simple, cheap material had been replaced. Polished wood of some dark grain filled the room. It was dark and menacing, and every chair and table was made of it, not to mention the floor and ceiling. Along the two longer walls were bookshelves stretching from floor to ceiling, packed with uniformly serious looking books, each marked with a number in ancient script. There had to be thousands, Felix had thought upon entering. They certainly weren't there the last time he had visited.

"What do you think of those?" he asked Furbo.

"Let's see…" the older man replied. He walked over and plucked a volume at random.

"Pick a number," he said.

Felix's mind went blank. "Uh," he mumbled, desperate to complete this unbelievably basic test of his mental acuity. He snapped his fingers, and all but shouted "Forty-two!" He looked a little too pleased with himself.

Furbo flipped the pages until he landed on Felix's choice, and screwed his eyes trying to read a passage. After twenty or so seconds of silence, Furbo let out a long whistle.

"*Quite* extraordinary. Take a look." He held open the page he was on so Felix could see. "It's not in Common, or even Elder, but some other language that I don't know even the name of. Yet… I can read the words. Go on, try."

Felix looked at Furbo, trying to figure if he was being pranked. Seeing only earnest on the older man's face, he moved his gaze to the page. The shapes on the page were quite bizarre. Circles, triangles, seemingly random splashes, scratches. It was as if a child had let their imagination run wild with whatever came to hand, be it paint, charcoal, a pencil. But it was… readable. As his eyes passed over the lettering, words formed in his head. He began reading aloud without meaning to.

"Thus, upon conclusion of the case of Hyyerii the Merciless, whomsoupon causes sacrilege by sacrifice of the unwilling for demonstrably selfish purposes must, upon death, face judgement from the incumbent soul-weighing deity and explain his reasoning, upon receiving no such reasoning the accused must expect five-hundred-thousand years of torment for each case of sacrifice, unless it can be demonstrated that the reasonable deity would—"

Felix shook his head. His eyes felt out of focus. He stared at Furbo, his mouth hanging open.

The two men turned to see Cherinda enter the room, trailed by Yetty, Helda and Racelsus. The light spilled from her and filled the room with radiance. The dark brown furniture seemed deep and warming, the books full of promise.

"Interesting, right?" Furbo chuckled. He turned to take in the rest of the room and clapped the book shut. "I'm going to make an educated guess based on what Cherinda explained to us a little while back." He gestured to the shelves. "I'd say these books contain precedents. A whole lot of them. Cases from humans, beasts, demons, perhaps. Am I close?" he said, turning to the Celestial. She smiled and nodded, looking pleased. Furbo nodded in return, then continued, encouraged. "That one you read out was just one part of one page. I'd say that book has at least…." He flipped the book open again and let a few pages flutter. "…two thousand pages. At a quick glance, this room has probably…" he rapidly flitted his finger a few times, speed-counting the rows. "…twenty-five thousand books, give or take a few? I don't know exactly how many cases there are per page, but it's reasonable to say that there's a whole lot of information here. I don't know if it's chronologically stored, or part of some system I can't comprehend. It's all quite fascinating. But, the point. I suspect that these books contain the sum total of anything anyone has ever deemed worthy of legal attention."

He idly picked at a fingernail. "I could be wrong."

Cherinda laughed pleasantly, giving him a round of applause. "Actually, you're rather spot-on!" Yetty joined in the light applause, with an expression of severe pomposity, and with a nasal voice, said:

"Oh, I say, very nice work, professor, you shall have to regale me with more of your parlour tricks, oh I say indeed."

Furbo gave her a good-natured smile.

Felix rubbed his eyes with a thumb and forefinger. "But why could I understand it? What I read, I mean. It was just… shapes."

"It's written in Allspeak," said Cherinda.

Felix looked at her as if she had said it was written by bees. He shrugged, in a 'what on earth are you on about' way.

"It's readable by anything that *can* read," she continued, then gestured to Furbo. "I'd put that back if I were you. It's technically heretical for non-higher beings or their direct representatives to handle them, punishable by… oh, what was it..?"

She walked over and picked a book from a seemingly identical shelf to those around it. Flipping to a page, she traced a finger down the page.

"Loss of one eye, one finger, one toe, one tooth, one ear, or equivalent," she said, snapping the book shut, and smiling at them.

Furbo's smile faltered and he looked pale. He handled the book as if it were a sleeping snake, and proffered it to Felix, who took it reluctantly. He put it back in the section of the shelf that it had come from. Yetty watched him.

"Do I count? Am I a… direct representative?" she asked.

The Celestial considered, then shook her head. "I don't think you count, I'm sorry. It's Felix only."

Yetty shrugged, but eyed the books again.

Cherinda coughed politely, drawing their attention, then gestured to the table in the centre of the room.

"Shall we?"

They settled around the table, and, for the last time, went over their prep. Felix got four minutes in before he turned to Cherinda, an exasperated look on his face.

"I'm conce—"

Just then, a knock at the door stopped him.

Is it time? I'm not ready… I need more time!

The door opened, and a short, fat man was waiting on the other side. He had a jolly face and was as wide as he was tall. His enormous moustaches drooped down to his belt, and his thick arms were holding a tray, balanced on his protruding gut. It was towering with cakes, biscuits, some sandwiches, and—

Felix sprang up and dashed over to the man, and all but snatched the steaming mug from the tray. Holding it in both hands, be inhaled deeply, the familiar scent massaging his frayed nerves. He didn't notice the man chuckle, then stride into the room, playing the tray in front of his team. He nodded to Cherinda, then left, without saying a word.

Once Felix had taken his first, beautiful sip, he returned to the table. Helda was onto her second tart already, and even Cherinda was examining something small, white and chocolatey. She turned to him as he settled, looking and feeling so much calmer.

"Better?" she asked.

Felix cracked his neck from side to side.

"Oh, yes. I'm ready," he said. And he meant it.

~

Cherinda sat resplendently at the other end of the table. Her usual glow had subsided somewhat since entering the chamber, and was gold tinged with blue. Felix thought this gave her an air of melancholic nobility, and once again was struck dumb by the sight of her. How many mortals had seen such perfection?

"Are you listening, Felix?"

He blinked and shook his head, only now aware that she had been talking to him. The others were bunched together at the other end of the long table, muttering about something. They were out of earshot. Felix smoothed his hair back, trying not to make it obvious what he was thinking about.

"Absolutely. Please, carry on."

She looked at him with a slight narrowing of the eyes before turning her head away, gaze downward.

"As I was saying… Jurrekker is not what people think. He isn't a being of pure evil. I'm convinced he doesn't want to kill everything for the sake of it. There are two halves of him. One half is similar to the legends. He is full of fire and fury, instinct and competition. The other half is driven by logic, cold and calculating. That is what drives him. As he has aged, his fiery side has diminished to an ember, and he is almost all ice these days."

Felix had felt, too, that as he had aged that he was more ice and less fire. He had begun losing patience with those of the opposite fiery persuasion, reacting more irritably than he might once have. He couldn't help but wonder if he and the demon would get on.

She looked at him again, and he had the terrifying feeling she could read him like a book. *Can everyone in this damn room read minds?*

Felix coughed, then started. "What difference does that make?"

"It means you can't appeal to his emotions. Time was, perhaps. But now, there simply is nothing there to appeal to. Emotions do not control him. So, you will have to beat him in other ways."

"Well, I was planning to beat him using evidence. I hadn't considered just asking him nicely."

His attempt at humour didn't work. She shifted uncomfortably then, her aura turning a dark shade of greenish-red.

"I'm going to explain something to you now that very few people understand. Higher powers, like me, like Jurrekker or Habeus, we are above you mortals in many ways you can't understand, and many you can. We are simply better."

"Don't worry, it won't all go to my head," scoffed Felix.

"Please, let me carry on. This is not easy for me to say. There are *rules*."

He remembered then that this wasn't just some ordinary person he was talking to. The sorts of things that go on in her head… He literally couldn't comprehend. He straightened up, all thoughts at joking gone, and listened. She looked at him then, directly in the eyes, and began speaking with some small strained effort.

"We have an understanding of the universe in ways you cannot fathom, I mean you *literally* cannot… but we are not infallible. We do not know everything, we make mistakes, we can be blinded by oversight and can simply get things wrong.

"We were similar to you, once. Long ago. Jurrekker and I have existed for aeons. All that we know we learned through experience. Jurrekker has been duped, tricked, humiliated and outwitted thousands of times in his long life, by kings and foolish farmboys alike. But, the difference is, each time… he learns. He remembers. And the next time someone tries to best him in the same way, they lose. He has lost in every way you can think of, and he hasn't forgotten a single time.

"What I'm saying is this: He has brought this case *now*, of all times, because he thinks he will win. He is *convinced* of it. He has bided his time, waiting, always waiting. I am blinded by my own experience, and, like him, cannot possibly see how he can fail to persuade Habeus. If it were up to me, if I were the one up there making the arguments... I think you would be doomed."

Felix frowned. *Doomed. That's not a word I expected her to use, somehow.* She stared at him.

"But there must be a way. There simply *must* be. You, Felix, must find it. You are the last hope of humanity. You must beat this demon at his own game."

She stopped, and Felix noticed she was flushed and out of breath. It had been an exertion for Cherinda to speak. She had never looked so dishevelled in the time he'd known her. Her aura was deep, muddied red.

"So, no pressure then," he remarked.

She smiled, and let out a long breath.

"Exactly. No pressure, but get this wrong and all life as we know it gets wiped out."

Felix rubbed his eyes with his hand. He looked over to see Racelsus staring at him. He frowned. Before he could speak, there was a knock at the door, and a spindly woman with hair that brushed the floor entered. She raised a hand as she spoke, palm facing outwards. It alarmed Felix when he spotted the mouth moving on her palm. It slid around as it spoke, gliding across the skin of her hand. The voice itself was harsh.

"It is time," the mouth said, and the woman left, leaving the door open.

The group exchanged glances. Felix stood, faced Furbo and Helda. He tugged at his collars, straightened his sleeves, and asked: "How do I look?"

They looked at one another, and Helda, fiddling with something in her pack, said: "Have you got anything a little less... boring?"

Furbo nodded. "I was thinking perhaps puffs and streamers would be just the ticket," he added.

"And some sort of floppy hat, with fur trims and a bell on the back," said Yetty, stroking her chin pensively.

Cherinda, peered at him. "You also need a cape. Pink and yellow spots."

Felix smiled despite the circumstances. "Great, now if I lose, I can blame my lack of frippery."

He strode to the door. They followed.

Journal Entry L: Necromancer

Reference case [BHvHK] (BeyHye v. HyrKin), year 1330, Judge Detson presiding.

I've never really had anyone close to me, so I haven't personally experienced loss. However, I'm human, so can, if not relate, understand how painful it must be.

I can, however, understand how painful it must be to see your recently deceased loved one's corpse reanimated and shuffling around performing menial labour for a careless Necromancer.

Necromancy: Magic Involving Death. Not everyone's first choice when enrolling for Magic College, I'm sure, but for some, it's their one true calling. Largely it seems to be concerned with either prolonging one's own life, or reanimating the bodies of us mere mortals. Or perhaps calling on the spirits of the deceased for all manner of bizarre circumstances.

My client, Beylia, had recently, tragically, lost her beloved. He had been fighting a terrible illness for months, and, after a bout of heightened symptoms, succumbed.

She had mourned, wept, attended his burial and had finally tried to move on with her life.

Then, she had bumped into him, quite literally, when out in the market some weeks later. His face was slackened, his gaze empty, but it was him. She had screamed and fainted, he had barely reacted at all.

It transpires he was under the thrall of a local novice Necromancer called Hyreit. Upon waking from her faint, Beylia had seen Hyreit placing a hand on her husband's shoulder, seen some dark magic pass from hand to body, and had realised what was happening with alarming acuity quite unusual for my sort of client.

She had then acted in a way that was not unusual for my type of client, when she had tried to elbow the necromancer in the face.

Our case argued that it was simply unethical to 'raise the dead', willy-nilly, without concern for the loved ones of the departed. We hadn't expected the defendant's legal team to whip out a consent form—signed, dotted, dated by the deceased—that explicitly granted full permission for Post-Burial Excisement and Bodily Re-Animation. Flabbergasted, our client demanded an explanation of the small, nervous death-wizard.

The witness for the prosecution at that moment had filled in the blank. None other than the ex-husband himself, or rather, his corpse, had taken the stand. His words were slurred, his movements clumsy, but for all that, he was here, testifying on own terms.

"Hi Beylie-girl," he had grunted. She had turned her head away, unable to look him in the eye. He carried on.

"I met Hyreit. We made a deal. No more pain. A year of ex-per-i-men-tal ser-vi-tude." His slack mouth had struggled with those words. "After, I come home to you. I had hoped not like this."

She had looked at him then, tears streaming, breaths coming ragged.

"I love you Beylie-girl," he moaned.

They had embraced then, all complicated emotions forgotten for one moment of forbidden affection.

Legally, with the forms all perfectly prepared and signed, we had no recourse. But, we requested that the other party offer information about the terms of this experimental servitude, which they graciously agreed to. The necromancer took the stand.

She explained, without ever making eye contact with the complainant. Effectively, once the body dies, it degenerates. The complex brain-machinery withers and rots, followed by the body. She had theorised that it might be possible to retain the brain in a state close to that in life, but it would need a willing participant to make himself available for 'reanimation' instantly after death. So, our novice had spent months hanging around hospitals, trying to find a good subject. That's when she had met our man. They had talked. She had learned of his illness and his pain, and his heart-breaking desire to end it all, but his conflict about leaving the love of his life behind.

They had found a compromise.

He would die, and she would try to bring him to life, as close to life as possible. She would perform a sequence of experimental necromancies to try and revive him, and, her data collected, she would return him to her beloved.

Unfortunately, the experiment was ruined by sheer freak chance, when the two erstwhile lovers had reunited during the wizards 'social conditioning' phase of the experiment.

They had come to a new agreement. In exchange for assistance in Hyreit's dark arts, Beylia and her husband would be able to reunite. Beylia would do her utmost to help her new employer in bringing her ambitious plants to fruition, and she would be able to spend her evenings with her true love, who was now more mobile than he had been in years, and pain-free.

For once, it seemed each party was happy. Well, every party was at least not distraught, which makes a nice change.

I'll be honest. I haven't checked in on these guys since our case a few years ago. I don't think I have the heart to find out if it worked or not.

~journal entry ends

5 – The Start

As he passed down the corridor between the chambers and the courtroom, Felix felt calm. He concentrated on putting one foot in front of the other. He ran over a few lines of his opening speech, but he knew he had it memorised. It was just a calming ritual, something to give him a sense of control.

Walking through the large double door to the courtroom proper, he glanced up, then frowned. The worn-out statue, the one that might have had wings and might have held rhubarb. The blindfolded figure. It was gone.

That wasn't the only difference. The courtroom was the same shape, the same size, it had the same no-smoking sign, but... There was something new about the place. The paint still needed redoing, but instead of feeling dank and mouldy, it felt resilient and ancient. As if painting over it would tarnish some piece of history. The smell was no longer unpleasant, but nostalgic. The scuffs on the wooden chairs and tables weren't shoddy, they were characterful. Was this the effect the case about to be fought, or was this his own homesickness, a feeling of coming home?

The court had been the first place he had felt a part of. He had fought his way up, and, through his own dedication, forged a path for himself. This courthouse was where he had done that, time after time, proving to others and himself that he was capable, that he was dependable, that he was useful. That he had a purpose.

He closed his eyes and banished that thought.

You can get all bleary-eyed once you've won.

If you win.

He shuffled past the galleries, through the small swing-door separating the crowd from the professionals, and settled himself at the table, followed by Cherinda, Furbo, Helda, Racelsus and Yetty.

Yetty produced a pipe, but Furbo tapped her shoulder and pointed at the sign.

"Bloody strange customs, these southerners," she muttered, putting her pipe away. Felix appreciated her acquiescence. He didn't quite fancy being held in contempt of court in this particular case.

Helda was finding room for her enormous bag. It took almost another person's worth of space. Furbo considered saying something to her, but decided discretion was the better part of valour.

Not for the first time, nor the last time, Felix thought: *I'd kill for a cup of tea.*

~

Felix had to admit, this was a new one for him. An actual universal covenant, old as time itself, being fought here, in the beaten-up courthouse of Placenamia. On one side, his client, the Celestial calling herself Cherinda, glowing gently, a picture of calm serenity. Across from him, the prosecution; the plaintiff, the demon known as Jurrekker, all wings, teeth, muscles, hooves, and smoke.

He was, in many ways, exactly what Felix had thought he would look like. Tall wasn't the right word—huge, more like. Muscled like a gorilla, enormous curled horns bursting from his head. He hadn't even glanced over at the defence yet, so Felix couldn't tell what sort of eyes he had. He'd be willing to bet they'd be dark, sinister, and terrifying.

Felix dragged his gaze from the monstrous form of Jurrekker and to what appeared to be his opposite: the prosecuting 'lawyer'. He was wearing an impeccably smart dark-brown suit. It had subtle beige pinstripes in a way not dissimilar to his own. As Felix looked closer, the vertical lines seemed to shift slightly, expanding and contracting like... like...

The suit wasn't breathing, was it?

Not a single crease or speck of muck could be seen on him. His head was completely bald, in fact, his whole face seemed utterly hairless, including brows and eyelashes. His eyes and mouth seemed a little too large, and perhaps a little too… off-centre. Almost like someone had tried to draw a human face but hadn't quite got the perspective correct. He was conferring with his client, a steady stream that occasionally floated loud enough for Felix to hear, but was in some language he couldn't understand.

Cherinda leaned over to Felix. Her whispered voice was like the susser of leaves on a summer's evening compared to the sounds coming from the prosecution. "It's Krurikkun, what you might call Demon-Speech. Rotten language, far too many harsh syllables and angry words."

She considered a moment. "Actually, some of their poetry is quite effective. The problem with Huleyah, Celestial-Speak, is that it's all very suitable for a wonderful story about a bluebird riding a current, or a seed sprouting in autumn, but it's simply awful for getting a good nasty bit of imagery. The best poets can use both languages in one verse. In fact, I think I see the poet Sheydele out there, why don't I see if—"

She noticed his raised eyebrow.

The Celestial blushed. "Oh, well, maybe that can wait. Let me listen…" she cocked her head slightly and waited. "The lawyer is saying something like, 'do not interrupt, no matter what you might hear', and the brute Jurrekker is replying, goodness his accent is thick, he's saying: 'I'm not above cuddling that human fool if he gets under my skin, and I could do it before anyone could stop me.' Is that cuddling, or flaying? It's hard to say. It really is a strong accent."

Felix coughed and suggested his opinion on the usefulness of debating whether the demon had threatened to cuddle him or flay him.

"Now he's saying something else, he's saying: 'I think that blathering Celestial idiot is listening to us, look at her concentrating so hard, she really is an idiot.'" She snapped her mouth shut and rolled her eyes towards the painted ceiling, studying the frescos with silent interest.

Felix turned to regard the audience. They were all arranged in the same way as any old crowd would be in the Placenamia courtroom; they sat in neat rows, chatting quietly to each other, just like ordinary people. Except—they were far from that. *Far* from that.

He wasn't sure what he had expected. Some part of him assumed there would be an audience made up of interested members of the public, or perhaps, more realistically, no audience at all. Instead, the galleries were packed with all manner of minor deities, celestials, demons, spirits, creatures of all shapes, sizes, auras and origins. Some looked human. Others were... not.

A creature seemingly consisting of nothing but a swirling mass of tentacles conversed with a solid floating cube of metal. An enormous brain, balanced on a single, worm-like leg, nodded as its neighbour, a giant furry water droplet explained something or other. His eyes were drawn to an ebbing hole of pure darkness. As he watched, the darkness seemed to grow, pulling him in. A voice in his head shook him back to focus.

Hello.

He looked down to see a frog, standing on the head of a stack of books. The books themselves didn't seem to mind. It was busy laughing having shared a joke with a spinning grey-green blur.

Felix's eyes widened, and he grinned as he recognised the speaker.

"Great Croaker! I hadn't expected to see you here."

The frog nodded. **Well. I am.**

Felix wasn't sure what to say. "So, you're a deity now, are you?"

Yes. I died. It's okay. The swamp is safe.

"Oh, I am glad." He racked his brains, trying to remember.

"How's—" and Felix made a sound like a burp trying to cough.

The frog didn't move a muscle, but a feeling of happiness emanated from him, washing over Felix.

Your pronunciation needs work. But not much. She is very good. She protects them now. Thank you for asking. But, my spawn is old. Soon she will pass. Do you still know the wizard?

"Oh, Huppity? Ah, I'm sad to say, he died a little while ago. Terrible accident. He was trying to stop a flood, but it sort of went wrong, and he... well, the details aren't important."

That is sad news.

There was a short silence. Despite the situation, it wasn't uncomfortable. Just peaceful, remembering old acquaintances.

The frog turned to hop away. The book beneath it giggled as if tickled. Great Croaker swivelled his head back to Felix.

Two pieces of advice. One. Death must, so life can. Two. Do not look at Mistress Black. She has no propriety.

Good luck, swamp-friend Felix.

And he hopped off.

"Friend of yours?" asked Racelsus, perched on the end of the defence counsel's desk, her cage once again polished and gleaming.

Felix took a moment to react, as he was trying to make sense of the words. Then he nodded, and meant it. "Yes. An old friend…"

The words drifted away, and Racelsus did not press him. He spent the next minutes in silent contemplation.

~

The sound of a gong rang, and up on the dais a door opened. An ancient man entered. He wore a simple robe of black, knotted with a thin belt, and he had a curious beard. It was enormously long and tied in a single knot, swinging as he walked. Felix stood up, his thoughts, arguments, everything forgotten. This was him, *actually him*, Habeus himself, the figure from legend upon whom it was said the first dispute was settled. Every snaking tendril of law's history winds its way back to that first moment, the creation of the pact.

He looked a little underwhelming.

As the gong faded, the room fell to silence. He introduced himself as Habeus, and said would be judging today's proceedings. He began to outline his expectations in a deep rumbling voice:

"I will be acting as the chairman of these proceedings today, as I am truly neutral. We have decided, the three higher powers selected, that we will rule on humanity's continued existence. If a unanimous verdict is not agreed upon, then a majority will suffice. We will take a vote before we begin, and will take more votes as we progress. If ever a majority is reached, the case will be concluded. Humanity rests in the balance."

He paused to let this line settle into the minds of everyone listening, and continued. His voice wasn't loud, but it drew the focus of the entire chamber effortlessly.

"However. The law is often not a simple black and white set of instructions. I am as aware as the lowliest lawyer"—and he glanced at Felix—"that the application of law is mutable and organic, it will grow and adapt to suit the circumstance. This applies not just to petty squabbles between mortals, but also to the laws we higher beings live by. With that in mind, I will remind the attendees here the Universal Truths, as set by the Universe itself. They are:

1. Each entity is entitled to exist upon its own terms and meet its needs for survival.

2. Death must, so life can.

3. Energy cannot be created or destroyed, only applied and moved, *and any being attempting to circumvent that deserves everything they get.*

4. Sentience begets superiority.

5. Virtue and Turpitude are relative and have no upper or lower limits."

Habeus sat down after this and looked around the room. Both Cherinda and Jurrekker met his gaze without faltering. He didn't bother to look at Felix.

"Let us take our initial vote. Those higher powers who agree that humanity should be revoked, raise your hand."

The demon to Felix's left lifted a meaty arm. Habeus nodded.

"And those who disagree, raise a hand."

Cherinda lifted her arm. Habeus nodded again.

"I abstain for now. Therefore, no majority. We are tied. The trial will go ahead as planned." He produced a small, worn gavel from a sleeve, and tapped it lightly on the plate in front of him. After slipping the gavel away, he gestured to the hairless man in the suit.

"You may now present your case."

~

The man nodded and stood, and it was only when he started talking did Felix notice he had no teeth. The arch of his mouth and the length of his slightly-too-long tongue gave his words a slurpy overtone.

"Thank you, judge. The case we have brought here today is concerning a most ancient matter, the matter of humanity, and their continued existence." He paused, seeing Habeus was about to interrupt.

"Rule One states that each entity is entitled to exist," said Habeus. His stare bored into the prosecutor, two inescapable blank eyes. The prosecutor bowed low, one arm tucked under, one arm outstretched.

"Rule One does state that, indeed, but we intend to present why the rise of the Human race in fact twists and perverts this natural law."

"Proceed," commanded Habeus, settling back into his simple wooden chair.

6 – Openings

The prosecutor straightened up and walked smartly to the centre of the concourse. The area in front of the judge's table was wide enough for a lawyer to stroll around while posturing, and any good lawyer knew that this was the way to draw attention to yourself. It is natural to follow movement, and apparently not just for humans. He held one hand behind his back, the other free to gesture for emphasis.

"Firstly, let us consider the wider picture. The natural life of a creature in the wild is thus: Born, survive, find food, reproduce, die. One must always be aware of predators and prey, but death must, so life can. Rule Two, of course. Some find themselves high on the chain, and must fear only each other, and some are low, and must remain cunning. The human is the only race that grips this state of affairs and tears it asunder, rearranging it to suit his own desires. Not needs, *desires.*"

He—*or, should we say 'it'?*—spat the word out as if it were a mouldy grape. A small amount of smoke and spittle vented from his mouth as he did.

"Humanity once, many moons ago, lived thusly: exploring the wilds, taking what they needed, hunting and being hunted, just like any other lesser being. If this were still the case, we would have no problem. Another piece of life, living as it must. Rule One." He paused then, and stopped walking, eyes closed.

"Then, they changed. Unfortunately, the world and the natural way of things changed as a result. Species *driven* to *extinction,* countless individual creatures born *just to die,* with no chance to fulfil their own divine right to exist, as per Rule One. For to exist is not simply to be born, it is to explore, to reproduce, to hunt or be hunted, to *live!*"

He had clenched his fists. He let them unfurl, slowly lowering his arms.

"Nothing else perverts this natural order. Nothing so impinges the sanctity of the First Rule as humanity."

Felix felt uncomfortable. How was he going to argue that humanity was not what it was? He had expected this argument, of course, but hearing it spoken in this context…

The hairless man continued.

"As if twisting the fate of all creatures humanity deems *lesser*—and I use that word *relatively*, of course—humanity has turned its eyes upon itself. Invisible divides split it into the haves and have-nots, the rich and the poor. The poverty-stricken and the immeasurably wealthy. They drive each other from hearth and home, other races and lower-status humans caught up in the tides of great wars they have no stake or interest in, yet are compelled to experience. Torture, pillage, slavery, all manner of despicable acts found nowhere else in nature. Humanity's crimes victimise everything, *humanity included.*

"Thus. Humanity has no place in the natural world, for he has turned his back on all things natural. They pace themselves ever faster trying to bend the universe to their will, caring nothing for the tide of misery and destruction in their wake. Their continual incline of population and consumption cannot continue forever, for soon their own planet will be stripped to a barren husk. Their treatment of other sentient life is abominable, their relentless consumption and destruction of their planet is reprehensible, and their short-sightedness can carry on no longer. We shall prove, through evidence, witnesses, and logic, that humanity must end—for the good of everything."

The man paused, then bowed his head.

"Thus concludes my statement."

He excused himself back to his bench.

Felix's throat was dry. Why did he never remember to drink? Habeus gestured to him.

"Your response, please."

Felix stood, and walked over to the podium with as much fake confidence he could dredge together.

7 – Felix

Felix could feel his heart in his ears. He clenched his teeth together, a bad habit picked up from somewhere. He stood at his post, staring around the room, trying the age-old trick of reading the judge's mood. This time was a little different. The judge wasn't just some old lawyer, enjoying the easy ride for a while after forty years long service. It was an ancient figure of legend, who happened to be completely, cosmically neutral in every way. The perfect judge, perhaps?

Wrong.

Judges are perfect in their imperfection. Their little prejudices, their experiences that shape how they see things. You see them react when you go into the gory detail, so you hammer that point home. You see them impassively trying to keep a brave face when you talk about the poor child victim, so you pluck those heartstrings. To break that steely exterior. That's the point.

We judge each other based on our experiences of life, and so justice is served.

Sure, judges are supposed to be blank slates, mere vessels for neutral justice—but that's not how humanity works.

Trying to sway Habeus was like preaching to a flowerpot.

The worst part though…. Was that the points the other lawyer were making… They were true. All of them. Humanity *is* disgusting.

We're a seething, steaming, boiling mass of scathing repugnancy.

But.

We didn't ask to exist. We weren't given the option. We were dragged from whatever primordial soup we were floating in and forced, kicking and screaming, to forge an existence. Yes, we have done things wrong. Yes, some humans are scum. But most are not, and we do not deserve to be punished for what anybody would have done in the same situation. You can't plant a weed and complain when it flowers.

Time to teach these cosmic bullies how humanity handles itself.

8 – Openings II

Felix leant on the desk behind him, looking like he didn't know where to start. He feigned indecisiveness. After pausing for perhaps a hair too long, he turned to face Jurrekker.

"How old are you, Jurrekker?" Felix said, barely reacting when the name caused him to taste fire.

The demon did not respond. Felix waited.

"Unless he is being cross-examined, he does not have to answer," Habeus intoned.

Whoops.

Felix gave a sad nod. "That's true. My apologies. Human error. I hope it doesn't count against me."

Habeus gave no indication either way.

Yikes!

"Suffice it to say, my learned colleague here is old. As are all you higher beings. Humanity is not. We are not higher beings, we do not have arcane intelligence, cosmic understanding. What we do have is a life, and dreams, hopes, dark thoughts, and the means to act on them.

"However, we never asked for these. We didn't ask to understand grief, or the feeling of worthlessness, or spite. We were formed in this way. Nature moulded us into what we are today. We did what we had to do to survive, and, piece by piece, we changed. No one human has stood up to declare humanity should be cruel. Individual humans discovered that on their own, through hard lives of pain. Humans hardened themselves to the world, and to each other, because without that, we would have become extinct. Anything else in the same situation would have acted the same way. Raise the slugs to feel what we feel, to know what we know, and before you can say 'pattern' they'll be farming out ants and fighting civil wars. Nature is cruel.

"However, there is good. For every nasty human, there is a kind one. For every thief, there is a charitable soul. For every murderer, there is a doctor, a healer, a nurse. We occupy every step of the spectrum, for good and for ill.

"It is my intention to show to you, and the court, that humanity did the best with the hand it was dealt, and we are deserving of a second chance. I ask that if you find, honourable judge, that you agree with anything I show you, then I ask you to find it in your heart to save us. Thank you."

Felix sat down.

"Well done," whispered Furbo, and Helda gave a thumbs up.

Habeus stood. "We will take another vote. Those in favour of the motion to erase humanity, raise your hand." Jurrekker voted in favour, Cherinda against, and Habeus abstained. Felix had expected this, but he had secretly hoped he might have swayed Habeus anyway. The judge stood and spoke.

"There is still no quorum, so we will continue. The prosecution and defence will alternate witnesses, and will each cross examine them. As per normal rules, a reactionary witness or piece of evidence may be called, out of the normal order, if relevant." Another tap of the gavel. "The prosecution will begin. Call your first witness."

He sat then, and the prosecution lawyer gestured to an aide, who opened a side door, behind which a small figure was waiting.

"We call our first witness… The goblin, Burrimo."

I know that name, thought Felix.

Journal Entry M: Wizard

Reference case [GCvGC] (GurTen v. GurTen/GurTen), year 1334, judge Purnisto presiding.

There was an interesting case involving a client of mine who had managed to split her essence in two, and was trying to reunite her splintered soul.

It started innocently enough. Gurrinko, who told me I could call her The Wizardess (though I'm not certain she was serious, but don't mess with Wizardesses), had reached a certain mature age.

She had begun to spiral into self-doubt, seeing her life stretched out before her. All she could see were shattered dreams and failed endeavours.

Classic mid-life crisis, basically.

After months of feverish research, she had discovered the means to perform a spell that would solve her problems.

It was to be a Rite of Splitting, she explained to her assembled entourage of colleagues and sycophants, and through it, if successful, she would split her essence right down the middle. This would create two copies of Gurrinko, each identical, allowing her to continue her life-long study of the arcane as well as pursue her childhood dream of being a baker. Each copy would, in theory, be 'incomplete' in some way, but that shouldn't cause an issue, she crooned.

The spell worked. Actually, it worked too well. Instead of splitting her twice, it split her three times. Immediately following the ritual, after the dust had cleared, three Gurrinkos stood, each eyeing each other warily.

The first had explained the situation to the others, as well as the plan, and the second had seen the logic and heartily agreed. These two splinters were full-figured and bright, each a mirror of the other. The third, however, did not want to go along with their plan. A plaintive, gaunt spectre of the once colourful Gurrinko, it strove to be reunited with its former soul-splinters, to feel whole again.

Many arguments resulted, as you can imagine. Bitter disagreements that did nothing but entrench their original positions. Eventually, the two primary splinters decided to abandon the third, casting her out into the wilderness. When she returned, more haggard than ever, they locked her in the basement of their house, feeding it morsels, daring not to let it die.

They had, after a few weeks of research, concluded that this third splinter had comprised all their bitterness and spite, and so deserved to be locked up. For the greater good.

Many moons later, the third splinter had escaped, and, with no other option, sought help from other wizards. Many ignored her. The two primary splinters held a lot of political sway, and being such a piteous wreck, this third splinter was easy to ignore. One wizard, however, decided enough was enough. Taking this issue right to the Council of Magery, this kind helper demanded financial support to take the heartless Gurrinko to court. The Council disagreed, and so the wizard came to Lunchers & Co, the perfect legal representative for the down-on-your-luck and got-no-cash-types of this great country.

Allegations of torture, false imprisonment and neglect; it was quite a heavy set of charges.

The case wound up getting all very metaphysical. Is it possible to torture oneself without one's consent? Clearly, these were three separate bodies. Were they three separate people? It didn't help that they all clearly shared some sort of mind-bond, and all responded in the same way to each question or point raised.

I had realised that if they did share feelings, then the two first splinters must be feeling rotten inside for the way they treated their soul-sister. They too must have felt the lonely, dark betrayal, yet they continued.

The judge ruled against us in that case, saying that as these people were in fact the same mind, they could not take legal action against themselves without all parties agreeing. But, it didn't matter. The first two shards had looked so tired and worn out by the time the trial concluded that they had all agreed to merge their soul again.

I chatted to Gurrinko's complete form once the ceremony was complete. I wanted to know if she felt she had learned anything.

"I have no idea," she had told me.

~journal entry ends

9 – The Goblin

Felix's eyes screwed shut, racking his brain, trying to remember. He clicked his fingers and turned to Yetty. "I know this goblin! He was a client of mine once, a long time ago. He, ah… oh."

Yetty clenched her teeth. "Is this the goblin who…" she asked.

"Yes. The one where we…"

"Oh, no," Yetty said.

"What is it?" Cherinda asked Felix, a look of concern on her face. Her aura was a pale pink.

Felix fidgeted with his collar as he explained. "We represented him after he was bullied mercilessly by a group of thugs… for no real reason. They tried to frame him with kidnapping and attempted murder of the princess of their household, but we had managed to get him off."

"Oh, that's good then. How did you prove it?" enquired the angel.

"Well… by pulling a few strings and possibly breaking a few laws… It was a rough case. They treated him horribly, and he deserved justice." Felix didn't look at Cherinda as he spoke, so he didn't spot her confused expression.

The door at the end of the chamber clanked open, and all heads turned to watch.

The goblin looked small and sad as he wandered over to the witness stand. He had clearly seen a few rough years. Whereas once he was slight, now he was scrawny. His hair was matted and had clumps missing, and his eyes, so full of life before, were empty. He looked up at Felix, who tried a smile, but the goblin didn't return it. Burrimo was tucking an arm into his body, leaning over it, hiding it in the folds of his ragged brown clothing.

Oh, what's happened to you, you poor creature?

Felix had hoped that after his case, the goblin would have found security and peace as a respected member of the royal guard, or perhaps some other outfit that would give him the life of adventure he so craved. The fact he was here indicated that this hadn't happened.

After the goblin was settled, Habeus spoke to the prosecutor.

"You may begin your questioning."

The bald man stood up and bowed slightly. *Sarcastically,* thought Felix.

~

"Please state your name for the court," asked the prosecutor, standing straight-backed.

"I'm Burrimo," mumbled the witness. His eyes were down, looking at nothing. He looked very small up in the stand, and his voice was quiet and hoarse.

"And what do you do, Burrimo?"

The goblin leaned back and gave the prosecutor a thousand-yard stare as he answered.

"Not much anymore."

"Why is that, witness?" the prosecutor pressed.

Burrimo ruffled a little, and unfolded an arm from the folds of his clothes. He raised it high for all to see. It ended in a mottled stump, halfway down the forearm. It looked painful and appeared to ooze slightly. The other arm remained tucked away.

"I'm going to ask you how you came to lose your hand, but first: have you ever been in a court before?"

"Hands."

"Apologies, witness, what was that?"

The goblin shuffled some more, and raised his other arm. It looked the same as the first. After a few seconds, he folded his rags over them as best he could, and retreated back into his robe. There was a sympathetic murmur from the watchers behind Felix, and he could feel the pity bubbling within himself. *How?*

"I apologise, witness. But, back to the question. Have you ever been in a courtroom before?"

"Yes."

"Why?"

"I was being bullied by a group of humans. They framed me for attempted kidnapping and murder."

Felix rubbed his forehead. *I can't object to the use of language here when I'm the bloody lawyer who got him off for being bullied... all this does is help show humanity as a rotten bunch of bullies... And I can hardly pick on such a dejected individual! What can I do...?*

"Bullied, you say?" pried the prosecutor, seemingly unbothered about opening old wounds.

The goblin nodded. "Spoiling or stealing my food, deliberately injuring me during training. And, of course, the attempted framing that I mentioned. That was probably the worst part." His eyes were back on the floor. The hairless man folded his arms.

"And why did they do this? To further some agenda, perhaps? To, let's say, collect a hefty ransom or unearth some valuable treasure?"

"No, nothing like that. It was proved that they just did it for the sake of it."

"Poor creature," whispered Helda.

"For the sake of it? No reason at all? Blind luck?" said the prosecutor.

"Well, no, not luck. They did it because they hated anything non-human, and I happened to be nearby."

Felix stood up, hand raised, and hated himself for doing it.

"I object to the suggestion that they hated anything non-human, perhaps they had something against this particular... individual."

"Prosecutor?" asked Habeus.

The prosecutor bowed his head. "Agreed, O Habeus. Could you please clarify, witness?"

The goblin stared at Felix and carried on. "They hated goblins. One of them went to rallies that taught how to hurt us."

I'd forgotten about that part. Damn!

Felix flumped down onto his chair and screwed up his eyes.

The prosecutor gave Felix a withering look and turned back to his witness. "What else did they teach at those rallies?"

"How to torture us in the most painful ways. The trick is to cut the ears. Goblin ears have many times the number of pain sensors that human ears have. Also, how to make jewellery out of our teeth. Apparently it's harder because our teeth are smaller."

The way the goblin flatly said these atrocious things showed just how jaded he had become. He talked of his own brutal treatment as if he were running a stock take at a cake shop. Felix noticed Burrimo's large ears were full of small cuts and nicks, and a few deep gashes.

The hairless man nodded sadly. "What happened after the case?"

"They threw me out."

"Who are they?"

"The Drakarian estate. Saw me as a troublemaker. I tried to find a new job, but no one would go near me. I was tainted. I had nowhere to go."

"Where did you go, witness?"

Felix didn't know if this was genuine concern in the prosecutor's voice, or if it was just an act. He thought of Ettyson.

Nothing new there, then.

"Eventually, having nowhere else to go, I was drafted into the army. I was to be used as a front-ranker. Given a spear and just left to stand in front of the more important people. At least they would feed me. I saw one engagement, but got shoved from behind as we moved into position. I was trampled by my own regiment. My hand was crushed, badly. They dragged me to the chirurgeon, who gave it one look and amputated. But he amputated the wrong one. I think he just didn't care. I also think he could have saved it. He just didn't want to, not with... not with..." Burrimo stopped speaking. His breathing was heavier than before.

"Witness, thank you. I will not ask you to recount anything else. No further questions."

Habeus nodded to Felix. "Your cross-examination, please."

Felix stood up.

Okay, here we go then...

~

Felix put one hand into his jacket pocket and the other rested on his chin. He hoped it gave an air of casual confidence. He addressed the goblin neutrally, despite the crushing sorrow that filled him at seeing his old client in such a way. "We've met before, correct, Burrimo?"

"Yes." He didn't look up.

"Could you explain where?"

"We were in a courtroom. Well, we met before that, in prison. I was in prison, you were visiting me."

"And why was I visiting you?"

"You were going to represent me for my court case after my mother talked to Mrs Luncher."

Felix remembered the strange way that Mrs Luncher had greeted Burrimo's mother. She was excitable, like a schoolgirl. Strange, the way these memories like to pop up at the most unusual times.

"And I did, and was I successful in getting an acquittal for you?"

"Yes."

"And I wonder, do you remember the fee I charged you?"

"Uhm, I can't recall…"

Felix softened his voice.

"It was a great, fat zero. We ended up settling our costs from the other side, and you were charged nothing. In fact, the question of charges never came up, not with you, your mother, or anyone. Win or lose, we were not going to ask you to pay anything, so willing were we to represent you." Felix smiled warmly, hoping the goblin would try to remember that not all humans were xenophobic, self-serving scum.

The hairless man stood up, languidly, hand raised. Habeus gestured at him to speak, and steepled his fingers.

The man paused, then cleared his throat lengthily.

"Objection," he said.

Habeus didn't react. "Yes, I assumed that. Well, on what grounds?"

The prosecutor turned, and Jurrekker handed his lawyer a large, heavy book. The man held it up.

"I believe it is important that the court understands the key details of this case—that have hitherto been quietly side-lined—before this cross-examination goes much further. Unless… our defence lawyer has objections to me reading out the details of the very case he defended over?"

Oh bugger.

In truth, Felix had been about to object. But… how could he now?

Felix swept an open palm in front of him. "By all means…"

The man flipped the book open theatrically to the correct page and stabbed a finger down seemingly without looking.

"Upon investigation, the case was concluded with the defendant, Burrimo, acquitted of charges, after it was revealed that the three perpetrators attended massed rallies designed to incite hatred and abuse of all non-humans."

Felix tried to cut this off and continue his questioning but was himself cut off with a finger.

"This case was conducted with a jury, an unusual custom typical of the East Country. In these 'juries', thirteen randomly selected citizens are chosen to decide whether, on the balance of evidence, the defendant is guilty or innocent." Still without looking, he flipped the page of the book. "The scribe notes with interest that the jury comprised seven goblins and only six non-goblins. Goblins, at the time, consisted of a mere 0.4% of the population."

He turned to Felix then.

"You wouldn't happen to know anything about this, would you, Defence Counsel?"

Felix coughed. "I don't believe I'm on the witness stand, unless I'm mistaken?"

Habeus turned to him.

"That might be true, but I would be interested in hearing your answer."

Felix thought fast.

"I personally had no involvement in the selection of the jury, and can attest that, to the best of my knowledge, no one in the defence team had anything to do with it. As far as I am concerned, it's blind chance, and my faith in civilisation is such that I am sure it would have made no difference to the verdict had the content of the jury been different"

Habeus looked unconvinced.

"And, as part of the Jury custom, no one is permitted to know the individual verdicts each member gives. It is up to the foreman or woman or indeed goblin of the Jury to give the majority. For all we know, six of those goblins could have voted 'guilty'."

Habeus looked even less convinced.

Worth a shot.

His mouth dry, Felix quickly turned back to the goblin, before he got himself in any more hot water. His voice took on a more pleading tone.

"You must have met some brave souls in the army? Brothers in arms who would lay down their lives for you?"

The small figure shook his head.

"No," he whispered. "They were rotten scoundrels to a man. Thieves and liars, and…"

Felix shot a side glance to Yetty, who shrugged. Affecting his warmest smile, he faced the witness again.

"Surely you can think of a single human being who you consider 'good'? Even just one, one human being that showed you kindness?"

The goblin's heavy eyes landed on Felix and didn't blink.

"Not one."

Felix felt himself deflate. He smoothed his hair back, and breathed deeply.

"What about—"

"Just stop, will you?" screamed Burrimo, tears in his eyes. He had leapt to his feet, and seemed to have trouble standing upright. He shook with emotion. "You pick and needle at these wounds, trying to find a perspective that makes you feel no guilt. Have I not suffered enough? Just leave me alone, for pity's sake!"

Felix was speechless. He felt shame, and couldn't look Burrimo in the eyes. The goblin slumped back down and wiped his face with his sleeve.

Felix walked over to Burrimo, and said quietly:

"I'm sorry. For what it's worth, I'm sorry on behalf of the species, and on behalf of myself. If I had known what was going to happen, I…" he couldn't complete the sentence.

The witness didn't react, other than to shift itself in such a way as to hide his stumps further in his jacket. He turned from Felix.

"No further questions," Felix mumbled, and Yetty patted him on the arm as he sat down.

The goblin didn't move until he was ushered out, through the double doors, and was soon out of sight, but not out of mind.

10 – The Selfless

"A re you okay, Felix?" asked Yetty, a hand still on his arm. He looked pale.

"I'm fine… I'm fine. Let's just get on with this, eh?" he replied, returning her concerned look with a cheery smile. Her expression didn't soften, if anything she looked more worried than before.

"Look," said Felix. "If I can't handle a few plucks at the heartstrings, we haven't got a hope. When this is all over, I'll have plenty of time to reflect and feel melancholy. For now, I have to focus on the job in hand. I'd appreciate it if you did as well."

That took the look from her face. Yetty never did take criticism well. But, on this occasion, she kept her doubtless acidic retort to herself.

A swift tapping sound, and Habeus's voice filled the air.

"Would the defence like to call their first witness?" he said.

"I think we need a bit of positivity. Don't you?" Felix whispered to Yetty, who nodded. "Let's try to brighten the place up a touch."

"Defence," said Habeus, a little louder. "Are you ready for your first witness?"

"We are, Your Honour. We call her to the stand," replied Felix.

The first witness for the defence was an old lady named Mrs Applebest. She wore sturdy clothes of good, hardy material, and a flowery apron over the top. Her tight white curls bounced on her head as she looked around the room, beaming at everyone she saw, be they man, beast, or cosmic monstrosity. She squeezed Felix on the arm as she walked past, and he guided her to the stand.

"Thank you, Mrs Applebest. I appreciate you taking the time to attend today," Felix said, inclining his head to his witness. She was the kindest woman in the land, so it was said, and had dedicated her life to helping any who knocked on her door, regardless of their circumstance.

Their line of questioning had prompted her, despite her embarrassed protestations, to go into details about the specific services she performed for the destitute.

"Oh, you know," she said. Her voice was a hot chocolate on a cold day, and her inviting smile and good-natured modesty warmed Felix. "I only do what any decent person would do. I dress wounds, I feed the starving. None leave my house hungry. None. When I was younger and a little fitter, I used to build shelters and bridges, that sort of thing. Nothing major, you understand."

Felix noticed that, despite her age, she was clearly fit. It was probably all that hard work in her youth, and doubtless she kept active into her twilight years.

"And what do you charge those who accept your help?" asked Felix.

She waved a hand at him, as if asking him to stop joking. "I ask nothing in return. I simply want to see the world a little better after I leave it than when I entered."

"What is your opinion of humanity as a whole, Mrs Applebest?" Felix concluded with. She thought for a moment, before adjusting her glasses and replying.

"I think that we all try our best, but sadly some people get lost along the way, dear. It's up to the rest of us to shoulder the burden and do our part to make the world a little nicer. I think there will be a time when we all live in peace and happiness, though I suppose I'll be long gone before then." She smiled a wide, crinkled smile, and Felix smiled back.

"No further questions," he said. She made as if to stand.

"Now, I've made a small box of biscuits for everyone, yourself included, Your Honour, dear. I think that people can get quite worked up in these court case thingies, and sometimes you just need a cup of tea and a little naughty treat to set you right again."

She reached into her purse and pulled out a wooden tub. "I hope you like lemon!" she said, proffering it to Habeus. He leaned over and took it, a curious look on his face.

"Excuse me, witness," came a wet voice. She turned to see the prosecutor. "You have not yet been subject to my cross-examination."

She slapped a hand to her forehead, and gasped. "Oh, silly me! I am so sorry, dear. I got all worked up thinking about my biscuits, you know how it is." She settled back into her chair. "Please, do ask whatever you need to ask."

~

The hairless man walked over to her.

"I wonder if I might ask you to recall a few details."

He paused. She didn't answer, just smiled at him.

"About your past."

Her smile faltered an inch, just for a second, but was back again instantly.

"Ask away, dear."

The man stared at her. "Actually, I will come back to that. Now, Mrs Applebest. Would you say the following is accurate: most of those poor, dejected people you help are hungry, often ill or injured, and have nowhere else to go?"

She nodded, curls bouncing. "Yes, dear. Often in a sorry state."

"I see. And, in your opinion, what would you say is the reason that most of these people are in this state?"

"Oh, well, I fancy I have no idea, dear. I don't pry," she said.

He nodded.

"The district you are from, the South Country. It is not a particularly poor district, is it?"

"Oh, I don't know about that. My views are concerning somewhat smaller things than national economics. I'm only an old lady who lives in the woods!" she chuckled.

The man smiled. Felix didn't like it when he smiled.

"I will suggest something to you now, and I urge you to stop me if you think I say anything untrue." He turned to Felix. "I offer the same request to yourself, *my learned colleague*," he said, putting emphasis on the words in a way that suggested anything but. Felix narrowed his eyes, but said nothing.

"Humans are hungry when they do not eat enough. If they do not eat enough for long enough, they starve. This causes them to become thin, sad, lost, mad, and they eventually die."

He waited for the objection, but none came.

"The South Country, specifically, is a rich country. It has wide, expansive forests, deep mines, and plenty of land for farming."

He paused again. Nothing.

"In the South Country, there is enough food to go around."

Felix stood. "Objection."

The man smiled again. "Please do."

Felix ignored him. "There is not enough food to go around, which is why there are these poor, starving wretches."

The man shook his head. "Ah, but. Our witness feeds them with the contents of her own stash. She saves enough to feed those that come to her, and none leave hungry. That is what you said, witness?"

She looked a little confused, and turned to Felix. He nodded.

"Yes, dear."

"Whenever you buy or farm or procure your supplies in whatever way you need to, have you ever been unable to buy enough to satisfy the needs of your patrons?"

"Uhm… No, dear."

"So, there is enough food?"

"Well…"

"It is just a matter of distribution?"

"As I said, I am not a politician…"

He spun to face Felix.

"Men overeat and grow fat in the cities, while those with less starve. The human world has *never* been so well provisioned. Yet, due to inactivity, or carelessness, or chasing a profit, men, women and children still starve."

Felix dropped into his seat. The prosecutor turned back to Mrs Applebest, pointed a finger at her.

"I move that the people you help are all in dire straits because of the very nature of humanity. If humans cared for each other, none would starve in the first place. If they put less faith in currency, none would sleep cold, or die of exposure. They are injured and cannot seek aid because the nature of humanity's self-serving agenda prevents it, unless the victim can pay. Therefore, if we remove humanity from the equation, the suffering reduces to nil."

Felix stood again. "But what about illness, or accident? That is suffering that is not human-caused."

The toothless man didn't miss a beat. "Then surely humanity would be best served if it bent itself to eradicating such cruel aspects of life. But does it, or does it pursue wealth, power, and other pointless, suffering-creating ends?"

Felix had nothing to say, and so said nothing.

The witness was looking at her hands.

"I don't ask how or why," she said in a quiet voice. "I just want to help."

The prosecutor turned to face her. "Witness. About my earlier question. You said you were a simple old woman who lives in the woods. I wonder. What drove you to seek a life such as the one you have created?"

"What do you mean, dear?" she asked, a smile back on her face. It didn't reach her eyes.

He reached into his pocket and produced a square of paper. He unfolded it and began to read. Then, after a moment, he addressed her again.

"Have you ever killed anyone, witness?" he asked, calmly.

She coughed and spluttered, and held a hand to her cheek.

"How could you ask—" she began.

"O Habeus," said the prosecutor. "Please remind the witness of the importance of her truth."

The judge turned to face her, leaning over her in the dock. "You will speak the truth, or be severely punished."

She looked pale and scared, but nodded.

"Witness," prompted the prosecutor. "I trust I need not repeat the question?"

She shook her head.

"Please state your answer."

"Yes," she whispered.

"Louder, please?" came the reply.

"Yes!" she shouted.

A few gasps and mutters from behind the court.

What on earth?

Felix ran his mind back to their discussion of the witnesses. He had personally researched this one. Her past had been empty, according to the records. Just a normal, everyday woman with a normal, nondescript past.

Mind you, it was curious how empty her record had been. Almost as if...

"I am going to read a list of crimes," said the prosecutor. "I would like you to stop me if I read one out that you have not committed." He looked at the paper again.

"Arson. Blackmail. Criminal Damage." He paused to let her interject. She did not.

"Unjust Beating of the Innocent. Theft. Kidnapping."

Another pause. Another silence.

"Torture. Murder."

"Please," she pleaded, gripping her purse with white knuckles. "I'm not that person anymore."

"What person, witness?"

"You know," she muttered. She looked old and deflated. Tears fell down her face.

"I do know. I do my research, witness," said the prosecutor, glancing at Felix. His look seemed to say, *"Unlike you, you amateur."*

He turned to the room. "Thirty years ago, Enola Thorngrasp hung up her boots. Do you recognise that name, Witness?"

"I..." she stammered. He plowed on.

"She had successfully evaded capture for fifteen years. She was a well-known and well-feared Forest-Ganger, and became rich from the fruits of her crime. How is it you made your fortune, witness?"

"Please..."

"It is suggested that this hardened criminal may have had an epiphany of sorts, a moment where she was faced with the severity of her crimes, and could not face what she had become. So, she vanished. Where did you spend your middle years, witness?"

She said nothing.

"I suggest that, perhaps, she tried to make up for that past life by correcting the balance she has tipped. The awful crimes she had committed. Perhaps she now feeds the hungry, the homeless, and the destitute, using the stolen wealth she has accumulated, to assuage her conscience, and nothing more. Can she undo the pain she has caused? Does that call her motives into question? Will she leave the world in a better place than when she left it? Of course, I cannot know that for sure…"

He returned to his desk and pulled out another piece of paper. A picture of a symbol shaped like an antlered head. "Though, I do know she had this symbol burned into her back, just between the shoulder blades. A message to the world, perhaps. A statement, saying: Here I am, and I am proud'."

Mrs Applebest stared at him. She looked haunted.

"I am not going to suggest we strip you, Mrs Applebest. Your confession will suffice," he said, in a reasonable tone of voice.

Felix whipped his vision from her, to the prosecution, back again.

"Witness. Are you Enola Thorngrasp?" asked the hairless man, a half-smile of triumph on his face.

She didn't answer.

"Witness," said Habeus. "Answer."

She looked up at him, fury in her eyes. It dissipated under the pressure of the judge's gaze.

"Yes," she said in a small voice. "But—"

"And do you now commit charity as self-imposed penance for your terrible, terrible crimes?"

"Yes, but—"

"And do you see how they might cause a reasonable person to call your motives into question, witness!" His voice was raised, his stare murderous.

She went to speak, but said nothing. He sneered.

"I suggest that you spread death and destruction in your youth, and now spend your twilight years trying to fix that which you yourself have broken. Except, you are bailing a ship that has long ago sunk. You are not a good person, and the world, on balance, is worse off for having you in it."

She made to speak. The prosecutor waved a hand, cutting her off.

"That will do, witness. I have no further questions. You are dismissed."

"But—!"

The doors at the end of the chamber opened wide.

"You may leave," he said. "And please do it quietly."

She looked completely crushed. All manner of emotions flitted across her grandmotherly face. Eventually, she stood, and strode from the room. The doors closed behind her.

Felix overheard whispering between Furbo and Helda.

"It wasn't like that," he heard Helda say, but he didn't know what she meant. He didn't much care at that point.

11 – The Beast

The prosecution had more witnesses. Many more. Disgusted as he was to admit it, Felix thought they were making a pretty good case.

Felix found himself trying, failing, to cross examine a *baby lamb*. The prosecutor had found this tiny slip of an animal, possibly the cutest, most lovable looking sheep ever to grace this fine earth. Some ensorcellment allowed it to converse in Allspeak.

"What do you want from life, lamb?" the prosecutor asked.

"Uhm-m-m, not much really-leally. Ju-just to wander about-ut, pla-play with others. I like-like sunshine, I do." It fluttered tiny eyelashes and turned its large eyes to take in the scene.

"I see. Do you think you deserve to be killed and eaten?"

"N-no-no?" it bleated, all wide-eyed and pathetic. It looked very small, perched as it was on a box in the stand.

Felix stood. "Objection. The circle of life means that, sadly, animals, even the cutest ones, must sometimes perish."

He sat down again. *Felix—Lamb Killer.*

The prosecutor nodded, and the lamb tilted his head at Felix. He couldn't meet the animal's gaze without feeling sick. The hairless man started again.

"That is right, that is right. Circle of life. Don't you agree, lamb?"

It quivered as it answered.

"Uhmmhm, my-my mother says some-sometimes we-we are taken away for-for-for-forever by the howlers, but-ut it's so that other-others can live, t'aint their fault they have to-have to-hah, uh, take-take us, they've no choice."

Oh no.

273

The prosecutor nodded sagely. "And what if you were taken away forever, to be killed and eaten, *not* because another creature needed to do so to survive, but because the other creature just *enjoyed* the taste of your flesh?"

"What! Why-why would they do that?" the lamb began trembling more.

"And what about the idea of being specifically bred *just* to live for a few weeks in squalor, only then to be killed for that purpose?"

The lamb's whole body started to shake, eyes darting around the room...

Felix was pressing into his eyes with his finger and thumb.

"I—I—Well—" whispered the lamb.

"No further questions," said the prosecutor.

Habeus leaned over. "Would the defence like to cross examine the witness?"

I could... or maybe if....

There was no use. There's no way he could spin this to make humanity appear anything less than monstrous.

He stood, and exhaled heavily. "No, thank you."

~

Felix watched as the prosecution interviewed all manner of tiny, impossibly cute creatures, following the same line of questioning.

"What do you want from life?"

"Do you think you deserve to be killed for fun?"

Animals bred to be eaten, animals bred to be hunted. Some bred to spend their sad lives in a tiny pen, or cage, to be gawked at by rich idiots. Even Felix found it hard to question the creatures humanity used for non-medical scientific experimentation. How could he justify experimentation for the sake of lipstick, for goodness sake?

Each one was another nail in humanity's coffin. Each one, the same story. Humanity using them for their own gain, not because they had to, but because they wanted to. Because it was easy. Or convenient. Or, worst of all, for *fun*.

"Prosecution," Habeus said, after a particularly fluffy calf was led out, crying. "How many more of these types of witnesses do you have?"

"Why, seventy-three more, O Habeus," came the smooth reply.

"I see. Might I recommend that we move on? I think we get the picture," he said.

The hairless man nodded. "Very wise, O Habeus. It does tear the soul to see such wretchedness, does it not?"

Habeus didn't say anything. Neither did Felix.

~

Felix sat up, an idea forming in his head quite out of nowhere. He whispered to Cherinda. "Can we call on... anyone?"

She nodded. "Pretty much. Except a higher being, of course."

"I have an idea..." said Felix. He whispered to Cherinda, who nodded and went to talk to an usher by the door. She shot back a thumbs up in his direction. Felix stood. "We'd like to call on our next witness."

~

"Witness! Witness, please, settle down!" Felix pleaded. His witness was jumping, clearly very excited.

"Haha! This is brilliant! Look at all these people, they all smell great! You're great! Fantastic!" it yelled. It turned in a circle.

Felix looked sidelong at Cherinda, who raised an eyebrow. Felix had envisioned this going better.

"Please, just tell me your opinion on humanity," he said, smiling through the panic.

The witness stopped, and tipped its head over to one side, its ears flopping over. "Humanity?"

It shook itself, slobber flinging from its mouth in strings.

"I love humanity! They're the best!"

It started itching itself on the neck with a hind leg.

"Witness! Please, focus! Oh, never mind. No more questions," Felix said dejectedly, waving his hands in the air and flumping onto his bench.

Jurrekker stared at the dog, which whined and recoiled. The prosecutor stood up, walking over it. It turned its large brown eyes to the hairless figure, the demon quite forgotten, and started panting again, its tail slowly wagging once more.

"The witness has told us of his opinion on humanity, which was..?" probed the prosecutor.

"They're great!" came the reply.

"I wonder if the witness would answer this: Does the witness ever eat excrement?"

"Poo? Yes!"

"And what do you think of…?"

"It's great!"

"Do you do anything else with—?"

"Oh yes! Eat it, roll in it, I love it."

"No further questions."

I should have seen that coming, thought Felix.

Journal Entry N: Muse

Reference case [JMvC/M/L] (JayMoo v. Con/Lut/Har), year 1335, judge Yellowbird presiding

I've never been musical. I mean, obviously I like songs, but actually taking the time to try and learn an instrument has never been something I much cared for. I might have been tempted by something in the woodwind family until I learned you had to suck up the spit that gathered sometimes in the instrument, so that pretty much confirmed it for me.

This case was unusual because it was a three-way case, in other words, three separate defendants, each with their own complaints. The reason the cases were consolidated like this was that their complaints were all identical.

They all claimed they were the true author of the song: Light on an Autumn Evening. A moist ballad about True Love's First Kiss, or something. Not really my kind of song.

A song writing contest had been posted on the walls of every alehouse in the city, with a prize of five hundred Golds and a hint at a royal patronage for the winner. The only stipulation: the song had to be original.

Enter our three musicians. It was the night of the contest, and the stage was literally set. An excited and nervous crowd babbled expectedly, a few waiting their turn, trying to size up the competition.

The lights were dimmed, and a hush settled on the room.

The first of our three clients took to the stage and began strumming his expensive harp, artfully tossing his impressive plumage-laded cap, and started singing his song. Not ten seconds later, outrage from within the crowd! A figure strode up, similarly pompously dressed, demanded to know how the thief had stolen the song he had written only last week, completely in secret, specifically for this contest?

Harp, of course, scoffed, but when his accuser recited the next four bars of his song, accompanied with a virtuosic counterpoint on his lute, Harp blanched. Imagine their surprise when a third gentlemen, scruffily dressed but no less earnest, burst from backstage, concertina in hand, reciting the next part of the secret song perfectly. Cue much name calling and scuffling, cue several bruised ribs and broken strings, cue much humiliation and being thrown into the streets, and, lastly, cue losing any opportunity to compete in this once-in-a-lifetime contest.

My client was the third man, Concertina. Being the last into this particular argument, his was the weakest position, but, as has been previously detailed, that's the sort of case Luncher can't seem to resist.

I looked at his weather-beaten clothes and asked him for his account of how he came up with the song. I expected that the only chance we had of winning was claiming that musically-trained spies had trailed him and secretly notated his song, word for word. What he explained instead was even more implausible.

He had been plumped under a rotten awning on a cold, cloudy evening. He was trying desperately to write a song for this contest to try to lift himself out of the gutter. All he had was his clothes, his wits, and his concertina.

Oh, for those unaware, a concertina is a ghastly little squeeze box that sounds like a cat being compressed, while handily recreating the movement of compressing a cat to further the illusion.

Anyway, there he was, no doubt sobbing into a mouldy handkerchief, when the clouds shimmer and part, and behold! A sparkling spectre appears before him, a beautiful maiden made of light, caressing his hands and filling his mind with such incredible music.

This vision swirls his inspiration into vivid, colourful explosions of harmony, and when his senses are returned to him, his hands move with a mind of their own, the words flow through him like nectar, and he creates the best song of his long, musical life.

"And the words, the tunes, they all just sort of appeared?" I asked, making notes.

He nods. "I was taken by the muse, she taught me to dance to her tune, and oh! It was special." A tear glistens in his one good eye.

I suspected, knowing what I knew about the other complainants, that their accounts would be much more mundane and technical, so I had hoped by repeating Concertina's tale to the judge, we might pluck at his heartstrings, so to speak.

I was in court, going through my well-rehearsed retelling of Concertina's story as part of my opening speech.

"...colourful explosions of harmony—" and I flourish my hands in the way I might expect some arty muso to do. I can't help but notice that, far from a haughty face of impatience from the other complainants, a curious mixture of outrage and disbelief held them, and not just them, their lawyers too. After interrupting me mid-flow, Harp's lawyer asked for a recess. Lute's agreed, and, backed into the corner as I was, I went along to this meeting with the other complainants and their representatives.

Concertina and I got there last and entered the back room to see the two other lawyers nattering quickly and quietly to each other. I slunk over to join in, and one turned to me, brow furrowed.

"Your speech. Colourful explosions of harmony. It's the same bloody story, almost word for word, that I had," she says to me, handing me a copy of notes she had taken. I glanced at them. It was a copy of my closing statement, which I hadn't read out yet, or even written down yet, written in another's handwriting.

"What is going on here?" I muttered, thankful that my counterparts responded to this apparent plagiarism with more decorum than our clients, who were ignoring each other, and making a great show of it.

"The muse!" exclaimed Lute's lawyer. "It must be her. We need to find her. Whatever she is, she's mucking with us all."

After entreating the judge for time to find a professional, we were able to call on a—and I'm quoting her job title here—'Metaphysique-Lunar Spirit Mystic'. An utterly mad old lady who happened to be the expert witness we needed. Harp's lawyer knew her from a different case and had thought she could help.

We met her a few nights later, under the full moon. With our expert intoning a few words and shaking a few burning bunches of something or other, sure enough, there stood before us a figure, seemingly made of light, eerie, beautiful, inspirational.

"Oi! You again I see!" spat Mystic Murrana, waggling a pointy finger at the spirit. "I thought I told you to stop stringing multiple fellas along last time we spoke, hmm?"

The figure looked abashed but didn't say anything.

"Okay gentlemen, I'll handle this, see you in court tomorrow morning!" the old lady said to us. When none of us made to leave, she turned and began yelling at us, so we scattered, quite unable to believe what was happening.

The next morning, as trial began, we collectively called the moon spirit known as Jayla to the stand, kept in check by our Expert Mystic. In a voice like moonlight, she explained that she was responsible for it all. She was fixated by adoration, and was tired of waiting for Mr Right to craft the perfect song, as it were, and so upped her 'visitations', appearing in the dreams of all manner of men (and women), and had decided to be less subtle and more overt in what she wanted. Under stern warnings from Murrana, she petulantly offered to stick to a single focus point from now on, and she was very sorry to waste everyone's time, but she just wanted to add that their songs were very nice.

The judge declared that technically she was the true songwriter, and so dismissed the joint cases from each complainant. And just like that, the case was over.

Oh, my speech? Why do you ask?

~journal entry ends

12 – The Elder

Felix met eyes with Racelsus, and she nodded. Or, at least he thought she did. He stood up and cleared his throat. "We would like to call our next witness. Elder Prastor."

At a signal, the double doors opened by themselves, and an ancient man shuffled in. His bald head was crossed with veiny wrinkles, and the skin under his eyes and mouth sagged. He walked with a gnarled stick as old as he was, and his loose yellow robes were simple, but well-maintained. He was stooped so low he had to lift his head to see where he was going.

As he passed through the gangway between the seats, a few onlookers turned to whisper to their neighbours. The demons in the crowd didn't say anything, but instead glanced nervously at Jurrekker.

It took the old man a full four minutes to reach the podium and climb into the chair. He looked as if he was minutes from death's door, he was so out of breath. He mopped his brow with a rag.

When he was finally settled, Felix had involuntary second thoughts. He leaned over to Racelsus.

"This is our expert witness?" he whispered urgently.

Her skull rattled slightly in its cage, which Felix had come to learn was her nodding.

"Appearances can be deceiving. Stick to the plan. You can trust me," she whispered back. His mouth felt dry when he remembered what they had discussed. He glanced at Helda, who gave him a thumbs up, and started reaching for something under her seat.

"If this goes wrong..." he considered his next words. "Well, I'll be dead anyway, so my threats are probably wasted."

She didn't reply. Felix sighed, then stood up.

"Thank you for joining us today, Elder Prastor."

Prastor slowly turned his head toward Felix, then gave a withered smile.

"Not at all, young one. Please ask me your questions, I have a long bath and a lemon tea waiting for me in the temple." His voice was thin and papery, and it seemed an exertion for him to speak.

"I'll try to keep this brief," Felix replied with a smile. He cracked his neck and took a deep breath.

"Elder, is it right for me to live in an empty hole in the ground?"

Prastor gazed at Felix. He pursed his ancient lips before responding, carefully, as if speaking to a madman.

"I suppose not, if that's what you like to do, child. Provided you have food, water, etcetera, I daresay you could live quite happily."

Felix nodded. "Is it right for me to build a house on top of that same hole, then live in it?"

"Again, I suppose so. You are your own man, you can live in a hole if you like," he chuckled.

Without missing a beat, Felix asked: "Is it right for me to enter someone else's house and start living there, quietly, without anyone noticing?"

The old man shifted uncomfortably and mopped his brow again. He coughed before replying.

"Well, if one isn't doing any harm… Parasites exist in nature in many forms. They can live quite comfortably without the host experiencing any negative side effects."

Felix considered this comment, then continued.

"You haven't given me a definite answer, Elder."

"Oh, haven't I? I am sorry, child. It's my old mind, it does get confused sometimes." His old face cracked into a warming smile.

A smile that didn't reach the eyes.

Felix felt a small relief, and exhaled. "Allow me to rephrase the question." He put his hands into his jacket pocket and leaned forward.

"Is it right for me to enter that house, beat up the occupant and his family, then threaten to kill them and burn his house down if he doesn't do what I say, when I say it?"

The old man's smile had dropped completely. A few mutterings floated from the back of the room.

The hairless man stood up, hand raised. Habeus nodded at him.

"Objection," he said.

"Yes. Well?" said Habeus to him.

"Honoured judge, this is irrelevant. This isn't a squatting case, and it is a waste of time to dwell on such pointless questioning."

Habeus waved him down and intoned. "I assume, I hope correctly, that the defence counsel has some relevant questioning forthcoming. If he doesn't, it will not look favourably upon him. So, I shall grant him the benefit of the doubt, for now." He turned to the witness stand. "Answer the question, witness."

The old man coughed and hawked up a gob of something wet and slimy. He looked very frail, and a touch frightened. In a quavering voice, he spoke.

"Of course that would not be the right thing to do." His rheumy eyes were wet with something. Tears?

Unlikely, thought Felix. He had the measure of this *man* now, and knew why Racelsus had suggested him. Felix leaned back on his desk, head down, body pointing towards the witness stand.

"Do you know the word 'possessed', witness?"

A few sharp intakes of breath from the crowd. Felix carried on.

"Allow me to spare you looking it up. It means, in this context, for a spirit to house itself in the body of another, physical being, almost exclusively unwillingly. Similar, perhaps to the example I gave earlier. Which, you remember, you said 'would not be the right thing to do'."

He let the silence lengthen, waiting for something. The witness did not fill it. He asked the silent question.

"You are possessed, are you not, Prastor?" he asked, nonchalantly.

A pause as the old man chuckled. His laughter was that of an old, kind grandfather, watching his grandchildren playing in the mud.

"Young man, I fear you are misinformed! Possessed, indeed."

Felix lifted his hands as if caught in the act.

"Ah, so you are *not* possessed? You are in fact, merely a frail old man? No other power has forcefully taken up residence in that body?"

"Quite so," nodded Prastor.

"I see."

"Defence Counsel," said Habeus. "I trust you did conduct your research properly prior to compiling your list of witnesses?"

Felix reddened. "Yes, oh Habeus."

Habeus didn't say anything. He leaned back into this small, wooden chair.

After a moment of silence, the old man spoke.

"Child, I am sorry for disappointing you. Am I free to go?"

Felix considered this, then nodded to Helda.

A spear, a full five feet in length and barbed wickedly, tore through the air at the old man. Helda was standing, flexing her wrist, watching the flight of her spear.

As the spear reached the old man, he exploded in light and fabric with a sound like a thunderclap. As Felix blinked the blindness away, the elder was gone, and an enormous, muscled man stood where Prastor had sat. He was easily seven feet in height and had a shock of yellow-white hair that glowed with light. One powerful arm was raised, holding the spear in one hand, its point an inch from his head. His eyes were two pools of white light as he stared at the spear point.

"Good aim," whispered Racelsus to Helda.

The man squeezed his meaty fist and the spear broke, clattering to the ground. Jurrekker applauded lightly, his hands sounding like two rocks as they clapped.

"Very impressive," he added in a voice like sulphur.

The figure in the witness stand flexed his arm and turned to regard the room. His eyes fixed on Helda. Helda met the gaze, and didn't falter. She blew him a kiss. He looked at Felix, who failed to suppress a smile. Felix took a breath, about to ask his next question, when the figure pounced.

He sprung, leaping over the dock straight towards Felix. He moved quickly for such a large man. Felix froze, a flash of terror across his face, ice filling his gut. Stupidly, he had never thought the witness would actually react in this way, not in front of Habeus. This... monstrous man was flying towards him, all muscle and raw power, and there was nothing he could do.

Felix could see him approaching in slow motion, one arm behind him for balance, one outstretched in front, preparing the single strike that would kill him. Felix knew that he wouldn't be able to dodge the blow, and so closed his eyes and waited for the end.

Another figure collided bodily with the attacker in mid-air, sending him sprawling sideways across the concourse. The two figures tussled bodily, grunting and shouting as they rolled down the walkway. Suddenly, both figures sprang to their feet, and began trading blows, each swinging huge punches at the other, the impact sounds ringing meatily throughout the court. The attendees were standing, keeping a wary distance. Only a few seconds had passed since the 'old man' had charged, and everyone was jostling to get a better view of the scrap. A well-aimed hit sent their saviour spinning around, and Felix recognised the huge, hairy shape.

"Bertruk!" he exclaimed.

The barbarian was giving as good as he got, but Felix could see he was being worn down. Blood and spit flecks sprayed from him with each hit, and his movements were slowing. He was avoiding fewer hits, dealing fewer blows, and was flagging. Pressing the advantage, the demigod delivered a fast series of gut punches to the barbarian's stomach, and when he doubled over, a brutal knee to Bertruk's face. The barbarian flew back and landed heavily, a few feet from the defence counsel's desk.

His head lolled to the side, and his eyes met Felix's. Blood dribbled from his nose and mouth. He grinned and gave Felix a wink.

The demigod was stretching his arm over his shoulder, flexing and unflexing his fingers. He advanced on the crumpled figure.

"Pathetic," he observed, in a voice like mountains. He began sprinting, cougar-quick, towards the fallen warrior.

Bertruk then swept to his feet with a roar, delivering a hands-clasped double-handed uppercut to the demigod's chin, which knocked him up, down, and back, landing heavily on his neck.

"Pah," he offered. One of his teeth flew from his mouth as he said it.

The figure grunted and pushed himself to his feet, bright blood streaming down his face. His eyes were blazing yellow fires. He took a step towards the barbarian, murder in his expression. A large, clawed hand reached out and held him by the arm.

"Stop," growled Jurrekker.

The figure snarled, then spat blood on the floor, before shaking his head. He pointed at the barbarian, and spoke in a deep, sinister voice.

"You are marked. Hear me, for I will have my revenge, savage. Your soul will know such torment," he promised.

Bertruk shrugged and spat out another tooth. "I've heard worse."

The muscled man was then enveloped in black smoke, which emanated from his body, curling to the ceiling. The smoke cleared as abruptly as it had arrived, and the old man was once again stood there, his smart robes torn into rags. His boney ribs and distended belly were visible. He sported a mighty bruise on his chin. His legs wobbled as he stood, staring bloody murder at Felix.

"I think the matter as to whether the Elder is possessed has been settled," Habeus intoned, tapping his gavel. "Let us take a short recess to, hmm, clean up the mess. Ten minutes." He left, walking through the door behind him.

The elder started conversing with the prosecution in the same language Felix had heard before. Others began standing and stretching, milling about, chatting excitedly about what they had just seen. Felix reached into an inner pocket, turned to Yetty and handed her five silver coins.

"What's thi—?" she began to ask, but Felix had already walked over to Bertruk.

"Colour me surprised!" he began, clapping the grizzled adventurer on his arm. "I figured I'd seen the last of Bertruk the Bruiser, gosh, many years ago!"

The years hadn't been kind to Bertruk. His hair had splashes of grey in it now that weren't there before, and, while still built powerfully, there seemed an unhealthy tautness, or leanness, to him. One of his eyes was scarred over, the white eyeball blinded, and he had barely any teeth left.

He grabbed Felix in a crushing hug, guffawing as he did so.

"Lucky you, huh, law-man?" His voice was deep and warm towards Felix. It sounded just the smallest part strained.

When Felix had extricated himself, he asked Bertruk the burning question.

"Where on earth did you appear from?"

Bertruk looked around him for the first time, taking in the crowd, the judge's table, the demon opposite. He didn't seem to react to it in the way a normal person would, as if this sort of thing was perfectly reasonable to walk into. He took a deep breath, shrugged, then began.

"I was making a fire in a cave. Resting. It was dark, I was cold. Colder than normal. It has been a hard winter. Then, I feel danger. A great shape walks toward me, horned, two-legged, big as a bear. I stand, ready to fight it off. I see it turn, then I see another shape, brighter, but smaller. Very puny. Something tells me it needs help, and I recognise him. I start moving towards it. The large figure breaks into a charge, so I charge him. As I get closer, he becomes less dark and more real, the cave changes, brightens, widens, and I see a man coming at you with blood in his eyes. So, I stop him. I dislike those who pick on the weak." He stopped his tale with a sweep of his arms. "Then, here I am."

Felix thought about protesting his own apparent 'puniness', but in the present company it really would seem rather ungrateful. Before he could speak, the barbarian started again.

"I don't think I will be here long. I can already feel myself being pulled away."

Felix didn't want him to go. "Where? Back to the cave?"

"No, somewhere else. Somewhere, hmm, beyond. I left my body behind," said Bertruk.

"I don't understand."

The huge man looked at him then, and grinned a toothless, bloody grin.

"Heh. Don't worry about it. I have no regrets, and I've repaid my debt. Now, it's up to you. Take this. Only give it to someone you trust. Once you give it, you can't take it back."

He reached into a leather pouch and handed Felix a small tube of brown powder. Felix took it, at a loss for words. Something tugged at his memory.

"Very strange company you keep these days, law-man," said Bertruk, looking at his companions. He winked at Helda, who blushed and averted her eyes down to the floor, nodded at Racelsus, before finally smiling once more at Felix. He turned then, and walked towards the door at the back of the courtroom. His body seemed more translucent with each step he took, and Felix was sure he had completely vanished before he reached the doorway. He looked to where the bloodstains were being mopped up by some attendants, but the blood had disappeared.

"Are you okay?" Yetty asked again from behind him.

"Yes, I'm fine, thanks," replied Felix. He pocketed the bottle, and rubbed his eye.

~

Habeus had stationed a number of aides after that incident, and instead of the slight, otherworldly figures that had hovered at the edges before, now there were bright, armoured watchmen, apparently called Finders, who stood with military attention around the room. The room itself had returned to a sense of quiet anticipation.

Habeus turned to the witness, who was still talking with the prosecutor. "Please return to the dock and resume your questioning, witness. And, I'm sure this goes without saying, but another outburst like that and you will regret it."

The old man stared malice at Habeus, but did as he was bid. Felix once again took his accustomed spot.

"Defence Counsel," said Habeus, in a warning tone. "Additionally, try anything else like that and you will be contempted. Am I clear?"

Felix nodded. "Understood, O Habeus."

I really don't want to find out what that means.

He turned to the dock, a wide smile on his face. He didn't have to care about irritating the witness anymore, so he didn't try to mollify him "So, *respected* Elder. Are you ready to hear my questions?"

The old man glared at Felix, then up at Habeus. Finally, he nodded imperceptibly.

~

Felix waited, stretching the silence for as long as he dared.

"Do you, in your opinion, have the right to occupy a human body?" he asked.

The old man spat as he answered, this time in a deep, booming voice completely at odds with his appearance.

"I have the right to do as I please. If someone has a problem with it, they can take it up with me personally."

Felix nodded, as if he were hearing the latest village news, not hearing threats from a demon.

"Forgive me if this sounds a little… hm, philosophical? But where did you come from?"

The witness frowned, thinking. "What do you mean, human?"

Felix continued. "Where were you born? How did you come to be? I fancy I know how a man is born, or a pig, or even what goes on with trees and plants, but the lifecycles of demons are beyond me."

"I don't have to—" started Prastor, before Habeus cut over him.

"You are compelled to truth, Demon," spoke Habeus with an air of calm authority.

The ancient man shook his head with an energy hitherto hidden. He resembled some beast drying itself after a swim.

"I just was. One day I wasn't, then I was."

"And, when you, 'was', did you have a body?"

"No."

"So you were, what? Gas?"

"Gas!?" the witness snarled.

"Gas, okay." Felix nodded, as if this was what he was expecting.

The old man jumped to his feet.

"I was a spirit, devoid of form, travelling the planes of torment! I was born of pain and suffering, malice and spite, all coalesced and condensed into a form of life!"

Felix gripped the table in front of him and leaned forward, fixing the demon with his best glare.

"In that time, you have taken physical form. When?"

"I don't recall, thousands of years ago, perhaps."

"And the host, were they willing?"

"…rngh…"

"Were they a willing host for your possession, demon? Answer!"

The demon slammed the wooden dock with a fist, then pointed at Felix.

"No! I waited until their heart was blackened by despair, then I tore their soul apart and wore them like a jacket!"

"And do you know what I say to abominable fiends like you?" Felix growled, eyes narrowed. The old man's eyes started glowing.

Felix stood straight, arms behind him, chin raised, eyes narrowed.

"I respect you."

A silence hung in the air. Glances from the defence team.

What was he playing at?

"I respect your right to exist. I respect your right to occupy the physical world in whatever way you need to." He spoke slowly and deliberately. His ears felt hot, but he carried on, and began to pace.

"You did not ask to be born so. You existed in, what? Torment, you said? Pain, nothing but brutal pain. You had no escape. Until, of course, you realised you could scratch your way into the physical world, taking the form of another, imprinting yourself onto them. Then you would be free." He stopped walking. "I respect that. I would probably do it, too."

He was an arm's reach from the demon. It was watching him with uncomprehending eyes.

"Humanity is the same. We did not ask to be born to the cold, harsh world. We did not ask to struggle with hunger or exposure." He turned to the room, back to the dock. "We! Did! Not! Ask! …to lack the wings of the birds, or the strength of the ape, or the cunning of the cat. We were given intelligence, and we used that to lift ourselves from misery. We did not ask for it, but we took it. We adapted. We have taken our place in an unforgiving world, grasping it with both hands. We didn't want to exist in pain, just as you didn't, but we weren't given the option." Felix turned back to the dock. "So, here we are. You and me. Demonkind and Humanity. Finding our way, despite the circumstances."

The demon stared at him with incredulity, unsure of how to respond. Felix nodded, and turned back to his desk.

"No further questions."

Habeus nodded, and invited the prosecution to cross-examine the witness. They declined.

Cherinda gave Felix a deep, searching look as he said down, her aura fading almost completely, but he didn't notice.

13 – The Final Witness

Habeus leaned forward, addressing both parties. He blinked slowly before speaking.

"Do either party wish to draw upon any further evidence?" he said. "Defence Counsel?"

Felix stood.

Was this it? Nothing left?

He racked his brains trying to come up with something, anything that could help them. Everything he thought of was either irrelevant, or too easily turned against him by the prosecution. He was trapped in a pit, and all he could ask for were nooses.

He swallowed. "No, Your Honour." Felix sat down again, trying not to think about what came next.

The prosecutor cleared his throat. "We have one more, O Habeus."

Habeus nodded, then sat down. He looked tired.

What now? Is he not satisfied?

"We call upon our final witness," said the hairless man, smiling a wide, putrid smile.

Felix turned to his colleagues. They were exhausted. He was, not for the first time, struck by their fortitude. He was thinking of the best way to phrase it to them, to try and give them some last piece of encouragement, when Racelsus spoke.

"Something's wrong," she said. Her voice was as uncertain as Felix had ever heard it, and quavered nervously.

"What is it?" he said. She clacked her teeth together.

"No…" she whispered, and fell silent.

The doors opened, and a figure in a cowl walked in, flanked by two armoured sentinels. They clasped one arm each, forcing him down the aisle. The figure stumbled, and jostled, and moved like a mad drunk, struggling against the strong arms guiding him towards the front. His head jolted sporadically in different directions, but his hood stayed up. The spectators shifted fractionally as they passed.

He had to be forced into the stand. Once he was pushed into the seat, he calmed down some, but would still jerk and twitch, sometimes just a touch, sometimes as if struck.

Racelsus was unsettled, and began to rattle continuously—with nerves or fright, Felix couldn't tell. Seeing her in such a state troubled him to his core.

"Who is this?" he said to her, but she didn't reply.

"Racelsus?" asked Helda.

The prosecutor stood.

"Witness," he said. The figure didn't respond to him.

"Witness!" he said, louder. The hooded head twitched slightly. "I'm going to remove your hood," he said, like a man trying to calm a rampant animal, hands forward, walking slowly.

The witness hissed. "I can do it myself." Its voice was scathing and airy, like acid rain. It flicked its arms up and shoulders back, head whipping jerkily, and the hood fell away. Racelsus moaned upon seeing his face.

His rotten skull gleamed sickeningly. He had no skin, no muscle, just bone, and the bone was pockmarked and weathered. His sockets glowed with green witchlight, and, despite having no eyes, Felix felt his soul being scrutinised by that terrible, terrible gaze. It turned its head to Racelsus.

"Hello, sister," the figure said.

~

"Racelsus?" Felix said.

"No, not like this, not like this…" she was mumbling. Helda and Furbo were exchanging glances, and trying to comfort the witch. Cherinda just stared at the figure, emotionless.

"Witness," said the prosecutor again. "Tell me your name and occupation."

"Why? What are you going to do?" snapped the figure. "Report me? Late for work again, was I? It must have slipped my mind. Or did my mind slip it?" he giggled, and reclined on the chair. The two guards flanking him didn't move a muscle.

"Witness, your name." The question was repeated, more insistently.

The laughter disappeared. "What's your name? Tell me yours and I'll tell you mine. 'Tis only polite, good manners, bad manners, bad spanners, span matters." His words seemed to slide between phrases, repeating but altered, so fast it was almost continuous speech. It would then abruptly stop.

With more patience than he had displayed since this case began, the prosecutor smiled and bowed to the witness. "I am Prosecutor Jeast."

I just realised I never knew that until now, Felix couldn't help but think. It was testament to his unsettled mind that this didn't bother him. In another case, not knowing such details would have left him feeling revolted with himself.

The witness tapped his head with a bony finger. "*Thank you.* My name is Peddin. Or I think it is. Was. Is. Was. Could be, would be, might be, flight bee."

Jeast nodded his thanks, or perhaps his relief. "Witness Peddin, tell us your story." He stood back, hands folded in front of him.

"Well!" Peddin said, with a flourish of arms, like an acrobat landing a perfect backflip. He swished his hands, then clapped them together. The impact echoed around the room. It sounded like a twig snapping.

"...that pretty much sums it up," he said.

After a pause, the prosecutor resumed. "...indeed. Are you alive, witness?"

The witness cackled. "No. Well, yes. I am, what you might say, functionally immortal. Just like my dear sister. Hello, dear sister!" He waved at Racelsus. "Sister dear, dear, my sister is a deer. Deers don't abandon each other, though, do they, dear?" His voice was suddenly murderous, deep and grating. "Leave each other to rot? Do they?"

Racelsus said nothing. *What is she not telling us?*

Peddin relaxed immediately, reclining back on his chair, stroking his skull with a finger. Felix noticed the finger was short, as if ground down. It was true of all his fingers, as far as he could see.

"Tell me of the Well of Eternity," said Jeast, ignoring this outburst.

The figure leapt to its feet, snarling, eyes blazing with green fury. The two chaperones grabbed him and forced him down.

"I'm not going back!" it screamed. "Never!" He collapsed heavily into the arms of the guards, his voice pleading and cracked. "Please.."

"No one is taking you back," said the prosecutor, "I promise."

The figure calmed with alarming speed, and began speaking conversationally, as if discussing favourite picnic spots. He had one arm resting on his elbow, propping his head up. The other waved in the air as he spoke.

"It's a bloody great big, deep, huge, never-ending hole in the ground that they throw nasty people in with the hope that the earth will swallow them up." He dipped his hand down, and mimed falling, moving it down, down, down…

"And—"

"Except! It's not never-ending. Oops, double negative. It isn't not ending. It hasn't not got a fake final point that you can't reach. Am I being clear?"

He picked at his fingers, flicking invisible specks of dirt from the gaps in his knuckles. The prosecutor continued, coolly. "Are you saying that this well *does* in fact have a bottom?"

"Yes, if you want to put it so complicated," the skeleton muttered, stroking his skull again.

"How do you know, witness?" asked Jeast.

"Oh, I was thrown in there. Or did I trip on a root and fall?" It started to count off on its fingers. "I did that, then he said that, she said she would find me, then…" He shook his head, then nodded. "No, I was thrown in, for definite."

"Who threw you in?"

"Some uppity church somebody or other. He's dead now, of course."

"Why?"

"Old age, I assume."

Jeast's eye twitched. "No, I mean, why were you thrown in?"

"Oh, normal reasons. People showing off. Showing off. You know, normal reasons."

"Showing off how?" pressed the prosecutor.

"Some priest or bishop or something wanted to quell un-sanctioned magickers, despite us not doing anything to anyone that didn't want it, so he rounded us up like fish, then dealt with us for having the sheer audacity to exist. Exist? Exist. Yes, exist. Can you *imagine*?"

A short pause, then the prosecutor continued.

"Did they know you were immortal?"

"Yes. It's pretty much the reason they didn't like us so much, I think." Peddin's voice was quiet.

"Did they know, or did they believe, this well was endless?"

"Yes, their god whispered it to them in a dream, or it was built by those who came before, or something mysterious." He was whispering.

"So, these people, knowing you were immortal, and believing that the well was an unending spiral of nothingness, threw you in the well, to gain prestige?" pressed Jeast.

"I'd say so, silly as it might sound, yes. They did worse to my sister. Look at her!" he gestured at Racelsus, his voice loud and intense. "They cut her body off!"

"Witness, please. What did you do when you were thrown in?"

He raised his arm again, miming the drop. "I fell, then I fell, then I fell, then I fell, before I finally hit the floor. Then, I didn't die, and slowly rotted while the world turned black and empty, and I turned black and empty."

"How did you escape this prison?"

Peddin was twitching again as he spoke. His head snapped from side to side.

"I climbed. I climbed, I fell, I climbed, I fell, I climbed, and my skin and muscles withered as I climbed, my fingers worn to the bone, then my bone worn to stumps, and my flesh peeling from me with age, and my mind must have been snagged on a rock at the bottom like a jumper in a twig, because the higher I got, the more my thoughts unravelled." His voice was completely level, and his head swung from side to side as he spoke. "Rational thoughts abandoned me. Cherished memories spoiled like old milk on a hot day. All I had were my inner monologues to keep me busy for all the time I climbed, I climbed, I climbed. Can you imagine sharing a room with yourself for that long?"

"How long were you in that well, witness?"

"Oh, who knows. Twentieth minutes? Fifteven years? Somewhere in between. Do you know?" he asked earnestly.

The prosecutor looked sidelong as Felix. "We estimate, based on evidence, around four hundred years," he said.

"If you say so. Plenty of time for one to completely lose one's mind, that's as far as I can tell you. Ha!"

Racelsus had said nothing up until this point. Felix wasn't sure if he should reach out to her, rest a reassuring arm on the cage she had become accustomed to. He decided against it.

"Did you see any other bodies in there?" asked the hairless man.

"Oh, no bodies, but lots of old bones. Bones for old stones, stones for old homes," muttered the figure.

"What happened when you reached the top, after all those years?" asked Jeast. Peddin swivelled his head to regard him, and Felix thought he could see that rotten skull *smile*.

"Why, prosecutor, you were standing there, waiting for me," said the witness. "And you said: I am compelled by the forces of the universe to stand witness in the trial for the fate of humanity, and if I did so, my greatest desire would be mine. So, I said 'sure, why not?', and here I am."

The prosecutor smiled, then nodded. "No further questions."

~

Felix.

The thought came unbidden into his mind.

What is it, Racelsus?

What are you going to ask him?

Felix paused.

I'm going to have to prove he's insane, so the court can't trust anything he says.

Oh.

I'm sorry. It's all I can do.

It won't work.

I have to try. I can't suggest he was dangerous, because that goes against the case I argued for you, and I would therefore contradict myself. We're hanging on by a thread as it is.

Felix stood, and walked over to the skeleton. It regarded him quizzically.

Felix opened his mouth to speak.

Ask him how he is… please.

"I—uh. How are you, witness?" coughed Felix, trying to make it sound natural.

"Am I under *oath* to tell the truth?" the figure said, amused.

Felix shrugged, and glanced to Habeus. "Yes, I think you are."

"Well, it's your cross-examination. I'm a little worn out, truth be told." He leaned back as he said it, sinking further into his chair.

Felix dipped his head, cracked his knuckles, and was about to start again. "Witness, wh—"

Ask him if he ever thought of me, as I thought of him.

"Did- did you ever, did you think of your sister, in that well? In those years?"

"Who?" asked Peddin.

"Your sister, Racelsus." Felix said. He gestured to the defence desk with his hand.

"Oh, yes." A pause. "I did. For a good few years, the thought of her kept me sane. She said, the last time I saw her, she said, well didn't say, she talked in my head, like I suspect she's doing to you now. She told me that she was going to find me, and we would be safe again. She was going to rescue me."

"And—"

"But, *obviously*, she never did. That was when I started losing it, I think, I think, when I realised she had lied to get me to agree to the worst of it, to get the worse punishment, if you like. I take the brunt, I go to the well, she goes to some cell, all done and dusted." His voice was growing louder.

Felix felt shocked. "She… lied to you?" he couldn't help but blurt out.

It's not true!

"Oh yes, haha! She said, she was better with magic, if I were to take the blame, she would come and rescue me, and we'd be off keeping to ourselves again soon. So, I did, brave as you like, and that turned out *well*, didn't it?" His voice took the angry tone again.

I have to get him off of this line of questioning.

"Witness, did—"

Prove him insane—

"Stop!" said Felix, stopping and shutting his eyes. "I will ask the questions I choose."

"Is that a question?" said the figure, tapping its chin with a bony finger. "Tough one to answer, that."

Felix shook his head, then looked back at Racelsus. She was averting her gaze. None on the bench were looking at him. He turned back.

"…Witness, you are, by your own admission, mad?"

Peddin's voice was conversational again. "Yes, I suppose so. But aren't we all?"

Felix shook his head. "No, I am not. I consider myself perfectly sane."

"Ah, that's the first sign."

"Witness, I am sane."

"Didn't you call a dog as a witness earlier?"

Don't rise to it, Felix, just carry on…

"Witness. How can we take anything you say as truth when you are— by your own admission—mad?"

"Because everything I said can be corroborated. In fact, it can be done so by your own assistant, my sister, Racelsus. She was there the whole time, and, if that's not enough, she can read my mind and learn the truth of it if she wants."

He turned to face the skull.

"Sister, do you want to read my mind? It's quite different to the last time you did so." He leaned forward, pate towards her.

"No…" she whispered. He leant back. His eyes were bright.

"Remember when you used to reach out to me? I used to hear your voice, sometimes, as I climbed. 'Brother, I'm here,' you would say. It kept me going. Then, it stopped. Why?"

He stood.

"Why did you stop?!" he screamed.

Habeus gestured, and the two guards held Peddin down. He collapsed without a fight. Habeus turned to Racelsus.

"Skull. Is this witness speaking truth, can you corroborate his statement, or is his perception clouded by madness?"

Racelsus hesitated, then whispered: "He speaks... truth..."

Racelsus! Thought Felix.

He stood and considered his options. None of them were good.

He stuck his hands in his pockets, paused, then removed them. "No further questions," he mumbled.

The skeletal figure clapped, then jumped up, pointing at the demon. Heavy hands on its shoulders tried to push it down again, but he remained on its feet.

"Great, now that's all over with, you said you could give me what I wanted, so if you wouldn't mind. I'm ready."

"What?" said Racelsus. "Ready for—"

Jurrekker stood, all cloven hooves and smoking horns. "The bargain was struck, payment will be delivered," he boomed in a guttural growl, and lifted an arm, pointing at the figure. His fingers began to glow.

Peddin looked at Racelsus.

"I wanted to say it was good to see you one last time, sister," he said. "But to be honest I don't think it was."

A beam of blackness burst from the hand of Jurrekker, meeting the skeleton straight in the head, narrowly missing the guards. His body spasmed as his head dissolved, before collapsing heavily on the floor.

"No!" screeched Racelsus, the skull flinging itself around the cage. Helda was on her feet, staring wide eyed at the demon. Furbo was holding the cage, trying to soothe Racelsus. Cherinda just sat, staring.

Habeus stood. "What is the meaning of this?" he shouted at Jurrekker.

The prosecutor produced a sheaf of paper from the air, curled and blackened. "A contract was signed between Peddin and Jurrekker—that Peddin will provide truthful testimony at this trial, and in return Jurrekker will provide obliteration. It was consented, signed and pacted." He strode over to the judge and handed him the paper.

Habeus read the contract, stroked his beard, then nodded.

"Please keep it out of the courtroom next time," he said.

Felix looked at his bench, his team. They were worn thin.

He was worn thin.

He looked up at Habeus, then sank into his chair.

I'm in over my head. We haven't got a chance.

He squeezed his eyes shut until he saw spots. When he opened them, he looked at his friends again. Racelsus was quiet and unmoving. Furbo was still chatting to her, and Helda was looking at the demon, hands moving unconsciously around her belt, searching for the weapons she wasn't wearing, but never settling on one for more than a second.

He looked at the Celestial, Cherinda. She was staring dead ahead, seeing nothing. *What is going on in her head?*

"Does the prosecution have any further witnesses or evidence?" asked Habeus.

"No, O Judge," said Jeast.

"Does the defence have any further witnesses or evidence?" he asked again. Irritation rose in Felix, but he quashed it.

"We have already answered previously, no," sighed Felix.

"You did? Oh, that's right," he said, slowly.

Something clicked in Felix's mind.

Did he forget..?

"Very well then," said Habeus, picking up his gavel.

14 – The Vote

"We shall take another vote," said Habeus. "The higher powers present will each indicate whether, in their view, humanity's continued existence should come to an end. We will begin with the prosecutor, then the defence, then myself," he gestured to Jurrekker.

Felix's mind was still racing. He remembered something Cherinda said.

"We do not know everything, we make mistakes, we can be blinded by oversight and can simply get things wrong."

The demon snorted, then said: "For."

Habeus turned to Cherinda. "And you?"

Cherinda paused. She looked at Felix and met his eyes for the first time in hours. He suddenly noticed her aura had reduced to nothing. His eyes widened at her level, empty gaze, and she regarded him with cold, empty eyes.

"Abstain," she said.

That one word turned Felix's guts to ice.

"I see. Then, it is down to me," said Habeus. He rose to his feet. "Unless I vote *against* the motion, humanity's fate is sealed, for to abstain as a majority means the remaining vote takes priority. Based on the testimony I have heard, and the evidence that has been presented, I cannot, on the balance, vote to save humanity. Therefore, I will vote for the motion."

Habeus lifted his hand and looked at his old, beaten gavel. He struck the plate in front of him.

"Thus rules Habeus."

~

Thus rules Habeus.

The words rushed through his head like a torrent of boiling steam. His mind shifted to the memory he was trying to dredge up.

*We need something! Anything! Or we're **dead**!*

Felix jumped to his feet. He bit his cheek accidentally, but he didn't even register the pain. With no idea what he was going to say, he slammed his fist on the table.

"Objection!" he yelled. *Think, you idiot! Think!*

"Ob…" said Habeus, quite unsure of how to respond. Anger threatened to manifest on his ancient face.

"Uh, that was the wrong word," said Felix. He could feel his face turning red, but he didn't care. It was now or never. "I move to appeal the decision immediately."

"You will have time to appeal at a later date," said Habeus, dismissively.

The thing that clicked in Felix's head before clicked again.

That's it!

"With respect, Your Honour, I don't think so."

Habeus considered this, brow lowered.

"…No, I suppose you're right. But there is nothing to appeal."

"Your Honour, if it pleases the court, I request a short recess for us to prepare our appeal officially."

"Pah!" growled Jurrekker.

Habeus shook his head.

"Defence Counsel, you are delaying the inevitable. You knew the terms when we started, and I have passed judgement." His tone was intended to brook no argument, but Felix plowed on.

"Please, honoured Habeus. Give me time to prepare. I want to check that there is no precedent we might have missed."

Take the bait, you old—

"No such precedent exists," intoned Habeus.

Felix took a step forward and gripped his hands to his sides.

"Honoured Habeus. Earlier this very afternoon, you asked the defence if we had any further witnesses or evidence. We said no. Then, shortly afterwards, you asked us the same question again."

Habeus looked puzzled.

"You told us we could appeal at a later date, but you forgot that we would not be able to do so as we would be, er, obliterated."

Habeus's face began to darken. Before he could speak, Felix continued.

"What I am getting at, Your Honour, is that your formidable memory is not completely perfect and reliable. There is a chance, however small, that there might be a precedent that you have hitherto forgotten, and if we are not given the chance to prepare an appeal, a great injustice may be performed."

Felix was at the base of the dais now. He looked up at Habeus.

"*Please.* My *species* will soon cease to exist. What is another hour?" He tried to sound as genuine as he could.

Habeus's dark expression lifted, and he waved a hand.

"Oh, very well. You have one hour. We will meet back here, where punishment will be meted out, if a precedent is not produced." Habeus banged his gavel once more.

"One. Hour," he said, before retiring to his chambers.

Felix rubbed his temples, then walked to the defendant's chambers in a daze, ignoring the hubbub and excitement that swelled in the courtroom.

15 – Time Borrowed

Felix slammed the door of the defendant's chambers. It bounced back from the frame with a crunch, but Felix didn't notice.

"We need a miracle," he said, looking at Cherinda. She had been in the room before them. She must have disappeared earlier, without him noticing. "What do *you* want?" He didn't try to hide the venom in his voice.

"Felix…" she began.

"I don't have time for this," growled Felix. "Just get out, would you?"

After a moment, she sighed quietly, then left the room. Her aura was still empty.

Felix looked around as the door sounded again. Helda and Furbo entered, trailed by Yetty. They looked downtrodden. "Where's Racelsus?" Felix asked.

"She wanted to be left on the bench to think," Furbo said.

Shaking his head, Felix exhaled deeply, then pointed at the wall of legal tomes.

"That wall is covered in probably millions of cases of legalese. I need just one. One that will give me some precedent, some lifeline, to keep us in this thing."

He looked at his entourage with as much earnestness as he could muster. He looked haggard and pale. They looked the very definition of despondent. He shook himself.

We have one more chance. We can mope when we're dead.

He clapped his hands and planted his hands on his hips.

"Look. Everyone. I know it's looking pretty bleak. But. It could be worse. We have one more opportunity. One more shot to show everyone that humanity isn't done yet. We're down, but we aren't out." He smiled. "But I can't do it alone."

They looked at him. Yetty stepped forward. Her face looked determined, her jaw set.

"What can we do?" she asked. He clapped her on the arm.

"I need you all to start looking, and looking fast. I don't care what it is. Anything. Find me something that will keep us in this fight. We have no rhyme or reason. No method. Just blind luck. We also have only one hour. Any questions?"

Furbo coughed. "Won't they, erm, dismember us if we handle these tomes? I distinctly remember a, ahehm, threat," said Furbo, looking at his fingers.

"I have no idea. Possibly. Probably. But, may I remind you, if we *can't* find anything, they'll do more than just that... and not just to us, but to the whole of humanity."

"Good point," said Furbo.

"Okay. Good luck everyone," said Felix grinning, managing a genuine smile for the first time in a while. Helda noticed blood on his teeth, as if he had been punched in the mouth. Before she could say anything, he had turned and picked the first book from the first shelf, and began leafing through the pages.

~

Furbo was moving rapidly between four open books spread in front of him. Helda was plucking books indiscriminately from the shelf, reading a random page, then tossing it behind her to pick another up. Yetty had taken one book to the furthest corner of the room, and was huddled over it, reading every line of every page. Felix held a book in each hand, and paced up and down, eyes flicking from one to the other. He muttered as he read, the two separate cases from each book melting together.

"...hereupon when two parties being equal in ruggedness of character should ensure both are agreed when in disagreement furthering their second hereupon..."

The air in the room was thick and dense. Books were strewn about, some in great mounds, some individual dotted around the floor. Everyone in the room was hot, stressed, and hopeless. They had less than ten minutes left.

Furbo spoke "Hmm, what about here? It says that Demonkind are forbidden from meddling in affairs of their equals... We could argue humanity is the equal of Demonkind? Or, well... bah." Furbo was clearly unconvinced by his own suggestion, and slammed his book closed in disgust.

Helda padded over and patted him on the arm. "Hey, it's the best we have so far."

"Well we need a bloody better one!" squawked Felix. His eyes boggled maniacally as he tried to read both of his tomes at once.

Yetty gasped loudly from the corner of the room. Everyone looked around to find her holding her book open, staring wide eyed.

"I think I have it," she whispered.

"Yetty," Felix said in what he had hoped was a calm, level way, but instead sounded the opposite. He dropped his two books and walked slowly over to her, hands gripped together. "What is it?"

She held the book open to Felix. He scanned the Allspeak, reading aloud. "Something about mixing of seeds, or carving into trees? I don't understand how this is relevant," he scowled.

Yetty shook her head. She looked on the edge of tears. "Look. Closer."

Felix took the book from her and stared at it.

And gasped.

~

Back in the courtroom, the air was thick with tension. People chatted excitedly with their neighbours, bets were made, nervous toes tapped on the floor.

"What could they have found?" Jurrekker snarled at his aide, who bristled.

"I can think of nothing, Mighty Jurrekker. There is no precedent. Over the last seven hundred years, I have checked every Tome of Precedent... personally." He smiled, showing two rows of pale gums.

"Then why does that human hold that book with such confidence?" the demon replied.

An eye twitch is all his lawyer managed in response.

~

A gong sounded, and Habeus entered and settled into his chair on the dais, casting his gaze around the room.

"I take it the defendants are satisfied with their recess?" he intoned, staring at Felix. "A reminder. Based on the evidence, witnesses and persuasion of the Prosecution, that being the demon Jurrekker, and with no precedent existing to guide us, this court *will* rule against the continued existence of humanity. Does the defence wish to present any appeal before judgement?"

Felix stood, tome in hand. He barely disguised the shake that threatened to overpower him. "We do, Habeus." The old man nodded, and indicated he should proceed.

Felix looked around him, from the terrifying figure of the prosecution, to the serenity of Cherinda. Despite her vote, she remained on the defence's bench. *No point arguing with her now.*

They all waited for him to speak. He realised, at this point more than any other, that no one knew what was going to happen. For all their millions of years of experience, their seemingly unending knowledge of the mysteries of the universe, their sheer arrogance at the superiority of themselves over humanity... he had them in his thrall.

He was a juvenile lawyer once again, revealing the key piece of evidence that would prove the baker was padding his loaves with coaldust. He was back explaining how he could prove why the longbow *must* have been enchanted with malicious intent, else how could it fire backwards?

However, this time, the stakes were much higher. But he was here.

Of course, this gamble would fail. But, it was his only option. He had no idea how this would go down. It was... *unprecedented.* All he knew for certain was humanity would go down fighting.

"This weed's got teeth," he whispered.

"Please speak up, Defence Counsel," Habeus said.

Felix cleared his throat and began.

"Precedent. It defines what we should do, which judgements we should make, based on what has been determined before. The wise minds of the past have deliberated, and concluded, and we adopt their decisions into practice, and into law. Rarely, we conclude that their way of thinking is no longer up-to-date. Perhaps an extenuating circumstance, or a change in attitude. Either way, precedent lets us understand that what we do has come before, and has been ruled on by those that came before, withstanding the test of time."

He glanced at the demon who was boring holes into Felix's very soul with darkened eyes. Felix turned, and could actually feel the heat of the stare on his back.

"We have striven to find a precedent for this case. Our great and wise Habeus has informed us just now that no precedent exists."

Habeus nodded, and moved to stand, to strike the gavel on humanity for the last time.

"However, I must beg our learned colleague to adjust his statement, for a precedent *does,* in fact, exist."

A monstrous silence filled the air. Habeus had frozen, half-standing, narrow eyed. He joined in the chorus of stares Felix felt were melting his insides. The room darkened slightly as what he said trickled through the room.

"Or rather, it *may* exist. I have here a copy of one of the Tomes of Precedent, written in Allspeak. It is my understanding that these books contain every law ever passed from the dawn of existence to this very moment. Any judgement handed down by any judge on any matter has been noted in these pages. Am I correct so far?"

Felix addressed this question to the room, and carried on before anyone could intercede.

"We have checked every page of every book, and I can honestly say we did not find a precedent," he conceded.

More silence. A creak as someone adjusted their weight in their chair.

"However," said Felix. It was the heaviest 'however' he had uttered, and he'd given a good few of them.

He flipped open the book in front of him, and opened it to the page Yetty had shown him.

"I ask the courtroom to consult book two thousand, five hundred and fifty-three, page eight hundred and eighty-one. I suspect all would agree that a detailed analysis of the mixing of seeds to be of little relevance, nor the carving of trees on the opposite page."

The prosecutor's brow furrowed, and he closed his eyes and began mouthing while twitching his finger, as if turning the pages of an invisible book. His eyelids twitched, and flicked open.

"That's not right…" he muttered.

"But! Draw your attention to the centre of page, O great Habeus, along the spine," continued Felix.

An aide carried the open book to the Judge's dais. He stood up immediately, knocking his chair flying behind him.

"A page is missing!" Habeus shouted. "Torn out!"

"Precise—" Felix said, before he was drowned out in the roar of raised voices. People chattering loudly to their neighbours, or no one at all. The buzz that filled the room was deafening. Habeus raised his hand, and they all fell silent, then he pointed at Felix.

"Continue," he said, with a hint of fury.

The prosecutor stood up. "This is clearly nonsense! There-is-simply-no-precedent! That page has some drivel about a frog, from my memory."

Habeus stared the prosecutor down, and he flinched, before sitting again.

Felix's throat felt dry; he spoke quickly. "Thus, great and wise Habeus, I must conclude: If this page is missing, then it is possible that there exists a pre-ordained precedent that might have an impact on the ruling. Without being able to locate the page, I move that it is impossible to dismiss the idea of a lack of precedent, and thus this case must be terminated, or at least recessed until this last page is found, for, if humanity was destroyed, and then the page was located and a precedent clearly stated that humanity should be spared, it will be too late, and a great, cosmic injustice will have been committed." He breathed, having almost run out of breath in that enormous sentence.

Felix stood, barely trembling, staring the old God down.

Habeus hesitated, then stood, and began to pace behind his dais.

Make or break. Felix thought. *A dodgy argument for all the marbles...*

Minutes passed.

"I can recall no such case in the history of existence that would have set a precedent that would be relevant to this case," Habeus stated. He stopped walking.

"But. As the lawyer Felix has taken great pains to explain, higher beings are not infallible. Therefore, it is theoretically possible that there exists, on this missing page, something that could decide the outcome of this case."

Felix almost choked but held his composure.

"Until such time as this page can be located, this case cannot be continued. Thus rules Habeus." He struck the gong behind him, and waited for it to quieten.

"We must therefore find this page, find who desecrated our holy texts, exact terrible punishment, and conclude this case as soon as we are able."

He turned to his armoured sentinel aide next to him.

"Make it happen."

The figure nodded, and turned, marching from the room. He waved his colleagues with him, and the column spread through the room and left by a multitude of exits. Habeus addressed the room.

"You are all temporarily dismissed. Court adjourned."

Felix turned to see Cherinda glaring at him.

"I suppose you thought that was terribly clever," she spoke, voice dripping with acid.

Felix rubbed his eyes. He was thinking of a comeback, but nothing came.

"Because it was," Cherinda said, and laughed. Her smile brought warmth back to Felix's bones. Despite himself, he forgave her instantly. He couldn't help it.

"Let's retire to chambers before I collapse," he said, and welcomed the arm from Helda, who took his weight and guided him out of the room.

Behind them, the demon Jurrekker's fist was clenched so tightly his claws had cut his palm, and black, steaming blood dripped from his fist in sinister droplets.

~

The atmosphere in the defendant's chambers was heavy. Helda was talking quietly with Furbo and Racelsus at the far end of the room. Yetty was nervously plucking at some threads on her outfit. At the centre, Cherinda and Felix sat at opposite ends of the table.

The Celestial looked at Felix. She stared past his eyes and straight into his soul. "I'm sorry Felix."

He shook his head. "Don't. What's done is done. Let's focus on what is happening now."

She shifted uncomfortably but didn't press the subject. "Never has anything like this ever happened to a Tome of Precedent," she stated flatly. "Never."

Felix shrugged with some difficulty and quoted: "It's always never until it happens."

Cherinda was unconvinced. "You know, if you *have* done something underhanded and sneaky… firstly, that will help to convince Habeus that humanity is in fact a bunch of self-serving hypocrites, and he might well rule against you."

She held up a hand when Felix tried to speak. "Secondly, before they destroy you and your kind, they will inflict such untold misery on you individually beforehand. Habeus will spend precisely *zero* time in considering whether to hand you over to Jurrekker and his ilk to punish you in the worst way they can imagine, and as you can probably guess, the worst way *they* can imagine is… unpleasant."

Felix hesitated, waiting to see if she was finished.

"I'm finished," she added.

Felix sighed. "Okay, heard loud and clear. I remember what you said about the wrong people even *touching* those books. Rest assured, none of us would dream of sabotage. We're in the clear. We haven't done anything underhanded, nothing sneaky, we're just exploring the avenues of legal possibility."

Cherinda closed her eyes, listening for something.

"They're making their way here. They're going to hold your mind, Felix, and search it for guilt. They'll search every edge and shadow, and will uncover the truth."

Furbo overheard. "If they can do that, why not do that on the stand?"

"They were," said Cherinda. "But the point wasn't about the truth— but the arguments." Furbo blinked, then nodded.

"Of course," he said.

"They're nearly here," said Cherinda. Felix could hear faint footsteps. "They'll check the occupants of the other rooms first, then come here."

Yetty squeaked from the corner of the room. Cherinda looked at her, levelling her considerable gaze. Her aura flared a noxious orange.

"Yetty..." she said. "Do you know something?"

"No!" Yetty said, not meeting the Celestial's eyes, who shrugged.

"It's not up to me, anyway. The Finders will dig it out. Not that there *is* anything, of course," she added, before walking past the cowering aide and out of the room.

Once she had left, Felix scurried over to Yetty and took a deep breath before adopting what he hoped was a kind, understanding expression.

"Yetty. I've known you for—"

"I ripped the page out," she blurted, quiet enough for only him to hear.

Felix had expected to hear this, but it still shook him. His blood turned cold, and his chest filled with waves of dread. He took her hands and waited until she looked into his eyes. Hers were bloodshot and erratic.

"Yetty... What have you done?"

"What I had to do!" she spat. "Humanity doesn't deserve this! What do they know? If I'm clever enough to outsmart the lot of them, maybe they aren't so high and mighty after all, and who are they to judge our entire species? Our entire *species* Felix! Everyone we've ever known, ever loved... Every old grandmother and new-born baby, judged and found wanting! How could they do it?"

Felix responded. "Yetty, I know you mean well, but this isn't the way. This is dishonest. If they find out, we're finished, and... oh god, the torture..." Felix closed his eyes, trying to shut out the image of a fiery monster out of his mind.

"What are we going to do, Felix?" Yetty blubbered. She was clearly out of her depth. She was *crying*. He had never seen her cry.

We're all out of our depth, mused Felix.

Yetty shook her head to regain her composure momentarily. "I... I think we can hide it. I told Racelsus... she says she can wipe my mind, just the parts of it that count, so they'll scan us and will never know."

Felix turned to the back of the room, and Racelsus's green sockets were focussed on him.

He went over to the group.

"Furbo, Helda, I need you to leave the room for a few minutes," Felix said. "I'm sorry, I can't explain why at this moment. I need you to go."

Furbo was going to protest, but Helda saw something in Felix's face.

"You look like a man with a heavy weight on him. Are you sure you're doing the right thing?" she asked.

"How much do you know?" Felix asked.

"She doesn't know," Racelsus said.

Helda and Furbo exchanged glances.

"Leave, you two, please" Racelsus spoke gently.

"...Okay," Furbo said, looking between them. "I trust you, Racelsus."

Helda nodded to them, and she and Furbo quietly left.

Felix gestured over to Yetty to join them.

"So, you can wipe part of our mind, erase all knowledge of the page?" Felix asked.

"Yes. I can manipulate it so you will know a page is missing, but not where or why or how. You will believe you are as innocent as anyone else here."

Felix closed his eyes.

You can read my thoughts, can't you Racelsus?

Yes.

Will it hurt?

No.

How did you learn of what happened?

Yetty thought it, I heard it. I looked at her, and she confessed.

I see.

Yes.

Does the Celestial speak the truth about the torture and the aftermath of the case?

I think she is perhaps even softening it somewhat. These creatures are truly abominable. They will break your spirit into pieces, but you will feel every splinter, from now until eternity.

Oh.

Yes.

Okay.

Okay?

Do it. Yetty first.

Yetty took Felix's hand and looked at him. As Felix watched, her expression slackened, eyes rolling, body teetering. Felix caught her before she fell, then she shook herself back into focus.

"Felix? Are you okay?" she asked.

"Yes, Yetty, I'm fine. Are you okay?"

"Yes... I think so... the strangest sense of deja vu..."

Your turn, Felix.

Racelsus, wait—

~

They filtered back into the courtroom in single file. The air in the room was full of weighted menace. Finders stood in great numbers, positioned along the edge of the room. Every eye tracked the party of humans as they took their seats.

Habeus was still at the dais, looking the very picture of ancient wrath.

Once everyone was present, he began.

"We have not found the page, nor anyone with any information on it or its whereabouts, despite scanning by the Finders. Therefore, I must suspend this case for the foreseeable future, until such time as we are able to locate it and conclusively rule out any precedent."

He lifted his gavel.

"Thus rules Habeus. Humanity is—"

"Wait."

Felix had stood, one finger pointing up from an outstretched arm. "I have something to add."

317

Yetty gripped his arm. "Felix! What are you doing! We're about to win…"

Murmurs from his entourage echoed these words. Other mutters from the courthouse expressed the general surprise at his outburst, but they quietened quickly.

Felix looked at his team. Racelsus's eyes were dark.

Well… here we go then.

He reached a hand into his inner jacket pocket and pulled out a page. It was large, it was covered in all manner of curious symbols, and it was torn along the long edge.

"Here is the missing page."

Jurrekker leapt from his seat, fire exploding from his back. Seven Finders rushed to restrain him as he started barrelling towards Felix. "You shall know such torment, human!"

"**SILENCE.**" bellowed Habeus, over the clatter and clash. His voice had a *power* behind it, and everyone in the room immediately stopped and waited, with the exception of Jurrekker. He didn't fight, but he flexed his shoulders, smoke drifting from his nostrils in angry puffs.

Habeus pointed at Felix.

"Explain this, now!" he roared.

Felix swallowed, taking one last look at his teammates.

"It is quite straightforward, wise Habeus. When we headed back for our hour-long recess, I took one of the Tomes of Precedent into the corner of the room, where none could see me. There, I chose a random page and ripped it out, slowly and quietly. I then tucked the page into an inner pocket, and… well, you remember the rest."

"And now you come forward to confess? Why?"

Felix pursed his mouth, thinking, ignoring the screaming inside his own mind.

"Because…" he hesitated, then shrugged.

"Because it's the right thing to do."

No one spoke, so he continued.

"Humanity has flaws. It makes mistakes. There are some evil people, some careless people. There are so many who lie and cheat and exploit their way to the top, or even to the middle… or anywhere, so long as it's above the next guy. Everyone sees it, the evil. Many sit by and let it happen. Some are scared to get involved. They fear for their safety, or comfort, or social status, and so permit evil. I performed evil, and my conscience stood by as I did it.

"I thought about this. I thought about the whole point of what we are doing in this case. I am here to represent humanity. Firstly, as its lawyer, but secondly… as a human. I am here with my esteemed colleagues, and their help and sacrifice have been vital to us getting this far. But, I am the one here, standing at the front, making the arguments. Taking the heat, dishing it out. I am, in this moment, the focus. I am humanity."

His voice broke, but he carried on.

"And, with that in mind, I stand up to be counted. When humanity had its back against the wall, I will not be the one who shirked. I will *not* allow dishonesty, dishonour and guile to be the reason we survived.

"I did what I had to do to buy us time… but it was misguided and deceitful, and it cannot be permitted to stand. Therefore, I humbly propose you take me in humanity's place. Do not wipe the species out. Instead, focus on me. I have represented us, and I have failed, so use me as the focus of punishment. I have earned it. I have tried to get one over on the very spirit of Justice. Give humanity a little more time, allow them to prove themselves, and in another thousand years, or hundred, or even one, test them again."

Felix stood straight backed and with his jaw clenched shut. He closed his eyes and counted his breaths. His eyes stung.

Habeus's eyes narrowed, but he didn't speak for some time. He gestured to Cherinda and Jurrekker to come up to the bench, and they began conversing in a language completely alien to Felix. Cherinda spoke in lilting musical tones, Jurrekker in harsh, scraped grunts, yet they all appeared to understand each other perfectly. They talked quickly, forcefully. Argumentative. Angry. Suspicious. Compromising.

"Felix…" Helda said.

He held up a hand to quiet her.

~

"We have reached a decision," said Habeus, before getting to his feet. Jurrekker and Cherinda flanked him. Without looking at Felix, he began.

"Without doubt, this is the worst crime ever committed against Law. A lawyer, no less, committing Cosmic Perjury, faking evidence, knowingly spreading falsehoods. Attempting to deceive everyone in such a callous way. For this, the most extreme punishment must be meted out. Unless you can give us any other mitigating circumstance we could take into consideration, perhaps to reduce your sentence?"

Felix tried not to react, but failed. His head dropped and his hands began to tremble.

"No, wise Habeus."

Habeus nodded.

"It is acceptable to all parties that in exchange for offering himself up as the guilty party, to be forever recorded in the Tomes, Felix will submit himself to an eternity of torture. Does the lawyer, Felix, agree to this compromise?"

Felix blinked back a tear of despair.

"Yes," he croaked.

Habeus nodded again.

"So shall it be. For such disgraceful behaviour, the punishment is appropriate."

Felix felt about to collapse into this chair. *Will I get to say goodbye..?*

"And yet, I feel..," said Habeus.

His hands stopped trembling; he snapped his head up.

"Alongside this, we see courage. Noble sacrifice. Offering oneself up for one's peers, however undeserving." Habeus's eyes darted over to Yetty as he said this.

What? Does he know?

"When given the easy way out, this lawyer, though tempted, resisted. Why? Because it was 'the right thing to do'. He stood up for his beliefs, and will pay most dearly for it. More dearly than anyone has ever paid for anything. And, I gather, he did so quickly, without hesitation?"

"Yes," spoke Racelsus.

Felix choked, letting out a meagre gurgle. "What?"

320

"He could have, at many points, said 'no'. Protected himself at the expense of others. But he didn't," said Habeus, and he smiled.

Felix looked around. All eyes were on him. He felt heat rising up his face.

"Humanity has extremes. Until today, I had seen nothing but the extreme worst. I have not experienced such selfless behaviour in a human before. Perhaps there is hope after all."

He lifted up the mace of office, and struck it once on the desk in front of him.

"The human Felix will be punished, but Humanity will not be. Thus rules Habeus."

~

"You will be allowed to speak to your colleagues before you head back with... him," Cherinda explained to him when they reached their chambers again.

Felix nodded, unable to answer. He was in a daze. He hadn't remembered the walk to chambers.

"I'll go and get them... Felix..." she said, but then left quickly without continuing. It was just Felix and Racelsus in the room. How did she get here?

Racelsus spoke to him.

"Are you sure you want to do this?"

Felix shrugged. "Yes... though what choice do I have?"

"You could explain it was Yetty's doing. I would back you."

"No..." Felix said, shaking his head. "That's not right... This is the best way. The only way. Oh, God..."

"I could end your life before they take you?" she offered.

"No... I don't want to compromise the result. At the end of the day, I'm just one person. What is my life against my whole race?" Felix spoke, and his cheeks were wet with tears. "This is the best way."

He remembered something then, his lawyer instinct taking over despite everything

"What did you mean, in the courtroom? You said, 'yes' to Habeus?"

Racelsus clacked her teeth and spoke loudly. Her socket twinkled. "Come on you old curmudgeon, surely that's enough by now?"

Felix looked at her with a puzzled expression.

"What?"

She ignored him. "Habeus!"

"Oh, very well." Habeus's voice filled the room.

The walls melted away, and Felix was standing back in the courtroom. It was as he remembered it, with Jurrekker and his lawyer across from him, his colleagues behind him, Habeus at the top. Felix stood at the table, tome in hand. He looked at it. There was no missing page.

What—

"Defence Counsel Felix. You have represented humanity admirably. You have shown that, despite the gravest of circumstances, even an ordinary person can make honourable decisions of importance, for the greater good of humanity.

"The balance of evidence left you wanting, this is true. But all things act in accordance with how they were created. I was unsure of the way to proceed, which is not a state of mind I am used to. So, a compromise was agreed, between myself and the higher beings. All shall be explained later. For now…

"I hereby judge: Humanity will not be erased, and the human Felix will be allowed to return home. Thus judges Habeus."

His gavel smacked against the gong behind him.

Felix blinked quickly, trying to understand what just happened. He turned to face his team, a confused look frozen on his face.

The demon Jurrekker howled in fury and leapt to his feet. He was bundled by Finders, who dragged him to the group. He managed to thrust one arm through and cast his hand out towards Felix. Black beams of balefire speared towards him, and hit him in the chest, billowing around him and consuming him in spiteful flames. More armoured Finders rushed to subdue the demon, but he had disappeared in a puff of black smog. Felix could feel nothing but pain, see nothing but smoke.

Soothing hands reached through and rested on his eyes, their cool presence spreading through his body. Within moments, the smoke had cleared, and he felt cold, but without pain. That is, except his chest, which still burned with poison.

He looked up to see Cherinda holding him, stroking his hair.

"What... where..." Felix managed.

"Later," she said, and held him until he passed from consciousness.

~

When he awoke, he was resting on a comfortable armchair, swaddled in blankets. His eyes burned, his skin sizzled. Through blurry eyes, he could make out the shapes of Helda, Furbo, Cherinda... and Habeus?

"Well done, Felix," Habeus said. He sat on a stool, hands folded in his lap.

"What..." he croaked.

"Humanity was indeed on trial. However, as I started to explain, you performed two roles. You were not just the lawyer, but the representative, as you somewhat grasped," Habeus said.

Racelsus's voice floated from somewhere. "We engineered multiple events to happen *precisely*... to test you. We had determined you were the perfect example of an 'average' human, so you were chosen to be the test case for humanity. Depending on how you reacted to these events, Habeus would judge the worthiness of humanity as a whole. Jurrekker agreed, thinking you would fail."

"You did brilliantly, Felix!" enthused Helda.

"Marvellous!" added Furbo.

"What... you two... in on it..?" Felix said.

"No, not at all, old chap. We're like you, we were caught up in the tide of the conspiracy. They explained it to us when judgement was passed, after you were hit by... that demon." Furbo's voice dropped.

"Demon..." Felix looked down at this chest. Where he should have had a heart, he had a gaping, black hole. He began to panic.

"Be still, Felix... I am keeping you alive and well," Cherinda said, resting a cool hand on his forehead. Her presence calmed him.

"What... is real...?" Felix said.

Habeus answered.

A. R. Turner

"All of it. Ah, you mean the courtroom. Once you asked for the recess to find precedent, we created a semi-reality for you. We knew there was no precedent, but Cherinda pleaded with me to give humanity one last chance, with you as the conduit. And, as I said, I was on the fence, to coin a human phrase. The higher powers agreed. One final test to see how you acted. From there, you were watched closely by the courtroom, and we… muddied the waters of reality a little. The case was very real, the witnesses and evidence real, but the whole missing-page saga was us. Come on now, you didn't really believe I didn't know there was no precedent, did you?" his eyes twinkled.

Felix's head was spinning, and not just from the pain.

"Yetty…" he spluttered.

She was there, in the background. She stood, and said: "Felix… It wasn't me. I don't know what happened, but it wasn't me."

Felix coughed, and the pain darted through him. He looked at Habeus.

"Humanity… Did… we win?" he asked.

"You did," said Habeus. "I am convinced. Humanity has potential. I wasn't sure for a while, but you… you tipped the scales, as it were. For now," he added, gravely.

Felix swivelled his eyes to Cherinda. "And… you?"

She had a tear in her eye as she spoke. "I'm sorry I ever doubted you and your kind. You have my vote, now and forever."

Felix tried to smile, but couldn't. It hurt too much.

"The demon..?" he asked.

Habeus looked instantly furious.

"A cowardly attack, completely unlawful. He shall be brought to justice, believe me."

A short pause. Felix heard a fire crackling from somewhere, and realised he had no idea where he was.

"Am I going to die?" Felix asked.

"That… remains to be seen," Habeus said.

Cherinda replied. "I am keeping you alive, but the demon Jurrekker is powerful, and he channelled all his hatred into that beam. I don't know what will happen to you, Felix." She was properly crying.

"I thought… Celestials couldn't lie…" Felix muttered.

Cherinda's hands gripped his tightly. His colleagues were all watching him. He looked at Racelsus, asking her a question with his thoughts. Her head shook slightly.

"I see," Felix said, grunting.

He regarded his colleagues. His friends.

"Thanks guys…" he coughed. They didn't know how to respond. Helda looked at the floor. Furbo was fiddling with his sleeves.

There was a pause. Felix turned to Cherinda.

"Can you… take me to the roof? I want to see the sunset, before…" he managed.

"I can do that, Felix."

The Celestial lifted him as if he was as light as a feather pillow and carried him gently to the roof.

Interlude – Habeus Becomes
~ *Very Long Ago*

Cherinda sat with Habeus, overlooking the dying forest.

"The trees won't last much longer," she said. "Jer told me they've got perhaps weeks before the last one dies."

Habeus frowned. He watched a bird fly overhead, snatching a moth from the air.

Nature…

He had seen the demon Krykk carving runes into that mother tree. He had stolen the form of that human. Corney, he called himself.

"What can we do?" she muttered.

Habeus considered.

"Where is Jer?" he asked. "I want to speak with her."

~

Habeus stood at the door. He took a breath, then knocked.

It opened, and Krykk stood there, a scowl on his face. "What do you want?"

Habeus straightened. "Do you know the farmer, Corney?"

Krykk shrugged. "Nope."

"I think you do. The fellow with the runes? The tree?"

"Can't say I recall."

Habeus stared at the demon, who shook his shoulders in irritation. "You're lying to me, Krykk."

"Prove it."

Habeus had heard enough. Shook his head, and walked back to his shrine, formed of leaves and stones. He placed his hand on the shrine and felt the warmth on his back. Turning, he held his face up towards the sunlight beating down on him. The searing brightness of that light formed a blurred smear across his vision. The shapes coalesced into a brief image of a blindfolded figure, then faded.

"Yes."

"I know."

"I accept."

His eyes glowed with white light as his back spasmed, arching him, twisting the emotion from him, wringing out like so much wet fabric. When he arose, he felt nothing. He cared for nothing but balance.

He was changed.

Returning to Krykk's house, he knocked once, firmly. As the door opened, his arm lashed out, gripping the demon by the neck with a grip like tree roots.

"You're coming with me," he said.

~

"What the hell is this, you old fool?" snarled Krykk from within his cage. He slammed at the bars, but they didn't move.

Habeus stood watching him. Cherinda was beside him, looking concerned, eyes moving between Habeus and the cage. She had, at his instruction, assembled Jer, Jurrekker, Ebo, and a dozen others to watch.

They all stood gathered around the stump of the Mother Tree of Midland Forest.

Habeus took a deep breath. "You stand accused of causing the doom of the Midland Forest," he said.

"I didn't do anything to your stupid trees," came the reply. "Now let me out before I do something you'll regret!"

Jurrekker stepped up to Habeus. "Explain yourself, old man. What is the meaning of this charade?"

Habeus turned to regard the demon. He waved a plume of smoke from his face as he spoke. Time was, the sight of those terrible eyes would have sent shivers down him. No longer.

"The great balance tips ever toward chaos. For too long it has been rudderless, drifting down a river of entropy. Left unchecked, the universe will unravel itself. I have petitioned those above, and have been granted the authority to change the course.

"It is time we set in place certain... *rules*. These rules shall be unmovable, unchangeable, unshakeable. They shall govern our actions and our philosophy.

"Should it come to my attention that these rules *have* been broken, then my punishment shall be severe. All shall be subject to these rules, myself included. These rules shall be named Law, and I shall be named Judge."

Jurrekker narrowed his eyes, but said nothing.

"I miss cheerful Habeus," whispered Sul the Jokemaker to a neighbour. "I wonder if he's ill."

"Despite this, I am not, however, omniscient, nor infallible," admitted Habeus. "Henceforth it shall be thus: Those accused of committing these acts shall stand before me, in what shall be called Trial. Whomsoever accuses them of these acts shall present, to me, evidence of the wrongdoing, either by witness or by physical object. The accused may argue these points, and present their own evidence. Once I have heard both sides, I shall decide on a course of action and a level of punishment as appropriate."

The assembled crowd looked at each other. Jurrekker shook his head. "This is not the way it should be. Nature sorts itself out. Intervention is not necessary."

Habeus thought of Corney.

"No," said Habeus. "This is how it shall be. Unless you wish to challenge me?" He let slip some of his power, releasing it as one would build pressure by leaning one's weight upon another.

Jurrekker averted his eyes, awed, and remained silent. Habeus chuckled mirthlessly.

"So shall it be. Worry not, for I shall be truly neutral. My... transformation has robbed me of much that defined me... before."

He turned to the cage.

"Now, I shall then hear evidence of this case, and every case hereafter, until such time as I designate a successor."

He turned to climb upon a rock that had been fetched. He lowered himself to a cross-legged position, higher than the rest, so that he might see everything.

His eyes glowed white once more, and he held a hand to his forehead. With a sound like a thunderclap, a flash of light burst from his hand. When it faded, he remained, but dressed in black.

"Jer. Come forth."

She did so.

"What do you allege?"

She hesitated. "That demon, Krykk, did, without reason or rhyme, set upon my forest a most dreadful curse, so much so that the trees die around me as I watch."

Habeus nodded.

"Krykk. You have been accused of the destruction of the Midland Forest. Do you admit to the crime?"

"No, you sanctimonious buffoon!" came the reply.

"I shall be respected, demon," warned Habeus, and the demon shrank back against the bars. He turned to Jer.

"Jer. Can you prove this accusation?"

"I can ask the man who the demon possessed, the one he controlled to do this terrible deed. I saw him before the mother tree before she died," said Jer. "His name is Corney, a human farmer."

"Very well. I shall call upon Corney, the farmer, who will explain to the court what he knows."

A wave of the hand, and Corney stood, pale and ghostly, on a small stone circle in the middle of the clearing. He looked between the demon in the cage to Habeus, barely reacting.

"What's this, then?" he said.

~

"Thank you, witness."

With a wave of his hand, the spirit was dismissed.

"You have been accused and a witness has corroborated the accusation. What say you?" said Habeus to Krykk.

"Excuse me, Habeus," said Khek the Hairless. "Might I debate on a few points?"

"You wish to argue on behalf of Krykk?" said Habeus.

"Yes, if you agree that I can. I would argue that, if truth is what we seek, then an independent observer might offer angles that the accused or accuser might miss."

"...Proceed," agreed the judge.

The hairless man nodded, and approached the centre dais.

"We don't know much of this farmer. For all we know, he is a liar and a scoundrel. Perhaps he has been paid to lie, bribed by the accuser? What of his character? And can it be proven that it was Krykk? Can the question be answered so that none hearing it would doubt? Those are the questions I would have answered before punishment is exacted."

Habeus looked between Jer to Khek. He looked at Krykk, and to the assembled watchers.

Yes. This is the way. Do you agree?

~

He was silent for a time, but eventually spoke.

"I have considered the evidence and the testimony. I have come to a verdict."

He turned to Krykk.

"Krykk the Demon: Of the crime you are accused, I find you guilty."

"Wait!" shouted Krykk.

Habeus stood, then plunged his hand into the stump upon which he had sat. He ripped a chunk of wood from it and held it high. He plucked a twig that jutted from the stump, and stabbed it through the chunk, forming a small, crude hammer.

"You have been judged by your peers, Krykk. You have been found guilty of perverting the natural order. I sentence you to obliteration."

The demon tried to reply, but Habeus lifted the hammer, and slammed it down in front of him, squatting as he did so, and the hammer collided with the floor in front of him. As it landed, the cage was crushed as if by some great weight, collapsing down upon itself with sickening speed. The screams of Krykk were cut off, and there were no echoes in the undergrowth.

Habeus turned to the rest, unphased by the death he had caused, and not noticing the terrified expressions of those watching him. He tucked the mallet into his belt.

"Let it be known. If you cannot settle your own arguments, or you threaten to pervert the natural order, come to me, for I shall judge. I shall hear all arguments from both sides, but know this: whether you agree with my decision or not, I am the final arbiter of what I shall call: Justice."

He stood.

"Thus judges Habeus."

~

Once the case was settled, almost everyone had left, contemplating what they had seen and considering what life would bring tomorrow. Cherinda approached Habeus tentatively.

"Habeus…" she said. He regarded her calmly.

"Yes?"

She hesitated, as if figuring the best way to frame a difficult question. Her aura, normally pale, was a dull orange.

"I was thinking. Thinking about what you said earlier. The great balance tips ever towards Chaos. You have so much... power... now. You could clap your hands, and it would be solved."

"And how would I do that, child?"

"You know who I'm talking about," she said, louder than she intended. She looked around, and carried on more quietly. "Those demons. Jurrekker, Krykk, their ilk. They delight in tipping the scales. Without them, life would flourish."

"Do you wish to bring a case, Cherinda?" intoned Habeus, his expression dark.

She turned her face away. "No..."

"We will not speak of this again," he finished, and left her standing there. She felt the embarrassment filter down from her face to her body, and her aura pulsed red. When she looked up, she saw Jurrekker, watching her from the shadows.

16 – The Roof

On the roof, Cherinda laid Felix so he could rest his back against a parapet. It was dusk, and the air was cold.

"Do you want to be left?" she asked.

Felix nodded. She stroked his hair once, then turned and walked back through the door to the main terrace.

Alone.

The city stretched out before him, and Felix swept his gaze slowly over Placenamia. He could see the whole city from here. Once, this district was his entire life. How small and distant it seemed now.

His heart burned.

There is good here. Somewhere.

The sun was almost set, flushing the sky with gold and pink.

He looked at his hands. His skin was starting to bleed as the taint spread, his blood and veins turning smeary and brown. The hole in his chest leaked brown sludge.

Brown...

His fingers felt thick and unresponsive as he fumbled with his belt pouches. He produced a small bottle and held it up in shaky hands. Glancing one last time over the city, he unstoppered and upended the bottle Bertruk had given him, scattering the powder to the wind. It was swept away, up and away, into the clouds.

Felix felt his strength leaving him within moments, and slumped down, head back, eyes to the sun. A final beam landed on his face. It was warm and he smiled.

~

"He's not up there." Helda was wide eyed and panicked. "I couldn't find him, he's not there."

"He's gone," replied Cherinda. She placed a hand on Helda's. "It's okay. He's moved on. He's in a better place." Helda's bottom lip quivered, before rage overtook her face.

"I'll kill that demon bastard! I'll—"

Racelsus clacked her teeth, and Helda stopped, shaken.

"I wouldn't be so sure he's gone. I can feel him. He's still here... somewhere..."

"What do you mean?" asked Helda, revenge forgotten.

The skull's eyes glowed blue, the colour of understanding. "He's got unfinished business. He won't be moving on for a while yet, I'd wager."

Yetty couldn't stop the tears. Cherinda embraced her, squeezing her tightly. Furbo was watching Racelsus, who turned to look out the window, a slight shadow passing over her.

~

Henria sat in darkness. Only the meagre light from the stars outside gave her anything to see by. She thought of her two infant children, sleeping on the floor in the front room.

Three days, she'd been given. Three days to leave. She had no money left to pay the landlord, and he had given them three days.

"Not my problem," he had said, briskly, when she had begged him to give them more time.

She picked up the letter again, the one she had read ten times. It was packed with awkward words she didn't understand, but she understood the message of it well enough.

It said: Three days.

Her husband had been killed in the war, five months past. She had received a small bag of silvers and a letter of condolences. It hadn't lasted long.

Her mind wandered back to happier times. The four of them. She had tried to live a good life. She gave back as best she could by helping those on the street when they struggled. Her children never worried about their situation for she kept the details from them. How had it come to this?

It was terribly cold this winter. The fuel had run out once she had had to save for food. She grabbed handfuls of her hair and lay her head on the table. She had no tears left.

There was no more hope.

"Please," she had whispered.

The light faded as clouds covered them. A chill passed her, and she shivered.

She heard the letter flutter in the bitter breeze. She would burn it if it got much colder. If she could find a match.

"It really is diabolical what some people try to get away with."

She snapped her head up, eyes wide with shock.

A pale figure sat opposite her, reading through the letter. It was as if he wasn't fully present, just a suggestion of a man. Yet here he was, reading, speaking, tutting, glowing slightly. He produced a pen of some kind and began writing on a spectral piece of paper that had materialised and was floating in mid-air.

"Oh dear, oh dear. Someone is going to have quite the comeuppance," the ghost chortled.

"Who are you?" she choked through terrified tremors.

The figure stopped writing and paused. He put down his appendages and looked her straight in the eye, smiling warmly.

"Why, I'm your lawyer, Mrs Henria. Now, let's get started…"

Acknowledgments

A book is a bowl of soup. It's a melting pot of experience, ideas, effort and imagination. Just like a restaurant is not a kitchen, a book is not a single person's endeavour. Without the small group of dedicated, intelligent, creative and detail-oriented people who volunteered their valuable time to help me, instead of a lovely bowl of warm broth, Advocatus would have been a rambling, inconsistent gallon of watery bland vegetable matter served in a bucket to a raccoon. The aforementioned wonderful people helped me reduce it, flavour it, blend it, serve it and market it, finally presenting it in the way I wished it would have been from the start. I hope you have enjoyed it! Just know that without the below people I can guarantee it would not have been half as good as I hope it is.

Thank you to Tom for his boundless imagination, for making me think about aspects of the story I hadn't considered, and for long nights talking about possible cases and future directions for each of the characters. Thank you to Dad, with his unerring anti-typo orbital-satellite laser-beam cannon, and for getting me to ask and understand 'why'. Thank you to my wonderful wife Anna for going over every sentence with a fine tooth comb and making me justify every word, strengthening the book page-by-page as she did so, and for making me put the Froggoboggo pies in. Lastly, thank you to Drew and the Cloaked Press team for welcoming me into their wonderful family. One day we'll share a cold cider in Hawaii, or somewhere else if it's too touristy.

About the Author

Born on the Isle of Wight in the south of England, Alex now lives in South Wales with his wife and cat, where he divides his time between reading, writing and board games. Having always wanted to read a book about a lawyer in a fantasy world (but never successfully finding one), Alex finally realised that there was nothing else for it: he was going to have to write it himself. His other passion in life is a board game called Blood Bowl. He talks about it often in his podcast and one day hopes to compete in the Chaos Cup or other big global tournaments. Check his podcast here:

https://anythingbuta1podcast.wordpress.com

You can find him on Facebook or Twitter.

https://www.facebook.com/A.R.Turner.ART

https://www.twitter.com/A_R_Turner

Printed in Poland
by Amazon Fulfillment
Poland Sp. z o.o., Wrocław
22 January 2022

1b2e17a0-64b9-4c30-a8a8-11986932830dR01